PRAISE FOR HEATHER BURCH

"Heather Burch has proven herself to have such an exceptional storytelling range that one might be tempted to call her 'the Mariah Carey of romance fiction.' *One Lavender Ribbon* blew my expectations out of the water and then swept me away on a wave of sweet romance. Don't miss this one."

—Serena Chase, contributor to *USA Today's* Happy Ever After blog and author of *The Seahorse Legacy*

"Burch's latest combines a sweet, nostalgic, poignant tale of a true love of the past with the discovery of true love in the present . . . Burch's lyrical, contemporary storytelling, down-to-earth characters, and intricate plot make this one story that will delight the heart."

—*RT Book Reviews* on *One Lavender Ribbon*, 4.5 Stars

Along the Broken Road

ALSO BY HEATHER BURCH

One Lavender Ribbon

Young Adult Novels

Summer by Summer

Halflings

Halflings

Guardian

Avenger

Along the Broken Road

THE ROADS TO RIVER ROCK SERIES

BOOK 1

Heather Burch

Montlake
Romance

Text copyright © 2015 Heather Burch

Published by Montlake Romance, Seattle

www.apub.com

Amazon, the Amazon logo, and Montlake Romance are trademarks of Amazon.com, Inc., or its affiliates.

ISBN-13: 9781477829875
ISBN-10: 1477829873

Cover design by Laura Klynstra

Library of Congress Control Number: 2014922411

Printed in the United States of America

For my dad, Jerry McWilliams, the man who taught me the most important thing we can do while we're alive is to touch the lives of others. There isn't a day that goes by that I don't miss you. Heaven is a brighter place because you're there.

PROLOGUE
AFGHANISTAN, PRESENT DAY

Ian Carlisle adjusted the backpack cutting into his shoulder and opened the journal. A light wind pressed against his back; the pressure of what lay ahead pushed against his heart. Off to the right of the base was a valley split in two by a green-banked stream. He sometimes went there in the evenings, boots off, no shirt, and wearing shorts with his dog tags clinking against his chest. After today, he'd return to American soil, where he could wade in water without the likelihood of a firefight. Ian touched his hand to the journal. With the base still quiet, he began to read.

I see you standing at the riverbank, your head tipped back, arms outstretched. The sun warms the locks of your golden hair. Does it warm your heart too? Or is it cold? That spot within your chest where you carry the hopes you dream and the pains you've suffered. But you aren't bitter about those hurts. You're strong. You welcome life. It's absorbed by you, your grace, your beauty, that spark that only you have. And as I stand here watching I wonder if you'll even remember me. Maybe I have no right to ask for a place in your heart. And yet, nothing will keep me from it. Nothing will keep me from reaching out to you. I can only pray your heart will hear me and you'll reach toward me as well.

———

Ian wiped the moisture from his eyes and closed the journal. Why that specific page haunted him, he couldn't say. Unfulfilled promises, he supposed. Broken dreams, the things a person planned to do, proposed to do, but never saw them through. Maybe there was a place in heaven where all the broken dreams littered a floor, reaching from side to side like a giant sea of disappointment and missed opportunities. There'd be a few with his name on them, for certain. Drawing a deep breath, he forced his attention to the world around him. The army base stretched before him anchored by tall mountains and what an Oklahoma boy would call tropical vegetation. It remained quiet for late morning, but that suited him fine. He needed a few seconds to adjust to what was happening. In essence, he was stripping off one coat and putting on another, the coat of a civilian. He hadn't done that in years and wasn't sure how he'd be at it. But fear was a useless thing. So he chose not to dwell on the what-ifs. A voice from behind took him by surprise.

"You Carlisle?"

"Yes sir." He turned to greet the man dressed like him in shades of gray-brown.

"All you got?" The soldier hoisted one of Ian's bags.

Ian grinned. "Like to travel light."

The guy tossed it into the back of the Humvee and motioned for Ian to get in on the other side. "Guess I'd leave all my junk here for a ticket home."

"No doubt." And that's when it hit Ian that he really, actually, *truly* was going home. It had seemed like a prank until now. Getting his paperwork, packing his belongings, all felt surreal, like someone would wake him at any moment or tell him, "Oh, sorry. We made a mistake.

You have to stay." His head knew he was leaving, but his heart hadn't assimilated it yet.

In less than forty-eight hours he'd be stateside. And that's when the real war would begin. The biggest mission of his life lay before him. And after two years in Afghanistan, that was saying something.

"Someone waiting for you back home?" the driver asked as he angled the vehicle toward the gates leading Ian away from base. This would be the last time he saw it. The last time he rode this specific bumpy road . . . away from one life and toward another.

He had to smile. "Yes sir."

"Good for you."

Ian peered at him across the Humvee. "I didn't finish. Yes sir, she just doesn't know it yet."

CHAPTER 1

Charlee McKinley had been painting when she got the news her father had been killed. His funeral was a who's who of military elite complete with majors, colonels, even a general offering their condolences. Everyone liked Major McKinley. Everyone except Charlee.

On the one-year anniversary of his death, she jumped into the lifted Jeep she used for working the grounds and drove it through the creek bed to her favorite spot on the entire property. The sun rose before her, lighting the landscape and painting the shadows with color. Night animals scurried back to their homes, a possum crossing the clearing and disappearing into the edge of the woods that framed Charlee's spot. She grinned when she saw the chubby animal as it waddled into the tree line. The thing that didn't make her smile was the fact that now, one year later, she still didn't know what to do with her father's ashes.

Off to the right, beyond a smattering of uneven evergreens, Charlee could see the shoreline of Table Rock Lake shimmering with the fresh morning light spilled across it. Sometimes in the early morning before the sun rose and when there wasn't any fog rolling off the water, she could see beyond the lake to the lights of River Rock, Missouri. The sound of gentle lake waves crashing onto the rocky shore filled her ears.

The constant hum was one of her favorite complements to the Ozark Mountain landscape and so different from the violent and tumultuous waves she'd seen on the East Coast during a college spring break she'd rather forget. Those waves were invasive. These were in harmony with the world around them. And harmony was something Charlee held dear.

Harmony *wasn't* what she felt when her mind drifted back to the urn perched on her fireplace mantel. Why her father hadn't given the task to one of her brothers, she couldn't fathom. Maybe it was some sick final joke. She thought about this as she hopped out of the Jeep and moved to the oak stump where she liked to sit. Two giant oaks had once anchored the spot, but one fell to disease and now offered her a seat while the other massive oak offered shelter from the rising sun. *Had it been a joke?* No. Her father had never joked when he was alive; it wasn't likely he'd begin now. And it's not that she hadn't loved her father. She had. Of course she had. She just didn't like him very much and the feeling was mutual. They were two people at opposite ends of the spectrum, separated by everything that made each who they were. They coexisted in a household after her mother died. They were cordial. Polite. Like strangers.

Now he'd been gone a year. Shouldn't her world have changed? Been different somehow? Yes, she was a grown woman, but shouldn't there be a longing for him? Instead there was a longing for all she'd never *had* with him.

When the first beads of sweat broke out on her forehead, Charlee left her perch on the tree stump and started toward the Jeep. The sun was a burning ball above her, promising yet another scorcher of a day. It had been unseasonably muggy and that made the artists cranky.

Charlee ticked off the list of chores in her head, turning her thoughts far from her father and to the world she loved, the artists' retreat she'd named after her mom. Her mother and she had planned it before her mother's illness took her life. At twelve, Charlee'd made a promise she'd see it through. And Marilee McKinley had believed her.

She'd touched her cheek and said, "You'll do it, Charlee. I know you will." And then her glassy eyes closed. Charlee knew that wasn't the last time she'd seen her mother alive, but it was the last real memory. And she kept it locked in a beautiful box inside her heart. The artists' retreat was a gift of hope to a little girl who would grow up without her mother to help her learn to wear makeup, to help her understand why boys acted so strange when they liked you, to snap pictures of a prom dress. This was her mother's way of giving her something to cling to. Something they'd share. Forever, even when death separated them.

Charlee cranked the motor on the Jeep and thought about her day, mentally listing things by order of importance. Mr. Gruber needed a bath. The other artists were complaining. He was one of the more eccentric artists who stayed on the property, often working days without sleep and sometimes forgetting trivial things like hygiene. The hot water in his cottage was shoddy at best and this gave him the perfect excuse not to bathe. She really needed to hire a handyman. Number seventeen on her to-do list.

The Jeep slogged through the creek bed and out to the open field where she could put her foot on the gas. The smooth terrain was mostly free of rocks on this part of the property, making it tons of fun to go fast during the rainy season. She could hit the brakes and spin the wheel, making perfect donuts in the mud—which she'd discovered was a great way to de-stress. As she rounded the curve and the compound came into view, Charlee smiled. She saw this same scene day after day, but mornings like this—after thinking about her mom and how pleased she'd be—Charlee couldn't help but feel a bit of pride herself. The cottages were arranged in a semicircle around an open yard with a giant wooden platform in the center. There were other cabins nestled in the edge of the woods alongside, but this was the hub of the Marilee Artists' Retreat. A large metal building used for gatherings anchored the platform and cottages, which sat six on the left of it, six on the right. They were spread apart just enough for privacy, but close enough to give one a true sense of community. Which was important for the artists. Artists, in her experience, were mostly solitary people, more comfortable in the presence of brushes and canvas, music and aloneness rather than in the presence of other human beings. This space brought them together, a wonderful gift to give them. Except when Mr. Gruber hadn't taken a bath.

Charlee spotted a door opening and a flash of white spiky hair with colorful tips. "Morning," she yelled as Wilma Vandervort propped her cottage door open with her rear end and shook a dust mop. The woman smiled, waved.

"How'd you sleep?" Charlee said, closing the distance to her.

"Like I'd fallen into angel's wings." Wilma held the dust mop handle to her heart and hugged herself.

"That's great, Wilma."

Wilma and her sister Wynona had come to the colony close to two years ago. They'd planned to stay for a weekend, but the time stretched and stretched and now, here they were fully moved in and with no intention of leaving. The sisters shared a cottage—which Charlee couldn't imagine in the 800-square-foot space—and both suffered insomnia. She didn't know their ages, but guessed they were in their mid- to late sixties. "Did Wynona sleep?"

Wilma shrugged. "Don't know. She's not up. Sounds like a busy lumberjack in the loft."

"I'm going to town tomorrow. Do you two want to ride along?" She tried to make sure the artists who'd taken up residency got out and about . . . into the concrete world . . . every now and then. And some of them liked that. Others felt it a chore beyond human comprehension. Wilma and Wynona were social creatures.

"Yes, we'll go." She pointed to the cottage at the left corner. "But I'm pretty sure King Edward wants to go to town as well. Said something about needing a haircut and new socks."

Charlee cast a glance to his cabin. "Well, there's room for all three of you."

"Who has dinner duty tonight?"

"You and Wynona." Charlee grinned.

"Thought so. What about tomorrow night?"

Charlee sighed. "That would be King Edward."

Wilma grabbed her throat, made a choking sound. "Will it be spaghetti with tuna again?"

Charlee nodded.

Wilma ran a hand over her head; the rainbow spikes sprung right back up after she did. "You know, he only fixes those horrifying meals because he wants out of the dinner rotation."

Charlee nodded. "And that's why we all just man up and eat it."

Wilma's chin tilted, eyes filling with nostalgia. "It's good for artists to suffer. It keeps us in a place of vulnerability. The best work is born in vulnerability." Wilma was a watercolorist. Her pieces were beautiful and delicate as spun sugar. Charlee swore each new work was better than the last. Wynona, her sister, had been a dancer. She didn't paint or draw or use any other medium to share her emotions, but the stories she told were incredible and she did have a penchant for decorating things with rhinestones. As a young woman, Wynona danced with the USO during the Vietnam War and though the United States took great pride in how safe they kept the USO entertainers, Wynona had a wandering spirit and would slip out late at night with one of the soldiers . . . or sometimes several of the soldiers. Charlee was pretty sure she'd seen much more than the US government would be comfortable with.

"I'll be out working on the fence line at the edge of the property today if anyone needs me." It wasn't actually the edge of the property. It was where her property stopped and her brother's began. The 200-acre plot had once been a kids' camp. Her colony took up the girls' section and a good mile away the boys' camp lay on the property her mother had left to her oldest brother. His stretch backed up to the national forest, but hers had the prettiest section of lake and the best cabins. Her other three brothers had a piece of the pie, with various structures on each. Her youngest brother, Caleb, had mineral springs on his stretch of land.

Charlee knew why her mother had bought the place. It was for the artists' retreat they'd always talked about. Something her brothers never did—and still didn't—understand. Who cared? This was her dream. And she'd never even thought of sectioning any of it with fence until her oldest brother, Jeremiah, told her he was thinking about finally doing something with that chunk of rocky ground. Good fences made good neighbors.

She bid Wilma good-bye and headed back toward the Jeep. Then she remembered. Mr. Gruber. Charlee sighed and angled to his cabin on the far right. A massive spinning metal daffodil caught her attention. The artist who created the giant yard pieces had come here a year back for a retreat. Most artists came to work, using the gorgeous Ozark Mountains as inspiration. But this particular artist, Javier LaFleur—she'd never learned if that was his real name or an eccentric alias—he'd come simply to rest, walk the property, and as he'd called it, romance the muse again.

Charlee understood that. It had been months since she'd painted anything except a mailbox and shutters. She missed it, having a fresh white canvas at her fingertips, opening the tubes and smelling the oil paint. Mineral spirits. At the same time, making a place for other artists to come and be inspired, well, that was priceless. Besides, she wasn't really a good artist anyway. She'd have time to paint when she found someone to take over some of the responsibilities on the property.

She stepped onto the small covered porch. All the cabins had them and evenings would find artists rocking in the wooden rockers and snapping photos of spectacular sunsets over the edges of the lush green mountains surrounding the retreat. In many ways it felt like a sanctuary, tucked so neatly against what had been dubbed McKinley Mountain. That wasn't the official name of the mountain that anchored the edge of her property, but the McKinleys had helped pioneer the small town of River Rock that lay only five miles away. Her father's family, *her* family—generations of hard workers who took more pleasure in a job well done than in having things named after them. *Good folk*, her dad used to call them, referring to his people, those quiet laborers, the silent workers. Her mother's side of the family was another story. *Old money*, that's what her dad called them . . . and there might have been a few other choice words.

Charlee knocked on Mr. Gruber's door. No answer. The screen creaked open and Charlee realized the knob was loose. She'd need to fix that later. Using her one hand to prop the screen open, she knocked again. "Mr. Gruber?"

A muffled sound came from inside. She took that as an invitation to enter. Light flooded the doorway. Deeper in the cabin she heard a yawn, but her eyes hadn't adjusted. The cabin smelled stale, like old sweat and older food. She'd pick up some air freshener in town. "Good morning."

The windows were covered with thick drapes so she moved to the front one and pulled it open wide. A hiss came from the bedroom. She dusted her hands. "Oh come on. It's not that bad."

He emerged from the bedroom wrapped in a dark green bathrobe that hung from his narrow shoulders. Mr. Gruber was in his seventies, thin as a rail with sunken cheeks and eyes and a patch of springy white hair on his head.

"What's good about it?" he mumbled. "Other than the beautiful woman who came to greet me?"

Charlee spun and lifted her arms wide. "You're too kind."

"Ha! I've been accused of many things; being too kind isn't one of them." He shuffled over to the kitchenette counter and peered into the coffeepot as if steaming hot coffee would magically appear.

She placed her hands on her hips. "When did you eat last?"

He grunted in answer and opened the coffee can to shake grounds into the filter. He never bothered to measure.

"I saw you got a package from your daughter the other day. What did she send?"

He waved a hand through the air. "Some box of candy from where they'd traveled in the Caribbean."

"Oh, that's nice."

The ancient coffeemaker rumbled to life. "It's exorbitant. Do you know what it must have cost to send? A box of candy not worth three dollars?"

"It's a very sweet gesture. She loves you. Just like we do." Charlee stopped at his feet and planted a kiss on his cheek. *Whew.* He was ripe. "So, did you finish your painting?"

He tossed his thumb toward the bedroom.

Without invitation, Charlee strode into the room and retrieved the sixteen-by-twenty canvas. She propped it on the easel by the front door, where the sunlight could illuminate it.

A hand went to her heart. A beautiful beach stretched across the entire piece. Turquoise water caressed by sugar-white sand, waves rolling gently with the sun peeking from a ribbon of brightly colored clouds. But it was the subject matter in the forefront of the canvas that took her breath. There, a woman with long, dark hair held up a chubby little baby girl, her mouth smiling, her eyes dancing. The woman wore a white dress that played in the breeze you could almost feel, her hair shimmering against the sun and the baby grinning a toothless grin as if the whole world were her playpen. "It's beautiful."

"Eh. It's okay."

"Was this from a picture your daughter sent with the candy?"

"Yeah. Had to make the baby thinner. She's a porker."

"Babies are supposed to be chubby."

He grunted again and retrieved his cleanest dirty cup out of the small sink.

"Well," Charlee said, turning her attention to the task at hand. "I'll be going, but I just wanted to let you know, it's going to be really hot today. A nice cool shower might make it tolerable."

He pinned her with a piercing blue eye framed with wrinkles. "What you're really saying is you haven't gotten my hot water fixed yet."

Charlee bit her lip. "Tell you what. You take a cool shower this morning and I guarantee I'll have it fixed by the next time you need a shower . . . in a day or two." If she had to call in a pro, she'd do it. But she'd really hoped she could hire a handyman. After a week, only three had answered the ad. And none of them sounded competent. But one offered to have his parole officer call her . . . as a reference.

She moved to the front door. "You really do have a beautiful family, Mr. Gruber." He waved in answer, but before Charlee could escape, she watched his gaze fan to the painting. A deep longing filled his watery blue eyes. His hands came together at his waist, fingers fumbling with one another as if he wished he could reach into the painting and touch the subject.

"Good-bye," Charlee whispered, not wanting to interrupt him as he stared at the image of his family. She understood that yearning, that emptiness left by those who'd once filled the now-hollow spaces of the heart. *I know how you feel.*

———

When Ian saw the Jeep, he whipped his motorcycle into the lumberyard's parking lot in River Rock, Missouri. He'd know that vehicle anywhere and just seeing it caused the first bits of tension to trickle down his spine. The familiar sense of a pending battle caused little sparks through his nerves. Though he'd been home from Afghanistan a couple weeks, the sensation seemed as normal to him as breathing. This could go well. Or horribly wrong. And there just wasn't any way to know.

He parked, threw a leg off his bike, and listened to her engine tick as he inspected the three people in the Jeep. The driver was MIA. Probably inside the lumberyard.

It was a strange crew to be sure. In fact, Ian would call them downright bizarre. He knew the Jeep though, knew it from a photograph when it hadn't been lifted, when the wheels and tires were more of a normal size and when it didn't tote three of the most unusual-looking characters he'd ever seen. A man squirmed in the passenger seat, a hat on his head and a kilt around his loins. He suddenly went ape-crazy, screaming about a bee and flying out of the Jeep. A moment later, he crawled back in and made no effort to cover himself as he bent to retrieve something from the floorboard. "Whoa," Ian muttered, turning to the side as he got the flash of white flesh beneath.

Two old women were arguing in the back, one with long white hair, the other with short spikes colored in an array that made her head look like a living firework.

Ian left his helmet on his bike and walked toward them, taking in the lumberyard and the tall, green mountains beyond. Surely, the driver would come out soon. And he hoped, one could even call it *prayed*, that it was whom he sought.

That's when she emerged. Thick curls of blond hair, long legs, tan. Gorgeous. The mountain breeze caught her by surprise, causing her hair to cover her face. Her chest and torso were also covered by a large bag of . . . well, if he had to guess . . . manure. Or maybe potting soil. The man in the Jeep turned to face her just as she ambled closer.

"Come *on*, Char Char." He lifted his skirt a bit and fanned it. "I'm roasting out here."

Ian cut him with his eyes and wondered why Fancy Pants was too good to get out of the vehicle and take the bag. Rather than point it out, he sailed in, jogging the last few steps to her. When his arms encircled the load, easily lifting its weight, she greeted him with a curious frown, mostly hidden behind a pair of bling-y Hollywood sunglasses. Her cut-off jean shorts and tank top didn't really go with the over-the-top shades, but so what? She was every bit as pretty as the photos he'd seen. "Let me help," he said when she continued to hang on to the bag, the two of them chest to chest, separated only by manure in a strange face-off.

"I got it."

He had to chuckle. "Yeah. I got it too, and we're a little bit pretzeled right now. If you let go . . ." Ian shifted his weight.

The frown deepened.

"Look, lady, I don't want to steal your manure, if that's what you're thinking." His face was a scant few inches from hers, close enough to see the tiny dimple at the edge of her pursed mouth, a mouth that, though framed with tension, was still full and moist. A mouth he could kiss. *Whoa there.*

Now it was her turn to shift her weight. She did, and the bag tilted dangerously to one side. His face broke into a smile. "Really, I don't mind helping."

She released her hold and Ian released the breath he'd drawn in, one full of the scent of vanilla and thoughts he shouldn't be having.

He nodded behind him. "You in the Jeep?"

She moved to the back of it and opened the little minidoor behind the spare tire. "Just cram it in." *Char Char* shoved a tarp and some other bags out of the way, making a hole half the size of the manure.

Ian frowned. "Cram it in *where?*" He rested the edge of the bag on the Jeep, and she must have taken it as an invitation to work the thing into the too-small spot because instantly she started shoving. And grunting. And shoving some more, feet firmly planted, butt wiggling from side to side. *That* was difficult not to enjoy.

Finally, the manure was in and a bead of sweat trickled down the side of her face. She closed the door by bumping her shoulder against it. "Thanks for the help." She flashed a white smile, spun, and headed toward the driver's door.

"Wait." He caught up to her. "Are you Charlee?"

Her foot stalled on the step, one leg up, hands gripping the handrails. She turned her head and looked at him.

Ian grinned. "I know your brother."

Charlee slid the sunglasses from her eyes and tossed them on the dash. She inspected him for a moment, gaze narrowed.

Ian sucked a fresh breath. Her eyes were a mix of gray and blue. Neither shade, but somewhere between. They were a storm brewing on a clear day. "Jeremiah. Your brother?"

"Four brothers. Jeremiah, Isaiah, Gabriel, and Caleb." She climbed on into the Jeep like she was going to leave, so Ian blocked her exit by positioning his body against the vehicle.

"I was actually headed out to your property."

Charlee retrieved her sunglasses and slid them on. Hollywood bug eyes stared at him.

"Jeremiah said you needed a handyman for the summer." He was pretty sure there was an eye roll accompanying her long exhale.

"There's an ad on Craigslist. And a place to send your resume."

When she started the engine, Ian reached in and placed a hand on the steering wheel. "I don't really have a resume, ma'am." Three sets of wide eyes watched the exchange from the passenger seat and backseat. The women had fallen silent.

The kilt wearer leaned forward and met Ian's gaze with a snarl. "Are you an ax murderer?"

Charlee chuckled and punched him on the arm. "Goof, my brother wouldn't send an ax murderer to work for me."

Fancy Pants folded his arms over his chest, indignant. "He didn't answer."

"No sir. I'm not."

The sunglasses dropped again, this time into her hand on the steering wheel as if she was ready to fight Ian for control if necessary. "No *sir*?" she echoed. "Yes, *ma'am*?" Her gaze shot down to his shoulders, where the straps of a military-issue backpack rested.

Ian watched her chew the inside of her cheek. Something was happening there, deep in those stormy eyes. They were softening, barely, but it was unmistakable. And something he could use. He hooked his thumbs on the straps of his camo backpack, dragging her attention to it again.

A long exhale from his blond target. "You just get home?" she asked, and for the first time since he'd met her, there was the tiniest hint of warmth in her voice. Her brows—the ones that had been slashed into a frown—were now raised on the inside edges . . . like she was looking at a puppy or something.

"Yes, ma'am. Been deployed in Afghanistan for the last two years."

She blew another breath into his face and he tried not to drag it into his lungs. He failed.

She pointed at him. "Stop with the *ma'am*. I'm not eighty. I'm twenty-five. You can call me Charlee."

Ian smiled. "Oh, we're about the same age."

"Me too," kilt man said. He was obviously at least twice that old.

The two women in the back piped up at that. "We're all twenty-five."

"I really could use the job, ma'—I mean Charlee."

The spike-haired woman reached forward and shook Charlee's shoulder. "Let's keep him," she said in a hoarse whisper.

Charlee turned, sending curls in an arc around her tan shoulders. "I don't want my *brother* choosing who I hire. It's none of his business."

"Oh, come on," firework lady pleaded. "He's so sweet and handsome, and I just want to squeeze his cheeks."

The kilt wearer checked his fingernails. "He'd be great for my nude study."

Ian blinked, removing his hand from the steering wheel like it had burned him. He took a step back.

Charlee pivoted to face him, a devious grin on her face, and eyes dancing with mischief. "You *really* want the job?"

A tentative "yes." But Ian's heart was pounding.

"Enough to do a nude study for King Edward?"

Giggles from the backseat and Ian had to wonder if he'd fallen right down Alice's famous rabbit hole. "Uh . . ."

Kilt-wearing King Edward nodded vigorously.

"I, uh, guess?"

"You know about building stuff?" Charlee propped a foot on the gearshift and Ian kept his gaze from trailing down to her tanned leg.

"I'm not bad."

"Minor plumbing, construction, a little wiring here and there?" She scooted around as if settling in to give him a thorough interview.

He nodded. "I'm pretty good. Worked with my dad all my summers growing up in his construction business. We did a lot of remodeling, lots of this and that."

"See, Charlee. He's a master this-and-thatter." From the backseat. "Can we see him with his shirt off?"

Charlee bit her cheeks, causing the dimple on the left to deepen.

Ian's mouth opened a little as his silent plea reached to her. He was pretty sure his face was blazing red.

Gray eyes sparkled. "Won't be necessary." But those eyes trailed over his shoulders and chest and dang it, it kind of made him feel like a piece of meat. It also sent a hot bolt shooting right into his gut. When the wind kicked up, Charlee gathered her mass of hair in a fist. "We'll give you a try for one week. But I'm warning you, it's not going to be easy. And I don't put up with any crap."

He nodded, for the first time feeling like he'd made progress and maybe, just maybe, he'd be able to honor his promise. He wasn't too surprised when she poked him in the chest with her finger. "And I swear, if you're here to spy on me and report back to my brother, I'll burn your clothes and send you into town naked."

Ian cleared his throat. Maybe this was the wrong Charlee McKinley. Oh, who was he kidding? She was everything he'd been warned about. And more. "Understood."

"Or worse. I'll turn you over to King Edward and he can paint you in the most *unflattering* and *smallest* of light."

Okay, so there could be repercussions, but it hardly mattered. He got the job. It was the first step. Maybe the most important because if she'd said no, everything might have ended right here. "Thanks for taking a chance on me."

An even stare was his answer. Without warning, she started the engine and popped the clutch on the Jeep. "Follow us."

She peeled out of the gravel drive and Ian jogged back over to his motorcycle. The dust trail marked her direction. He followed, hoping he hadn't bitten off more than he could chew. Could he meet this challenge? He was a six-year military veteran with two years deployed in Afghanistan under his belt. And one conversation with Charlee McKinley had him feeling like a new recruit.

CHAPTER 2

They turned on the second dirt road and Ian couldn't help but appreciate the rugged beauty of the land. Would be great for hunting, he decided when he passed a deer trail at the edge of the road. For what felt like the first time since being in the states, he took a deep breath. Finally, things that had to come together were. For Ian, it was the first step in a new beginning, complete with a dirt road leading deeper and deeper into the Ozark Mountains. The path was canopied by giant oaks and evergreens that towered above like sentries guarding the forest. He loved the woods. Loved being outside, loved being home from the Middle East where there was no sand and no one shooting at him.

When the property opened up before him, he tried to take it all in. It looked like it could have been a camp at one time, but everywhere—and he meant everywhere—there were signs of a much artsier handprint. The artists had claimed every inch of space, from the brightly colored tennis shoes hanging in one tree to the large metal animals resting atop spears in the front yards of really cool cottages. Giant metal flowers dotted the area where real flowers should have been planted. They ranged in size, but all were gigantic and whimsical and really, to him, a little bit creepy.

Charlee jogged over as he took his duffel off the motorcycle. "So, you can choose one of the cabins. I mean, I'm assuming you need a place; if not, that's fine. You can show up each morning at eight and leave at five. I know it's long hours, but there's a lot I want to get done."

Did she ever stop to take a breath? Ian readjusted his backpack.

"So, do you?"

He blinked. "Sorry. Do I what?"

She kicked a clump of dirt with her foot. "Need a place?"

"Oh. Yes ma'am."

She speared him with her eyes.

"Charlee."

"Better." Her head tilted and she gestured in an arc.

"There are several cabins empty here in the hub."

Ian's heart dropped. The hub was close enough that if he woke up screaming, someone would surely hear and he'd get fired before even getting a chance to prove himself.

"There are also some cabins around the property." She pointed. "Along the woods over there are the nicest ones. Others aren't habitable yet."

Ian smiled. "Perfect." When she started walking toward the edge of the woods, he followed, leaving his stuff at the bike. "One of the woods cabins will be great."

"They're a little bigger. Especially the first one. But you may not want it. My garden is alongside and I work there early some mornings."

"How early?" But even as they neared the dwelling, he knew he wanted it. It was framed on one side by a beautiful garden overflowing with an array of plants. It smelled like home. Garden and green and fresh.

"Sometimes eight o'clock."

That wasn't early, but he decided not to point that out.

He inspected the green tin roof, as if still deciding, but he'd already fallen for the place. "This should work."

Her hands went to her hips. "Don't you even want to compare it to the others?"

"Nah." He smiled, but didn't meet her eyes. He really didn't want her to see how excited he was to be here and how relieved he was she'd taken him on.

"Do you want to go inside?"

"Oh, sure." She was trying to figure him out. That he could tell. They stepped in and right away he noticed the artwork. Some of it was fantastic; some was, well, really crude.

Charlee chuckled. "You want to play poker later?"

He forced his eyes from the walls and stared at her. "What?"

She threw her head back and laughed. "I think I just read about fifteen expressions on your face, everything from joy to horror."

He ran a hand through his hair. "Yeah. These are . . . well, some of them are . . ."

Charlee stepped over to one. "You don't like them?" It was both a question and an answer.

"No. I like this one." He touched the edge of a black-framed beach painting where massive waves crashed on a shore that was barren save for one rainbow-colored beach umbrella. Off in the distance the sky changed from bright blue to a murky gray.

"It's called *The Storm*."

They continued to look at it.

"Makes you feel something, doesn't it?"

His eyes left the painting and settled on her. "Yes," Ian whispered.

"I love it too. It was done by Mr. Gruber. You'll meet him later."

Shock came in a quick rush. "He's here? The artist who did this is here?"

She laughed. "What did you expect? Finger painting? Amateurs? Some of the best artists of our time have wandered into the Marilee Artists' Retreat."

For some inexplicable reason, watching her say that, the proud tilt of her head, the fact she'd named the retreat after her mother—another woman he'd been told about—made Ian want to reach down and take her hand while they studied the piece. Like something about it caused them to have a connection.

"Oh, come look at this one." And then she did it. She reached down and closed her delicate fingers around his wrist to pull him over. Ian's skin turned both hot and cold at the same time. His nerve endings flickered to life.

Her fingers lingered there for a few seconds as they stood staring at a blotch of red on a white canvas. Other than a little drop of yellow, the red splotch was the only thing on the canvas. "Can you guess what it's called?" she said, her soft words echoing in the otherwise quiet cabin.

"*The Palette?*"

She giggled, a deep rumbling sound that clawed its way over Ian's skin. "That's funny, but no. It's called *Blue*."

He pointed. "Of course it is."

She shot him a look, so he winked. "Why not call it *Green?*"

She bit back a wickedly sexy smile. "Well, that would be stupid."

Ian turned from the painting and gave the cabin a quick once-over. "At least I won't need to buy anything for the walls."

"We can remove all of these. Or you can keep a few if you like." She crossed the smallish living room and opened the blinds of the big picture window. "They've all been donated by artists who've stayed here."

The cabin was laid out perfectly for a bachelor. The A-frame roof sat above a second-story loft. The bulk of the downstairs was a living room and kitchen. One doorway led into another room. When his gaze fell on it, she moved there and opened the door. "Bedroom and bath."

"Got it. How soon would you like me to get to work?"

She sighed. "Yesterday."

"Ah."

For the first time since they met, Ian saw the stress. She'd looked so light and happy gazing at the paintings; now a heaviness settled on her at the mention of work. "Do you have other help?" He hadn't meant to ask that, but it slipped right out of his mouth.

"Who? Like a landscaper or lawn service or cleaning person or anything?"

"Yeah, this would be a lot to take care of on your own."

"Well, the artists each keep their own places clean." Her shoulder tipped up. "Mostly. And we take turns fixing dinner each night." Something devious entered her silvery gaze. "So King Edward is cooking this evening. You're gonna love it." But her eyes rolled and he watched her bite into her cheek. That dimple again.

Charlee moved to the front door. "You can get to work today if you're game. I've got a hot-water problem that needs to be fixed. Settle in, then come find me. I'll get you started."

He was slow to nod, wanting just another second to look at the woman he'd been told so much about. When she started down the steps, he hollered after her, "I'll keep *The Storm*."

She paused at the foot of the steps and turned to look back at him, a smile of approval lighting her face. When she didn't move, it was Ian's turn to roll his eyes. "I'll keep *Blue* too."

Charlee nodded and started back toward the hub, her denim-clad rear end swaying as she moved.

When she was gone, Ian took the backpack from his shoulders and rested it on the table. Zipped inside, wrapped first in a gallon-size Ziploc bag, was the real reason he'd come. The solitude of a cabin in the woods surrounded him. He could sense the overwhelming power of a world unscarred by man just beyond the property borders. The thought was both exciting and terrifying because he'd spent his fair share of time in quiet places that in an instant erupted into chaos. That needed to not happen here. Outside, birds chirped, reminding him he wasn't really alone. The plastic bag crinkled as he withdrew the contents.

It was an expensive journal, leather and worn down by time. The kind purchased by those willing to invest in the written word, those who knew its power. Black corners were frayed like a favorite pair of jeans and the binding opened easily, as if inviting one to step into its world. Ian pulled a long breath and opened to a random page in the middle. His one hope was that he could read through it without breaking down and crying. So far, each attempt had failed. But now he had a mission. There was an objective and that made the circumstances different. He had a job to do. Failure wasn't an option and there was no room for compromise. Ian worked to muster everything within him. He could do this. He had to. He had a promise to keep.

But he hadn't counted on Charlee affecting him the way she did. He hadn't counted on that dimple in her cheek or her fierce desire to maintain her independence. He hadn't counted on her being everything he'd imagined.

Ian was in over his head. And the one person he could always count on to point him in the right direction was gone.

Heart hammering in his ribs, Ian touched the page as if he could still see its author, pen in hand. He forced the image from his mind when his nose tingled. Ian sniffed and began to read.

Dear Charlee,

Below me is a dry, dusty landscape scarred by mortar shells and interrupted by the indentations of a thousand army vehicles that cut a path to the base. This is a war zone unlike any other. And yet, all are the same in so many ways. Different enemies, same bloodshed. Different faces, same injuries. A new set of recruits has come out and they are exercising on the ground below my high perch. They are the best my country has to offer and they are ready and willing to lay down their lives to defend its freedom. They humble me. They remind me that life is precious. They remind me about the unstoppable human spirit. Each one has touched my life already and only now am I first seeing them. If I can leave them with one truth, it would be this . . .

Life is a river. It flows, turns, gives nourishment. It twists, spins, gives hope. It is a home for those who will step in; it is a shelter for those who cannot breathe the air.

Life is a river. It changes the world it touches and it heals the parched land. And if you open your banks and invite the world, you will forever alter it. It will carry a piece of you forever. Life is a river, Charlee. Never forget that.

Ian pressed harder onto the page. Only teary-eyed this time. That was good. He swallowed the lump in his throat. The one that always settled there, sneaking up from his heart. He pulled out a picture from the back of the journal. When the image blurred, he blinked several times and put the journal back in its plastic bag and into the backpack. He'd unpack later. Right now, he needed to get to work.

———

Before leaving the cabin, he took a few moments to look at the painting, *The Storm*. When he tugged the door open, he spotted Charlee immediately, standing at the edge of the hub and dumping something onto the ground. He hustled over and asked if she needed help.

"I'm good. We're being invaded by ants and this stuff is supposed to get rid of them." It was hot outside and she'd been working. Dirt smeared her white tank top. She returned her attention to the task at hand. Charlee gave the bag a shake. "Take *that*."

Ian swallowed a laugh.

"I'm usually all about *live and let live*, but ants . . . they get into everything. If we don't stay after them, they invade the cabins and it's impossible to get rid of them."

He took the large bag from her. It seemed to be growing more difficult for her to grasp as contents flooded the ground. For once, she didn't fight him. "You don't have to make excuses for killing the ants. You have a right to defend your property."

Every muscle in her body seemed to screech to a halt when he said this. Her jaw cocked, reminding him of a curious bird. "I'm not making excuses."

Ian hauled the package to the next anthill and dumped some of it. White powdered the mound. "Well, you do have a right to defend—"

"Yeah, yeah." Charlee brushed her hair back with the back of her hand. "So, you want to tackle the hot water?"

"You're the boss."

"I'm pretty sure it's the water heater. What I don't know is if it can be cleaned out or if we'll need to replace it. Well water here. Hard on the water heaters; fills them with lime."

He followed her as she traversed the lawn and across the edge of the big wooden platform in the center of the hub where patio tables and chairs made it almost feel like an outdoor restaurant. Ian stepped up onto the six-inch rise and stopped. "Question?"

She'd already stepped down, but turned to face him.

"Did you build this platform here in the center of the cabins? And why? Also, what's that big rectangle building?"

Charlee took the ant poison from him. "Give me two seconds and I'll answer all your questions."

He watched her put it in a small building that sat beside the larger one. As she returned, she gestured to the small outbuilding. "All the garden stuff is in there. Lawn mower, weed eater, bug sprays and such. Got it?"

He nodded.

"So, this used to be a kids' camp. Years ago. I even came here one year when I was eight."

He tried to imagine her as a child. Bright eyes, long hair, probably into everything.

"The large building was the main gathering place—you know, if it rained or anything. There's a full kitchen with an industrial dishwasher, long stainless steel counters, the works. We cook dinners in there, but always bring the food out here and eat alfresco."

Ian coughed. "You mean in the nude?"

Charlee's perfectly arched brows winged up. "No, *alfresco*, not *au natural*. It means outside, in the fresh air, under the stars."

"Whew." A hand went to his heart. "I was worried there for a second. I think seeing the kilt wearer naked would make me lose my appetite."

Charlee shook her head, sending curls scattering in the breeze. "So, we eat dinner together. It's nice. The wooden platform was for the kids' camp, but we put it to good use. There are four people staying here right now, but it always changes."

"So, the people I met earlier?"

"Yes, King Edward—who, by the way, you'll be sitting for—Wilma and Wynona—"

"Sisters, right?"

"Wilma has the short, spiky, rainbow hair. She's one of the most brilliant watercolor artists alive. Wynona doesn't paint, but she decorates sunglasses and glues rhinestones and bobbles to just about anything. So keep your bike covered." She took her sunglasses off and showed him Wynona's handiwork. "And she was a dancer. You'll meet Mr. Gruber in a few minutes. He acts like a cranky old man, but inside he's soft as mashed potatoes."

"Are they always old?"

She considered this. "No, and don't let King Edward hear you call him old. He's only fifty. I guess it may be easier for older artists to have the freedom to come here. Not as encumbered."

"And they stay for how long?" Really, Ian just wanted to keep her talking.

"Up to a month."

"So how long has King Edward been here?"

"A year and a half."

"Uh-huh. And the sisters?"

"Going on two years."

"Mr. Gruber?"

"Almost three." Charlee started to open the door of the toolshed, but Ian's hand on it stopped her.

"How do you do it?"

She slid the sunglasses to the top of her head, trapping her hair. "I don't know what you mean."

He motioned with a hand. "This is a lot to maintain. How do you keep up with it?"

She squared her jaw, and some little bits of fire shot from her eyes right into him. "Your paycheck is secure. You don't have to worry about it."

Ian's gaze dropped. That wasn't what he meant. "I just meant all the work," he mumbled. When he looked back up, her eyes had softened too, if only marginally. Standing face-to-face with her, he wasn't sure if he should apologize or just go on into the toolshed. When he started to move, she stopped him by placing a hand on his chest.

Ian swallowed, followed her gaze down to the place on his shirt where her fingertips touched a spot just below his collarbone. Could she feel his heartbeat quicken? He hoped not. After a few more moments, Charlee dropped her hand.

"I'm sorry," she said. "I assumed you were referring to the cost of a place like this. I realize a twenty-five-year-old woman running a money pit of a business and having no other means of income is an unusual sight. My mother bought me the property before she died. There was a trust set up by my grandparents. It became available to me after I finished college. It funds the retreat."

Ian took a step closer to her. "Charlee, it's none of my business. I didn't mean for you to explain."

A smile tilted one side of her face. "It's okay. I'm your livelihood now; you have a right to know." A gentleness framed her eyes that, to him, looked perfectly right on her. A softness that hinted at the real

Charlee McKinley, a woman who wasn't constantly fighting a money pit and trying to keep quirky artists in line.

His study of her intensified. "Is it worth it?"

Charlee looked out over the grounds and he could easily see two conflicting emotions running the gamut in her mind; they both played across her smooth face. "It is. But—"

"But?"

She sighed. "It's hard too. I didn't expect it to be quite so challenging. Almost four years in, I don't know. I thought it would get easier."

"Yeah, I know what you mean." He'd thought that too, about being deployed. Thought one day he'd wake up and it would all just fall into place. But he'd never fully acclimated. Every day was too different from the last. And yet, sometimes it felt like they were all the same. It was such a weird, conflicting blend of feelings.

"But I love it." Her words were final and held more determination than passion. "It's all I ever dreamed of." Charlee's fingertips disappeared into the pockets of her jean shorts.

Ian watched the nostalgia appear, first in her gaze, then in the tilt of her head, finally, on her lips.

"My mother was an artist," she whispered. "When she got sick, we'd spend hours drawing together. All my best memories of her are wrapped around art. Besides, if I didn't do this, I don't know what I'd do."

He wouldn't push the fact that not knowing what else to do wasn't a viable reason to continue something that had run its course. "I had a commanding officer who used to tell me that fear of the unknown was the second most powerful force on the planet." With that, Ian tucked into the toolshed and began gathering tools.

He was aware, shockingly aware, of Charlee still standing at the door chewing on his words. Atop a small cabinet, he found a tool belt. He placed it low on his hips and adjusted the strap. "Fits," he said.

She stepped into the shed and for a moment he thought he saw a tear in her eye, but it must have been the dust he'd kicked up inside the small metal building, trapped by the movement of air. She retrieved a hammer from the counter. "Here you go." No, there was something there, a mistiness, a glassiness. He tried to meet her gaze, but she dropped her eyes, hooding them with long, dark, half-moon lashes. The air around him actually felt thicker.

He stepped back and raised his arms. "How do I look?"

"Fine, soldier. Just fine." Slowly, she turned and walked toward the door. Once there, Charlee paused. "That was my dad's tool belt. Take good care of it."

Something in Ian's heart snapped. Wrapped around his waist was the utility belt of Major McKinley. Ian's hands came down and ran slowly over the smooth leather pouches. He swallowed hard. Charlee's dad had died a year ago. For a moment he thought he should take it off, but he didn't. Instead, he gently placed the hammer in its place, filled the nail pouch with a handful of trim nails sitting nearby, and hooked a wrench through one of the loops. It was a few more seconds before he could bring himself to leave the shed.

Outside, the sun was rising to the center of the world and chasing away every bit of shadow and shade. It was going to be a hot one. Charlee stood in the center of the hub waiting for him.

When he reached her, she asked, "What's the most powerful force?"

"What?"

"Earlier you said fear of the unknown was the second most powerful force on the planet. What's the first?"

Off in the distance, a crow split the silence with a piercing squawk. "Passion for the journey."

Charlee's brow quirked. Her face was the most interesting thing about her. Alive with determination one second, curiosity the next. She wasn't used to being thrown off base, that much was evident. *Passion for the journey.* He could almost see her repeating it in her head, weighing it, seeing if she agreed. When neither moved, she nodded slowly and headed to Mr. Gruber's cabin. Halfway there, a surprise breeze met them, coursing around the mountain and pushing against their backs. It drove Ian and Charlee forward. And in it, Ian could smell the scent of hope. His hands came down to his sides to the tool belt as he followed Charlee onto the porch.

She knocked a few times, but there was no answer. "Mr. Gruber?"

"I'm here," came a voice, from the side of the cottage.

They both turned to see him coming around the corner. Confusion flickered in Ian. *This* was the man who'd painted *The Storm*? Couldn't be. He was thin and frail and weak looking and the painting was nothing if not powerful and bold and commanding. The wide sweeps of the brush made for a violent oncoming storm. This man looked as if he could barely lift the canvas onto the easel.

"Mr. Gruber, this is Ian. He's going to fix your water today."

"I wish I'd known. I took a cold shower earlier. I could have waited." His narrow blue eyes studied Ian. "Nice bone structure. Have you modeled?"

"No sir." Oh Lord, here we go again.

Gruber reached up to his face as if he were a scientist and Ian a newly discovered species. "Look at his facial structure, Charlee."

She reluctantly leaned closer.

"See how his cheekbone narrows here?" A cold, wrinkled finger grazed Ian's cheek.

"Mm-hmm," Charlee said, but it sounded forced. She cleared her throat.

"It would be garish if not for his lovely jawline. See how the squared jaw creates the uniformity?"

Charlee licked her lips.

"When I studied in Paris, we were often offered models of this quality. Not anymore, though." There was a distinct nostalgia in his tone, sounding like the kind of man who gloried in days gone by more than the present.

"King Edward is going to paint him."

Ian's skin crawled at the thought. Had he really agreed to that?

Gruber poked him on the shoulder. "Don't let Edward destroy you. He has no sense of true artistry. All passion, no training."

Ian raised his hands. "I just want to fix the water."

Charlee and Gruber took a step back, as if the strange inspection was complete. Charlee grinned. "Okay, I'll leave you two guys to it."

Mr. Gruber opened the door for Ian. "Go right on in. I'm going to sit in the swing for a bit. I'll be back along in a while. Make yourself at home. If you need to move some things out of your way, feel free. But stay out of my loft. I have paintings in process up there."

"Understood." Ian gave him a salute and went inside, thinking he just might like Mr. Gruber. He did, at least, until his eyes adjusted to the lack of light in the cabin. "Lord Almighty," he whispered, half in disgust, half in prayer for immediate deliverance.

Ian wasn't sure where to rest his eyes first. The small couch was covered with clothes and papers. The coffee table supported a mix of plates and half-empty glasses crowded together; one cup sat so dangerously close to the edge, he couldn't imagine why it hadn't toppled off. "Ignore it," he told himself. "Not your business." Touching as little as possible, he looked for the closet that likely housed the water heater. There in a pantry separating the living and dining rooms, he found it. The door was blocked with an overflowing trash can and three bags of canned vegetables. Irritation whooshed up from deep inside, but he fought it. He was here to fix the water heater.

For ten minutes, he moved and moved again the items in his way. Maybe Gruber was a hoarder. He'd heard about those people. But when Ian pulled the cabinet doors open he found . . . nothing. "You gotta be kidding me." Gruber had room to put things away; he just didn't do it. When Ian stubbed his toe on yet another bag of unemptied groceries, he exploded. He sailed across the cabin and flung the front door open wide. "Gruber!" Hearing the tension in his voice, he took a breath before continuing. "Need a hand in here."

Slowly Gruber stood from the swing and started across the lawn. Ian counted to ten while he waited.

When the older man stepped inside, Ian's hands rose in question. "Are you kidding me?"

Gruber's bushy brows tilted into a frown.

Ian gestured around the house. "You've got bags of groceries sitting on your floor where you have to step over them while your cabinets are empty."

Gruber blinked, the lines around his mouth deepening.

Ian pointed toward the kitchen. "Don't you care? Doesn't it matter to you . . . the state of your home?"

When Gruber just stood there, Ian moved to the front window. "I can't work in this." Years of soldier training had done a number on him. This kind of irresponsibility was unacceptable.

The window groaned as he opened it. He pulled the curtains open, filling the space with light. Ian moved to the other windows with Gruber standing aside watching him.

"This morning Charlee showed me the most amazing painting I've ever seen."

Gruber threaded his hands together, and though he looked a bit like a child being scolded, Ian didn't stop his rant. "*Your* painting, *The Storm*. I can't quite assimilate that to this. Where I come from, you take pride in your work."

Gruber's chin rose. "I do take pride in my work."

"No. You don't. Or you'd have more respect for yourself than this."

Gruber's eyes darted around the cabin. "I've . . . I guess it's gotten a bit out of hand, but that's just how I do things."

"Look." Ian knew his temper had taken over and that could just as easily get him fired as anything, but no one should be okay with this. "It just needs to be picked up. Let's get it done. I can't complete my mission until this stuff is out of the way." Before Gruber could answer, Ian was gathering glasses and dishes and taking them to the sink.

Gruber carried a trash bag around and silently filled it with papers, crumpled potato chip bags, plastic cups, empty water bottles.

"While I was deployed, I watched some of the hardest workers in Afghanistan. Know who they were?"

"The foot soldiers?"

"No. It was the guys who kept the vehicles clean and running smooth. If you don't have a vehicle you can count on out there, you're screwed. Everything fills with dust, sand, dirt. Everything clogs. It's a constant battle, even when the vehicles are sitting at base. We could do our best work when our vehicles were up to the challenge."

Gruber paused, a half sandwich in his hand. "What are you saying?"

"Well, you're like that vehicle."

He tossed the sandwich in the trash, brows high on his head.

"You're an artist. What's the most important component to your artwork?"

He shrugged and the bag made a crunching sound. "My brushes."

"No."

"Paints, canvas, inspiration." Gruber huffed when Ian continued to shake his head. "You're losing me, soldier."

"*You* are your most important component. You can have all the paints in the world but without *you* to give it life, there's nothing. You are your vehicle. It needs to be kept up so you can do your best work."

Gruber emptied one bag of trash into another. "Hmm. I've never seen it that way, but perhaps you have a small point."

Once Ian was able to get to the water heater, he quickly discovered it needed to be replaced. Mr. Gruber kept cleaning. By the time he had the old water heater pulled out, the cabin was spotless. And Gruber looked . . . lighter. Even younger.

Gruber folded a shirt and glanced around. "This place is roomy with all the junk picked up."

Ian nodded. "Yes, sir."

The older man scratched his ear. "Thanks."

"Yes, sir." Ian muscled the water heater out the front door. He'd need to find Charlee and see about getting to town to buy another one. Dripping with sweat, he figured a shower couldn't hurt. She might want to drive him there and he didn't really want her to have to smell his essence of sweat and stale cabin.

He turned to Gruber, who held the front door open for him. "If you see Charlee, could you tell her I'll be at my cabin? We need a new water heater today. I'm gonna grab a shower."

Gruber saluted. "Sure thing, Soldier Boy."

Ian wiped the sweat from his hands onto his jeans. "See you later."

———

Anger shot from Charlee's gut to every appendage. After her conversation with Mr. Gruber she headed straight to Ian's cabin, burning up the ground with each step. She banged on his door. No answer.

She should have known the innate problems associated with hiring a soldier for . . . well, anything. Already her artists' retreat felt smaller with him there. More cramped, a bit stifled. She wished she'd listened to the inner voice that told her, *Danger, danger! Soldier in need of work and a world to absorb.* But he'd looked so sweet standing there at her Jeep door. So sweet and so . . . lonely. Alone in a world he'd gone away to protect. Curse her romantic notions about life and patriotism. They were going to bring her nothing but trouble.

She knocked again, this time letting some of her fury out with the pounding of her knuckles against wood. And she kept pounding. And kept pounding until, just on the other side of the door, she heard him yelling, "Okay, okay!"

Ian threw the door open, met her angry eyes with his own, and barked, "What? What is so important it couldn't wait until I dried off?"

Bare chest, tan flesh, jeans, bare feet, wet, wet, wet. Water dripped from his dark hair onto his face and trailed in rivulets down his chest.

He took the towel in his hand and rubbed it over his eyes. "You want to come in?"

"Yes." She took a step, stopped. "No."

He tossed the towel over his shoulder and the muscles in his arm bunched. There was a narrow scar on his left arm and another across his wide chest.

A flash of amusement entered his gaze. "So which is it? Yes or no?"

"Yes," she said, but her voice sounded shakier than she liked. She breezed past him, hoping to gain some equilibrium. "You shouldn't answer the door half naked."

She hadn't turned around, but could feel him inching closer. "You, uh, didn't give me much choice."

Before her, the wall was a nice steady place to focus. No dripping wet muscles, no dark eyes. For an instant she forgot why she'd been mad.

"Are you here about getting the water heater?"

Oh yes, that brought it all back. She turned to face him. "Mr. Gruber said you yelled at him about his house."

Ian used the towel to scrub his hair then smoothed the strands with his fingers. "Someone needed to."

She tried not to watch. "Look, this isn't a preschool and it's not our job to teach these people how to take care of themselves. You were way out of line."

Ian threw the towel on the kitchen chair and moved toward her so quickly, Charlee wanted to step back, but she didn't. She'd learned with four brothers, you never back down. Never show fear.

When he didn't speak, she continued. "You're the handyman. Not the camp counselor."

He stopped at her feet where their bodies nearly touched. "And I shouldn't have any pride in my work?"

"Of course you should."

"Then, to work well, all that crap in his house needed to be moved."

"Look, this isn't the army, Ian. You're being paid to do a job. That's it."

"So, I've gotten my first complaint."

His eyes scanned hers. She wanted to create some space between them because he was standing too close. Close enough she could see tiny flecks of gold in his dark brown eyes, close enough she could pick out the scents of spice and pepper in his aftershave. He'd shaved, she realized. The day-old stubble gone, revealing surprisingly smooth skin. Charlee swallowed. "I'm sorry. What was the question?"

"Mr. Gruber complained."

Her shoulder tipped up. "Actually, it wasn't really a complaint."

She watched as he released a bit of the tension from his shoulders.

"He wanted me to come in and see how his place looked." Her gaze fell to the floor when she said it. His bare toes, tan and manly, were almost touching the toes of her work boots.

"He was proud of it," Ian whispered. And though she would have expected him to rub that in, he didn't. He just seemed pleased.

"Yes, he was. Very. But, I don't want to have to worry about some-one treating my artists badly."

"You know, when I look around, they all look like big girls and boys to me. Not so much in need of a mommy."

Frustration shot into her gut. "Then stop trying to be one."

"I'm sorry. That was out of line. You're the boss." He was used to subordination.

"That's right." She turned from him and headed for the door, hop-ing the air outside would be clearer. Hoping it wouldn't smell like pep-per and sin. But her feet shuffled to a stop when she thought of Mr. Gruber's face when he'd asked her to come in. "Look, I may seem a little overprotective, but they're artists and they've spent their whole lives being misunderstood by society. I give them a safe place where they can just be themselves without fear of . . ."

And then there he was. Right behind her again. "What about you, Charlee? Have you been misunderstood by society?"

Off in the distance, McKinley Mountain towered over the retreat. Was she misunderstood? Yes. Not just by society, but by everyone she'd ever cared for. Except her mother. There was heat at her back. Ian had moved close enough to change the temperature around her. She took one step forward, turned her focus back to Mr. Gruber and the incident. "I don't want this to happen again."

"I get it. But *I* gave Gruber something today too."

She angled just enough to see Ian over her shoulder and waited for him to answer.

"Self-respect."

She couldn't argue with it. She should have known she'd have a war on her hands if she hired a soldier. They were always looking to put things in order, always landing on the side of discipline. "This is a safe place, Ian. I want to keep it that way."

He smiled; it was slow and genuine. "Sounds good to me."

Was there a hint of longing in his words? Charlee wasn't certain so she chose to focus on the task ahead. "I can drive you to town in an hour."

"Yes, ma'am." Whatever had been there was gone, replaced by a distinct playfulness to his tone.

She walked away mumbling, "Stupid army men."

CHAPTER 3

"Nice truck," Ian said as he climbed inside the late 1980s model Chevy Silverado. He'd already placed the water heater in the back and sandwiched it with a concrete block so it wouldn't roll around. It was three in the afternoon and the sun was a vindictive ball of flame above them.

"Thanks," Charlee said. "Sorry there's no air."

"Windows are good." He watched her shift into reverse to back it out of a garage nestled behind the main hub area. He hit the button and his window went down. His gaze scraped over to her legs. There was something inexplicably hot about a pretty girl driving a truck with a stick shift.

"I called the hardware store. They've got the same model as this one." Charlee used her thumb to motion into the back of the truck.

"Sorry it wasn't reparable."

"Eh, I figured." She brushed a hand through the curls snaking around her cheeks as they picked up speed on the dirt road.

She turned the radio on to a country station and Jason Aldean's voice filled the cab. "So," Charlee said and smiled over at him, "what are your plans after the summer?"

He rubbed his hands along his pant legs. Well, that really was the question, wasn't it? "My sister wants to introduce me to someone who may want to hire a foreman for his construction business."

When she reached the main road, Charlee peeled out, throwing gravel. Once the wide truck tires met the paved road, they screeched. "Why wait? Why didn't she plan to introduce you right away?"

Because of you. Instead, he said, "He's not ready to hire for a couple more months. My sister's getting married and he'll be at the wedding. The guy is a cousin of her fiancé. She figured it would be a great time for him to get to know me." Plus, Ian had a mission. And he wasn't sure how long it would take. He'd told his sister the soonest he could meet the guy would be August at the wedding. That would give him several weeks to accomplish his task.

"That makes sense, I guess. More social. Might give you the upper hand over the other applicants." Her brows rose in a quick motion and a smile touched her mouth. "Did you meet Jeremiah in Afghanistan?"

Oh, this could get sticky. He really needed to deflect too many questions about that, at least for a little while. "Well, I was there for two years. Did he ever tell you about the terrain?"

She glanced over. "The mountains? How it's not all sand like people think?"

"Exactly. It was really pretty in some areas. A little like home, but tropical."

"Where's home?" She rested her elbow on the window.

"Oklahoma."

"Oh, not too far." They reached town and Charlee went inside the hardware store while Ian helped the workers load the new water heater. She came out with her arms full. She held two potted plants in one hand and a receipt in the other. The fragrant greenery filled Ian's nose as he moved in to take some of the stuff. For the first time since they'd met, she gave the load to him without flinching. His face split into a smile. "Hey, I think you're getting used to me."

She quirked a frown, her brows disappearing beneath those rhinestone sunglasses, and she got into the truck.

Just after she pulled out, she slowed the truck. "Do you like ice cream?"

"Yeah." Who didn't like ice cream?

She pointed to a small, cone-shaped building just off the road. "Mind if we stop?"

"Sure."

Charlee pulled into the gravel drive and hopped out of the truck. He followed her toward the walk-up counter, barely glancing at the offerings.

She screeched to a halt halfway there and turned to face him. "Don't tell."

His brows rose. "Excuse me?"

She huffed. "You can't tell them when we get back. You have to promise."

"Uh." But really, what was there to say? She was a grown woman. Did she really have to have approval to eat ice cream? This was getting too weird. "Why?"

Frustration at having to explain flickered in her gaze. "Because it's King Edward's night to cook and the rest of us have an agreement not to eat before dinner. We all have to suffer through together."

Amused at her, he tilted closer. "You told me I'd love King Edward's food."

Charlee waved a hand through the air. "Oh, let's face it. No one loves his food. It's horrible."

"Aaah, so you're a liar?" he teased.

"No." Innocent eyes blinked. "I like to think of myself as more of a person who goes by the spirit of the law, not the letter of the law."

He tilted a touch closer, his face coming down to where only a few inches separated them. To the unknowing onlooker, they might look like two lovers on a date discussing which type of milk shake to share.

Body language was everything. And he'd learned to read it while deployed. Charlee wasn't backing away. But he figured she didn't have much of a flight gene. With her it was all fight. She probably didn't have the sense to back down from an angry rattlesnake. "Well, I think your secret's safe with me. But it will cost you."

The wind grabbed her hair and tossed it right into him. He fought the urge to breathe it in.

"How much? A hot fudge sundae is only worth so much."

"I'll think about it and let you know. Better yet, I'll just let you know when and how you can pay up." He hadn't meant for that spark of sensuality to accompany his remark. But he knew it did because he saw it reflected in her eyes, eyes that darkened if only for an instant, then returned to the shade of a swimming pool at dusk.

He moved to the counter to order. The guy standing on the other side was wearing a red-and-white striped shirt and hat. He craned his long neck to look around Ian, practically ignoring him. "Hi there, Charlee."

She stopped alongside Ian, her arm scraping against his. "Hi, Rodney." Sweetness in her tone. "How are you feeling?"

As soon as she said his name, red snaked up his throat and settled on the apples of his cheeks. "You know, I'm doing okay."

Ian glanced over, watched her smile broaden. "No hug?"

Rodney wiped his hands on his towel and came around the counter through a screen door. He pulled Charlee into an embrace that lasted a little too long for Ian's comfort.

When Rodney finally stepped back, she looked him up and down and Ian had to swallow a couple times because something was stuck in his throat. Heat flashed down his arms. That's when it hit him he didn't like seeing Charlee be so nice to some other guy when she barely tolerated him.

Charlee took the tall, skinny guy's face in her hands. "You look great, Rodney. Gaining some weight, right?"

"Not fast enough. Who's your friend?" Rodney seemed concerned, but returned to his post on the other side of the counter.

Charlee placed a hand on Ian's shoulder. "This is Ian Carlisle. He's working for me for the summer. He just returned from Afghanistan."

Judging by the frown on striped guy's face, he must not have liked the fact that Ian and Charlee would be together for the entire summer. Ian held a hand out, shoving it right through the window. "Nice to meet you, Rodney."

Rodney stared at the outstretched hand a few seconds then slowly lifted his. Ian gave him a firm handshake—an act of mutual respect.

"You too, Ian." It was almost a question.

Geez, he'd only been gone from the states two years. Didn't anyone shake hands anymore?

Rodney turned his attention to Charlee. "The usual?"

She nodded.

Ian looked down at her and for the briefest second, it felt like a date. He forced that image from his mind. "What's the usual?"

"Hot fudge, bananas, marshmallow, and extra whipped cream."

"Ew. Seriously?"

She challenged him with a wide-eyed stare.

Ian turned back to Rodney. "I'll just have a hot fudge sundae with pecans."

Charlee drummed her fingers on the counter while they waited.

Rodney returned with Charlee's concoction and a good old-fashioned hot fudge sundae for Ian. He handed them out the window. "No charge."

Ian had already dug a twenty out of his wallet. He held it in midair.

Rodney nodded to it. "Really. No charge. Thanks for serving our country."

Ian would have argued, but what could he say? Slowly, he slipped the twenty into his wallet. "Thanks. Very much."

It wasn't the fact that someone was willing to offer him a few bucks' worth of ice cream. It was the fact that they remembered, were aware that young soldiers put their lives on the line every day, living on foreign soil, missing out on time with their families.

As they turned to walk to a picnic table, Charlee bumped his shoulder. "Nice gesture, huh?"

Ian was a little choked up. "Yeah. Seems like a good guy." He wasn't fishing, no, not really, wasn't trying to determine the relationship between this guy and Charlee.

"He's a good friend. Known him forever." Charlee slid onto the seat across from Ian and took a bite. "Mmm." Her eyes closed and Ian was glad because that sound wrapped right around his gut and shot downward.

Charlee opened her eyes and winked. "I don't think he really liked you at first."

"I think what he didn't like was that I was with *you*."

"What?" Her spoon dug into the whipped cream again.

"He's got a crush on you, Charlee."

She pointed at Ian with the spoon. "Don't say that. He does not."

Ian's sundae was melting so he took a giant bite. "He totally does."

Charlee shook her head, concern pinching her brows. "No. He couldn't; I mean he knows about . . ."

This brought Ian's gaze up. "About what?"

Charlee looked lost in her own thought. "Not what. Who. And you know what? I don't want to talk about it." She flew off the picnic table bench and headed for the truck.

Ian remained seated, took another bite. "How you gonna eat that and drive a stick shift?"

She squared her shoulders and came back over to the table. "I can't."

Ian grinned up at her. "You can sit down if you'd like."

She plopped onto the seat. "Okay, but as far as that other stuff, I don't want to talk about it."

He shrugged. "No one's asking you to."

"Oh," she said. "Okay then."

And they finished their ice cream with Ian wondering just how far he was going to let this go before he admitted the real reason he was there.

He pushed the thought aside. It wasn't something he could just come out and say to her. He knew that. Had been told that. She'd need time. She'd need someone she could trust. But how much would she trust him when she learned the truth? His appetite for ice cream was gone.

He wasn't doing this for himself; that's what he needed to remember. This was to honor a promise he'd made. Whatever the outcome for him, it couldn't matter. Helping Charlee understand was what mattered. And that would take time. But at least he was seeing some cracks in that granite shell of hers. At least those walls seemed to be eroding just a touch.

"You okay?" Charlee's voice. Soft and tender.

"Sorry. Got lost in my own head there for a few seconds."

There was a speck of whipped cream on her lip. "I saw that. You know, I understand that it's got to be pretty difficult to enter society again after being deployed so long." Her tongue captured the whipped cream while her fingertips grazed the edge of her dish.

Ian stayed quiet. It was. For so many more reasons than he could say.

"If you ever need to talk . . ."

His eyes came up to meet hers. Sincerity drifted from her, that tiny glimmer he'd noticed when they first met and she'd softened when she realized he was a soldier. It made sense. She had four brothers in the military—as far as he knew, they were all deployed right now—and her father had died a military hero. "Thanks." It was all he could manage because what made life in society difficult for him was her. Her and the secret he carried. Her and the truth that had to come out. Her and the fact he needed to change her mind about things she'd been resigned to for a long time.

Charlee stood. "Let's go home."

Ian swallowed. She'd chosen the word, *home*, specifically. He already knew her well enough to know that. Home was the safe place. Home was where you worked out your problems. Home was . . . it wasn't his home and it would never be. But that was okay. He appreciated the gesture. Ian painted on a smile. "Yeah. Let's go home."

———

Charlee stood at the kitchen window staring out over the hub. Wynona and Wilma were placing a row of white lights around the umbrella of one of the round tables. The new lights gave a soft glow to the space. Charlee loved it. She loved the hub and the platform where four round patio tables anchored the dance floor. The *dance floor* was what Wynona had dubbed the large square space, and it really did resemble a dance floor. Of course, it had never been used for that purpose since she'd opened the retreat. Charlee grinned as she watched Wilma and Wynona string lights on the other tables. Tiki torches in full flame also helped illuminate the space and kept the bugs and mosquitoes to a minimum. Along with the whimsical decorations of a hundred artists who'd left their mark, the dinner space looked magical. This was one of her favorite times of the day because it was her opportunity to recharge, relax, and just enjoy. It was the one time of day she felt most connected to the purpose of Marilee Retreat. It was when she was just another artist, not the proprietor. Not the fixer of things, not the redeemer of lost items or the smoother of arguments.

Behind her, standing at the long stainless steel counter, King Edward continued fixing his spaghetti and tuna. "What do you think of the soldier?" she asked as she turned to face him.

He pursed his mouth and shrugged.

The smell filling the kitchen was slightly nauseating. Charlee chewed her cheek and thought about her new hire. "Seems kind of sad to me." He'd proven himself on the water heater, no question. If she was honest with herself—which she'd already decided not to be—she enjoyed his company. He reminded her of her brothers, only Carlisle was not as stiff and seemed less neurotic. Easy to talk to. In fact, she'd almost told him about Richard. At the thought of his name, the nausea increased. Richard, her epic mistake. He'd sailed into Charlee's life and swept her off her feet. He'd acted interested in her artwork, the retreat, every detail of her life. It all seemed to fascinate Richard. For once, Charlee had felt like the center of someone's attention. Until she found him at the Neon Moon with a redhead. That night, she learned his real intentions where Charlee was concerned. It wrecked her. And she wasn't one to recover quickly.

"I'm not certain the soldier isn't an ax murder."

Charlee chuckled, letting the tension of Richard's betrayal go. She had more immediate things to ponder. Like Carlisle. "Well, we don't know for sure. I tried to call Jeremiah about him, but never got through."

"Jeremiah is in North Carolina, right?"

"Yes. He's on a hunting trip for another week, then he'll be back at base." It helped knowing at least one of her brothers was on American soil. Now, if she could just get the other three home. "As far as your thoughts, I'm pretty sure Ian isn't an ax murderer."

"We'll all end up dead like those kids in the horror flicks."

Charlee spun and leaned her weight against the sink. "Don't be so dramatic. Ian's my hire. My responsibility. You're not going to die a Hollywood death and as far as who I put to work on my property, it's none of my brother's business. I don't have to call him. Get his approval."

"Hate to tell you, but you had already decided that when you first met Ian." King Edward grunted as he came toward her. "Char Char Baby. Can you hold the strainer since you're hogging the sink?"

"Got it." Steam rose from the hot noodles as they flopped into the colander. All that lovely spaghetti getting ready to die a horrible death smothered in red tuna sauce.

She shook the noodles and dropped them back into the pot. "I'll follow you."

King Edward took the lead. They were greeted with applause when they stepped outside and Charlee couldn't help her eyes from flittering over the gathering of people in search of a certain dark-headed handy-man. Then, across the lawn, she spotted him. He'd changed his work jeans for a fresh pair that were faded and looked soft as velvet hugging his strong thighs and narrow waist. There were holes in the knees and for some reason that made him distinctively sexy as he moved toward her. A tight black tank stretched across his chest and Charlee hadn't realized she'd come to a screeching halt until she heard King Edward's voice in her ear. "Oh honey. You *do* look hungry."

Charlee blinked several times, feeling the heat rise to her face. Across the lawn, Ian reached down and captured a dandelion. He looked so comfortable, one hand sinking into those snug jeans, the other with the dandelion between his finger and thumb. He looked so *at home* cross-ing her property like he owned it. "Well, if our little soldier can stroll a little faster, we might get to eat before it's cold."

King Edward clucked his teeth. "I'm sensing some sexual frustra-tion coming from you, Char Char."

She speared him with her eyes.

King Edward continued to talk, taking no notice of her disap-proval. "I wouldn't call that a stroll. I'd call it a saunter."

Suddenly, Charlee was aware of the other inhabitants in a semicircle around her. All eyes in the direction of Ian Carlisle. Wilma placed a hand on her shoulder. "Yes, definitely a saunter. Oh or maybe a swagger."

Wynona agreed. "Swagger. Absolutely. And look how effortless he makes it. My my my, if I'd had a dance partner that smooth, I could have conquered the world."

Charlee's heart was a hammer in her chest. But she found it difficult to move from the spot.

"Conquer the world, my darling," Wynona said again and pointed at Ian. "That's what a man like that can make you feel like."

A fresh wave of emotions washed over Charlee. The world spun back into focus. She knew that feeling. Powerful and bulletproof. "Yes. A man like that can. Right before he runs you down like yesterday's roadkill."

Wynona sighed.

King Edward placed the sauce on the table. "All I know is it's going to be one hot summer."

Charlee hoped not. She was tired and frazzled and the last thing she needed was her already-unsteady equilibrium being shifted further. Too many things were going wrong in her world, and if not wrong, too many things were changing. One of the biggest, the way she felt about the retreat. Every morning she had to drag herself out of bed to face the day. And that wasn't like her. Love was turning to chore. And across the lawn she saw both an answer and a problem in Ian Carlisle. But of all the things she didn't know, one thing was clear. Ian needed a little time to adjust to life in the real world. And one thing she could offer was a retreat, a safe place for those who didn't quite fit into society. Where Charlee was concerned, Ian was just a different type of artist who needed a place to land.

No problem. She was good at that. But she'd guard her heart also. She had a soft spot for soldiers. Charlee needed him to be like her brothers. Like her father, because those were the kinds of men who could never approve of her life's work and who could never understand it. They were warriors, leaders, fighters. But they weren't alive inside the way she'd need a man to be. They weren't artists or passionate or even spontaneous. They were ordered and disciplined. And soon enough, Ian would be driving her crazy with his type A attitude. Of course, he would. And that kept her safe. In some ways he already was.

"Evening." Ian had a dangerous smile. Slightly crooked, curling up at one edge and exposing a line of white teeth beneath succulent lips.

Charlee mumbled a greeting. When she moved to sit down, she was surprised to find a lap rather than a wooden seat. "Oh, sorry Wilma." Embarrassment caused her to laugh. She hadn't even seen Wilma there. Keeping her eyes on Ian as he sat at the table across from her, she moved to take the seat next to Wilma. The scraping sound drew her attention. Charlee looked back to find Wynona stealing her chair.

After Wilma tossed an empty cup at King Edward, understanding dawned. Wilma gave Edward a sharp look. He shrugged; her eyes widened and shot to one of the empty seats at her table. Wynona had already taken Mr. Gruber by the hand and was leading him to the fourth and final seat at the table Charlee had tried to claim as her own. This of course left Ian alone. Sitting under the butterfly lights with the flame from the tiki torches reflecting in his dark eyes.

She would have expected him to laugh at the scene. At her. But he didn't. Ian Carlisle drew a deep breath and let his head fall back to gaze up at a star-studded sky. And Charlee's heart melted by a tiny increment.

Above them a sky filled with diamond specks glistened. It was beautiful and under the right circumstances could be wildly romantic. But this wasn't the right circumstances because what she imagined that sky represented to Ian was a place he could—for possibly the first time in a long time—close his eyes and rest without the fear of waking to mortar shells, combat. War.

Ian was finding home. She knew this because her brother Isaiah had told her about it when he first returned from Iraq. He'd been there a year and she'd been so happy to have him stateside until he was sent to Afghanistan. The joy had been short-lived. And might have done more harm to her than good. She understood the struggle soldiers go through, at least to some small degree.

When Ian's eyes opened, even though she'd moved from her previous spot, his gaze fell straight to her. And there he sat while she stood, and for the briefest of moments something passed between them. What it was to really come home. And what it was to know someone understood.

Charlee pointed to the seat across from him. "May I?"

Light danced across his features. "I'd be crushed if you didn't."

His humor lightened the mood. Charlee cocked a hip. "I highly doubt that."

Ian's face split into a wicked grin. "I'm beginning to think you're going to doubt everything I say."

"Until I get to know you, yes." She lowered herself onto the seat and pretended not to notice Ian's careful scrutiny as she did. "I've learned men aren't the most trustworthy of beings." Why had she said that? Charlee pulled her hands through her hair, shaking off the past and all the memories with it.

"Learned from?"

Richard, she wanted to say, which really was strange because she never wanted to talk about him to anyone. "I learned from my brothers."

"Ah."

"The ones who fed me a spoonful of celery salt and told me it was cinnamon sugar, the ones who duct-taped me to an oak tree. The ones who swung me by my arms and legs and dropped me into the river. I could go on, but I think you get the point."

"Jeremiah is the oldest, right?" Ian threaded his hands together on his flat stomach.

She tried not to notice, but her gaze dipped to the spot where his jeans met his shirt. "He's thirty-one. Isaiah is twenty-nine. Gabriel, twenty-seven. And Caleb is the baby."

"Younger than you?"

"By a year." The breeze rose and carried the scent of honeysuckle to them. It grew wild along this side of the toolshed. "I suppose I shouldn't call a man who carries an automatic weapon every day a baby, but he's still my little brother."

At the table behind them King Edward dished up plates of spaghetti; utensils clinked against china. A moment later he was hovering over their table.

Charlee swallowed as the nauseating scent of hot tuna and tomato sauce filled the space between them, obliterating the honeysuckle. Edward smiled. "An extra large helping for our soldier?"

Charlee's eyes widened at Ian then she gave her head an almost imperceptible shake back and forth.

Ian watched her, unfolding his hands from his stomach. "I did work pretty hard today."

When Edward's grin spread into what Charlee could only call a sadistic smile, she cleared her throat, catching Ian's eye. Again, the head shake, which she quickly quelled when Edward's laser gaze moved to her.

The sound of Ian's hands slapping together brought everyone's attention to the table. "Give me a double helping, Edward."

Poor Soldier Boy, Charlee thought. She'd tried to warn him. Why did men always insist on learning things the hard way?

Evil. Pure evil reflected in King Edward's eyes. He knows his food tastes like crap. He's doing this on purpose.

Ian lifted the plate under his nose and inhaled deeply.

Charlee leaned back, ready to dive under the table lest he spew. "Smells amazing."

What? What? Charlee blinked. Edward's smile deflated.

"Put one more scoop on there, Eddie. I'm starved."

The empty ladle hovered in the air for a few long moments while Edward's curled top lip ticked. Finally, with a huff, he slapped another scoop on top and went back to his chair. "Dive in," he mumbled.

And Ian did just that. The air stilled as Ian lifted the first bite. He took it in, eyes fitted tightly on Charlee as he chewed twice and swallowed.

She waited for the sound of gagging. But there was something more going on here.

Ian dropped his fork to the plate. "Wow. I mean, wow."

Charlee's gaze flittered from him to the other table, where four sets of round eyes watched Ian intently.

"King Edward, this is fantastic."

Charlee sucked a horrified breath. As did the patrons at the other table. Ian, well, Ian spooned mouthful upon mouthful until his plate was nearly empty.

Food gone, he wiped his mouth with a napkin. "You gotta give me that recipe, Edward."

Edward didn't bother to turn around or reply so Ian's gaze skittered to Charlee, eyes flashing with not just tiki illumination, but something else. Something more. His tongue darted out and moistened a mouth that was too perfectly shaped, too sexy to belong to a soldier who lived on her property. His brow dipped and that's when she saw the smirk.

Without drawing attention, she pointed to the plate and mouthed, "Good?"

Ian looked around her at the other table then leaned closer. "Awful."

Charlee slapped a hand over her mouth and squeezed her eyes shut until she had her desire to laugh out loud under control. Behind them, the other table had finally engaged in a conversation about museums.

Charlee lifted a hand. "Why?"

Ian shot a glance left then right, then motioned for her to move closer. He too leaned in and Charlee refused to admit—even to herself—the intimacy caused emotions to stir inside her.

When she was right there, two breaths from his face, both their chests pressed against the table edge, Ian said, "My commanding officer always told us to never ever let the enemy know your fear. Fear is the only power he has over you. Don't give him the match to light the cannon."

Charlee felt her face spread into a slow smile. Ian smiled back and the two sat there, looking at one another and sharing the art of war. "Sounds like one smart commanding officer."

Ian swallowed, the muscles in his throat tightening. "He was the best."

Charlee stayed quiet and let him reminisce. The scars of war and remembrance colored Ian's features.

Finally, he returned to the present and addressed the table behind him. "So, Edward, did you ever think of adding Vidalia onion? Maybe a little more basil?"

Edward turned and glared.

"I love tinkering around in the kitchen. If you'd like, I can swing by on your next meal shift and maybe we can concoct some more original dishes."

Charlee spun to look at the other table, where wide-eyed artists seemed more than a bit off guard. Wilma's and Wynona's heads tilted like lilting boats while Edward looked almost relieved he'd have help in the kitchen. "If you like cooking so much, take my shift," he said.

Ian leaned back in his seat. "Nah, it'll be more fun if we do it together."

When Edward sighed and turned away, Charlee scrutinized the soldier before her. His dark eyes filled with amusement; his lips spread into that dangerous half grin. His hands pressed flat against the table. He'd managed to uproot and undo not only Edward, but the other artists as well. Except Gruber, who just seemed bored with the whole thing. Finally, those dark eyes broke their hold on her and he winked. "Don't worry. I can cook."

"Aren't you tricky?" she whispered back. "I believe your CO would be very proud of you right now."

One blink. Two. Ian's gaze moving to the horizon, then far away. His mouth—full of mischief moments ago—lay lax now, slightly open. She watched as the light in his eyes dimmed. The mischief faded, being replaced by something darker, deeper, and if Charlee wasn't wrong, much more painful.

The pain of a soldier come home.

Did people really know the sacrifice these men made? Ian was damaged. Of that, she was sure, but how damaged? She hoped one summer could repair the hurt. He had a right to enjoy a life free of the sorrows of war.

Her thoughts shifted to her brothers on foreign soil serving their country. Becoming damaged. Would they return with the same ghosts she saw in Ian's eyes? Would they *all* return home?

It was a moment before she realized her hand had warmed. Charlee glanced down to see Ian's hand gently covering hers.

He whispered, "Are you okay, Charlee?"

No. She wasn't okay. She was a woman who'd lived her dream, only to discover she wasn't sure it was what she still wanted—and if she didn't do this, who would take care of the Mr. Grubers of the world? She was an orphan. She was a girl who prayed every night her brothers would make it home and a girl who worried they wouldn't.

In her own way, she was a soldier. And she was damaged.

Without answering, Charlee rose from the chair. Fear and love drove her across the dance floor, across the yard and around the corner where a tree-lined path led to the sanctuary of her front porch. When she reached the steps, tears stung her eyes because she'd been foolish to think she could have a soldier living on her property without feeling his pain—her brothers' pain—every day. She loved her brothers, bullheaded as they were. Charlee had convinced herself they'd all come home. Jeremiah was stateside, but that still left the other three. Her dad had died in combat last year. In her mind, her family had given enough. But now she knew there were parts of a soldier that never came home. There were things they left there, on the battleground, things one could never get back.

Charlee continued to cry as she entered her dark house. She cried for her brothers. And she cried for the innocence they'd never have again. When her eyes fell on the urn sitting on the fireplace mantel, she wanted to throw something at it. *Don't you know I'm not equipped for this? I can't hold a family together when they're halfway around the world and you're . . . you're gone.* The kitchen light shone against the smooth porcelain of the urn. No answer from it, no reassurance. Charlee headed to bed without bothering to lock her front door. There was no reason. No one came out here. She was alone.

―――

"I'm not sure what I said." Ian retraced it in his mind as he stood from the table and moved to the four onlookers. Mortified that Charlee had run away and he'd been the cause, he stopped at the feet of those who knew her best.

"Sure have a way with the ladies," Edward joked.

Wilma jerked, in unison with a muffled thump under the table. Edward jumped. "Ouch. You kicked me."

Wilma pursed her mouth. "Don't you worry, Ian. You didn't do anything wrong."

Wynona reached out and snagged his hand. "That's right, honey. It wasn't you."

Ian ran a free hand through his hair. "Could someone tell me what it was then, so we don't have a repeat?"

Both sisters opened their mouths, but no words followed.

Edward took a bite of spaghetti. "Personally, I think it was you."

He shifted his chair so Wilma couldn't land another strike.

Wynona squeezed Ian's hand in hers. "Charlee is a very special kind of creature." Wide, expressive eyes rimmed with tiny wrinkles blinked up at him as if willing him to understand. "She's unique."

"Yes," Wilma agreed. "Unusual. Complex."

Ian coaxed them on, but neither woman said more. He wanted to understand Charlee. Needed to, if his mission was to be accomplished. "And complex, unique, unusual people frequently fly away from dinner without warning?"

Wilma scooted in her chair. "No. Charlee feels the blows of the world deeply. She's an empath."

A what? Okay, this wasn't helping. It was like another language.

Mr. Gruber dropped his hand to the table. "Oh good Lord. What they're trying to say, soldier, is that you don't get to know someone like Charlee in one night. She's got layers. The strongest women sometimes have the weakest hearts. Charlee didn't get upset with you . . . Whatever you did. You got into her heart and for her that's a little bit scary. Understand?"

Around them, the wind kicked up. Yeah. He did understand.

"Eloquently put, Arnold." Wynona released Ian's hand and patted Mr. Gruber's. Gruber made a face and pulled away.

"So, what should I do now? Go after her?"

At the same moment he heard two different answers from the four different artists. The men landed on the side of yes. The women landed on the side of no. He opted to listen to the women on this one.

"Give her time," Wilma said and the nod of Wynona's head had her agreeing. Long white strands floated around Wynona with the breeze, a soft, encouraging smile on her face.

Ian realized she must have been some knockout in her younger days. And a dancer too. And he had a suspicion she'd been a bit on the wild side. "Okay. Give her time. I can do that."

By the time he got back to his cabin, he wasn't sure. Something about being around Charlee threw him off guard in too many areas. Only one summer then life could move on. With that in mind, he found the journal in the dim light the moon cast through the open window shade.

Ian angled himself in the chair so that moonlight lit the page. Not that it needed to; he'd memorized so many of the entries all he needed was the first few words to get him started.

Some were titled; some weren't. But all were important, each one cutting right to his heart.

Charlee,

The eyes of my mind picture you. Standing on the front porch watching a sunset. It is sunrise here. Bullets zinging over our heads, but that doesn't change the blue sky. Its umbrella covers us, reminding the boys it's the same sky they grew up staring at when they were young and would lie on their backs and make shapes from the clouds. I can picture each one as a small child. I can see a father scooping each into his arms. It wasn't that long ago they rode bicycles and skateboards, not that long ago they learned to drive and perhaps experienced a first kiss. Oh, I look into their young eyes and I see the children they were. But they're men now. Each one a man with scars and memories no one should have to live with. Of course, it's not all bad here. They're building who they are and who they'll be for the rest of their lives. They're learning that all days must end. That's what I tell them. "Keep your head down and your spirit up," I say. "This day, like all others before it, will end. How it ends is your choice. Who you were this morning and who you'll be tonight—that's up to you. You can't control what happens to you, but you do have a say in how you handle it." Those are words for you too, Charlee. You can't control what happens to you. But you do have a say in how you handle it.

Ian closed the journal. This was going to be harder than he imagined. Though he didn't know what he expected, Charlee was a lot more—what was the word Wilma used?—complex than he'd thought. And his physical reaction to her didn't help. He'd heard so much about her, he felt he already knew her before he came. And seeing her, meeting her, well, he'd assumed that would destroy the fairy-tale person he'd created in his mind. She was just flesh and blood. He needed that fairy tale destroyed. Because he already cared about Charlee much more than he should. And because of her stubbornness, once she knew the real reason he was here, there was a very good chance she'd throw him out. Caught between two McKinleys, Ian had no clue what to do. On one side, there was duty. On the other side, a woman he'd grown to love from afar. There was no easy way out. If he'd thought the war was difficult, this was a thousand times worse. And he was the one calling all the shots. He had to go ahead and tell her. About the journal, about everything. He couldn't wait any longer. Though there'd been specific instructions to let her get to know him before dropping the bombshell, it was just wrong to be here, to have this agenda and not come clean about it. He was going to tell her. At the very first opportunity.

CHAPTER 4

The next day, Charlee was gone but had left instructions for him on what work to do for the day. Done by noon, he searched out Mr. Gruber.

"Morning," he said, at the foot of Gruber's steps.

Gruber offered a rare smile. "Nice work with Edward yesterday. I'm assuming you can cook."

"Yes, sir. I actually attended a culinary school before joining up."

Gruber pointed to his own coffee cup. "You want one?"

Ian was already drenched in sweat. Coffee didn't sound good. "No thanks."

"Why'd you join if you were in culinary school?"

"Uh, well." Ian sighed. "I got the administrator's daughter into a little trouble one night and was given an ultimatum."

Gruber leaned back, brows furrowed and looking instantly angry. "You get his girl pregnant?"

Ian blushed. "Oh, no. Nothing like that. I just . . . well, for kicks we broke into a college's private swimming pool. I got stuck in a locker room when the door shut behind me. Someone called the cops and they arrested her. Didn't find me. It didn't sit well with her father."

Gruber's face was twisted into a disapproving frown. "I expect not. You don't seem like a rabble-rouser to me, Carlisle."

Ian nodded. "Back in the day, I was. Not now. Joining up changed all that."

"Yep. Had a bit of wildness in myself back in the day. Joined up at age seventeen."

"You were in the military?"

Gruber sat a little straighter. "Beginning of Vietnam."

"Army?"

"Navy."

Ian's finger trailed the wood on the banister. He wasn't here to chat about the military. He needed answers and though Gruber was a crusty, temperamental old man, he also seemed to be the one who knew Charlee the best. "Is Charlee avoiding me now?"

Gruber was wearing a sweat-stained ball cap. He lifted it and rubbed a hand over the springy hairs on his head. "Ah, I wouldn't think so. Women are easy enough once you understand them."

"And how long does that take?"

Gruber's face broke into a crooked smile. "Not sure; I'll let you know when I get there."

Ian chuckled and set the rocking chair into motion. The squeak, squeak, squeak of wood against porch floor calmed his nerves.

"Before she passed, my wife used to say, 'I don't need you to fix it; just let me talk about it.'"

Ian's chair stopped abruptly. "What's that mean?"

"Means shut up."

He nodded, wished there was a manual, planted those words deep into his psyche. "Shut up, got it."

Gruber pointed a long, slender finger at him. "But you better talk when they need you to or they say—" and for the next few words, the edges of his mouth went down and his voice went up, "—we never communicate."

Ian drew a deep breath. "Should I be taking notes?"

"Nah. It's simple. Shut up and talk. And while you're thinking about all that, you could go work on the fence line." Gruber closed one eye and pinned him with the other. "It's real important to Charlee to get that fence line complete before her brother moves onto the property next door."

"Charlee seems like she loves her brothers. Putting up a fence suggests they don't get along. What's your take?"

"They all get along fine." Gruber drained his coffee cup and sat it on the porch floor where a water ring waited for it. "Just doesn't want them in her business. Doesn't want people dictating what she does. That's her business, not theirs, and I agree with her. Both her parents are gone and she doesn't need someone trying to take their place."

Oh boy.

"About that fence . . ."

———

Charlee spent the day in town to avoid Ian. It wasn't him particularly; it was just the whole thing. He made her miss her brothers. And worry about them even more. Really, more worry was the last thing she needed. But when she looked in his eyes, saw the pain he was trying to leave behind, saw the fight and the battle that still plagued him, well, her nurturing gene kicked into high gear. After leaving town, she drove home and found Ian at dinner with the rest of the clan.

"I hadn't expected you to work on the fence today," she said, stepping up to the table where he sat chatting with the sisters and King Edward.

Mr. Gruber was just dishing plates when she arrived. He motioned her with a spatula dripping with cheese. "Sit. I don't want it to get cold."

Ian grinned up at her. "Bossy, isn't he?"

"Mmm. You have no idea." She spun and moved to the empty table while Gruber placed a generous helping of lasagna on Ian's plate. "Thank you, sir."

He picked up the fork and was just getting ready to take a bite when Gruber barked, "Now get outta my seat, Lunch Box, or you'll be eating that through a feeding tube."

Charlee rolled her eyes. Ian hustled out of the seat and moved to her table, plate in hand, fork perched on the edge. "May I?"

Her hands covered her face. "I'm so sorry about this." She leaned in. "They're hopeless busybodies."

From above her, Ian winked. He really was a lovely specimen to look at, with his easy smile and toned body. She'd spotted him earlier through the tree line as he worked. He'd been bare from the waist up, his jeans worn and snug on muscled legs, his tool belt hanging carelessly and at just the right angle to draw a girl's attention. Whew. It was hot out tonight.

"You want me to turn on the fans?"

Oh, dear Lord! She hadn't said that out loud, had she? "What?"

"You're holding your hair up."

Oh. She was. She'd scooped the mass into one fist and held it off her neck. Ian's gaze drifted down from her eyes to her throat and all that exposed skin of her neck. He licked his lips and something in her stomach thudded.

"No." She dropped the mass and hoped it would cover her. Stupid idiot of a guy made her feel naked. "I'm not hot."

A twinkle, a blink. Ian sat down and she was pretty sure she'd heard him mumble, "That's highly debatable."

Gruber paused at their table and filled her plate. Here they were again, alone and having dinner. This could so quickly turn into a disaster. Best to stick to business. "The fence."

"I got your list done and was told that was your ongoing project."

"You did a great job." Charlee scooped a generous helping of Gruber's cheesy lasagna into her mouth. There was no need to act dainty. She wasn't dainty and this wasn't a date where she had to pretend to be sweet and demure. This wasn't a date at all. Even though the night's sky was dressed in perfect romantic fashion, the kind lovers stargazed at while planning their futures. Even though the giant trees swayed with the softest of breezes creating a gentle whisper like a song for couples only. She could feel sauce at the edge of her mouth but didn't bother to wipe it away. Definitely not a date.

When Ian's gaze stalled there, her tongue darted out to catch the runaway sauce. But what entered his eyes didn't help the situation. He actually looked hungrier.

He leaned back, lungs expanding and showing off the tone of his pecs. "I finished the other stuff, so I figured why not?"

"Well, it shows a lot about your character."

His fork paused halfway to his mouth. "I was thinking the same thing."

"Huh?"

"Putting up a fence to keep your brother out shows a lot about your character." His gaze dropped as soon as he said it.

Charlee huffed. Below her line of vision was a lovely helping of lasagna that Soldier Boy had just ruined. She used her fork to move the ricotta cheese around on her plate. "Look, you don't understand and you don't need to." She actually had a whole bunch of words in her head to spew at him, but he already looked sorry for saying it.

"I, uh, tend to say all the wrong things at all the best times. I'm really sorry. Stupid mouth gets me in more trouble."

Well then. Charlee didn't know exactly how to handle that. So, she didn't.

They each took a few more bites. But her mind kept spinning. "Look. I love my brothers, but they are all up in my business all the time when they're around."

"Do you see them often?"

"They all four wander in and out when they're on leave. Our family home is still here, in town. It remains their home base."

"Have they always been so protective of you?"

Charlee thought back. "Yes. I think it got worse after our mom died."

"How so?" Ian pushed his empty plate away and leaned forward.

"They went into hyperprotective mode where I was concerned. I went into nurturing mode. Thought it was my job to raise them all. Even though Jeremiah is almost six years older than me and I was only twelve."

His dark eyes grew troubled. "That's a lot for a young girl to carry."

"I didn't mind it. Unfortunately the boys still treat me like I can only survive on my own when they're away at war. And I'm going to shatter into a thousand pieces when they get back if they don't rescue me. I don't need to be rescued."

And that's when he did it. Ian rested his forearms on the table and trapped her in that dark gaze. His words were barely a whisper and all but lost in the sound of the breeze. "Everyone needs someone to rescue them." One second ticked by. Then two. Then three. And something in Charlee's heart twisted because there was a place, a place deep, deep inside her where she wanted a shining knight on a white horse. Someone who wouldn't just lift her, but someone who would give her wings. And that, she knew, didn't exist.

Flickering lights above her twinkled their own Morse code. If only they could flash the answers to life. The wind intensified, mountain gusts moving the treetops, the rustling sound increasing until it drowned out the questions. Ian had a right to his opinion. And Charlee had a right not to give a crap what he thought about her.

Noise from the other table drew her attention. She realized it had been a while since she'd spoken and Ian wasn't the least concerned. He'd turned around in his chair and was locked in some good-natured argument with Gruber about army versus navy. His hand was flat on the table. Why she reached out and snagged it, she didn't know.

He turned to look at her and the talk at the artists' table went on without them. She gave his fingers a light squeeze. "I'm really sorry about last night."

Ian held her gaze as she slowly released his hand. And though they were no longer touching, she could feel the sear of his flesh against her skin. She wasn't good at apologies. Growing up with her brothers, one tended to get it right the first time or suffer unimaginable goading. Or clam up, set your face as flint and hold your ground no matter how wrong you were.

When he offered the faintest of smiles, Charlee pulled her lower lip into her mouth and bit down. "I . . ." *I what?* She couldn't easily explain what had happened last night.

"No need to apologize. And no need to explain. Okay?" His velvet voice offered assurance; the tilt of his head and open demeanor exemplified his willingness to let it go.

"Okay." She took another bite. "No. It isn't okay." Charlee squeezed her eyes shut for a few moments and nodded toward the other table. "They're kind of . . . protective of me."

"The artists?"

Charlee could tell he wasn't certain if she meant them or her brothers. "Both them and my brothers. But right now, the artists. I was in a bad relationship a few months ago and now I think they're bent on playing matchmaker." She motioned at him with an upturned palm. "Unfortunately for you, you've passed their bar."

"Lucky me," he joked, but a flicker of relief and, dare she say, anticipation skated across his features.

"I'm not looking for any kind of relationship deeper than employer and handyman."

Ian tilted toward her. "My CO said the best things in life happen when we aren't even looking for them."

Charlee bristled. "As do the worst."

"Touché."

She flashed a quick smile. "So, now you know my secret."

His eyes leveled on her. "You're safe with me."

Fire shot right into her stomach. Safe with him? She doubted that. She couldn't even trust her body's reactions. Cold and angry one second and . . . well . . . hot and bothered the next. "You mean *my secret* is safe with you?"

Tiki light danced in his smile. "Yes, Charlee." It wasn't exactly patronizing. It was patient, willing to wait. Blasted soldiers knew how to wait for the right moment, then sail into a guerrilla attack and make the kill. "Your secret is safe. In fact, one day I'll tell you mine."

Seemed fair. But as she watched his shoulders tighten, noticed the muscles of his jaw harden, she knew Ian wasn't ready to talk. "When it's time," she said, and was shocked at the display of emotions that danced across his face. Relief, seeming to lead the parade.

"Really?"

"When you're ready to share your secret, Ian, I'll be ready to listen." The sound of other voices and banter had all but disappeared around them.

The seriousness of the conversation was palpable enough to grow legs and walk away. But it didn't. It stayed right there between them.

Ian worked the muscle in his jaw. "You mean that?"

She could almost hear the gears turning in his head. Weighing something. "Absolutely."

"Friends, then?"

"Of course." Liberation flooded her. Friends, she could handle.

One side of his mouth slid into a smile. "Is it too early to ask for a pay raise?"

"Darn it. I was just going to ask if you'd mind a pay cut."

Charlee returned to the lasagna she had lost interest in. It wasn't until Mr. Gruber served dessert that the conversation between Ian and Charlee picked up. "What about you, Ian? Any bad relationships in your past, or is that topic off-limits? You know, with the new rules about telling secrets and all."

"Uh." Ian wiped his mouth and spread the napkin in his lap, leaning back. "Bad relationships? How about all of them?"

Charlee took another bite of key lime pie. "Can't be all that bad." She had figured whatever his deep, dark secret was, it had more to do with where he'd spent the last two years than what was in his little black book. *Relationships seemed so easy for guys. You have one, you don't. Life goes on.*

His dark hair glistened in the tiki light. "It was all bad, trust me."

"One in particular?"

When he looked up at her, Charlee saw it. The same pain she'd felt when Richard betrayed her. An older wound perhaps, but a severe one.

"I was in love once. Her name was Brenna."

Charlee choked on the bite she was trying to swallow. Guys didn't typically throw around words like *love*. "What happened?"

"I guess my whole life I've been a bit of a screwup." He laughed without humor. "So, you can probably guess."

"Was it recent?" He'd been deployed for a long time; had he fallen for someone there?

"High school sweethearts."

"Oh." That was a long time ago if he was about her age.

"I messed it up then. And when we reconnected right before I joined up, I messed it up again."

"I'm sorry, Ian." And she was, because whatever happened still weighed on him. And that was a brand of pain she understood.

"It wasn't until I was in the military that I learned what it really is to be a man."

"War can do that to a person."

"It wasn't the war. It was my CO." Ian reached for his dessert plate and lifted the fork. "If not for him, I'd still be a screwup."

"I doubt that."

Ian shrugged. "And if you consult my father, I'm *still* a screwup."

"Don't feel bad about that. I think most of us feel like our parents don't understand us. It's human nature, I guess. My dad never understood me." She motioned around her. "This place. Thought it was a huge waste of money and throwing away my college education."

"And your mom?"

"This was her dream first. She talked about it so much, it became real to me before it even existed. What little girl wouldn't dream about living where she can paint pictures all day and eat dinner under the stars every night?"

"Do you get to paint every day?"

Charlee looked beyond him to the mountain range. "No. Too busy. But now that you're here . . ."

Ian smiled.

It was a nice smile, filled with interest in her words. Charlee shook her head to clear it. They really needed brighter light out here. Glaring, ugly, incandescent light. Yes, that's what they needed.

Wilma cleared their plates and followed Mr. Gruber into the kitchen while Ian and Charlee stood and gathered their utensils and cups. Before they could move away, Wynona sailed in and grabbed their things. "We're cleaning up tonight to help Mr. Gruber. You two would just be in the way. It's a lovely night; why don't you go for a stroll?"

Charlee opened her mouth to speak, but nothing came out.

Ian to the rescue. "I'm beat. Maybe some other time. But, hey, Charlee," he lightly punched her shoulder, "I'll walk you home."

It was such a brotherly gesture, Charlee had to bite back a smile at Wynona's look of disapproval. "Sure. Whatever."

With a wide berth between them, they headed off in the direction of Charlee's house.

When they were out of earshot, she leaned a bit closer. "I'll give you props for the arm punch."

"Good. Props has to be better than a knee to the groin . . . like I was expecting."

"What? That's stupid. Why would I do that?" The path home was well worn and she knew where all the stumbling blocks were.

"You grew up with brothers. I just thought the arm punch might cause a flashback."

She stopped to turn and face him fully. "You were expecting that, really?"

"Noooo," he said, but as he did, his open hands came together as a shield below his belt.

Charlee threw her head back and laughed. It was good to laugh. It had been a long time. It was good to stroll to her house with a clever conversation passing between herself and someone else . . . someone under the age of fifty. And that's when she realized, maybe it was too nice. Too easy. Something squeezed on her heart. Charlee turned from him and kept walking, picking up the pace just enough to outrun the feelings shooting through her system. But Ian picked up his pace too and suddenly they weren't only walking, they were close. His arm nearly scraping her shoulder. When he stumbled forward, obviously not knowing the path as well as she, instincts took over and she reached out and grabbed him.

He'd bent at the waist, but gathered his feet under him and stood, moving closer to her rather than farther away. Her hand was still clamped on his upper arm as if she'd be strong enough to catch him if he fell. He was two hundred pounds of solid muscle. Charlee's fingers seemed to have a mind of their own, staying planted on his rock-hard arm. *Let go, let go, let go.*

Ian turned into her. "Thanks," he whispered and she could smell the scent of key lime on his lips.

"No problem." But she was lying. This wasn't just a problem, this was an epic fail because he was right here and too easy to lean on . . . or grab . . . whichever the case may be. And Charlee was feeling the stone-solid walls of her resolve crumbling.

Ian sniffed. "Can you smell that?"

Charlee used her free hand to brush the hair from her eyes. "It's peppermint I planted some years ago and now it grows wild along the side of the kitchen. There's honeysuckle by the toolshed."

"It's incredible." But she could see in his features, the way his gaze lingered on her eyes then her mouth, he wasn't just talking about mint. Charlee swallowed, took a minimal step back.

Ian knew something had changed; she saw it reflecting in his eyes. "You okay, Charlee?"

The wind had kicked up and tossed her hair in front of her face. She wished she could just hide behind it. But she couldn't. This needed to be handled. Head-on. "You're a good man, aren't you, Ian Carlisle?"

"I'd like to think so."

Charlee let her hand drop from his arm. "And you wouldn't break your word, right? It's a code among soldiers. If you give your word, you have to do it."

"Yes."

"Then I want you to make me a promise."

In his eyes, she saw the war. And the tiniest part of her felt bad for putting him on the spot, but the biggest part of her knew she had to.

Ian swallowed. "Anything."

Charlee's heart stuttered to a stop because in this moment, with this man, she knew she could make any demand and he'd accomplish it or die trying. It was such a stark realization it nearly took all the wind from her lungs. "I want you to promise me we won't become more than friends."

Ian looked like he'd been punched. Which was crazy. They'd only just met. But sometimes, sometimes an instant was a lifetime and that's what it felt like with Ian. He rubbed his hands over his face as she tried to breathe, but there was no oxygen and spots were flashing in her periphery like tiny ghosts trying to find their way home.

When Ian's eyes landed on her again, there was a new strength in them. "You know, on the battlefield when someone gets wounded, the medic looks to see if it's superficial or if it's deep. Superficial, you can keep fighting. Deep, you need to leave the battlefield."

Charlee's gaze stayed riveted to his as he closed the small space between them. And then, his hands were there, against her arms, fingertips moving ever so gently. "I get it. You were wounded on the battlefield."

And for some inexplicable reason, all the pain of Richard's betrayal and the hurt she'd suffered surged to the surface. Charlee choked back a sob.

Ian moved even closer, his face only a few inches from hers. "Is it superficial, Charlee? Or is it deep?"

She wanted . . . wanted so badly to say it was superficial, that the right guy could help her through it. And she was going to, the instant she opened her mouth . . . she was going to tell him that. But she heard herself saying, "It's deep."

Ian nodded slowly. His hands became a caress; he leaned forward and rested his forehead against hers like the words had stolen the strength from his body. Eyes closed, their bodies were communicating though their mouths were silent. He sighed, a sound filled with resignation and sadness. Charlee stiffened because she knew it would be painful when he drew away. And Ian was undoubtedly going to draw away from her, of that she was certain. Mustering his strength, he took a tiny step back and squared his shoulders. "I give you my word. What's between us won't go any farther than friendship."

Right then and there, Charlee crumbled. He had no idea the gift he was giving her. Relief rose like the giant swell of a tsunami, but right on its heels came the heartbreak. She'd spent many nights crying herself to sleep in the last six months. Alone. Always alone, rarely in front of anyone else and now, it seemed impossible to stop the tears. Giant drops filled her eyes and she couldn't hold back the flood anymore. Charlee tried to turn from him to take the last few steps to her front porch, but he caught her in his arms. In the next moment, the scent of pepper and spice and Ian surrounded her just as his arms wound so tightly around her body all she could do was collapse under the pressure. He didn't stroke her hair or speak. He didn't move except to breathe. But he held her there, steadfast. Like a brick blanket. A safe house. A port in the storm. When their breathing slowed and the fast tears became slow ones, with her head against his chest, Charlee knew what it was to feel not just protected, but cherished.

Ian didn't move until she slowly pulled away. It was only fair for him to see the mess that was her. He'd been there when she needed a good cry. He used his thumbs to rub away the remaining tears from her cheeks. When she opened her mouth, he placed a thumb over her lips. "Good night, Charlee McKinley. Sweet dreams."

And then he strolled, no sauntering, no swaggering, off into the darkness. And Charlee was left with the very real possibility that it might be more difficult for her to keep the promise than it was going to be for Ian. In fact, a tiny bit of her heart might already be gone.

CHAPTER 5

"You want to get out of here for a while?" Charlee asked Ian as she jumped out of the Jeep. She'd slid to a stop in front of his cabin. So, he hadn't run her off completely, he decided. That was good. For hours last night, he'd stayed awake listening to a killer thunderstorm shake the mountains and rumble his cabin walls. Ian had always liked the rain, its cleansing power, its ability to purify the land. But last night had left him unsettled, as if the heavenly show was a forerunner to disaster. A disaster he could no more control than the storm that shook the retreat.

It was twelve hours after her crying episode and four hours after the mammoth storm rocked the mountainside. Wearing jean shorts and a ripped tank top, Charlee looked hot enough to melt iron. Ian reined in his libido as she—smiling like a Cheshire cat—hopped up onto his porch step. The morning sun was rising over McKinley Mountain. That's what they called it, he'd learned, the mountain that shot into the sky, cutting the horizon.

He handed her a steaming coffee cup.

She frowned. "Were you expecting company?"

"Yeah, met some girls in town late last night after I walked you home."

She came to a screeching halt on his top step. Eyes jabbing him like a fireplace poker.

"It's a joke, McKinley. Geez, lighten up."

Her shoulder tipped up, eyes landing heavenward. "None of my business."

But her tone was tight and red snaked across her throat and the bare section of her upper chest. This was jealousy. Oh. He liked seeing that on her. "I was awake half the night with that storm."

She took a sip of the coffee. "Good ole Ozark Mountain storms. It rained buckets." And that's when he saw the glint in her eyes.

Ian had been concerned about the morning. Charlee had bared her feelings last night, letting him see her in a true moment of weakness. She'd been a downed wire and him, the puddle of water the frayed lines landed in. Electricity and water, a dangerous combination and a fair description of the two of them. "Gruber said he might stop by this morning, but I haven't seen him yet."

Charlee dropped into the wooden rocker beside Ian. "He can get his own coffee."

"You like the rain?" he asked her.

"Yeah, I guess. But mostly I like hitting the trails on the property after the rain. I thought you might like to go with me."

He smiled over at her. "I'd love to." *I'd go anywhere with you, Charlee.* That part, he needed to keep to himself, but in all honesty, the more time he spent with her, the more he wanted. This was all working in reverse of what he'd planned. "Charlee, can I talk to you about something?"

She stopped rocking and angled in the seat to face him. "Sure."

"At dinner, when we were talking about secrets . . ." How to finish this? He needed to just tell her the truth. Tell her why he was there and what was supposed to be accomplished.

"Ian, I meant what I said. We all have things, skeletons in the closet. It's okay to take your time." She moved her coffee from one hand to the other and reached over. Her fingers were still hot from where she'd gripped the mug.

"What if that secret would change the way you saw me?"

Understanding entered her gaze. "Ian, I'm getting to know you now. Who you are. We're building a friendship based on *now*. Not on the past. Not on what you've done or what's happened to you. I choose to know who you are by experience. Okay?"

Could he leave it at that? He guessed so, for now. But soon, there'd be a right time to tell her what his true mission was. If he revealed too much too soon, she'd run; that's what he'd been told. He'd imagined the conversation would come up naturally, but it hadn't yet. What had seemed like waiting for the right timing now felt like dishonesty. He didn't like it. And he didn't know how long he could hold out. Without realizing it, his hand fell to his front pocket where he kept a folded page of the journal. He'd been instructed to make copies of the pages and when the time was right, begin.

Obscure. Infuriating. Necessary.

"Where's your mind, soldier?"

Ian jumped. The words, words he'd heard many times, took him by surprise. It was Charlee's voice. Not the one he knew so well. He angled to face her. "Can I read something to you?"

Her smile faded. "Okay."

Ian's heart pounded as he reached into his jeans and withdrew the page. It crinkled as he unfolded it. "It's a letter home."

Charlee placed her coffee mug on the railing and gave Ian her full attention while off in the distance, the sound of early morning birds pierced the sky.

The woods were still wet from last night's rainfall, the sun glistening off the trees, making them appear trimmed in a diamond garland.

He didn't read the heading.

In three days you'll celebrate your birthday. I wish I could be there. To see your smiling face and watch you greet another year of your life. Sometimes it feels like I've already been gone for an eternity. And each new day I think the separation will get easier. But loneliness is always there, my constant companion, my closest friend. I've been here a long time. And I know this is where I'm supposed to be. But I feel like everything I've left behind is crumbling, seawater beating against the rocks, wearing them down. The corrosion of time taking what was once mine and layer by layer destroying it. You know the thing that keeps haunting me? I wonder if you remember the sound of my voice. Can you close your eyes and hear me? If I whisper something here, will it travel to your heart there, so many miles away? Close your eyes. Am I there? Do you hear me? Or have I waited too long? I love you.

Charlee's hand landed on his. "Ian, that's beautiful. Beautiful and tragic. I don't know how else to describe it."

Ian nodded, folded the page and slipped it back into his front pocket. "Yeah."

"So much love in that letter." Her gaze fanned to the mountains before them where evergreens reached to the sky, their branches stretching upward, searching for sunlight.

"Do you think the person who got the letter knew how much she was loved?"

Charlee's shoulder tipped up. "How could she not? It's so evident."

"Some people have a hard time coming right out and saying things." Careful, here. He knew he needed to tread lightly.

Charlee turned to face him. "You'd have to be an idiot not to know how that person feels."

Ian nodded and made the decision, now was the time for Charlee to know. Everything. Right now.

"Okay." She turned to him with a smile. "Enough deep talk for one day. Let's go have some fun. I hear your boss is a complete slave driver."

He could push, maybe even should, but fear kept him from it. "Don't forget she's also a control freak."

She squeaked and put a hand to her heart.

"And a complete narcissist." He looped a finger through one of the small holes in her tank top. She glanced down at it, shrugged.

Charlee pinned him with a finger. "You better take off those nice jeans, Pretty Boy. You're going to get dirty today."

Those words—innocent as they were meant to be—wrapped around his gut. He should drag her into his cabin. Instead, Ian disappeared inside. Alone. He hollered through the closed screen door, "She's bossy too. Orders me around like I'm her personal servant."

"Is that right?"

"Yeah." He slipped out of his jeans and found a pair of gym shorts. Ian inspected his T-shirt in the mirror, decided all his shirts were old and left it on. "If it gets any worse, I may need combat pay."

Through the window, he watched her fold her arms and drop her weight against the doorjamb. "I don't give combat pay, soldier."

He brushed past her, stepping into the fresh sunlight and shaking off the heaviness of earlier. "You should." After tromping through the mud, Ian jumped into the Jeep and waited.

Charlee climbed into the driver's seat and gave him a wicked smile. "Anything you're scared of?"

His eyes widened. "I'd prefer to not have a bucket of snakes dropped on my head; other than that, I can't think of anything."

She pushed the clutch and revved the motor as the Jeep lurched forward. "Good. I'd hate to make fun of you if you're a chicken. But I'd do it."

"Hit me with your best shot, little girl. I think I can handle anything you've got."

———

After climbing the first mountain and half sliding, half driving down the next, Ian wished he'd added a few things to his list of fears—death, for one. Charlee was a daredevil. Or crazed. Or had a death wish. Or all of the above. When he finally became confident in her mountain driving off-road ability, she was on to blasting through mud puddles and creek beds. Okay, so it was fun. More than fun, great. Adrenaline-pumping, heart-hammering great. Their flesh and clothing were spotted with enough mud they could easily camouflage themselves if need be by disappearing right into the ground.

After a couple hours, they stopped for lunch. Charlee dragged a cooler out of the back of the Jeep and tossed a blanket to Ian. They were along the creek where the water rushed down a four-foot waterfall and landed in a pool at the base. They were in a lush green valley and all around were mountains reaching to the sky. "We can clean off at the creek." Charlee sat the cooler in the center of the blanket. She had dried mud on her hands, making them look ancient and cracked.

"You scared me half to death, you know?" He bent and scooped some water.

"Ah, only half?" She slipped her feet from her tennis shoes and stepped into the creek where shallow water bubbled over the rocks.

"Cute." Ian didn't bother taking off his shoes, but stepped in beside her.

"Careful! The rocks are really sl—"

Splash! He disappeared below the water and came up sputtering.

"Slick." Charlee laughed.

"You could have told me before I got in." The water was cold and felt great after being pelted by mud that had hardened in the sun.

"What kind of an idiot gets into the creek without at least removing his shoes?"

He tucked under the water, then came up fast, flinging the water in his hair in all directions. "The same kind who agrees to work for a slave-driving, bossy, know-it-all boss."

She raised a finger. "You forgot narcissistic."

He gave her a long look up and down. "I've decided to recant that."

She splashed water onto her legs and arms, leaving a trail of mud in the sun-dotted creek. Ian found it difficult to stop watching.

To cool off, he ducked under again.

Before long, they were on the blanket eating sandwiches and chips. A few droplets still shimmered on Charlee's tanned legs, but Ian felt surprisingly dry—between the heat outside and that generated by his internal temperature rising while he watched Charlee remove mud from her skin—yeah, his flesh was cooking.

"This had to be a great place to grow up." He reached for the bag of chips.

"We lived at the edge of town. The house is still empty except when my brothers are on leave. We couldn't bring ourselves to sell it. It still has too much of Mom." She smiled sadly. "And now too much of Dad to get rid of it."

Ian swallowed hard. She'd lost both her parents. He and his dad didn't get along, but he couldn't imagine a world without his parents. "You always lived here?"

"You sound surprised."

He shrugged. "Military families. Usually move more."

"Dad was stationed at Fort Cradler. It's about an hour from here. When my mom got sick, we were never asked to move. After she died, Dad actually took a desk job at the base until me and Caleb could graduate."

"A desk job?"

"Drove him nuts not being in the field. But he knew we needed one parent home. And Mom was gone."

"Caleb is your younger brother, right?"

She took a bite of her sandwich. "By one year. He enlisted as soon as he graduated. Loves the army. The army and water, Caleb's two passions."

"Water?"

"He's a swimmer. Would have gone into the navy if he hadn't been afraid Dad would disown him." Charlee handed Ian a bottle of water. "So, were you and Jeremiah close?"

"No. Not really." Ian dropped his gaze and took a long drink.

"Did you know him when he was in Afghanistan?"

"Yeah." He needed to move this conversation in a new direction.

Fact was, it wasn't Jeremiah who'd told him about the job. When he'd reached town he'd filled his tank at the gas station and inquired about the artists' retreat. The guy behind the counter asked if he was there for the handyman job.

When Charlee opened her mouth to speak, Ian swallowed and angled to look at the waterfall. "It's really cool here. Love the falls."

"Yes. We're on Caleb's property right now. It's a bit more rugged than mine, but Caleb is a total outdoorsy guy. It suits him." She studied Ian for a few moments. "You know, you haven't done the study for King Edward yet. Has he mentioned it?"

"No. And I hope he doesn't. I can't imagine stripping my clothes so he can stare at me naked."

"It's art, Ian. Not porn."

He shuddered. "It's my body, Charlee, and I don't particularly like the idea of it being exploited on a canvas for all the world to see."

She bit back a grin, causing the dimple in her cheek to deepen. "Why? Hiding something?"

"Go on, make a joke of it, but if it were you having to pose nude, I think you'd feel differently."

"Well, if it helps, I could see if Edward will let me do the study rather than him. Would that be better?" She blinked wide, innocent eyes at him.

"Yes."

She wadded the empty bag of chips and threw it at him. "I knew it. You're just a chauvinistic jerk. It's okay for a young woman to stare at you naked, but not for an older man."

He blinked once, twice, and again. "At the risk of sounding old-fashioned, yes." A smile spread across his face. "Whenever you want to stare at me naked just let me know."

She stood and stormed off toward the creek. "Idiot. Stupid army jerk." But there was a hint of teasing in her tone and a definite sway to her hips.

He followed her with enough stealth she didn't know he was there until he spoke. "You're a control freak and I'm a jerk. Seems like we're pretty evenly matched."

She turned around to find him close. Her mouth opened, but nothing came out. His brows rose. She rolled her eyes. When they landed on his, they softened. "Ian, was it you who wrote that letter?"

He wanted to tell her yes even though it would be a lie, to tell her he was capable of a ridiculously beautiful thing like that, but he wasn't. Ian didn't have a romantic bone in his body. "No."

She tilted her head. "Would you tell me if it was?"

"No." He wouldn't tell anyone because he simply was inept at letting people know how he really felt. It was in him, in his head, in his heart, but the words got all tangled up.

"Here." She slipped something into his hand.

He glanced down to find the Jeep keys.

"You can drive."

"I'd love to." Before she could comment back, he gathered the blanket and cooler and headed toward the Jeep.

Charlee hustled the artists into the Jeep and Ian followed on his Harley. They were headed to the Neon Moon. It had been a long week and they all deserved a night on the town, though Charlee had some reservations about Ian going along.

Her fence was halfway done thanks to Ian's constant attention. He'd been sweet and friendly for the last several days since their little talk about deep wounds versus superficial ones, but that smoldering look in his eyes had all but gone. She appreciated that. And missed it. The day mudding had been fun and everything between them seemed to be at a nice, smooth, *safe* pace.

The Neon Moon was a bar and grill with peanut shells littering the concrete floor and farm equipment attached to the scarred wooden walls. It had been a barn in its former life but served the best burgers and homemade potato chips on the planet. And it was the only good restaurant within a five-mile radius of the retreat, making it not only tasty but convenient. When she was young, her older brother Gabriel would bring his guitar and sing on stage on open mike night. Gabriel had an incredible voice, and there was a time Charlee was certain he'd follow his dream to Nashville. But after her oldest brother had a short-lived and unfortunate brush with fame, Gabriel stopped talking about his dream of singing onstage. The guitar was put away in the top of the closet and the dream died.

Mr. Gruber was sandwiched between the sisters in the backseat of the Jeep and though he scowled for the ten-minute drive, Charlee had the distinct impression he really didn't mind being trapped between the ladies. King Edward occupied the passenger seat, hairy knees spread and his kilt flittering in the night breeze. He wore a brightly colored African hat on his head. One he swore had been given to him by a shaman when he'd visited their beautiful country for a photography safari. King Edward's stories were colossal and Charlee barely knew where fiction began and fact ended. Especially since she'd found the hat in the laundry once and noted the tag inside, *Made in India*.

In the rearview mirror she watched Ian. He leaned into the corners and she wasn't sure why watching him made her heart beat faster. She hadn't wanted to invite him along because, well, because this was an *away from the retreat* event and that made it feel too social. But it would have been rude to leave him there. Charlee chewed the inside of her cheek and whipped into the gravel parking lot.

The place was alive and thumping with country music and laughter. Charlee ran her hands through her hair to smooth the strands—which never really worked, but she figured she'd get points for trying. When she turned to see Ian doing the same thing, she chuckled. His cheeks were flushed and his face smiling. "Good to be out?" She hopped out of the Jeep and slammed the door.

He laughed as she stepped over to his bike. "I like riding at night. You have to be careful though."

"Traffic?"

"No. Bugs. Windshield helps. But I learned the hard way to keep my mouth shut."

He was in his customary jeans and had just placed his helmet on the seat when King Edward came over. "I've unfortunately never been good at that."

They both turned to face him.

"Keeping my mouth shut."

Ian slapped him on the shoulder. "You don't have to tell us that, Edward. We already know." The three entered the restaurant behind Wilma, Wynona, and Mr. Gruber.

―――

This was Ian's kind of place and it felt great to be out in the real world. He was from Oklahoma—one state over—and his home state boasted hundreds if not thousands of restaurants like this one. Greasy spoons and dive bars where you could get a great burger or catfish dinner, where you could tell your secrets to a wizened old bartender and be called *Sugar* by a gum-smacking waitress. He felt right at home here. It was a lot like home, in fact. Except it didn't have all his past mistakes to taint the present. Inside, the space glowed with canned light, and the general radiance of happy people chatting about their week.

Ian glanced over to find Charlee bobbing to the song. Her shoulders bumped, hips swaying ever so lightly. Oh God. His mouth went dry. He was pretty sure she didn't even know she was doing it—which made it that much sexier. "I need a drink," he said over the noise.

She turned to face him, face alight. "What?"

Her light eyes sparkled; her cheeks were rosy with the flush of fun and anticipating a great night out, and, with little desire to control himself, Ian wanted to reach out, grab her and drag her onto the dance floor. He wouldn't, of course. They'd end up a tangled mess lying on the floor. Which actually didn't sound bad either.

Charlee leaned closer and cupped a hand around her ear. "Did you say something?"

He leaned in and was blasted by her scent of vanilla and life with the faintest hint of mineral spirits. It was an intoxicating mix. "I'm going to the bar to order us some drinks. What does everyone like?"

Her face clouded and she shot a glance at the group of artists behind her. They were just settling at a round table in the far corner. She took hold of Ian's arm and pulled herself closer.

Ian froze as her free hand cupped his shoulder and she stood on her tiptoes. A moment later, her lips were at his ear and hot lava was trickling down his neckline. It was just her breath, he realized, but it was fire.

"I forgot to tell you, we don't drink." She shot another look to the far table. And Ian took the opportunity to give her a confused frown. When she turned back to him and pressed even closer, her lips brushed his ear. Oh yeah.

"It's for Mr. Gruber. We all took a vow. He's an alcoholic, sober for the last eight years. It's our way of supporting him."

She leaned back just enough to look Ian in the eye. Lord, he didn't care if they were there to drink gasoline, he just wanted to keep her talking. When his blank expression gave nothing away, she leaned in again. "Of course, you don't have to not drink. I mean, it's fine. I'm sure it won't bother him. Just a decision the rest of us made."

Again she tilted out and chewed her lip while Ian tried to keep the nonchalant frown of interest on his face. All he really thought was, *Keep breathing in my ear and on my neck.*

Charlee kneaded her bottom lip. When Ian realized she was going to go move away, he asked, "So what does everyone like?"

"I'll have an iced tea, same for Mr. Gruber. King Edward usually orders a Shirley Temple. And the sisters like root beer."

When she turned to go to the table, he reached out and grabbed her. She turned and came easily back to him where her body pressed against his. Now it was his turn. Rather than yell over the din of noise, Ian used his hand to lift the hair off her shoulder and move it behind her. Ah, there was that long, gorgeous neck. Slowly, he leaned in and though Charlee had been moving to the music, she stopped. Even her breath seemed to catch in her throat. In a fast swoop, Ian tilted down until it was his lips against her ear. He drew in a breath before speaking and was pretty sure he felt it quiver over her skin. "Save me a seat beside you." His upper and lower lips teased the delicate skin on her ear and if he wasn't mistaken, a little bit of Charlee melted. He couldn't help the satisfied grin on his face when he tilted away and she looked *deer in the headlights* glazed. His eyes made a quick trail down over the white T-shirt and jeans she wore. When she didn't move, he took her by the shoulders and angled her toward the table of waiting artists. A little press on her lower back had her walking to them. But really, Ian only did that so he could watch. Back pencil straight, she dropped into the seat and had them scoot over so Ian could sit beside her.

Ian ordered drinks at the bar, waited for the tray of beverages, then turned to go back to the group. When he caught sight of what was going on, the hair stood on the back of his neck. Two guys hovered over the table of artists and from wide-eyed, nervous looks on the artists' faces, they weren't welcome guests.

Ian bullied his way between the two men and sat the tray of drinks in the center of the table, quickly changing the atmosphere and joking about how hungry he was. He slid in beside Charlee and gave her a long, slow look, perfect easy smile in place—to let the guys behind him know they were no threat. When he finally turned to face them, they'd puffed their chests a bit more, elbows angled out and standing a little taller.

"Who's your friend, Charlee?" the one on the left said. He was dressed in camo with a tight ball cap shoved down over his forehead. Light brown hair curled over the hat rim and he wore a short-bladed pocketknife in a sheath on his belt. Ian knew how to handle a guy with a knife. He continued sizing up the enemy in case this conversation went south.

Ian stood, easily, held out a hand. "Ian Carlisle. I'm working for Charlee."

Knife guy didn't shake his hand, but Ian hadn't figured he would. The one on the right grunted. "If you need male attention, Charlee, you can hire me for free."

Fire shot from Ian's ears into his gut. He could feel the fury building, but it was King Edward who spoke up.

"You wouldn't be hiring someone if it was free, moron."

The guy on the right leaned over the table into Edward's face. "What did you say?"

Edward leaned forward to put himself nose to nose with the man. "I said—"

Wilma's hand clamped over Edward's mouth. "If you don't mind, we're tired. We just want to eat a burger and have a nice evening."

Ian stood toe to toe with Curly. The guy's hand stayed close to the knife on his hip, an intimidation tactic that might work on civilians, but didn't on him.

Charlee spoke up and Ian cast her a quick look. She wasn't afraid, wasn't nervous. Just . . . looked frustrated.

"Excuse me." She pushed past Ian and Curly. "Dean, you've had a lot to drink. Why don't you go home to your wife?"

Dean pointed to Edward. "I want an apology from Sissy Britches over there. Anna said he flashed her. On purpose."

Wilma's hand had fallen away from Edward's mouth until he spoke up. "Afraid you can't measure up?"

Wilma sucked in a breath and this time slapped her hand hard enough it made a loud clap.

Charlee reached out and placed a hand on Dean's arm. A gesture Ian found not only revolting but irritating. "Dean," she oozed. "Please.

Edward has a big mouth and admittedly doesn't know when to keep it shut." She threw Edward a harsh look.

His eyes grew wide with his shrug.

"I'm tired," she purred. "I've had a hard week and I don't want to have to babysit one of my artists in the hospital."

Ian had lost interest in Curly; his eyes fitted tightly on Charlee and how she melted the room by soothing this guy. "Please. Can we let this one go? I promise to do my level best to keep King Edward on a short leash." And then, she batted her eyes and it wouldn't have taken much more than a feather to knock Ian right off his feet.

Dean swallowed, cleared his throat. "Okay, Charlee. For you."

Was there a dude in town that *didn't* have a crush on her?

"Thank you." She stood on her toes and dropped a peck on Dean's cheek.

All the air left Ian's lungs. Dean and Curly walked away.

Conversation picked up at the table, but Ian didn't care. He couldn't seem to drag his thoughts from watching Charlee stand, pucker up, and land her lips on that jerk's cheek. It was a moment before he heard someone say his name.

"Looks like someone's been struck by the green monster." Mr. Gruber had finished his iced tea and was using the straw to clink the ice around in the tall plastic cup.

"Shh," Wilma warned.

Gruber just smiled his crooked grin.

The rest of the evening passed with the weight of the earlier interaction looming over them, though no one seemed that bothered by it except Ian.

When they left and the cool night breeze hit them just outside the door of the Neon Moon, Ian decided he was too keyed up to go home and try to go to sleep. "I'm going for a ride," he barked as Charlee dug the Jeep keys from her jeans pocket.

"You're not going back with us?"

"No."

She angled to face him. "What's your problem, Carlisle?"

He took a dangerous step toward her. "What's my problem? How about the fact that two idiot rednecks insulted your friends and you reward one of them by kissing him."

Charlee brushed a hand through the air. "Is that what you think?"

His hand fisted at his side as the image played over in his mind. "I watched it, Charlee."

"Mind your own business, Ian."

When she spun from him to storm off, he grabbed her. "You kissed him."

She jerked from his grasp and Ian was quickly reminded this was a woman who'd grown up with four brothers and didn't get intimidated easily. "And you're the one who's being a jerk right now." She shot a hand behind her. "I've known Dean my whole life. Since kindergarten, okay? He's not the outsider here, you are. So stop trying to rescue me because you'll only make things worse."

His hand dropped to his side. Honestly, he didn't know how to take that. She started to walk away, got three steps and turned to light into him again. "And for your information, King Edward did flash his wife! He flashes all the ladies in town whenever he gets the chance. Most of them just know to glance the other way when Edward leans over to pick something up. Dean was trying to defend his wife."

Ian opened his mouth, but nothing came out. "I'm sorry, Charlee."

She held up a hand. "You know what? Save it. I knew bringing you tonight was a mistake." And then she walked away, pausing for only a moment before climbing into the tall Jeep. He watched her shoulders rise and fall, then she cast a glance behind her to him and he must have looked like a pitiful excuse because when she blinked, there was regret in her eyes. Charlee tilted her chin and got into the Jeep. He watched as she peeled out of the gravel drive and headed in the direction of the retreat.

For several minutes, Ian sat on the curb by his bike. He wasn't in the mood for a ride anymore and he wasn't ready to go home. *Screwup.* The word rolled over and over in his mind. Maybe the only time he wasn't a screwup was when he was in the military. Maybe he didn't have what it took to make it on the outside. Maybe he just didn't belong anywhere.

When the Neon Moon's front door swung open and out came Curly and Dean, Ian decided it would be best to go. He didn't want to make matters worse—as Charlee said he would—by provoking the two who'd been looking for a fight the better part of the night. He started to get on his bike when a hand landed on his shoulder. Ian pulled a deep breath because he knew how this was destined to end.

———

Charlee took turns watching the clock and the long winding dirt road leading to Ian's cabin. She paced, made tea, paced some more. Scolding herself for saying such harsh and hurtful things to him. *He's not one of my brothers.* This, she'd repeated like a mantra because Ian was all man and man defended woman. It was in their genes and under normal circumstances with a normal woman was really a sweet gesture. But Charlee wasn't a normal woman. She'd had four brothers growing up and never got to fight her own battles until one by one they left and she had to learn how to use her wits to get out of tight jams. They had, in fact, done harm to her by not letting her fight her own wars, and she'd grown up with that survivor part of her still in its infancy. But as an adult, she'd learned; oh, she'd learned. She'd fought and clawed her own way to the top of Respect Mountain. And hated when her brothers showed up and knocked her off her throne. *You're not one of my brothers.* Oh boy, was that easy to remember when he'd touched his lips to her ear. She lifted a hand to the spot and could almost still feel the sting. Ears were so sensitive. She'd never noticed before, but his soft mouth against them caused ice in her stomach and sweat on her brow. When she spotted the single headlight coming down the road and into his drive, Charlee grabbed her flashlight and ran out, not bothering to slip on her shoes.

There was a wide path through the trees that led from her front door to his. She walked it most mornings and could do so with her eyes shut—which was good because now she ran barefoot over the path. "Hey!" she yelled, but he didn't turn around at the wave of her flashlight. She didn't blame him. She'd said some hurtful things but she was here to make amends. "Ian, wait."

No answer as he parked, stepped off his bike and headed for his porch. She ran the rest of the way to him and noticed he was moving slowly up the steps. Charlee reached forward to grab his arm and spin him around. When he yelped, she dropped the flashlight. It crashed to the ground and rolled, the light flashing across his face. A face red and swollen and—*oh my gosh*—bloody. She grabbed his shoulders and tried to make him out in the dim moonlight. Her eyes searched him frantically. "Ian, what happened?" He must have wrecked his bike.

He slumped toward her, and Charlee gathered him in her arms. He draped over her like a bearskin and smelled like sweat. She could feel fear creating tears in her eyes. "Are you okay?"

Ian clung to her as she helped him into the cabin. She flipped on a light as she passed through the door and hustled him over to the couch. Ian collapsed there, and with his head lying back on a throw pillow, she got a good look at his face.

Her hands came up in horror. One eye swollen and bruised with dirt and blood caked at his temple. More blood on his mouth, and coming from his nose. There was a footprint on his T-shirt and anger shot into her gut that someone would stomp on him while he was down. "I'm calling an ambulance."

"No." He grabbed her hand, stopping her. "Please, Charlee. Just stay with me."

At that, her knees gave way and she floated down until she was sitting on the edge of the couch. When he didn't let go of her hand, she used the free one to brush the dark hair from his forehead. "What if your lung is collapsed?"

He opened one eye. "It's not."

"What if you broke ribs and they punctured your spleen?"

At this, he frowned, then smiled. "My ribs are bruised, maybe cracked, but my spleen is fine. Believe me, I've had worse."

"Ian. I'm so sorry. What happened?"

His eyes opened and focused on her. It seemed to take great effort but she could tell he didn't mind. "You're beautiful," he said, words coming from cracked lips.

Her heart stuttered to a stop. One brow winged up. His fine dark hair was a mess of tangles clumped with dirt and small splatters of blood. He sported a rakish five o'clock shadow. "So are you," she whispered. For a moment she took his hand and held it against her beating heart. "Although it's hard to see you under all that dirt."

"I'll go clean up. Just . . . just promise me you won't leave." He started to lean forward, winced, and she used her hands to push him back down on the couch.

"Stay here. I'll take care of you." And in this moment, there was nothing she wanted more than to take care of beautiful, damaged Ian Carlisle with the handsome face and haunted eyes.

She rose and found a first aid kit in the bathroom and a bucket and washcloths under the sink. She filled the bucket and returned to her patient. Water ran in rivulets from her hand as she squeezed the excess from the rag. It made tiny little tinkling sounds filling the quiet. When he tried to scoot over to give her more access, he winced and she dropped the rag back into the bucket. "Shirt first."

Ian had wide, powerful arm muscles and when he tried to wrestle the shirt from his own torso, it proved a futile task. He lay back, breathing heavily. Charlee took scissors from the kit and began at his waist. "It's ruined anyway," she said, blinking several times and brushing the hair from her eyes as bit by bit she exposed the taut, long muscles of his abdomen. A swatch of springy dark hair rose and fell with his breathing and disappeared into the waistline of his pants. She continued to cut, forcing her eyes to follow the line upward. Soon, his chest was exposed and Charlee pressed her lips together hard. There was a jagged cut beneath one of his pecs. A smooth spread of flesh that should never be interrupted by such a crude slice. She'd bandage it first because when she looked at his face she wanted both to cry and to drop beside him just to nestle against his body.

He trembled as she ran the cloth over his chest, removing traces of dirt and the sweat he'd accumulated. The single light of the cabin was enough to illuminate the cuts and scratches. It was soft light, the kind couples danced to before slipping off into an adjoining room to make love. At that thought, Charlee's eyes darted up to Ian's face, expecting to find him watching her. But he wasn't. Mouth slightly open, body lax, eyes closed, and she could only imagine what he must be thinking. When a long, surrendering sigh escaped his lips, she knew. He'd been deployed a long time. And been home only a short time. Had female hands been on his body like hers were now? Charlee used her forearm to brush the hair off her brow. Gently, she pressed her fingertips, then her palm, to his flesh. The cloth was in her other hand, gliding over his skin. Another sigh from him and the sound, so soft, so intimate, wound around the lowest part of her stomach.

Her fingers wrapped in cloth continued to trail and now the other hand joined. When she'd find a bit of gravel or dirt, she'd remove it, then continue as her hands cruised over his flesh. "Okay," she whispered, her heart hammering. "Now the face."

She thought she'd find his eyes still closed, but was surprised to find them open wide, dreamy and locked on her. Charlee tried to smile. "I'll get you cleaned up, then we can put some bandages on." She didn't need to tell him—the steps of wound care were pretty universal—but she needed to fill the air with more than just the thick tension of her hands so intimate on him.

Ian blinked. One side of his mouth tipped up ever so slightly. It didn't matter to him, the pain; he had a smile for her. "Thank you," he said and the words hung in the air between them like magnets drawing two helpless pieces of metal together.

"Be quiet," she whispered and attempted a frown. "You're ruining my focus."

Ian lay back, let out a long sigh and said, "Really? Because you're perfecting mine."

Trembling fingers hovered over his neck. The cloth dangled from her hand and dripped onto the hollow of his throat and there, Charlee McKinley was stalled because she'd never been anyone's focus before and if she had been, it was surely that she'd gotten in the way of that person's true purpose and destiny.

And something about Ian Carlisle made her feel powerful. Strength born of determination. Power born of a desire not only to care for someone but also to nurture him. Nurtured. That's what she'd felt like while Ian held her when she cried, and she wanted, needed, to return the favor. Nurtured was different than protected. Oh, she'd always felt protected. By her dad first, then her brothers. But she'd never felt important. Never felt as though she mattered. She was a footnote, a detail. A possession one protected because it was one's duty.

But Ian made her feel different. Like she was the focus. And that was scary.

She continued cleaning his wounds and exchanging the dirt and blood for fresh, clear water. Soon, his face was a wash of clean skin interrupted by the cut at the edge of his mouth, one small one above his eye that zigzagged into his brow, and a strawberry-like scrape on one cheek. After she'd applied Neosporin to the wounds, refusing to notice how the slick slip of it glided between her fingertips and his flesh, she placed bandages on all the sores except the one at the edge of his mouth. When she leaned in closer to it—in an attempt to make sure he didn't need stitches there—she was surprised to find hands landing gently on her back. Strong, warm hands. Touching ever so lightly. When he spoke, her eyes flickered up to his.

"Charlee." The single word rolled off his tongue and created a hot pool in her gut.

She let out a few quick breaths in answer because she knew he'd hold her there if she tried to pull away. And she didn't want the fight. She didn't want the struggle. She just wanted . . .

His eyes opened and focused on her. "I made you a promise, Charlee, and that's something I don't take lightly."

Her mouth was cotton and when he moistened his lips, she wished he could do the same for hers. And she cursed herself for wishing that. "I know."

And now his hands were moving slowly, rhythmically, like she was an instrument and he was the master. Fingertips glided over the bumps of her back ribs, finding the hollow, tracing the space until his hands were at her sides. "And I swear I'll uphold that." His eyes opened wider. "I swear, Charlee. But . . ."

Her flesh heated with anticipation. "But?"

He lay back again and let his eyes shut. "But I'm weak right now. And I'm finding it very difficult to not kiss you."

When she moved closer, his eyes slid open to find her there, less than a breath away. She'd pay for her weakness later. Of that she was certain, but right now, she very much wanted to be kissed. And not just kissed by anyone, but by Ian Carlisle, a man she was certain knew exactly how to give her what she needed most. So she leaned in.

Their mouths came together, her hair creating a blanket around them. His fingers dug into the strands and angled her so that he could taste more, touch more, feel more. His lips were salty and soft and as his mouth parted ever so gently as if exploring a new discovery, Charlee couldn't stop the tiny moan that escaped into his mouth. This changed the momentum. What had been tender and soft, morphed into a deep, full kiss that had her dragging her hands up over the chest and fighting not to rake them into claws. Hands at the sides of her head, he broke the kiss.

Desire, heat, fire, all of those and more flew between them as they sucked the oxygen-depleted air from the scant few inches that separated their faces and mouths. He started to pull her in again, but she froze. A moment later, after he licked the taste of her from his mouth, Charlee lost all thought of tomorrow and started to tilt toward his lips again, drawn by his tongue and the desire to quench the thirst for more. This time it was Ian who stopped her. His eyes shut tightly, he tried to slow his breathing, as did Charlee, but she was helpless, and a lack of oxygen made her giddy and stupid and if she didn't get up—rise up right now!—she was going to dive in so deep she just might drown. "I have to go," she whispered, and he locked his hands into fists at the sides of her head and brought her forehead to his own.

"I know," he whispered into her mouth. For a few long moments neither moved. Then, Ian's eyes popped open and he gently moved her away from him. In his gaze, she saw he was the soldier, the warrior who could put personal feelings aside and accomplish the mission. And that gave her strength too.

"Before you go, I have something I need to tell you."

Suddenly, he looked tired, spent. Finished. Her heart bled. "Tell me tomorrow, Ian. I'll come by in the morning to check on you, okay?"

"I'll be here." He grinned.

"Are you going to be okay alone?"

Irony entered his gaze. "I fought in a war, Charlee. I'll be fine."

She nodded. "Okay. Okay, so I'll be by at first light."

When she got to the door, his voice stopped her. "Thank you. This won't happen again."

She paused, wondering if he meant the fight he'd obviously not done well in or the kiss. Charlee was surprised to find she hoped it was the first and not the second. If she'd thought he'd know how to kiss her, she'd been wrong. He didn't just know. He instinctively moved to every whim of her desire. This man could thoroughly wreck her. If, of course, he hadn't already.

CHAPTER 6

Eight hours and two cool showers later, Charlee was once again at Ian's door. She knocked, listened, jiggled the door handle. Still unlocked. She opened it a crack and peered inside. "Ian?"

No answer, so she stepped in to find the couch empty. A coffeepot gurgled on the counter; that was a good sign. She walked to the sofa and stared down at the place where his body had been. Blood stained the throw pillow. Beyond her, she could hear the shower running and this fact gave her tremendous confidence that all was well with the world. She needed all to be well . . . with Ian. Needed him to be fine and not in need of a caretaker.

Planning to busy herself until he was out, she strode to the kitchen in search of a washrag to scrub out the bloodstain. Drawers *whooshed* and *clinked* as she went through them. She pulled the far right drawer open to find a leather journal resting atop the washcloths. She tried to reach beneath it, but the towel snagged so she pulled the journal out and sat it on the counter edge. She chose an old washcloth and started to return the journal to its spot when a photograph slipped from between the pages and fluttered to the ground, landing upside down.

Charlee started to return it, but curiosity got the best of her. Was this a photo of Ian's first love? A picture he still carried to this day. When she flipped the photograph, her breath caught. Black spots appeared before her eyes, and everything in her periphery began to fade.

Charlee stared down at a picture of herself.

Her free hand lurched out to grab the counter, her knees weak. She knew this photo but hadn't seen it for a long time. Mind spinning, she tried to make sense of it. Ian hadn't been in her house, couldn't have retrieved it from there, and besides, it had been years, *years* since she'd seen the photograph of herself.

When she heard noise behind her, she spun around to find him mouth agape, staring at first her, then the photo, then the journal.

"Where'd you get this?" Her voice was high with panic.

But the look in his eyes told her this was no innocent mistake.

"How long have you had this?" She slashed the photo through the air.

But Ian didn't answer. The cuts above his eye and at the edge of his mouth looked better today, less swollen, but his eyes were pleading and filled with pain. It twisted her gut, but she couldn't let it, so she took a shaky step and slammed her hand on the table. "How long?"

"A long time, Charlee."

She sucked a breath. "Before you met me?"

He nodded, shame blanketing his features.

Her mind couldn't, *wouldn't* wrap around this. "You carried a picture of me before you met me? Did Jeremiah give it to you?" She tried to remain calm, slow her heart, but the Mack Truck that had just run her down seemed to be circling back to make another pass.

"No, Charlee. I tried to tell you last night. I've tried a couple times."

She stumbled back, hands flying up beside her face. "Get out." Her head shook from side to side as she moved toward the door. "Get your things and get out."

Dark eyes filled with tears and if she wasn't so freaked out by the whole thing, Charlee might have been tempted to let him explain.

"Please. Just give me five minutes so you'll understand."

Her hand closed on the doorknob and squeezed for support. "There's nothing you could say to me to make this right."

————

Desperate, Ian rushed to her but she slipped through the front door and slammed it shut. He stood just on the inside but it could have been a hundred miles away from her. His hand fell on his heart, fingers twisting into a fist. *Nothing could make this right.* He knew that was true. He could see it. Everything he needed to accomplish here was destroyed. *Screwup.* Why had this task been entrusted to him?

In silence, Ian moved around the cabin in a daze, packing his things into his military-issue backpack. He'd have nothing to remember her. She'd taken her picture, leaving him utterly alone. Empty. And at the back of his mind, a voice teased him that it was destined to turn out this way. He could handle himself on the battlefield, but Ian Carlisle was no match for the battleground of the heart.

He'd need to stop by Mr. Gruber's cabin before leaving. Though Ian didn't have much in the way of belongings, it took him an hour to gather his things. He wrapped the journal in plastic bags; it would need protection from the elements. At one point he was tempted to stop to read a few lines, but what did it matter now? Charlee was gone from his life and he'd let down the only person he swore he wouldn't. When he got outside and looked at his bike, he was well aware he had no destination. So for a long few minutes he just stared at the chrome and leather as if it would indicate where he needed to go. His body ached with the abuse he'd taken last night and now his chest ached with a deep and hollow sensation of real pain. Heart pain. The kind he'd hoped he'd never feel again. By comparison, he'd take a beating from three guys any day over this.

————

"My goodness, he looks like a lost puppy," Wilma said, standing in her doorway with Charlee. On the other side of the hub, Ian readied to leave. His movements were slow and mechanical as he tied a duffel on his bike and rested his backpack on the ground beside it.

"I just want him gone."

Wilma draped an arm lovingly around Charlee's shoulder. When King Edward and Wynona stepped onto the porch, they all pivoted to watch Ian. "Honey, are you sure you shouldn't let him explain?"

Charlee's breath caught. "Does the word *stalker* mean anything to you?" Everything with Richard had been a lie. This had all the same earmarks.

Wynona left to collect Mr. Gruber. King Edward sniffed. "That boy's no stalker. Drama, drama, drama with you women."

Charlee gave him a harsh look.

Wilma rubbed a hand up and down Charlee's arm. "I just don't see Ian as dangerous. Maybe your brother gave him the photo."

Really? They'd known him less than two weeks and were defending him rather than consoling her? "I asked him if Jeremiah gave him the picture. He said no." She held it up. "And look how worn it is. He's been carrying this a long time."

"Did he say your brother didn't give it to him or that he hadn't gotten it from him? Maybe he saw it, thought you were beautiful, and took the picture without permission."

Charlee could see the writing on the wall here. She had to deal with this or the artists would be driving her crazy for weeks. "I'll be out in a minute." She disappeared into Wilma's cabin.

"What are you doing, sweetheart?" Wilma called.

"Calling my brother."

Three minutes later, and with a fresh new wave of anger, Charlee stomped past the gathered artists, burning up the ground to Ian Carlisle. He was just getting on his motorcycle when she reached him. Before he could sling a leg over, she grabbed his arm and jerked. "My brother doesn't know you."

Ian's eyes closed.

"I called him." Her teeth were clenched so tightly, she thought the back ones might break off. "He says he's never met you."

Shoulders curled forward, Ian nodded and faced her fully to take the abuse she was ready to dish out.

"Admit it." This time, Charlee landed a fist against his chest.

Ian grunted and she remembered the cracked ribs and for a hot instant felt bad. But the moment faded quickly. "Admit it."

He pulled a breath and lifted his gaze to the sky above. His eyes were wet. "I don't know your brother."

Charlee's heart closed on the words. Even though she knew it, had known it since talking to Jeremiah, hearing Ian say it from his mouth, a mouth she'd tasted and had trusted, caused her body to want to shut down.

She slowly turned from him and started walking back to Wilma's cabin. But with each step anger and fear and confusion rose. She spun and marched right back to him. "Why?" Charlee's head shook from side to side.

A fat tear trickled off Ian's cheek and she wanted to wipe it away because you should never have to see a soldier cry. And the fact that even now her heart was tender to the man who'd done nothing but lie to her caused an ever-deeper surge of pain. "Why did you come here, Ian?"

He rubbed his hands over his face, then dropped them at his sides. "Because I promised your father I would."

Slam! Some intangible force hit her in the torso and slung her backward. She stumbled as the world shifted, going from a place of solid ground to liquid around her. It was a moment before she realized Ian's hand was holding her arm. She pulled away from him.

"I promised your dad. And I was so afraid I'd screw it up . . ." Now the tears came in great streams down his cheeks, causing his giant dark eyes to swim, to plead. "And I *did* screw it up." Wide shoulders quaked under the strain.

And Charlee realized there were tears on her face too. "My dad?" Still, she couldn't grasp what was happening around her or how Ian and her father were connected.

"He understood you better than you thought, Charlee. And, oh my God, he loved you more than life."

Again, she felt as though she'd been punched. Her *father*? There was grass beneath her feet and below that, good rich Missouri dirt. And below that solid rock, bedrock or granite. Firm, unmovable. But where she stood, it all felt like sand sifting with each word.

Ian took a tentative step closer. "The journal you saw in the drawer. That's his. I was supposed to bring it. To give it to you, but not just hand it over. I'm supposed to read it to you, one page at a time. But I—I couldn't seem to . . ."

"The page you read me?" She sank her feet into the ground, hoping for equilibrium, hoping to feel a little of that bedrock below.

"Your father wrote it to you."

Her fingers clamped on his wrist when she swayed. "But why?"

"Because your dad wants you to know another side of him. A side you never saw because he was busy trying to prepare you for life. You and your father are more alike than you know."

Charlee shook her head. They were polar opposites.

"Will you come inside with me? I can read you the first page."

Her gaze fell to the mountains in the distance. Solid, strong, their unwavering sight grounded her, if only a bit. Still in a cloud, Charlee let Ian take her hand. Gently, he tugged, pulling her to his cabin and into her past.

———

I am a man who is undone. Torn between what is right and what is necessary. In the eyes of my mind I see another life. Home, chores, long quiet dinners, long silent nights. But that is only the place I live in my dreams. My reality is different. My reality is guns, rations, war, death. But the other world that waits for me makes it tolerable. And though my heart is there, my responsibility is here. To them. To the kids who arrive daily and die daily. My responsibility is to their mothers and fathers to give their children every resource to succeed in this war. Will young men and women survive and even thrive because of my commitment? Yes, they will. And will I one day return to that other life? A place of green grass and clear streams. I hope. But whether I return or die in this desert landscape, I have done what is necessary. I can only hope those I left behind will understand. Will you, Charlee? Can you forgive me for being here when I should be there?

Charlee sat at the table, back straight, arms folded over her chest and hugging herself. "Me," she whispered. "He's talking to me."

Ian nodded.

"My father was a poet."

Ian drew a deep breath because since she'd first followed him inside, he'd half expected her to bolt. She sat quietly, the fire gone out of her eyes, but replaced with a nostalgia, a flicker of the pain that only now was becoming an ever-deeper loss.

"I'm so sorry I didn't tell you right away. I didn't know how."

Her gaze left the floor and rose to him. He wished he could read her better. "You knew my father well?"

Ian hated the fact that tears again were threatening, his nose tingling, his throat tight. "Yes, Charlee. I knew him very well. He's the—"

"He's the CO you keep mentioning. The one with all the wisdom."

Ian nodded.

Her head tilted and curly blond strands fell from her shoulder. "Why you?"

Careful here. She was much like a wild cat and if he gave her too much attention, she would run. "Your dad . . ." And as Ian began to speak of the man he'd looked up to, the man he loved, he realized he hadn't only agreed to this for Charlee's sake. He'd also come for Major McKinley. And Ian had come for himself. "We got close because I was from Oklahoma and he was from Missouri. A lot of common ground. But he took an interest in me right away. Man, I wanted to quit so many times, even considered going AWOL. I was a hard case, Charlee. One of the worst. But he wouldn't give up on me."

Charlee smiled. It was slight, tentative, but there.

"One day I asked him why. He said I was a tough nut to crack, but if he got through to me, he could reach anyone." Ian pressed his hand to the journal cover. "And then he started talking about you. Wow, was he proud of you."

Charlee leaned forward. "What?"

"He was. You could see it in his eyes."

"All my dad ever did was try to talk me out of doing this."

Ian shrugged. "Just because he didn't want you to do it, doesn't mean he wasn't proud of your accomplishments."

Charlee pressed her hands to her head. "This is a lot to take in."

"Yeah," Ian agreed and stood to put the journal away.

"Wait." She pointed at it. "You're not giving it to me?"

He turned slowly. "No."

"But I just thought since . . . you know, the way things went—"

Ian returned to the table and set the journal between them. "His last request was to share it with you one page at a time. I'd like to honor that request, Charlee. Your dad always had a reason for the things he did. I'm sure there's a reason for this." As an act of trust, and allowing her to use her own free will, Ian shoved the journal toward her.

Charlee chewed on her bottom lip. Ian could see the war. Cold shot down his spine when she reached for the journal. But rather than take it, she pushed it back to him. "Okay," she whispered.

And Ian's heart almost exploded from his chest. He was going to get to keep the promise he made to Major McKinley. Now, he'd have to work on the promise he'd made to himself.

———

Charlee figured Ian wouldn't be too surprised when she showed up on his doorstep early the next morning. She held up a Stanley thermos as he answered the door. "I brought coffee."

"Come inside or sit on the porch?" He didn't even look sleepy, though she was pretty sure she'd woken him up. Soldiers.

Her gaze flickered to his bare chest. "Porch."

Ian turned from the door to grab a T-shirt. "You're the boss."

"Oh, wait. Can we go out to my spot? Maybe have coffee there? I was thinking you could read me some more of the journal. Plus, it's not too hot this morning. That heat wave finally broke."

One side of his face tilted into that devastating smile he had. Ian was no longer just the hot soldier living on her property. He was a link to her father, a man she felt like she'd never really known. They climbed into the Jeep and made their way to Charlee's spot.

"Why is this your favorite place on the property? I mean, it's pretty and all, but so are lots of other spots."

She hopped out of the Jeep and looked around. Table Rock Lake shimmered with the sun's rays dancing across it. "I don't know. I just feel safe here."

Ian nodded and unwrapped the journal as Charlee sat on the oak stump.

"I found this spot after clearing some of the brush. But . . ." She paused, eyes going to the lake and thoughts far away.

"Charlee?"

"But even when I first saw it, I recognized it. I'd been here before. I knew this spot."

Ian followed her gaze. "Did you come here with your mom?"

"Once. She was pretty sick and it took us a while to get back here. The trail was hard to find."

"Was your dad with you?"

"No." But then, something occurred to her, a memory, from long ago. She took hold of Ian's arm. "You know, I think he was with us. But he stayed back. Didn't want to interrupt Mom. She was telling me how I could accomplish anything I wanted. Even if she was gone."

"So, this is your favorite spot because of your mom. That's nice, Charlee."

The memory cleared as she thought back. Her mother's words hadn't been anything different from what she'd said a thousand times to her. That wasn't what made it monumental. "No, I don't think that's why."

And then, like a flood, like a rushing river, the memory cleared. "It was my dad." Charlee planted her hands on either side of her because, suddenly, it felt like the hundred-year-old oak tree she sat on was swaying beneath her.

"My mom walked back to the truck parked beyond the trees. But my dad was staring at the lake and when I stepped over to him, it surprised him. He looked down and I saw tears in his eyes." Charlee swallowed as the memory of her father materialized. "I'd never seen him cry. I guess he didn't know I was still there until I slid my hand into his."

Beside her, Ian sniffed and Charlee realized this was probably hard for him too. She reached over and took his hand in hers. "It was just a moment, but in that moment, he was someone else. He cradled me in his arms and told me he loved me. Told me everything would be okay. Mom would always be watching over us from heaven."

Ian's face was wet with tears.

"Then he squared his shoulders, smoothed the wrinkles out of my shirt, and put on his soldier face. He told me to be strong and I promised him I would. I never saw him cry again."

"I did." Ian's touch became a caress, holding her hand in his to give her strength.

Charlee frowned.

"The last time he talked about you."

Her eyes closed. Her mouth quivered.

The early sun's rays trickled through the shadow of the mighty oak nearby, causing slashes on the ground. "Charlee, do you want to hear another journal entry?"

She inhaled the crisp mountain air around her. "I'd like that."

Ian gave her hand a squeeze and released her to open the journal. Across the lake, a great blue heron landed, tapped his beak at the edge of the water and searched for food. Above him, the sky was softening shades of morning, peaches and pinks that would eventually burn off to deeper hues. But right now, it was gentle. Charlee slipped her hand back into Ian's as he began to read.

Dear Charlee,

I spoke with your brother yesterday. And the sound of his voice made me think about what a fortunate man I am. I hear you in his voice. I hear your mother. Why an amazing woman like her ever chose a man like me, I'll never know. It's like God dressed an angel in flesh and sent her to me. Only, once she was gone he realized heaven wasn't as bright a place. She always wanted a little girl. Dresses and bows and ribbons. And then you arrived and wouldn't wear a dress to save your life. She'd just shake her head and blame me. Then one day when you were nine or ten, she found you drawing. I had a stack of important documents and you'd found them and decorated the whole lot. How could I be angry? She was so elated that you'd spent so long on them. Your mother loved to draw and paint when we were young. But being a wife and mother, she'd put her paints in a drawer. Until you showed interest. More interest than a normal child should. It was her excuse to dig out her paints again. I'm telling you this because I don't think you know . . . you're the one who gave that gift back to her when it was all but gone. You made that last couple of years even better for her. And that made them better for me as well.

Charlee pressed her lips together. "He loved her so much. Can you imagine love like that?"

Ian's hand came up to touch her cheek. "Yes, Charlee. I can."

———

For three days Charlee and Ian worked side by side on various projects while Charlee worked to process what having her father's journal meant to her. It was like glimpsing into the past. In some ways, it was like having the conversations with him she'd never gotten to have. In the journal, he spoke of things he'd never talked about. His love for her mother, what it meant when one of the boys called him to visit. She hadn't called him often because most of the time was filled with crackling dead air, and she always felt like she was keeping him from more important things.

Ian gave her room to digest. She needed that because the man in the journal was a very different one from the father she'd grown up with. But somewhere in her heart, she'd always known there must be more to him than discipline and order. Had she seen glimpses of that tenderness when her mother was alive? Maybe those memories were buried beneath the years of running a tight ship once her mom was gone. Charlee had determined to help him. Cook the meals, keep the boys in line. Make sure everyone had clean clothes. Make sure Caleb remembered to wear underpants.

Ian gave her space to contemplate, time to absorb. He didn't ask questions, just let her be. For the last three days she'd worked mostly in a comfortable silence with Ian at her side. They'd cleaned every gutter on every cabin, moved piles of wood to a new location and even erected a lean-to to keep the firewood dry. Ian had shared two more pages of the journal with her and in each she learned that though her father had loved his job, his heart was far away. In Missouri. With Charlee.

As she stepped from the Jeep on her way to Ian's door, her eyes trailed to the toolshed. Her dad had rebuilt it when he'd visited her six months before he died. His tool belt was now a constant adornment on Ian's hips and for the strangest reason, that felt right, like it was meant to be. Charlee forced the thought away. She and Ian had a job to do. She'd arrived a few minutes early and found Ian's door open wide but she still knocked. She wouldn't want to catch him naked or anything.

Inside, Ian passed from the bedroom into the living space, ear tipped to his shoulder and his shirt in his hands. He motioned for her to come in.

Something jerked in Charlee's stomach because—though she'd seen him with his shirt off before and rather enjoyed the view—she couldn't stop her system from reacting, and that spelled trouble. The kind she didn't need.

Charlee stepped in and could tell Ian was frustrated. The phone between his ear and shoulder must have been the source of aggravation. He only gave Charlee a fleeting wave then turned from her, planting his feet on the floor near the table.

Charlee's gaze drifted over him. Shoulders, narrow hips, jeans that fit so amazingly, and work boots. His body was tan from working in the sun and it only added to his beauty. She'd love to sketch him. Her artist's eye drew the line of muscle along his side, then his lower back where a spine split the area into two powerful parts. Seams of muscle ran along—

When his words into the phone snapped her attention, Charlee blinked.

"Love you too."

And the conversation went on, but a flash of red snaked across Charlee's vision. Love you too? It bothered her. And then it bothered her that it bothered her.

"Kristi, you look beautiful in anything you drape on your shoulders. Don't worry about it."

Kristi? At that moment, Ian turned, gave Charlee a wink and mouthed the word *sister*.

Charlee released the air she'd been holding and hoped he wouldn't notice.

But Ian's eyes stalled on her, first narrowing, then widening with surprise and, if she wasn't mistaken, a bit of amusement.

"Whatever you want, Kris. You know that."

He hung up the phone and stared at Charlee, who'd become fascinated with the hem of her tank top.

"You okay?"

Arghhh. Why couldn't he leave it alone?

She waved a dismissive hand through the air and gave him her best flat stare. "Of course. Why?"

His laser eyes penetrated right through. "You look a little flushed. Like a woman does after . . ." He let the words hang in the air.

Charlee swallowed. "Nope. Nothing here."

"My sister wants me to dance at her reception."

Charlee shrugged. "Doesn't everyone dance?"

Ian pulled his shirt down over his head and covered his fine chest and stomach. "No, like an organized dance thing. I have to dance with her after her new husband, then my dad, then my Uncle Phil. So stupid."

Charlee chuckled. "Yeah, who does she think she is?"

At this Ian laughed too and grabbed Major McKinley's tool belt from the side table. "Not like it's a big day for her or anything."

Charlee put her hands to her hips. "Right. It's not like she's probably been planning it since she was ten or something. You should just tell her no. She'll get over it." She enjoyed joking with him. It was a nice reprieve from all the serious moments they'd had lately. "Why even bother going?"

"Yeah. You're right. She won't miss me."

Charlee bumped his shoulder. "Nah. Who'd miss you?"

They jumped into the Jeep and headed toward the deeper part of the woods along the creek where Ian had spotted a beaver dam that needed to be removed and had told Charlee about it. Today would be hot, sweaty, dirty work. And Charlee couldn't wait to dive in.

———

By dinnertime, Charlee and Ian were both spent. Tearing out a beaver dam had proved more strenuous than he'd imagined and now his body bore the abuse. His ribs were still a bit tender and he'd never admitted the truth to Charlee about what had happened that night. She knew it was Dean and J.C., the guy he'd called Curly. But she didn't know details like how he had them both on the ground until a bruiser of a guy jumped him from behind. Three on one was a little more than he could handle, though he'd fared okay. They all had looked worse than him.

The artists had stopped throwing him and Charlee together at a table alone—which he missed. Those had been intimate little moments with dancing firelight and mountain air. But Charlee wasn't interested in him—no matter what had happened when he was injured. Florence Nightingale syndrome, he figured. Maybe men were more appealing when they were flat on their backs and wounded. Tonight, he sat with Wilma and Wynona. Wilma had a smear of paint on her cheek, making her look childlike and adorable in the tiki fire and the glow of tiny lights trailing the tables. She talked on and on about the painting she'd been working on and how she'd discovered—quite by accident—a new way to manipulate the paint, giving the dry work a luminous glow.

"She's crazed," Wynona leaned closer to Ian and whispered.

He laughed. "It's good to be passionate."

Wynona's chin dropped. "It's very good." She followed his gaze to Charlee, sitting at the other table between King Edward and Mr. Gruber.

When Ian realized her suggestion he shook his head. "Nah. Nothing there. She's told me."

"We'll see." Wynona folded her hands in her lap.

Wilma spun toward them, spiky hair shifting. "Charlee?" She pointed at Ian and closed one eye. "She's got it bad for you, young man. She just doesn't realize it yet."

Ian swallowed and searched for a subject change. "So, my sister wants me to do some stupid dance with her at her wedding reception."

Wynona clapped her hands together. "Oh, I love weddings." Her head tilted back and all that long white hair flowed behind her. Gently, she swayed side to side as if the words alone had transported her to the event.

Mr. Gruber spoke up from the other table. "Weddings. Humph. Thousands of dollars thrown away on people you don't care about and party favors with little white ducks on them."

Wilma raised a hand in his direction. "Doves, Arnold. Not ducks. Those delicate little birds you see are doves."

"Doves, ducks, whatever. All a big fat waste of time and money. At least my Ashley never put me through that."

"Ashley?" Ian asked the sisters, but Wynona was still swaying—and now humming, lost in the wedding in her mind.

Wilma leaned closer. "Arnold's daughter. She's an attorney. Has a lovely little baby girl, but no husband. Arnold doesn't talk about the details."

"Oh. I've seen her picture in a few paintings in Gruber's cabin."

Wilma cupped a hand around her mouth as if the other table might hear. "He has dozens in his loft, but won't show them to anyone."

Wynona's eyes popped open and leveled on Ian. And something, something very strange and frightening, was in that solid silvery-blue gaze. "What dance?"

Ian swallowed, feeling as if he'd stepped into a powder keg holding a match. "Uh, the Sunbee, no. Som—" Shoot. He'd meant to write it down.

Wynona's eyes grew wide. "Samba?"

"Yes. That's it."

She flew up out of her seat so fast, her deck chair toppled over. And suddenly, the sixty-something woman was swaying at the table. Hand to her stomach, hips practically disjointed beneath the long sheath dress she wore. "I love the samba."

Somewhere below the table, her feet were moving as well and her shoulders dipped and curled until Ian himself could almost hear the music. He couldn't move, of course, could only stare up at her.

Wilma leaned closer to him. "Close your mouth, honey."

He did as instructed.

When Wynona stopped dancing, applause from the other table—complete with a few catcalls—filled the night air. She offered an airy smile, bent at the waist, and gave an elaborate bow. She was accustomed to this type of attention, he realized.

Charlee's face was beaming. "Wynona! Why haven't we ever seen those awesome dance moves before?"

Wynona's smile took on a sad, nostalgic look. Slowly, she righted her chair and sat down. "I haven't danced since my Horace died."

And all the light humor and fun surged out of the moment, leaving the sadness of loss in its wake. Wynona's head tilted back. "My Horace loved to dance. I told him if he'd get well, we'd dance for the rest of forever. If he didn't, I would never again." Wilma reached across the table to take her sister's hand. "And oh, did he try. Horace was a mountain of a man. Divine, with thick black hair and giant eyes. But he was so light on his feet, like a feather gliding to the ground from the wing of a dove." She glanced over at Mr. Gruber and winked. "Or a duck."

Ian didn't know what to say, but felt the need to say something. "I'm so sorry, Wynona."

"Well," she said, smiling over at him. "I won't have my student making a mockery of the most beautiful and easily one of the most sensual dances there is."

Student. Sensual. Mockery. Ian wasn't sure which word to focus on or lose his dinner over.

"When's the wedding?" Wynona said, tone sharpening, a bit insistent.

"Uh, end of August."

Wynona tapped the table with a slender finger. "That gives us six weeks."

Ian tried to swallow, but his throat was closed off. "Us?"

Wynona blinked. "Did you expect the dance fairies to sprinkle you with glitter and you'd be able to go to your sister's wedding with Fred Astaire feet?"

He hadn't really thought that far in advance. He just figured he'd Google *samba lessons* and it'd be okay. He shrugged.

Wynona stood, hands to hips. "Get up. On the dance floor." When he hesitated, gaze shifting from her to the onlooking crowd, she yelled at him. "Do you want to make a fool of yourself? Your sister? Get up!"

"Yes, ma'am." Ian stood and rubbed sweaty palms down his thighs. He quirked a smile when the other table applauded his bravery.

All he could think was, "Help." He cast a glance to Charlee. But she'd turned her chair to have a fully unobstructed view to the dance floor and sat there waiting like a kid at a carnival sideshow.

Wynona lifted Ian's hand and placed hers with it. "Lead me to the floor," she instructed.

He stepped out feeling like a giant spotlight was on him.

Wynona had him face her. "Now, a dance is an exchange between two people. It can be friendly." When she said this, her hands went out to her sides and she bowed her head. "Or intimate." And with that, she slid right into Ian, pressing her body to his and looking up at him with serious eyes.

Oh Lord.

Wynona took his hand and turned him toward the audience. "You must forget about them. It's only you and your partner and the music." She tapped a hand to her cheek. "Which we don't have yet, but no worry. By tomorrow night's lesson, we'll be utterly prepared."

"Tomorrow night's lesson?" he echoed. And really, he needed to put a stop to this. "Look, I have two left feet. I can't even do the electric slide. And . . . and you said you don't dance anymore. I don't want to interfere with a promise—"

Her hand flattened over his mouth. "Be quiet. Desperate times call for desperate measures, and Horace would understand. In fact, he'd be furious at me for not helping you." Wynona smiled and removed her hand from Ian's mouth. "Horace has been gone for fifteen years. It's time I put my dancing shoes back on."

Well, whaddaya say to that? Ian was leveled, a little freaked. But okay. Dance Lessons 101. Fabulous.

"Now, the samba is about beat, passion, pulse, rhythm. The rhythm *is* a pulse. You have to feel it, sense it. Be part of it."

Charlee came out to them. "Here, Wynona. I Googled *samba music*. Push this button when you're ready for it to play."

Wynona's hands came together. "I just love technology! Brilliant. Absolutely brilliant."

When Charlee spun to leave, Wynona caught her hand. "Where are you going, young lady?"

Charlee froze.

"Ian needs a partner."

"But I thought you . . . ?"

Hands to Charlee's shoulders, Wynona turned her toward Ian. "I'm the instructor. You're the partner."

Charlee's gaze drifted up to his. The last time they were this close, this face-to-face, was when they'd shared a world-rocking kiss. For a quick instant it all flooded into his mind. Her hands, fighting not to clench into fists, the sweet taste like sugar and heaven of her mouth, the tiny moans that escaped.

Charlee released a ragged breath right into his face. Something was swatting his calf. Slap, slap against his leg. Then, he realized it was

Wynona's bony hand slapping the inside of his leg. "Stance! Widen your stance. Goodness, soldier, I hope you weren't this slow to react on the battlefield."

Ian spread his legs.

Charlee smiled up at him. "I think we're in for all kinds of abuse."

He winked. "I'm not sorry, if you're looking for an apology."

"What I'm looking for is a dance partner who can hold his own."

Wynona continued manipulating their bodies like marionettes without strings. Ian's rogue hand slipped around Charlee's lower back. "I'm a pretty quick learner if I've got the right motivation."

A harsh tone interrupted their banter. "Are either of you listening to me? Good heavens, it's like herding cats." Wynona clapped twice. "I need a switch."

Charlee's and Ian's eyes widened. Had they heard her right?

"King Edward, go find me a nice limber switch, maybe from a birch tree." Edward headed off toward the woods.

Ian whispered, "We may be in over our heads."

Charlee giggled.

After Edward stripped the leaves from the switch with a sadistic smile on his face, he handed it to Wynona. She bent it between her hands, testing the tension, then she sliced it through the air making whipping sounds. "Perfect."

She pointed the stick at Ian and Charlee, who both straightened a bit. "Now, the samba is from Brazil. Brazil is known for its movement, its passion. The dance was born out of desire. So as you work together, keep that in mind."

She hit the button on Charlee's iPhone and music erupted. "Listen. Hear the drums? Samba is heavy on percussion. Feel each beat."

"Are we going to learn the steps first?" Ian asked. It was a dance. There were steps. He was a linear thinker; he needed things like step one, step two.

"No. Samba steps will do you no good whatsoever if you don't understand the passion driving the music and ultimately driving the dance."

When both Ian and Charlee remained stiff as boards, she stepped between them, creating some space. "Both of you close your eyes. Now, feel the music. Come on. You're young people. Charlee, imagine yourself in a club surrounded by your girlfriends. Just let your body react to the music."

Ian opened his eyes to slits to find Charlee's hips moving side to side and oh but he wanted to feel that. Wynona stood behind her, disappearing except for the occasional whip of long white hair and her hands planted firmly on Charlee's hips to instruct. "That's it," Wynona purred.

Oh yeah. He could watch Charlee do that all night. When Wynona moved to him, he squeezed his eyes tighter. "For you, Soldier Boy. I've trained a lot of men to dance and let me tell you, soldiers are the easiest."

"Really?" His eyes opened.

"You're used to using your bodies as a vehicle to accomplish a task. Think of belly crawling under barbed wire, light on your feet you are. You just have to use different muscle groups." Now her hands were on his hips. "Where your partner is swaying side to side, you're going to thrust your hips."

Okay, whoa. Ian stopped moving and looked at her.

"Trust me. You are making a cradle for your partner. You see? She must have a foundation. You're that foundation. Your movements are in sync with hers, but aren't exactly the same."

That made sense. Whatever. He just liked the idea of being a cradle for Charlee. His sister? Not too much. The strong percussion made it easy to move along. Wynona's hands on his hips helped, and when he moved incorrectly, she used the switch beneath her arm to swat his leg gently.

He was surprised that after a few minutes, sweat was on his brow.

"Okay, that's it for tonight."

When he opened his eyes, he got another surprise. Everyone was gone. Dinner plates were cleared and Wynona was already walking off in the direction of her cabin, leaving him and Charlee. Her cheeks were flushed and she was breathing heavily. "That's a workout."

"Yeah," he agreed and reluctantly moved a few steps away from her, reminding himself there was always tomorrow night. "I actually am sorry I got you into this."

"It's okay. It's kind of fun."

"Except the welts on my thighs."

Charlee crinkled her nose. "She's a tough teacher."

They slid chairs under tables, the last bit of cleaning up that needed to be done. "Ian?"

Hearing the change in her tone and feeling it in the atmosphere made him stop. "Yes?"

"Were you with my dad when he died?" There was so much sadness in her words, he wanted to reach out and take her in his arms. But that wasn't what Charlee needed right now so he pulled out a seat for her and then took one of his own while the gentlest of breezes worked to soften the words he was going to say.

"I was."

Her fingers threaded together on the table. Above them a clear night sky twinkled with thousands of stars. "Can you talk about it?"

He couldn't. But for her, he would. "We were pinned down. Separated from the rest of the unit. It was the last of a three-day mission. There were a lot of stray bullets and . . ."

"I know he was shot in the neck."

All of the memories rushed into his mind. The smell of blood and wet concrete, the sounds of bullets firing, then striking. Concrete flying, hitting him in the eyes. "I tried to stop the bleeding."

Charlee's teeth clenched to block the words.

"He . . . talked about you, Charlee."

This brought her head up. "What did he say?"

"He gave me instructions about the journal. Every detail specific." Ian rubbed a hand over his face. "He said he wouldn't be able to be here to share it with you and that task was up to me now. His writings, his words. He . . . he wanted to bring you the journal himself. That was his plan, to share it with you. He was going to get out. Retire. Spend the rest of his days close to you."

Her eyes closed. "I could have gotten to know him while he was still alive. I would have liked that."

"I'm sorry, Charlee."

Her eyes opened and settled on Ian. "It's okay. He sent you to me."

Ian smiled, but there was no humor in it. "He knew I didn't get along with my own dad. Maybe he thought this would help me too."

"What happened between you and your father?"

Ian rubbed a hand over his chin. "He used anger to try to reach me when all I needed was validation."

"Have you two worked things out?"

"No." He pointed to himself. "Screwup, remember? He has a construction business and though I was expected to help out summers and eventually take over, I liked being in the kitchen with Mom more than being on the job site."

"So you rebelled and went to culinary school."

"After I rebelled and did the goth kid thing. Black hair, black eyeliner, and the real kicker, black nail polish."

Charlee's mouth dropped open. "No way. There's no way I can picture you like that."

"Believe it. He was so done with me at that point. I was a huge disappointment to him. Not just a disappointment, an embarrassment. You can imagine. He'd built a reputation as a strong, tough contractor.

"So, I packed my black hair color and black clothes and went off to culinary school."

"And?"

"And I discovered you get more chicks without having black nails. It took a few months, but little by little the clothes and all became more normal."

"And?"

He dragged a hand through his hair. "And that's when I met the administrator's daughter."

"Wow. I heard the story from Mr. Gruber. She actually got arrested?"

"Yep. It would have been pretty hard to stay, so I quit. Seems to be a pattern for me."

Charlee let her gaze drift to the horizon beyond them. "I don't quit."

Ian's heart sank a little deeper.

"I run."

"What?"

Charlee pulled a breath. "I run. When things get too hard. It's my big character flaw."

"More than your stubbornness?"

She narrowed her eyes, but the smile toying at her mouth betrayed her.

"More than your self-destructive independence?"

She pointed at him. "You know, you can be replaced."

"Undoubtedly. Easily, in fact. That is, if you can find someone willing to work alongside a temperamental female."

Her nostrils flared.

"My point exactly."

Charlee let out a little laugh, but her eyes grew serious. "There's no way I could replace you, Ian. You're the link to my father."

"Charlee, he knew what he was doing when he left word for you to spread his ashes."

The color drained from her face. "You know about that?"

He nodded. "He said for you to not worry. You'll know when . . ."

She finished for him. "And I'll know where."

Somehow, his hand had moved across the table. Ian realized his fingers had threaded through hers. "Come on. I'll walk you home."

He didn't bother to release her hand and she didn't bother to draw away. And there they were, two people who both loved a man who was a father first to one, then to both.

When they reached her front porch, Ian dropped a peck on her cheek and turned to leave. But Charlee's voice stopped him.

"He must be proud of you now."

Ian turned to face her, the light of her porch making a halo around her head.

"Your father. He must be proud now."

Ian wished that were so. "He's not. But it's okay. I know Major McKinley is proud of me. To me, that matters the most." With the wind at his back, he turned and walked away.

———

The following week, and after several dance lessons that had Ian's libido working overtime, he hauled the wood he'd cut to Charlee's favorite spot and went to work. He knew she loved it here, beneath one oak tree and sitting on the stump of another, but Ian wanted it to be grander for her, more comfortable. He hauled the wicker bench from the back of the truck—he'd purchased it in town—and set about building the pergola roof that would shelter it. Large floral cushions would complete the look, and the lights he'd purchased would give it a whimsical glow.

Just before dusk she found him. He'd planned to bring her there tomorrow morning to check out the work, but Charlee was nothing if not nosy and she must have sniffed him out.

"Oh my gosh!" She hopped out of the Jeep.

The sound of her excitement cut right to his heart. "You like it?" He'd been a little worried; she was so bossy and particular. He wasn't sure if she'd like it or be mad at him for taking the liberty without permission.

Her hands flew out beside her. "It's incredible!" The sun was setting beyond the mountainside and casting long strips of gold on Table Rock Lake. He'd angled the bench so she could watch the sun go down, the shadows lengthen and disappear, clothing the lake in darkness. She turned to face him. "I don't know what to say."

"You haven't seen the best part." He motioned for her to come closer and took her by the hand. Ian led Charlee to the edge of the pergola and pointed to the post. "Flip the switch."

When she did, the roof of the pergola lit up with what looked like a thousand fireflies. She squealed.

"Now, flip the second switch." Her eyes met his in the golden light, glowing with a mix of anticipation and excitement, and the whole thing sent Ian's heart right over the edge.

When Charlee flipped the other switch, the lower branches of the oak tree lit up with the same firefly lights. She gasped. "It's the most beautiful thing I've ever seen."

Her hand was on her heart and she might just as well have reached physically into Ian's chest and squeezed his until it stopped beating. Mission accomplished.

"Will you sit with me for a while?"

He was covered in sawdust and dirt, sweat and a few drops of blood. He didn't want to ruin her first sunset with his stench. "Yes. As long as you want."

They sat on the bench and watched the stars brighten above. "Ian, this was really sweet of you."

He smiled in answer.

"I hope one day the woman you end up with knows to appreciate you."

He swallowed. "I'm a pretty easy guy to please."

"You deserve someone really special."

He couldn't agree more.

Charlee's eyes narrowed in concentration and he could almost see the wheels in her mind spinning. "What's the most important thing to you? You know, in a woman?"

That her name be Charlee McKinley. He cleared his throat. "The most important?"

She angled to face him, her eyes having gone curious, almost catlike in that manner they had. "Your deal breaker."

He thought about it. "I gotta have someone who's got my six." When he opened his mouth to explain it, meaning, someone who has his back, he stopped because he could see she understood.

Charlee nodded. "Yeah. I know what you mean."

Ian smiled. "Someone I can count on. Everything else is negotiable."

She laughed. "Everything?"

"Eh." He shrugged. "I'd prefer if she didn't have a mustache."

Charlee scooted closer to him and took his hand in hers. "Thanks for doing this. It's really a special place to me and you made it even better."

He tilted her hand to his lips. "I'm glad you like it."

"Will you read to me?"

He left her only long enough to go retrieve the journal from the truck.

Dear Charlee,

It's quiet this morning at the base. The sun is rising over the edge of the building across the street from where I sit.

Yesterday was hard.

I received bad news about one of my young soldiers. His name is Kip Reyser, a wealthy kid from Lansing, Michigan. He'd recently found out he was going home.

He'd never bragged about being a rich kid. He kept his head down, worked hard like all my soldiers do. But when he knew he was going home, we started hearing the stories about summers in the Hamptons, his dad's private jet, flying to Europe on a whim. That happens when a soldier knows he's going home. Life and excitement bubble out of him. He was no exception. Even those who try to hold their composure fail. There's a fresh light in their eyes. It's beautiful, Charlee. I wish you could see it.

Yesterday I got word Kip's parents were killed in a plane crash. I had to give him the news and watch him die inside while all his plans for returning home to a loving family disappeared. He kept swallowing, nodding his head, saying, "Yes sir."

Finally, I told him, "It's okay to break, soldier."

And he did. Right before my eyes, Charlee. I held him while he cried. And I'm not ashamed to say I cried right along with him.

And when I leaned back to look at him, I saw you reflected in his eyes. I saw that same bewildered look, that orphaned look you had when your mother died. I also saw your brothers there, swimming in that young soldier's tears. And every single reaction you each had when I told you Momma wasn't coming home. Jeremiah, trying to be strong for the rest of you, Gabriel, looking inward and finding solace in his music. Caleb, so small then, only eleven, stiffening his mouth, trying to be brave like his big brothers. Isaiah, the quiet thinker, roaming around the house putting things into place. And you, Charlee. You took my hand and held it in yours. So frightened, but so determined to be strong.

Charlee, something happened when I told that young soldier about his family. I realized time can be short. I've spent a lifetime as a soldier and now I think maybe it's time to spend the rest as your dad. I'm getting out, Charlee. And I think you and I need to devote some real time to getting acquainted all over again. I know I tried to do that a while ago, but I guess I wasn't ready. I'm not good with talking. You'll have to teach me.

I want to see what you've done with the place since I was there last. Is my toolshed still standing? Do the shutters need paint? To be completely honest, I need to know if that frightened little girl I remembered yesterday . . . I just need to know she's okay.

A stream of tears ran down Charlee's face. "He really was going to do this. Come here himself to share the journal with me."

Ian nodded.

The soft sound of her crying became louder as her mind undoubtedly wound around the injustice.

Ian opened his arms and she moved silently into that place of safety. He held her while she cried with the firefly lights twinkling above and the soft sound of the lake nearby.

He hoped sharing this with her here, now, hadn't damaged how she felt about her spot. Ian knew something about this place Charlee didn't. This was where, someday, she'd spread her father's ashes.

CHAPTER 7

The next five weeks passed in a blur with Charlee throwing herself into work. It was how she processed things, and Ian had been great to give her the time and space she needed, all the while ready with a journal entry at any given moment. The retreat was looking good for all their hard work, and Charlee and Ian spent days slaving away in the hot sun and evenings talking. That is, when they weren't in dance lessons after dinner.

But this morning had been rough. She'd had a dream, a bad one, spurred by the journal entry Ian read to her the night before. These days he mostly read straight out of the journal, but had made copies of each page so she could keep each message once he read it.

Her mind turned to the dream. Her father was in a giant glass bubble filling with sand and she was on the outside, screaming at him to get out. He couldn't hear her. Over and over throughout the night she'd dreamed the same thing. Charlee reached to the nightstand, where the newest journal entry lay on the top of the stack. Once they reached the end, he'd give her the journal. And she'd already decided to give him the copied pages. Her father was a man Ian loved. She'd like him to have a copy of his words.

Charlee had run the gamut of emotions in the last few weeks. One entry would make her sad while the next happy. She wished she could have seen her father like this, like the man of the journal, because as she remembered him, it was almost as if he and her father were two completely different people. Charlee reached for the letter and placed it before her eyes; as the bleary words cleared, the smallest voice told her not to reread it, but she couldn't stop.

Dear Charlee,

The chaplain came by yesterday and shared a story with me. A parable, he called it, about how a good shepherd will leave the flock to go after one lamb that's gone astray.

I can't stop thinking about the story. Many times I've left the safe place to go after one of my men. Worked my way under the radar, found myself in hostile territory. I've saved lives, sure. That's my job and why the army sees fit—even at my age—to keep me right here on the field. It's my commitment to my troops. They've put their trust in me and their very lives in my hands. I don't think I've failed them, Charlee.

And yet . . .

And yet I have to wonder . . . What if you're the lamb that's wandered away from the flock? Out there, alone and exposed, calling for help with only the wolves close enough to hear your plea.

And what if I'm the shepherd who is supposed to find you? I'm not even there, Charlee. And that makes me think about life. What if I was given one task? One treasure was entrusted to me? And what if—in spite of the lives I've saved and the good I've done— what if I failed the only mission that really mattered? You, Charlee. I don't want to have failed you but I fear I have. Even though I plan to return to you soon. What if . . . what if it's already too late?

Charlee folded the paper and crawled out of bed, refusing to focus on the letter and instead on all the things she needed to accomplish.

An hour later, she was splitting wood beside her cabin when Ian rounded the corner, his hands full of vegetables from her garden. "These looked ready, so I thought I'd save you the trip."

She sank the ax into the wood and brushed at her brow. "Thanks." Charlee turned and headed into her house, where country music drifted from the stereo. A classic George Strait ballad.

"You okay?"

Just inside the door, she spun. "No. I'm not." She turned back around and continued on.

Ian followed her. "What's wrong, Charlee? Did something happen?"

She huffed and dropped the greens on the kitchen counter. "It's not fair that I didn't get to know him when he was alive. I'm twenty-five. I've been an adult for a long time. He was here, Ian. Eighteen months ago. Six months before he died. He'd told me we were going to spend some real time together. But all he did was work. That was his chance." She brushed away angry tears.

"I know you miss him."

"No. That's just it. I don't miss him. We were on different planets and I was sad when he died, but sad for all the things we never had. And that was okay because people can't give you what they don't have."

Ian crossed the room to stand closer, but gave her plenty of space. Charlee needed that—space. Especially when things got to her.

"But there was an artist, a poet inside him. We could have shared that. Talked about the books he loved, how he saw the world through not only the eyes of a major but through the eyes of a poet. And he was right here."

Ian knew the major had visited Charlee months before his death, but he'd not talked much about the trip, just the list of things he'd accomplished to help lift some of the weight. "In the journal entry we read at your favorite spot, he said he'd seen you but he guessed he hadn't been ready to talk."

"For two weeks he was here and all he did was work on the place. Fixed the holes in the cabin walls, cut back the trees overhanging the walk paths, built a new storage shed. Right here, Ian. I could have known him in that two weeks' time and do you know what that would have meant to me?"

Ian stepped closer, gently placed his hands on her shoulders. "I know."

"He spent more time clearing brush than talking to me." A tear threatened, but she wouldn't give in to it. She was done crying over the could-have-beens.

"He thought he was doing the right thing for you, Charlee. Right or wrong, he was trying to help."

She let a long breath slip from her mouth. But a nauseating sensation followed it up from the very depths of her being. "I just wish I could miss him, instead of missing everything we didn't have. I miss the man in the journal, but it just doesn't seem like it's really my dad."

Ian pulled her into his arms. She didn't resist. She went willingly. At this point, they'd spent many hours in each other's arms with pounding samba music in the background and an audience of aged artists. But this was different. Intimate but firm. Strong but tender. They were alone. Charlee and Ian. And in each other's arms. She tilted back to look at him.

Ian dropped his forehead to hers. "How can I make you better?"

She was surprised at the ideas that shot through her mind. "Dance with me?"

A slow smile spread on his face. The music in the background, a mournful love song, took center stage as Ian's right hand slid to the small of Charlee's back. His left hand drifted down her arm and interlocked their fingers. Rather than draw their arms out in true dance fashion, he let his arm bend, folding her into him, their clasped fingers resting near their hearts. With confidence born of many nights of dance lessons—though the music couldn't have been more different—Ian spun Charlee around her kitchen floor until all the tension and sorrow melted from her.

———

If he could only make it melt from him as well. He tried not to crush her against him, but everything in him wanted to hold on tighter. With so many of the journal entries read, he'd started to feel as if Charlee might be slipping away. Summer would end. The wedding was in a few days and that marked the end of August. Time was closing in on them. On him. He had introduced Charlee to the sensitive side of her dad, but she still had so many unresolved feelings. Would he be able to stay long enough to help her sort through all the emotions? Or would summer's end and the job offer—if it came—cut their time off when the first signs of fall emerged? In two days, he'd be leaving for the wedding. In two days he'd have to face his father, his mom, entertain a potential boss, and dance a samba. Wynona, his dance instructor, had given him an A-plus, something she swore she never did. And that meant one more thing he and Charlee shared was ending.

When the music stopped, he continued to dance, but angled to look down at her. Ian brushed blond curls from her face. "Do me a favor?"

She looked up at him.

"Miss me while I'm gone."

A saddish smile touched her lips. "You'll only be gone for a few days," she reminded him, then sighed. "But, yes. I'll miss you."

Ian drew her closer, closed his arms around her, and held her tightly because a few days away from Charlee was going to feel like an eternity. That's how it was when you were a soldier who had finally found his way home.

CHAPTER 8

Charlee sat a glass of iced tea at the table and chuckled at the sight before her. Mr. Gruber had bought a cell phone and Wynona was teaching him how to use it. The group of artists lounged in deck chairs and had just watched a brilliant sunset beyond the mountain. Ian would have loved it, Charlee realized, the way the reds and oranges set fire to the mountainside. She hadn't lied to him. She really did miss him and he'd only just left.

Mr. Gruber had received a box of candy from his daughter and King Edward was stuffing his face.

"Shhh!" Gruber yelled, pressing the phone to his ear and pointing at it with a crooked finger. "It's Ian."

Charlee stood behind him and didn't want anyone to see how excited she was to hear if Ian's time at his parents' place was going well or not. She knew there were issues with Ian's dad and she hoped for the best.

Gruber listened, then placed his hand over the bottom of the phone to address the artists who'd gone quiet. "He doesn't sound good." That was all Mr. Gruber said and Charlee's heart lurched. She came around the table and sat where she could watch Gruber's expression.

"Just one more day, son. And you can come back here. I know your momma's proud of you for coming and I'm sure sorry about that

Brenna person." Gruber was so tender it melted Charlee's heart, until she heard the name *Brenna*. Ice chips in her veins. That was the girl Ian once loved.

When Gruber hung up the phone, Wilma waved her hands. "What? What's happening?"

He rubbed a hand over his jaw, concern deepening the lines around his eyes. "Well, it's about what Ian expected far as his dad's concerned. But the kicker is this Brenna girl."

Charlee flattened her hands on the table. "She's there?"

"Oh, she's there all right. Even staying in the next room with her new fiancé."

Charlee's hands fisted. A strange sensation of first jealousy then anger scalded her insides. "They put his ex-girlfriend in the room next door with her fiancé?" There weren't words to project her disgust.

"How insensitive," Wynona said.

"Poor dear." Wilma shook her head.

Charlee just couldn't quite wrap her head around it. "Next door? As in *in the same house?*"

Wilma's hands covered her face. "Oh, this is just awful."

Wynona slammed her hands on the table. "We have to do something."

Charlee's gaze skittered to the sister with the long flowing hair.

Edward swallowed a mound of candy. "What can we do? We're here. He's there."

Mr. Gruber straightened. "Yep. I agree. We gotta have an intention."

Wynona placed a hand on his. "I think you mean intervention, Arnold."

Wilma paced the dance floor, clucking her teeth. "We're going. All of us. We're going to that wedding."

Gruber scratched an ear. "I'm not real up on manners and all, but I don't think you're supposed to crash a wedding."

Wilma turned to face him. "Oh, we're not crashing. We're Ian's gift."

Edward choked on a piece of candy.

"It's perfect. Gruber, call Ian. Let him know we're on the way in two hours. I'll be taking photographs at the wedding and you will use one of them to do a portrait of the happy couple after the day is over. Wynona, you'll be blinging anything and everything the bride wants to sparkle at the reception. Now we don't have a lot of time, so Arnold, make that call."

Just as he was getting ready to hit "send," Wilma stopped him.

"Wait! Charlee, you're the most important piece of the puzzle here. We have to know you're on board."

On board? With four crazy artists getting ready to scam their way into a wedding? Oh yeah, she was into that. But then Wilma's words caught up to her. "What do you mean, I'm the most important piece?"

Wilma shrugged. "You don't really think the four of us showing up will make things any better, do you? We're just moral support. But you . . ." Wilma came around the table and lifted her hands out to her sides. The next thing she knew, Charlee was being scrutinized by the others as well as they turned and prodded her. "You are the star."

Around her she heard comments like, "We'll need to clean her up. Wrangle that hair. Makeup."

"Whoa!" Charlee stepped from them, realizing the plan and her part in it. "You want me to act like his girlfriend, don't you?"

"Of course." Edward patted her back. "Geez, Char Char. For a smart girl, you sure are dense."

"Now, do we need to go shopping?" Wynona's bright eyes blinked expectantly.

"No. I have clothes."

Four flat stares doubted her words. "I do. Really. I have dress clothes, heels and everything, you've just never seen me in them."

Edward wrinkled his nose. "They're not camo, are they?"

Charlee rolled her eyes. "No. You all just worry about yourselves. I'll be ready in an hour."

Edward leaned closer, sniffed. "Does that give you time to shower?"

She cut him with a look then dropped her gaze on Mr. Gruber. "It gives us *all* time to shower." Although, since Ian's arrival and his interaction with Mr. Gruber, the man was staying cleaner, keeping house, and even walking a little taller. She'd even caught him and Wynona flirting. Maybe in a world of artistic chaos there was a little room for discipline.

When she turned to her house, she heard behind her, "Go. Go, Cinderella. The prince is waiting."

———

King Edward drove the Jeep so Charlee could sit in the back with Wynona, who gave her an over-the-road manicure complete with oil being rubbed into her cuticles and massaged into her calloused hands. No polish, thank goodness, the Jeep's shocks weren't what they used to be and painting could have been a disaster. But Charlee admired her nails, trim and neat and without the usual dirt clumped beneath. Wilma had invaded her closet and chose a white sundress for today and a more formal dress for the wedding tomorrow. On her hands and knees, Wilma had discovered the stiletto heels Charlee had purchased on a whim while in Cabo during a spring break. She also had tall wedge sandals that complemented the sundress. It had been so long since she'd actually dressed up, she had barely recognized herself in the mirror. And now she was wishing she had backed out of this whole thing.

Her hand fell to her stomach as they turned off the highway and began pulling down the long winding driveway that led to Ian's family home in good ole Oklahoma, just one state over.

"Nice digs," Mr. Gruber said from the front seat as the sprawling home came into view. It was a multilevel ranch style that wasn't so big it looked pretentious, but big enough for a good-sized family with lots of kids and grandkids. The Oklahoma grass was thick and green and the landscape similar to home.

Seeing the place where Ian grew up had Charlee fighting a powerful dose of nerves. Acting like a girlfriend could cause all kinds of residual problems later.

"Remember." Wynona squeezed her hand. "*Be* the part."

Mr. Gruber angled to look back at her and scowled when the streetlight reflection hit his eyes. "That boy was overjoyed when he found out you were coming."

Charlee swallowed. "Really?" Poor Ian. It must be horrible here.

"Over the moon, little girl, so you just pour it on thick and make that Brenna rue the day she agreed to stay here."

Charlee bit her bottom lip until Wilma shrieked. "No! Your lipstick. Please, dear. Don't ruin all our lovely work."

Charlee had allowed the sisters to darken her makeup. It wasn't like her, but she had to admit, she looked pretty. Even if it took Wilma five watercolor brushes to paint on the shimmering smoky eye shadow. If Ian needed someone in this situation, she was glad it was she. "I got your six," she whispered to no one.

They stepped out of the Jeep and Charlee smoothed her sundress as the front door swung open. It was a wide double door with ornate etchings in the oval glass. A couple of young kids came rushing out with a middle-aged lady right behind them. She was all smiles and arms already open wide. As she neared the Jeep, Charlee could see the resemblance to Ian. Same tilt of a dark head, same almond-shaped eyes. This had to be his mom. The woman was tall, trim, and headed straight for her as if on a mission. Charlee stiffened as arms wrapped around her and hugged, words gushing from the woman's mouth. "Just beautiful. Of course, you're Charlee. Ian's told me so much about you."

The wind grabbed Charlee's hair and threw it behind her back. "He has?"

"I'm Rosy." And Rosy hooked her arm through Charlee's. "Everyone, please come in.

"It's wonderful to meet you all." She stepped toward the house and the horde followed, no one bothering to talk, because with Rosy, it just wasn't necessary. She could carry both sides of the conversation. "Wilma and Wynona, we have room for you here in the main house. And Mr. Gruber and is it . . . King Edward?" She didn't pause for him to answer. "I've put you two in the bunkhouse. But don't worry, the bunkhouse is really quite lovely."

Charlee stuttered to a stop. "Oh, we don't want to impose." And her heart was hammering because in the list of rooms and who belonged where, Rosy had left her out.

"Impose? No! It would be an *honor*. You all took in my boy and from what I understand have been treating him like family for weeks."

"Really, we can get hotel rooms in town," Wilma said, the obvious impending scenario easily read on her face.

Rosy brushed a hand through the air. "Why, I wouldn't hear of it. You'll be much more comfortable here. We've got a big family and they're spread out all over town at various houses. I got rooms ready for them that are sitting empty. A good bit of our out-of-towners are at Ian's uncle's ranch. We come from cattle ranchers, both Ian's father and I, but he wanted to be a contractor." She threw her hands into the air. "Voilà. Here we are. Contractors sitting in the middle of cattle country."

"Your home is lovely. I thought it looked like a *real* ranch," Wilma offered.

Charlee had to agree. The sprawling home, white fence line, smooth, rolling hills. Very ranchy.

"We own the land from the road to that far line of trees. Beyond that is my family's property." Rosy had pivoted to show them the space. She squeezed Charlee's shoulders. "We've got lots of room for your friends, Charlee. I'd be heartsick if they went to town to stay."

Charlee forced a smile. Then she paused because a strange sensation crawled over her. Eyes on her. Someone watching. She tried to gather her hair, but the wind was unmerciful, blowing it around and fluttering the dress she wore, causing it to cling to her flesh.

Rosy stepped away, leaving her at the base of the steps, and Charlee felt suddenly alone. And a bit panicky.

Wilma leaned over and whispered in her ear. "Remember, be the part."

And that's when her eyes came up and she saw him. Standing at the front door, hands in the pockets of his crisp new jeans and mouth hanging open. His gaze trailed from her head down, lingering, pausing, stalling on her legs in the tall wedge sandals. Charlee swallowed.

From behind someone gave her a little push in his direction.

She mounted the steps focusing on Ian's dark, sparkling eyes. He mouthed, "Thank you," and for some inexplicable reason, those silent words drove Charlee to him. Her breath caught as she read all the emotions that swam in his eyes. Relief, happiness to see her, maybe even a little desire. There was also a bit of shock seeing Charlee all dressed up like a Barbie doll and all for him. Her feet chewed up the ground and the sounds of everyone behind her faded into oblivion when she realized all Ian had done for her in the short few weeks he'd been with her and all she could do for him right now. As she neared, a car pulled into the driveway, horn blasting. Though her focus was pinpoint, something made her turn. And there, in the passenger seat, was Brenna. She knew instinctively the dark-haired woman had to be her.

Charlee turned from the oncoming car and set her focus on Ian. His face, his mouth, still open in an *O*, and his beautiful, beautiful eyes. *Be the part. Just be the part.*

As she neared, his hands slipped from his pockets slowly. When Charlee finally reached him, it was like a tidal wave had held her back. She threw her arms around him, one over his shoulder, and pressed her body to his. Her other hand tangled into his hair and Charlee found his mouth with hers and pressed a kiss that had him first stunned, then warming, melting into her and drawing every ounce of strength from her.

Somewhere behind she heard someone say, "Oh my."

When Charlee broke the kiss and opened her eyes, the former pain she'd seen on Ian's face seemed gone. He quirked a smile and didn't loosen his grip. She smiled too. "I was instructed not to mess up my lipstick," she whispered, for his ears only.

His dark gaze, now filled with desire, flickered down to her mouth. "You're incredible."

She started to pull out of his grasp, but he held her there. "Did Brenna see it?"

He flipped his hair to get a quick look without anyone realizing. "Yep. All bug eyes and mouth hanging open."

"Good."

Ian still held her while everyone else waited for the two lovebirds to finish their reunion. "You're incredible."

"So you said." She blinked innocent eyes and decided right then and there she needed to dress up more often.

Rosy spoke up. "Good gracious, son. You've only been gone from her a day or two. Poor girl, you look like you're ready to eat her."

Ian chuckled, slid his arm firmly around Charlee, his *girlfriend*, and they all headed into the house.

———

Three hours later, Ian was still trying to get a grip. Charlee. Wow. His mom had put her things into Ian's room and this was a problem because . . . well, the male part of him couldn't think of a reason, but the protector part of him knew this put her in a precarious position.

She came out of the en suite bathroom with an empty makeup case in her hands. "You think Brenna was surprised?"

He didn't want to think about Brenna right now. He wanted to think about Charlee and that dress and how it was only one piece of clothing. He cleared his throat. "Yeah. She was really rubbing it in yesterday. You know, the whole engagement thing. How surprised she was when he proposed; how happy she is."

Charlee dropped onto the edge of the bed. "She's with him, Ian, but probably wishing it were you."

He let out a humorless laugh. "Yeah, 'cause I've got so much to offer."

At this, she stood and walked to him. He sat in a chair at a small table in the corner of the room. She came around him and dropped to her knees at his feet, where she could look into his eyes. "You have a lot to offer for someone—"

"For someone who's looking."

Her gaze fell to the floor.

"For someone who's not already wounded."

Charlee rose slowly from the spot and went to unzip her small suitcase.

Before she could finish, he was there, behind her, breathing into her hair. "I'm sorry. This place gets to me. Forgive me?"

She turned and landed in his arms. "If you make me a promise. Let's pour it on thick for Brenna, okay? What kind of insensitive person stays with her new fiancé next door to an ex-boyfriend, especially a soldier who's just come home?" She tipped her head. "And how did this even happen?"

He inhaled, thinking how well Charlee fit right there, in his arms. "She and my sister were really good friends growing up. My dad is the one who invited her. My mom wasn't happy about it."

"But next door, Ian? Why not down the hall or in the bunkhouse?"

"Brenna picked the room while Mom was gone. By the time she got home, they were all moved in."

"Your mom seems like a sweetheart. I couldn't imagine her doing that."

There was a strand of hair that kept falling in front of her face. His fingers itched to touch it. Ian's hand rose to the side of her head and threaded the strands. "And you, Miss Dirt and Grime, really clean up good."

She shrugged a delicate, tanned shoulder. "Eh. Some women go to the gym. I go to the woods."

He tilted closer and for an instant wanted to claim her mouth, but he knew he had to play it cool. There was no one around to see the act right now. Ian dipped and pressed his lips to her jaw. When he felt her quiver, he drew back a bit, satisfied with himself. "About sleeping together . . ."

She sucked a breath and he busted up laughing.

"Don't worry, fair maiden. Your honor is safe with me. You can have the bed. I'll take the floor."

She chewed her lip, ruining her lipstick. "I don't want you to have to do that."

He wiggled his brows. "There is the alternative. I mean, if we really want to make this act seem convincing."

She swatted at him. "The floor for you, soldier."

He sighed. "Fine." But before he released her, he gave her a nice full-body press, and a confident twinkle sparked in his eyes. "But you don't know what you're missing."

He left her there, frozen, blinking, and he was pretty sure judging just how true that statement was.

———

Off in the distance, Ian heard mortar shells, the *bap, bap, bap* of gunfire, soldiers screaming. He tried to rise, but his body was trapped. Thick black liquid held him from the neck down. He yelled, trying to get someone's attention, but no one came.

His mouth was dry, and his weapon rested only a few feet away. He twisted, trying to get an arm free, but his body could barely move. Up ahead he could hear the enemy moving closer. He stopped thrashing for fear of drawing their attention, but when he did, the black tar he was stuck in made him sink even deeper. Now the back of his head was in it. He had to do something. Hands shook him. Someone was there. Someone was either trying to help him or preparing to kill him. They shook him again, a voice. This time there was a voice. High, panicked. He needed to focus on getting free, then he could help them. Hands closed on his arms. Pain, like claws. Ian jolted. The room was dark except for the smallish figure in front of him. The voice again, soothing this time, saying his name. Through the dark haze, she materialized. It was Charlee.

He drew breath after breath to slow his racing heart. He hadn't had a nightmare in over two weeks and had thought they were all but a memory. His breath came in short spurts, as did hers.

In the darkness he heard, "Are you okay?"

Was he? Only a moment ago he was trapped. Sinking. Dying. A hand went to his forehead and he found it slick with sweat. He fell back onto the pillow.

"Ian, are you all right?" Now there was an edge to her words, a panic.

"Yeah. I'm sorry." He felt hands reach out and smooth his hair, fall onto his chest where his heart was pounding like a hammer.

"You were having a nightmare." Slowly, her fingertips glided over his arms, his pecs. She was using her hands to calm him. And it was working.

"Did I scare you?"

"I was just scared for you. It sounded horrible." Again, her fingers brushed at his hair.

"Yeah, it was."

"Do you want to talk about it?"

No. He just wanted to stay there with her hands on him. Rather than answer, he opened his arms.

Even in the dark he knew she was contemplating the situation. When she disappeared, Ian dropped his hands and tried to concentrate on the ceiling fan above. But then she was back, dragging the blanket off the bed and using it to cover them. She nuzzled into the crook in his arm and rested a flat hand on his chest.

There was a new kind of tension now, but Ian let it go. He let it all go. The dream, the memory, everything that had happened in Afghanistan, everything he saw and everything he'd done. There were still safe places in the world. And this, right here, with Charlee folded into his arms, this was one of the very best.

⸺

The next morning Ian hadn't wanted to leave Charlee's side but he figured the gentlemanly thing to do was let her sleep in and get the heck out of her way when she woke.

He'd showered, shaved, and slipped into a pair of running pants and a T-shirt. He had quite a bit of pent-up energy to release and figured a nice long run would help. Plus he loved running here, on his family's land. He used to take off down the winding drive and out onto the tree-lined road, early in the morning while the world was still asleep. It was almost daybreak and he paused in the dark kitchen to see if there was any coffee left over in the carafe.

"I just drank the last," a voice came from the open patio door.

Ian closed his eyes. His dad. He was hoping to avoid conversations without the buffer of his mom.

"I was just going for a run. Won't be gone long." He turned toward the front door—his escape route.

"Sit down."

His father completely ignored the fact that Ian had another destination. Grinding his teeth, Ian stepped through the patio door and chose a seat. *Might as well get this over with.* "Your mother will be up in a bit to make coffee."

That burned all the way down. "If I want coffee, I know how to make it myself."

His dad laughed without humor. "That's right. You're right at home in the kitchen."

"Were you wanting to talk to me about something?" Ian could feel the tension settle behind his eyes where he'd probably have a nasty headache if this went on too long.

His dad was still for a few moments and as the emerging sunlight made its appearance on the horizon, Ian caught the first morning's glimpse of his dad. The shadows of early sun deepened the wrinkles in his face. Bags rested beneath his eyes and the gray at his temples was getting whiter, growing longer, overtaking the dark hair of youth.

Ian swallowed. For the first time in his life, his father looked frail.

"So, I saw the McKinley girl, your *employer*." The last word was said with enough disgust to cause Ian to close his eyes. "She's pretty, I'll give you that."

Ian chose not to speak for fear of tearing into his father.

"That motley crew of artists is weird enough. That one man always wear a skirt?"

Ian never thought he'd find himself in a situation where he actually had to defend King Edward. And now, he'd been in two. One at the bar and presently with his father. "It's a kilt, Dad."

"You're not planning on taking up wearing one, are you?" Thomas Carlisle sniffed.

"Was there some point to this conversation? I thought you wanted to talk to me about something." *Like, glad you made it home alive, son. Proud of your service to our country.* But Ian choked down those words because they were ones he'd never hear from this man.

"So, this handyman gig. Done in a few weeks, right?"

Ian chewed the inside of his mouth. "Yeah." And the realization settled in. End of summer meant end of his time with Charlee.

"Well, I need you. Know your sister is wanting to introduce you to some hotshot from Tulsa, but I need you here." His dad's hands threaded together in his lap. This was hard for him, Ian realized. And for that he felt bad, but he and his dad working together? No. Not ever.

"Sorry, Dad." He tried to sound genuine. And a tiny part of him was. "It's not really part of the equation."

His dad looked over with steely blue eyes. "What's that mean? You're back. I need the help. You finally get home—and the army turned you into something I couldn't—why would you go to work for someone else when a job's waiting here?"

Ian pulled a long breath. "I don't think we would work well together anymore." And they never had. But back when Ian was young, he took the abuse and kept his mouth shut. "And what do you mean the army turned me into something you couldn't?"

Thomas's hands unthreaded and rode over his thighs. "Guess I failed in the father department. You left looking like a vampire girl and came home . . ." He raised a hand to gesture to Ian.

Ian finished for him. "Looking like a man." There was irony in his tone. Thomas's hand fell with a *clop*.

"So, this is about you." Ian knew he shouldn't be surprised at his dad's selfish pride. But the sting hurt nonetheless. "This is about me finally being what you always wanted and you being able to walk around town with your head up because your prodigal son finally ditched the eyeliner and came to his senses."

At the word *eyeliner*, his dad recoiled. "Just trying to offer you a job. You want to stay a handyman in a geriatric commune for crazies, suit yourself."

"They're good people. All of them. And if I could stay there forever, fixing leaky sinks and cleaning gutters, I'd be honored to. Because life isn't just about having the right job or the right career. It's about people, Dad. The difference you make in their lives, how you help them. How you honor them." Ian stood. "That's something you never did understand. Guess not much has changed around here."

His father stood too, the light of a beautiful morning casting a glow on the side of his face. He looked hurt by the words, but right now, Ian didn't care about that. He just wanted to go, to leave, to run because—just like old times—if he ran hard enough and fast enough he could outrun the pain his father was to him.

———

As the day went on, Ian found himself with a surprising case of nerves. When Charlee asked if he was okay, he'd smiled, kissed her cheek, and told her he was going to find his sister. The wedding planners were set-ting up chairs outside where a beautiful arch of flowers and greenery anchored the wedding area. Ian rounded the corner and knocked on his sister's door. "Come in," she yelled, voice a bit of a squeak.

She wore a white bathrobe, and a giant white dress was hanging from the doorframe behind her. Kristi Carlisle was two years Ian's junior. Her hair was curled and sprayed, creating long tendrils around her face. When he opened his arms, she came willingly, smashing the curls.

"Nervous?" he said.

She pulled away to look at him. "I guess. Yes. I don't know."

He chuckled. "Three answers to one question, I'd say you're a bit nervous."

Her slender, manicured hand went to her stomach. "I'm a little nauseous."

"Have you eaten breakfast?"

Kristi blinked and Ian realized she was wearing fake eyelashes, which he couldn't figure why because Kristi had always had long, thick lashes like him. "I don't think I could hold down any food."

He gave her a half grin. "I could make you crepes."

Her eyes, glittery with a smooth splash of gold, lit up. "With crème fraîche?"

He shrugged. "Of course."

Her hand fell from her stomach. "Good. I'm starved."

He squeezed her shoulder. "That's my girl. Come on. The kitchen is still fairly quiet. On the way, you can tell me about the plans for the day."

"The reception is at three. In that big tent at the edge of the house. It's really going to be beautiful." Arm around her, giving her the sup-port she needed right now, Ian listened to her yammer on about the day. "Oh, thanks for Wynona. She's been gluing rhinestones to the place settings, the decorations, she's like a machine. It looks great."

"I have a confession, sis." Ian leaned closer.

Kristi stopped at the top of the steps and blinked those giant hooded eyes at him. "What?"

"The artists came for other reasons." He leaned closer. "They thought I needed some moral support with Dad and also with Brenna staying here."

Kristi's giant eyes narrowed; a smile played at the edges of her mouth. "Charlee's not your girlfriend, is she?"

He leaned back. Nothing ever got past Kristi.

She poked him in the chest. "If she were, she would have come with you. What girl doesn't love going to a wedding?"

Ian rubbed a hand over his face. "She's not your typical girl."

Kristi shook her head, causing long curls to bobble. "Undoubtedly. And you've got it bad for her. So, what's the problem?"

What was the problem? "She was in a bad relationship recently. Think it tore her up."

Kristi shrugged. "And she's too stupid to spot a good thing when it lands on her doorstep?"

He laughed. "I'm just trying to take it slow, you know. One step at a time."

"Do you remember when we were kids and we went to the swimming hole?"

"The one with the rock ledges?" He remembered. There were rocks you could climb and jump into the water from varying heights. Only the bravest went to the top.

"Yes," she said.

"You didn't bother to test the lower ledges the first time I took you there. You climbed straight to the top."

Kristi laughed. "And froze. Everyone was laughing at me."

"You were braver than most of them for just climbing to the top."

"I started to climb back down, but you came up. You wouldn't let me back out." She reached out and squeezed his hand. "Do you remember what you told me?"

He remembered wanting her to jump. If she didn't then, she never would.

"You told me to jump. You said my courage was waiting for me at the bottom of the ledges."

Ian pointed to himself. "Smart guy."

"And you were right. There was no fear after that. At the end of the day you said, 'Good job, kid. I wanted to swim with my sister today.'"

Ian cast a glance heavenward. "How do you recall all that?"

"You were my hero back then, Ian. My big brother hero."

He kissed the top of her head, unconcerned with what it might do to the curls. "Come on, let's get you some breakfast."

———

Ian sat in the front row with Charlee at his side. She looked amazing in a pale pink dress that made her tan look three shades darker. Her hair was down and her lips shimmered with a juicy splash of dark pink gloss. She needed to be kissed. He hoped the day would warrant that. When Charlee crossed her legs, one angled toward him. Tall heels elongated her luscious legs and it was a darn good thing they were leaving to go home after the reception because he didn't think they could stay in the same room again and he continue the gentleman act. The slit in her skirt offered a glimpse of skin that also shimmered and he wondered if she'd used some kind of lotion with glitter in it.

Charlee leaned over. "You're staring at my legs."

"Was I?" he said, trying for innocence, but just sounding ridiculous.

"Mm hmm." He watched her bite back a smile.

Ian's eyes narrowed. "And you like that, you little vixen."

Charlee filled her lungs, causing her chest to expand, and recrossed her legs, causing the slit to ride a bit higher and exposing more of her flesh.

He leaned closer and growled in her ear. "You're lucky you're going home tonight. I promise you'd be in danger if we were in the same room again."

This caused a bright red stain to settle on her cheeks as he watched the thought of that tick over her features. Her silvery-gray eyes danced and if he wasn't mistaken, she was breathing a little harder.

It was a moment before they realized something was wrong. The earlier case of nerves returned as Ian cast a glance behind him, only to see people getting fidgety. He looked down at his watch. Twenty minutes late. Probably not that unusual, except they'd seated everyone and all the preliminaries were complete. There should be a wedding march.

"What do you think is going on?" Charlee whispered.

"Don't know. Think I better find out." And he slipped off the seat and out the side so he wouldn't make more of a spectacle.

Ian made his way into the house, where he found his mom guarding the library door. Her face was a wash of horror, pale and frightened. Ian rushed to her. "Mom, what?"

"He's gone. Allen. He just . . . flew in and told Kristi he wasn't ready for this, and he left."

Ian's mind spun to catch up. It was rather difficult to have a wedding without the groom. His heart sank for Kristi. He pointed to the door. "Is she *alone*?" Surely not, her mother would never leave her.

"She wanted to be. Asked me to leave, give her some time, but your dad barreled in there."

Ian didn't need to hear more. He sailed past his mom and into the room. Kristi was sitting on the edge of the long leather couch, her perfect hair a strange frame for the tear-swollen face. Makeup gone, save for streaks on her cheeks. His dad stood staring out the window.

He figured it wouldn't help to say the *I'm sorrys* so instead, he walked to her, dragged her up from the spot and held her in his arms. Within minutes the tears stopped. "What can I do, sis?"

Behind him, his dad shifted to stand closer. "We gotta send these people home. Someone's gotta tell them. Guess that'd be my place."

Kristi raised her eyes to look at Ian and his heart broke. She was shattered. "Sweetie, what do you want? How do you want this to go?"

Because Ian knew his sister and knew that a simple "sending everyone home" wasn't her style. "This is your call." And he knew it was a little bit like the rock ledges.

Kristi mustered her strength. He watched determination enter her, the tilt of her head, the squaring of her shoulders. "All our family is here. Some of them came from twenty hours away." As she spoke, her voice grew stronger. "No one is leaving. We've got a beautiful party facility set up. We're not going to let it all go to waste."

Ian smiled. Proud of her. So very proud of her. He cast a look to his dad. "Can you tell them the reception is now a party? And any of the bride's guests are welcome to stay."

Thomas Carlisle, hands in his pockets, frowned. "I . . . I can do that." His piercing eyes landed on his daughter. "You sure, honey?"

"Positive." A hand went to her mouth. "Oh, Ian, I'm so sorry, but Allen left with his cousin, the one who had the job."

He took her hands in his. "Kristi, I don't care about that right now."

She smiled up at him, thick fake lashes flashing as she blinked. "You're the best brother anyone ever had."

Ian wiped the tears from her cheeks. "Change into some party clothes, sis. I'm not letting you sit this one out."

She hauled a ragged breath. "I guess you wouldn't, would you?"

———

To Ian's surprise, his dad handled the situation well. Explaining there was no longer going to be a wedding, and please don't ask the bride about the situation. Sometimes people get cold feet and come to their senses later. Only a quarter of the people—Allen's people—left. The others migrated to the party tent. Ian was glad to find the artists had swooped in and removed much of the "wedding specific" decorations. He held Charlee's hand as they walked across the tent.

"Wynona took a bucket and filled it with the little dove accents and the table decorations with the tiny gold rings," she said.

"Good call." Ian tilted her hand to his lips and kissed it.

"It's still pretty fancy, but not so wedding-ish now." She pivoted to face him, sadness in her eyes. "How's your sister?"

"She's really strong. Got a good dose of that from our mom and just enough of Dad's stubborn pride, she wouldn't allow the day to be completely ruined." Still, his heart ached for her.

When the orchestra started up, Ian cringed. "Think these guys know anything but wedding music?"

Charlee shrugged.

Ian left her and made his way across the floor. Charlee watched as he grabbed a few guys on the way and dragged them to the low stage where the orchestra was set up. Minutes later, he was back beside her.

"What just happened?"

Ian pointed. "That's my Uncle Phil. He plays harmonica. That's Roy, bass. And over there is my Uncle Jeb. He plays lead guitar in a country band. But he's only got his banjo with him."

"Are they replacing the orchestra?"

Ian grinned. "Nope. Joining them."

Charlee's eyes widened.

"They all know country music, Charlee. They may be classically trained, but they live in Oklahoma."

She wound her fingers around his forearms. "Aren't you clever?" And she hoisted herself up to kiss his cheek. Tables lined the outer edge of the tent and as Charlee pressed her lips against Ian's cheekbone, she spotted Brenna at one of the tables. A Chris LeDoux song filled the space. Almost instantly, the stuffy wedding atmosphere became alive with toe tapping and even some singing along.

The heaviness of a wedding gone wrong disintegrated. No one even noticed when Kristi slipped into the tent and sat in the far corner, watching.

Ian left to go find his mom and Charlee took it as a divine signal to search out Brenna. The woman sat alone, her shoulders hunched, eyes far off. Charlee glanced behind her to see what she was looking at and realized Brenna's fiancé was spending more time at the cash bar than with her. For a quick instant, Charlee felt bad for the girl, until she remembered that Brenna had accepted an invitation to stay at the house.

"Can I sit with you?"

Brenna's shocked expression disappeared with a smile. "Sure." Her gaze went right back to the cash bar.

"So, you knew Ian back in his wilder goth days."

Brenna seemed surprised by the attempt at conversation, but a fast glance to Charlee softened the shock. "Yes. It was what drew me to him."

Okay, she hadn't expected that. "Really?"

"Yep. Wanted a bad boy, I did. My dad had always told me I'd end up with a loser. Guess I thought I'd find one and make it a short trip."

Wow. Charlee couldn't imagine. Her dad had always expected so much, too much, she figured she'd be a disappointment if she didn't become president. But he would have never told her she'd end up with a loser.

"But Ian was so much more than black clothes and black hair." Brenna looked directly at Charlee and the tension mounted as they discussed the man who'd obviously made a deep impression on both of them. "He was . . . in a word . . . perfect."

Perfect. That was a pretty stiff assessment. And Charlee got the impression Brenna still cared deeply, a little too deeply to suit her. Not that she had any claim on Ian. She didn't. She couldn't. But Charlee had the distinct feeling that if she didn't move forward, she'd one day be sitting alone at a table and looking back. She swallowed the lump in her throat.

"What happened between you two?" She couldn't help herself. She had no right to ask. And knew in her heart, she didn't want to know, not really.

"I guess you could say he betrayed me. Once with another girl in high school. I'd broken up with him, but I didn't really mean it." She rolled her eyes. "It was high school."

But ice spiked through Charlee's veins. "And the next time?"

Brenna let out a long sigh. "Not another girl, just wasn't there for me when I needed him. I probably overreacted. Ian is a loyal guy, but once you kick him to the curb, he's gone. I shouldn't have handled it so badly, but old wounds . . . you know."

Yes, she did. Across the room her eyes found Ian, who'd just stepped over to his sister. Old wounds. New wounds. They'd all messed up what could be. If she hadn't met Richard and believed his lies about wanting to build a life with her, she'd feel differently about Ian. But she had, and that had soured every bit of romance in her system.

Beside her, she heard the words, "Yes, he is."

Charlee turned to face Brenna. "I'm sorry, what?"

Brenna let out a little laugh. "I was agreeing with you. You said, 'He's a good man.'"

She didn't remember saying that. Was thinking it, though. When Ian held his hand out for his sister to take, Charlee chewed her lip. He was a very good man.

CHAPTER 9

Kristi's eyes were wide. "Ian, what are you doing?"

He left his hand extended toward her. "Come on. I want to dance with my sister today."

She frowned, eyes flittering around the tent where people had started watching them. "I was fine in the corner."

He worked the muscle in his jaw. "We're Carlisles. We don't hide in corners. And we don't climb off cliffs. We take the hard route."

She stared at the tent ceiling for a few moments. "Not going to let me out of this, are you?"

"Come on," he encouraged with the flick of his hand. "Your courage is out there waiting for you."

"I'm not up for a samba. Sorry you learned it for nothing." Kristi placed her hand in his.

"No samba today." Although he hadn't minded the hours of spinning and twirling Charlee beneath the stars at the retreat. He angled to the band. "Tim McGraw," was all he said. And they started a ballad that was neither slow nor fast, but a comfortable tempo between. Within minutes, the dance floor was littered with other couples swaying and turning to the tune. After a while, his sister pressed her cheek to Ian's chest and cried.

Within an hour, Kristi was inundated with a myriad of dance partners, mostly guys from town, old family friends, and she was actually laughing.

Thomas Carlisle came striding across the dance floor to where Ian stood. He stopped at his feet. "Good job, Ian."

Ian blinked, waiting for the irony. Waiting for the sarcasm. When it didn't come, he uttered, "Thanks."

Thomas took him by the arm and pulled him out from under the tent through an opening not far away. The music was muffled there, softened, and the lighting dim. Thomas turned away from his son and toward the house. "I uh . . . wouldn't have handled things like you did."

Here it comes.

"This was . . . this was good. She needed it. Hold her head high, no scrawny jerk from the city going to make a mockery of us."

Ian closed his eyes, because though he wanted to remind his dad this wasn't about the Great and Powerful Thomas Carlisle, he knew his dad was trying. "I didn't want her seeing family at Christmas, Thanksgiving, and having it be the first time they saw her since the wedding. It'd bring it all back. Now it's done. She can move on." Ian turned to go back inside but his dad caught his arm, stalling him there.

"You got this one right, Ian. And . . . I'm sorry about earlier."

All the air left Ian's lungs. His dad had never apologized for anything.

"It's okay, Dad." He started to turn again, but this time stopped himself. "Really."

"Think about that job offer, okay?"

Ian nodded. "Okay."

———

When Ian led Charlee onto the dance floor, he felt better, lighter. And if someone had told him he'd feel this good at his sister's botched wedding, he'd tell them they were crazy.

Charlee came easily into his arms, her flesh cool from the night breeze that slipped into the tent, her skin soft as silk. His hand slid over her bare shoulders. "You feel incredible," he whispered in her ear as he felt a little tremor run through her body.

Charlee tilted back to look at him. The motion caused her hair to tumble over his hand. "And you look like a man who saved the day."

"Careful, I'll get a big head."

"You mean bigger than it already is?" She blinked up at him innocently. And those beautiful eyes, the ones that looked sometimes gray and sometimes blue, beckoned him to kiss her. She wasn't saying that, of course, but it was there, deep in her gaze. He spun her to the center of the floor where tightly pressed bodies would make a wall for them. When his lips parted and he moistened them with his tongue, Charlee's gaze went glassy. Maybe it was the spinning, maybe it was the anticipation, whatever. He didn't care; that look was filled with excitement and expectation. Her body pressed into him, and he relished the feeling of someone who could make him both hot and cold at the same time. Someone who could make him want to move faster, and yet slow time so he could relish every moment. His hands came up to cup her face. For an instant, her eyes drifted shut, and she nuzzled against his touch; when her eyes opened, there she was. The woman who'd traveled four hours to act like his girlfriend, the woman who'd given him a job, not because he was qualified for it, but because she knew he was a soldier who'd just come home. The woman who lay on a floor with him after a nightmare. The woman he . . . the woman he loved.

Oh God. He was in love with her. The kind of love that plants your feet and makes it impossible to walk away, ever. Ian had been infatuated with Charlee McKinley from the time Major McKinley first started talking about his headstrong, willful, uncontrollable daughter. He'd fallen for a picture of a pretty girl standing in front of a Jeep. But now, now he *knew* Charlee. Knew everything she was and everything they could be together. And that was both exhilarating and terrifying. "Charlee, I need to tell you something."

Her eyes opened and in them he saw his future. He saw everything he wanted in life.

She blinked, thick caterpillar lashes shrouding her gaze. Her fingertip touched his mouth. "This is a perfect night," she said. "Tell me something beautiful."

And love allowed time when it would rather rush. So he swallowed the words he'd been ready to speak and instead of telling her he loved her, he simply said her name.

Charlee wound her hands into his hair and pulled his mouth to hers. She was a woman who knew how to get what she wanted, and Ian was more than willing to give. The kiss was long, full, and caused the world to spin away from them. The music faded, the colors surrounding them drained until there was only Charlee—the light for his path. And for Ian, a man who'd spent a long time in darkness, she was all he'd ever need.

———

When she finally broke the kiss with heat rising from her toes all the way to her cheeks, Charlee glanced around her to see who'd been watching them. To her surprise, no one. And yet she felt bare, exposed and naked though she was fully clothed and in the middle of the dance floor. Her eyes found Ian's. She allowed herself a tiny laugh. "I guess we put on a pretty convincing act, huh?"

He pressed into her and every cell of her body screamed. His hand shifted against the small of her back and if he didn't stop it, she was going to explode. "Did you mess up my lipstick?" she said in a rush, needing to focus on something else, anything else.

"Yeah." It was a word and a victory all rolled into one. His dark eyes sparkled and that devastating half smile tilted his cheek.

Charlee's heart pounded unevenly. Off to the right, she noticed commotion. "Is that—?"

Couples were moving to allow room and as the floor cleared they saw it. Charlee sucked a breath. There, Mr. Gruber had Wynona in his arms and for a frail man who walked slowly, he moved along the dance floor with Fred Astaire grace. Wynona's long hair flowed, a silk white scarf behind them, and she knew just how to snap a turn so that it whipped as they spun.

Ian pointed. "Did you know he could—?"

"Un-uh." That was all Charlee could say with her mouth hanging open. It took her a moment to realize there was a light tap on her shoulder. Her gaze left the two aged artists and focused on Ian for a moment before turning. His look had soured. Charlee pivoted.

"Could I cut in?" Brenna.

Ice shot down Charlee's spine. She swallowed, not trusting her voice to speak. Brenna's dark eyes were warm and fitted on Ian. His grip on Charlee tightened ever so gently.

Brenna blinked and turned to look at her. "Just wanting a dance with an old friend. That's all." Something about the words, something desperate and pitiful made Charlee start to step away. Again, Ian's grip tightened, this time obviously, and Charlee watched the motion register on Brenna's face. Her gaze dropped to the ground and she mumbled, "I'm sorry, never—"

And that's when Charlee squirmed free. She gave Ian a hard look and placed a hand on Brenna's shoulder. "Absolutely," she said with more vigor and confidence than she would have ever thought possible while turning Ian over to his ex-girlfriend, a woman who still had feelings for him. "I'll get us some drinks, Ian. Meet me at the table when the song is through." And she strode away, proud of herself for giving him a one-song limit. The look of anger and shocked betrayal in Ian's gaze would lessen if he had a nice glass of punch to wash it down. He wasn't interested in dancing with an old friend. But he had such unresolved emotions about Brenna. Maybe an opportunity to air things out would help him move on. Let him know he was not the screwup his father claimed. Plus, it was his dad who gave Brenna the okay to stay there. If he'd planned to embarrass Ian, seeing Ian and Brenna being civil might send an overdue message to Thomas Carlisle. *Your son is a much bigger man than you give him credit for.*

She got two glasses—not three—she didn't want to give Brenna an excuse to hang around. Charlee found a table where she could see the dance floor and focused her attention on Ian and Brenna.

"They make a nice couple, don't they?" The words were slurred and before Charlee could turn around, she knew it was Brenna's fiancé. His hand fell on her shoulder, heavy and with the scattered clumsiness of a drunk. "Saw you at the bar."

Bar came out as *brrr* and Charlee wondered how rude it would be to hop up and leave.

"I'm James. Came with Brenna." Which sounded more like *Brennann.* "But she's busy, so I got you a drink." He plunked a glass on the table with his own. It was three fingers full with two perfectly square ice cubes. The dark amber liquid sloshed a little as he slid it under her nose; the tart bite of whiskey rose in her nostrils.

Charlee swallowed and wondered if this was going to get difficult to get out of. "No thanks," she said.

He drew his chair closer to hers, his shoulders crowding her as he moved. James finally settled with his head close enough to hers that when he breathed, the same strong scent rushed into her face. "Come on. It's a wedding." Then, he frowned, thought about what he'd said and shoved the drink at her again. "I mean, it *was* a wedding. Now it's just a party."

Charlee stared down at the glass, then searched for Ian and rescue from the dance floor. His focus was on Brenna, and he seemed to be listening intently as her head shook from side to side, and her shoulders rose and fell with . . . whatever words she was saying. Charlee couldn't read him from here. The temptation to grab the glass, down it, and allow a little liquid courage to send her across the dance floor was great. When the smell intensified, she realized James was holding the glass just beneath her nose. It smelled like courage. James had gone still, except for the glass that now he touched ever so lightly to her mouth.

Charlee was surprised when her tongue darted out to find a bit of the liquid on the edge of the glass. The tip of her tongue zinged deliciously. And very suddenly, almost uncontrollably, she wanted more. She snatched the glass from James and started to tip it back, the scent again, fresh and fire, filling her nose. Just as she opened her mouth, another hand closed over hers, stopping her. Charlee blinked, looked up, angry at the interruption to find kind, blue, aged eyes staring down at her. Thick brows in a frown, but the look was softened by the gentle smile on Mr. Gruber's face. His hand closed more tightly on the glass and though she was reluctant to let go, she did.

He shifted his weight. "We have a promise to keep to one another, remember?" And Charlee did. As the glass disappeared, along with James, who'd been hustled away by King Edward—heaven only knew what Edward had done to him . . . or shown him . . . to get him to disappear so quickly.

Ashamed, Charlee stared down at the table surrounded by her artists. Wynona, cheeks still rosy from the dances she'd shared with Mr. Gruber, Wilma, who'd exchanged her rainbow-colored spikes for wedding-appropriate pastel ones, King Edward in his dress kilt, and Mr. Gruber, a recovering alcoholic, sober for eight years now, who had saved her from making a huge mistake just moments ago. "Let's go home," Charlee said and rose from the chair.

Mr. Gruber placed an arm around her and they followed the rest toward the edge of the tent where a lighted path would lead them away. Gruber leaned closer. "Don't be ashamed, honey. Whiskey, she's a seductive one."

Charlee placed a hand to his cheek. "Thanks."

"Eh, you'd do the same for me." His wild white brows rose on his forehead. "Aren't you going to go get your man?" He motioned to the dance floor, where Ian was just separating his body from Brenna's.

Wynona leaned closer to her. "Yes, dear. If a woman insisted on fondling my man like that, I'd skin her like a hog."

Mr. Gruber's approving smile shot to Wynona.

She blinked innocently, folding her hands in front of her. "Well, I would," she whispered.

"He's not . . ." But Charlee couldn't finish the sentence, because it tasted like a lie. She shook her head. "He's not . . ." When Brenna reached up to touch his cheek with her open hand, and Ian gave her a friendly smile, Charlee's hands fisted. "Be right back."

She crossed the dance floor, back rocket straight, and stopped at their feet.

Brenna spun around to look at her and the wide smile on her face brought Charlee to a screeching halt. And then, the woman grabbed her arms and kissed her cheek.

What the—?

Words were flowing from Brenna's mouth but Charlee was still stuck in the let's-be-best-friends moment a few seconds ago. She shook her head to clear it, caught Ian's gaze—who chuckled and slipped his hands in his pockets.

Words. Why wouldn't Brenna shut up? Charlee caught snatches. "Clearing the air. Thanks so much. You two are great together. Really makes me want to hold out for the dream." One line she heard clearly. "So, thanks again, you two. I gotta go. Some things I need to take care of." And Brenna marched off in the direction of James.

Charlee had a headache. "What just happened?"

Ian dropped his hands on her upper arms and slid them down, trapping her against him. He chucked a nod in Brenna's direction. "She deserves better than that creep."

Red. Fire red materialized before Charlee's eyes and she for the first time understood what Tinkerbell felt all those times she lit up with jealousy. "She deserves better?" she repeated, slowly.

She watched as the emotion she felt registered in his gaze. Smug, smiling. Stupid soldier. Why couldn't Charlee hide her feelings?

"I had a *loooong* talk with Brenna." His eyes twinkled. "Thanks so much for stepping out of the way."

That was it; Charlee spun to get away from him but found her body unable to move. The strong hands of a soldier clamped down on her upper arms. She was trapped. And he was enjoying it. "Let me go," she growled through gritted teeth.

He frowned, smile fading. "Charlee." Now the eyes that were mischief a moment ago were filled with concern. "I'm just kidding. I don't have any feelings for Brenna. At all. I hurt her twice in her lifetime and you gave me the opportunity to apologize. That's it."

Her chin jutted forward. "Are you completely dense? Or is it just where women are concerned?"

He blinked, surprised.

"She still loves you, Ian. A rabid dog could see that."

A long exhale came from his mouth and right into her face, and dang it, she didn't want that because it reminded her of the moments, those intimate moments when their breath had become one. The kisses, lying beside him, tucked beneath his arm last night.

"She doesn't love me, Charlee. She loved the idea of holding out for the real thing. And maybe she thought it could be me, but you don't pursue someone who's already in love with someone else."

All of the fight left Charlee. Drained, right from her head to her toes, leaving her a melted mound of goo. "What?" she whispered.

Ian's head tilted back. He stared at the angular tent ceiling for a few long moments. "Look, we need to get home. Everyone's waiting on us."

Had there been a short time warp from a few seconds ago? Because she was pretty sure she'd asked him a question and he didn't answer. Charlee mimicked her father's voice and words. "I asked you a direct question, soldier."

Ian blinked once, twice, then again as if recognition and surrender were warring in his mind. Then, all the doubt disintegrated as his eyes focused on hers. "You sure you want to know?"

Now, she really needed to run. Because if she stayed everything between them was going to change. Shift. And though her mind wasn't ready for that, her heart longed for it.

"Charlee." His voice brought the calm.

She closed her eyes, needing to go. She could run. Right out the side of the tent and away.

He repeated her name and the calm and certainty in it caused her to open her eyes.

"Charlee, I love you."

The world slipped away. Her heart swelled as her mind shattered. It was such a dangerous thing, love. Such an emotion with sweetness and claws. Ian Carlisle loved her. She sipped the air because her lungs didn't have enough oxygen. Where was the oxygen in this tent?

After a few moments, he said, "Did you hear me?"

Of course she did. *Don't say it again. Whatever you do, don't—*

"I love you, Charlee."

Good Lord. What was he thinking? It was as if speaking the words somehow made it okay. She needed to answer. Say something that could either discourage him or lighten the mood. Yes, that was it. Something clever and detached. "All right." Wait. That's not what she meant to say.

First his brows pulled down into a frown. Too close. She could read every emotion on his face. He let out a humorless laugh, then rubbed a hand through his hair. "All right," he said, slowly as if he'd never heard the words. Then, to her utter dismay, Ian threw his head back and laughed.

Charlee blinked.

His arm came around her, drawing her to his side as if she needed someone to lead her out. She didn't. Nope. Knew how to walk on her own. Bend one knee, raise foot, step. Bend other knee and so on. Somewhere behind her, the artists fell into step with them. She was vaguely aware of stopping to say good-bye to Ian's parents and sister. She had mumbled words . . . parroted what Ian and the others said. He led her to the driveway, where they had already placed their suitcases in the Jeep. Ian stopped at the driver's door, waited there a moment, then lifted her in his arms.

"She going to be like this the whole way home?" Gruber grumbled.

Ian shook his head. "Nah, she'll snap out of it eventually. Shell-shocked, that's all." Charlee rose in the air and found herself deposited into the backseat.

She should say something. "I can drive."

A pregnant pause followed by a hail of laughter around her. Anger set her jaw; this was ridiculous. The only thing that had happened was Ian told her . . . and it all rushed right back. The dance floor, the scent of Ian and Brenna's flowery perfume and him saying . . . saying . . .

Someone leaned in and kissed the top of her head. She followed the motion until all she saw was Ian. Eye to eye. His arms folded on the window frame. "Don't worry, Princess. I'm not expecting things to change between us. I made you a promise, remember? And I keep my word."

She opened her mouth to speak, but nothing except air came out. *Things won't change between us? Won't change?* They'd already changed, and the terrifying thing was she was both scared and happy about that. Ian Carlisle loved her.

Before she could speak, or scream or panic and run off into the woods, King Edward jerked the Jeep into reverse and gave Ian a flat stare. "You following us, Lover Boy?"

He shook his head. "I'll be a couple hours behind you."

The lights of the ranch home and the sound of the party alongside faded as they wound down the drive. Charlee's head felt detached from her body, floating somewhere above as the Jeep bounced onto the main road. She looked over. Wynona sat beside her. Charlee's mouth opened. "He loves me," she whispered.

Wynona took Charlee's hand in hers and patted the air-cooled flesh while the wind filled the car and every cell of her body. "Of course, dear. We were all wondering when you two would figure that out."

CHAPTER 10

She didn't see Ian the following day after they got home. He was giving her space, time. He always did. Time to deal with the fact he loved her. And didn't expect things to change between them. It was ridiculous. A little bit wonderful and when she thought about it her heart was happy, so she forced her thoughts to something else. Her father. The man in the journal. In the back of her mind she knew they were one and the same. The tender writer of the letters to her was also the strict disciplinarian raising five kids alone. Wow. Five kids alone. When she put it in that perspective, no wonder he'd been rigid.

Charlee had taken the entire day to paint. She hauled a steaming coffee cup into the living room, where an easel held her newest obsession. Before there were four permanent resident artists living here and it was only she, back when it didn't matter if the mailbox was eroding off the screws that held it in place, and it didn't matter if weeds overtook the walk paths, Charlee could spend long hours lost in a painting. She'd done that yesterday. Because Ian loved her and that made it impossible to get any real work done.

The tip of her index finger was green. She'd played in the paint until each leaf on the giant oak was exact. A stretch of glassy lake ribboned through the background and a gazebo dripping with firefly light anchored the foreground. She'd fallen asleep thinking about her new piece of artwork and now, with the morning sun cascading in through her windows, she loved it even more than she had last night.

This was what the artists' retreat was supposed to be about. Not clearing paths so no one fell. She'd all but forgotten the joy of a newly completed painting. She'd all but forgotten how painting made her feel at all. Until Ian. He'd reconnected her to her passion. And carried the load of busy work so she could indulge in the one thing that had always made her happy. And as a bonus, he loved her.

It was still bright and early Saturday when he knocked on her door. She opened it to find him with a batch of homemade oatmeal chocolate chip cookies—her favorite, although she didn't recall ever telling him that.

He smiled, held the plate beneath her nose, and waited for her to sniff. She did, drawing in the scent of brown sugar, oatmeal, and dark chocolate. Her eyes closed and the smell took her back in time. She was twelve and determined to be the woman of the house after her mother died. Baking cookies and all.

Ian stuttered to a stop when he saw the painting. "Wow, Charlee. That's beautiful."

She tried not to swell with pride. "You like it?"

He stepped closer, examined the tree, the intricate yellow lights that cast a glow on the ground around the gazebo. "It's perfect."

Her attention went back to the cookies. "How'd you know?"

Ian carried them to the kitchen. "That they're your favorite? Your dad told me."

Charlee grinned and reached to take one. Ian pulled the plate away. "Not without cold milk."

He sat the cookies on the table and retrieved two tall glasses from the cupboard. Charlee reached for a piece of one that was broken. She popped it into her mouth and melted right there on the kitchen floor. "Mmmm."

"You little sneak."

She shrugged, took another bite. "They're still warm." Just the way she liked them. Warm and so soft they fell apart in her hands. She sat down at the table and pulled the plate closer. "Wait. My dad remembered that oatmeal chocolate chip cookies are my favorite?"

Ian looked surprised. "Yes. Even told me how you discovered that."

Charlee thought back to when she was twelve, and the memory flooded her. "Oh my gosh. He liked oatmeal raisin and I hate raisins. So I—"

"You swapped the raisins for chocolate chips. You thought he wouldn't notice."

She laughed, leaned her arms on the table. "That's right." Charlee touched the plate, letting her finger trail the edge. "It all worked out. He liked these better anyway."

Ian laughed. "He hated them, Charlee."

Her head came up quickly. "What?" She searched her mind, remembered all the times after that her dad requested oatmeal chocolate chip.

"He hated them." Ian nodded to prove his point. "But he knew you loved them and you were trying to take your mom's place, take care of everybody. So he ate them."

Charlee was leveled. Slowly, she slid the cookies and milk away from her. "Why?"

Ian leaned closer, took her hand in his. "To make you happy."

There were still so many things she didn't know about her father. It was like each new day, a new discovery met her. "Ian, will you read me another page in his journal?"

He nodded. Smiled, reached into his back pocket and pulled out a folded piece of paper. "You want to hear my favorite?"

He'd come prepared. Of course he had. He'd been trained by the best.

I look down at the miracle in my hands. Never have I felt a moment such as this. Ten tiny fingers. Ten wrinkled toes. I count and recount them. Perfection in a pink blanket and my heart is already gone. My heart is already lost to this tiny girl who makes me want to both laugh and cry in the same instant. Her nose crinkles, eyes close, a yawn escapes her bow-shaped mouth. She has no care and no concern because she's been placed within my arms, the safest place in this world. I will protect her. I will love her. I will keep every harm from her so she can grow up knowing she's not alone and there's nothing to fear. Nothing will stop her. No one will stand in her way. Her hand falls against her cheek. She makes a tiny fist. I place my finger there, in her palm, and swear I will hold her hand forever.

Silently, Ian folded the page and slid it across the table to Charlee. She opened it and stared down at the words. "It's taken me long enough, but I can actually see my dad doing this, making this commitment to protect me. There was a time I wouldn't have been able to, but now I can."

"Major Mack had one soft spot, Charlee. It was you."

"And that's why he ate cookies he hated." There were things her father had done because he loved her that she'd never known. Her gaze leveled on Ian. "I think I'd like to have the journal, now." She no longer wanted a page at a time. She wanted to hold it in her hands, read for herself, flip pages at will. Read it cover to cover.

Ian sat straighter in the chair. She knew that stance; she had brothers. He was readying for a fight. "No, Charlee."

That wasn't how this was supposed to go. She stood. "We can't have many pages left. Ian, he sent the journal to me."

Ian stood too, slowly, and she knew he wasn't trying to intimidate her, though his stance was hard. "I promised him I'd share the journal one page at a time."

She spun from him and paced into the living room. "But I'm really beginning to understand who my father was."

"You have the pages I've copied."

She folded her arms in front of her. "Why won't you just give me the whole thing?"

Ian dropped his gaze.

"Or, don't you have an answer for that?"

"He had his reasons. Please, let that be enough."

"Sorry, but it's not enough. There can only be a few more pages. I want the journal."

Ian worked the muscles in his jaw. "You can't have it. Not yet."

Her instinct was to reach out and hit him. That's what she would have done to her brothers. When they played keep-away with her in the middle, she'd learned a fist to the stomach . . . or lower, if she was mad enough . . . would gain her the ball. Rather than hit him, she shoved him. "Then you need to tell me why. Is all this leading up to something? Some great revelation at the end?"

Again, Ian looked away.

Her eyes narrowed. "Or don't you know?"

"It was his dying request."

"Why?" she yelled.

And Ian's temper flared to meet hers. His words came out in a rush. "Because he said if you got too much at one time, you'd run. Okay, Charlee?" His hands flew through the air, angry at her, maybe at himself. "He said you'd run just like you always do."

The world spun, thrown off its axis. Everything disappeared to one tunnel before her, all else dark and far away. "I'd run." She repeated the words in a whisper.

"That's all he said, *all right*? I don't even know what he meant."

And then, without so much as a hint of a warning, the night at the wedding flooded her mind. Something triggered the memory. Something he'd said. *All right.* That was it, because when he told her he loved her, she'd said, *all right.* And really, in a normal world with normal people there was nothing *all right* about that. But this wasn't a normal world. It was filled with artists and dancers and poets masquerading as military majors. It was filled with Ian and Charlee and the mess that was their nonrelationship. And for some inexplicable reason, that made Charlee chuckle.

Ian stretched out a tentative hand. Not a hand in invitation but the kind one stretches out when a loved one is about to check out of reality and enroll herself in the nearest nut farm. He didn't speak, just hung there, hand offering to steady her.

She smiled. Shrugged. Smiled some more. "All right."

His head tilted as if testing the air, the words, her sanity. "All right?" And then, she watched it dawn on him and she knew he was replaying the night in the tent. She hadn't lost her mind; she was surrendering to her father's wishes.

"All right." She repeated it again, this time letting all the remaining tension drain from her.

Ian did the same. Finally, he smiled. "You in the mood for ice cream?"

Had she heard him correctly? "It's ten in the morning."

"Gorgeous day out, let's take the bike and go for a ride. We'll end in town and get ice cream for lunch."

Her head jutted forward. "For lunch?"

"Maybe wash it down with a burger and fries at the Neon Moon."

"What about your homemade cookies?"

"We'll save them for dinner tonight. King Edward and I are fixing seared ahi tuna with mango chutney."

Charlee kissed his cheek. "Thank God we don't have to suffer through tuna spaghetti anymore."

He laced an arm around her. "Come on, the road is waiting."

———

They spent the better part of the day winding down country roads. By lunchtime, Ian was hungry, but in no hurry to stop. After all, the woman he loved was on the back of his Harley, her arms wrapped around his stomach. Life was pretty good. No, great. She hadn't run screaming when he told her he loved her, and that was a good sign.

After lunch at the Neon Moon, he swung the motorcycle onto the gravel drive of the ice cream shop.

Charlee groaned. "You trying to kill me?"

"Nah, just fatten you up a bit."

"Oh. Well, *that's* a relief."

Near the front corner of the drive, a pickup truck was selling puppies. Ian cast a long look in their direction as he stepped off the bike. He'd like to have a dog. One day. Once he was settled. He could picture that in a future with Charlee. But he didn't know how long it might take her to come around, and summer was almost over. When Charlee jogged off in the direction of the puppies, Ian started to follow. But then, he paused. He needed to be careful not to sink roots too deep. His time here was coming to an end.

He neared the ice cream shop and intended to order, then decided to just sit and wait for her. He took a seat where he could see Rodney at the window and Charlee, now holding a yapping ball of fur.

"Can I sit?" Rodney came out and hovered over him, blocking the sun.

"Sure." To Ian's surprise, the lanky, skinny guy sat but kept his shoulders back and his back straight. Ah. One of *those* conversations.

Rodney's cheeks were sunken, his chin narrow. "So, I've known Charlee my whole life."

"Yeah," Ian said. "She told me you guys were in kindergarten together."

"We've been there for each other over the years." Rodney lowered his chin, mouth a straight line.

Ian nodded, chewed his cheek, wondered if he was going to be called into a duel at dusk. "I'm sure she appreciates your friendship."

Rodney shrugged. "I'm there when she needs me."

Dude, if you've got a point, could you get to it before we die of old age?

"Like when Richard dumped her." Rodney's forearms fell to the table, widening his posture.

"Yeah, she hasn't really told me much about that."

This seemed to please Rodney—he was in while Ian was on the outside. "Well, it was really hard on her. Really bad. She was happy with Richard." Then, his eyes narrowed. "Like she's happy with you. And the guy just left."

Rodney cast a long look to Charlee. "He just quit on her. You know?"

The words burned, because Ian himself was one who had quit on others . . . like Brenna. But he'd never do that to Charlee. He was a different man now. "I'm not going to do that, Rodney."

Rodney cleared his throat. "You better not. Because I'll hire someone to kick your butt if you do."

Ian's eyes widened. "Okay. I think we understand each other. Man to man."

Rodney stood up. "I wasn't always like this, you know."

Ian frowned.

"Weak." Rodney spread his arms out at his sides. "I was sick. For months. Lost a lot of weight."

"I hope you're okay now, Rodney." And he meant it, because the young man was fiercely devoted and that deserved respect.

"I'm fine. Just more frail than I'd like. I won't always be. I'm gaining my weight back."

"That's great. Hey, if you ever need someone to work out with . . ."

Shock registered on Rodney's face. Then a smile. "Yeah. Okay. I'll call ya."

Ian pulled the cell phone from his pocket. "What's your number? I'll call you and you can put me in your phone."

Ian noticed he'd missed three calls from Mr. Gruber's number. He should call him, but they were headed back to the retreat after ice cream and he just wasn't ready for the day alone with Charlee to end.

"What do you do for fun, Rodney?"

"Not much time for fun." He hooked a thumb toward the ice cream shop. "I grew up working for my stepdad. He owned a construction business."

Ian leaned forward. "So does my dad. We have a lot in common."

"My stepdad died when I was eighteen and my mom couldn't keep the business going. She ended up selling, but if I'd been a little older, a little wiser . . ."

Ian understood. Life could be filled with regrets. Some of your own design, some you had no control over.

"Anyway, I was running jobs for him. I was good at it. Really good at it." His eyes widened when he said that. "And now I'm working in an ice cream shop for twelve cents over minimum wage. Up for a six-cent raise in another three months. Funny how life works out, isn't it?"

Ian's heart went out to Rodney. Funny, no. Not in this circumstance. Rodney leaned over the table and extended a hand. "Good talking to you, Ian."

"You too, Rodney."

He grinned. "My friends call me Rod."

"Okay." Ian stood and shook his hand again.

Rodney started to walk away, then turned. "It doesn't change what I said about Charlee. Don't hurt her. Or you'll answer to me."

Ian couldn't stop the smile. "Duly noted."

Charlee jogged to the table, her hair—wind wild—flowing behind her. She was beautiful. The most incredible woman he'd ever met. And she was going to be his. Just as he let that thought settle into his heart, another raced to the surface. Something dark, intangible, but real nonetheless. *It's all going to crumble around you.* The thought, so stark and unwelcome, shot through his system. He rejected it. Pushed it away. Wouldn't give it a chance to root.

His phone buzzed on the table. As if she'd forgotten she even had a cell phone, Charlee pulled hers from the small shoulder purse she had across her body.

Ian grabbed his phone and answered while he watched Charlee push her hair back. A frantic voice on the other end of the phone caused him to look away from the woman lighting his world. Ian's heart lurched into his stomach with each word being hurled at him through the phone line. Slowly, he lowered the phone.

"What?" Charlee said, panic rising in her voice. "What's wrong?"

"We gotta get to the hospital. It's Mr. Gruber."

———

Charlee squeezed her eyes shut and held on to Ian while the onset of tears stung her nose. The worst things in life could happen at the most beautiful moments. The air was the perfect blend of sunshiny warmth and cool wind off the Ozark Mountains. One moment, she'd been holding a squirming puppy, belly swollen and breath smelling like milk, the next she was on the back of a motorcycle racing to the hospital and fighting panic.

Cold first, a chilling blast that shot from her flesh inward, settling in her chest. Then blackness as she imagined a world without Mr. Gruber. They'd had no details to go on, just a few sentences of rushed words. *We called an ambulance. They've taken him to Mercy Medical Center. We'll meet you there.* If Ian knew more, he hadn't shared it. And Charlee knew it was bad. In her heart, she knew. It had to be because when it wasn't bad, people gave you plenty of specifics. None of that. No, oh, he just slipped and fell and hurt his knee, or, silly man, tried to pry open a can with a kitchen knife, now he needs stitches. No, this was not like that. Charlee laid her head against Ian's back and closed her eyes. Even on the road, she could feel his lungs expand and deflate, and the motion was soothing. Mr. Gruber would be okay.

Ian sped across town and by the time they were in the hospital parking lot, Charlee's emotions were a frazzled mess. She ran inside the emergency entrance with Ian's footfalls right behind her. The nurse pointed them to the ICU waiting area. As they rounded the corner, Charlee saw King Edward sitting in a chair facing the TV. Wilma stood at the window and Wynona was pouring a cup of coffee. "What happened?"

They all turned and Wynona got to Charlee first, leaving the coffee cup behind. Quick on Wynona's heels was her sister, who took Wynona's hand. "Wilma saw Arnold first thing in the morning. She said he seemed fine. I went to his cabin around eleven. He'd told Wilma he had something for me. When I arrived, I found him facedown on the floor. He'd knocked over the easel."

Charlee's hands went to her mouth. "Is he okay now?" There was panic in her voice; she could hear it, alarming and uncontrollable. Ian's hand rested on her back, offering strength, but she just didn't think it was enough to keep her upright. He had to be okay. He must be okay.

"They don't know yet, honey."

And a look passed between the sisters that Charlee hated. Hated because it was the look her dad and older brothers shared when her mom was dying of cancer and everybody in the entire world was trying to protect her rather than let her be part of the world she loved. Charlee gritted her teeth. "Is. He. Okay?"

Wynona's eyes filled with tears and Charlee hated that she'd caused them. "He's still unconscious."

The room darkened around her to one tiny tunnel of light. Her knees gave way, and had it not been for strong arms shoring her up, Charlee would have collapsed. The world swayed as they helped her to a chair. Ian lowered her to the seat, but kept both hands firmly on her shoulders.

This wasn't happening. Couldn't be happening. She'd lost her mom and her dad and now the possibility of waking every morning and looking out at an empty cabin where Mr. Gruber once lived . . . no. She just couldn't. He was going to be okay. "Can we see him?"

"They're running tests. Not sure if it was just a heart attack or a heart attack and a stroke." Wilma shook her head.

"Both? They think it could be both? Wait, he's been unconscious the whole time?" She wasn't sure why she needed to know that, or what it mattered, but somewhere in her mind, she felt that if she pieced all the pieces together, she'd have a clear picture and he'd be fine. Crazy, of course. Insane. But she needed more details. "Had he complained about not feeling well?"

Wilma shook her head. "No. In fact, this morning, he seemed extremely chipper. Smiles and everything." And that's when Charlee realized Wilma and Wynona had already done what she was trying to do. Make sense of it. Put it all together so a clear picture emerged. But there was no clear picture to have because when it came to things like illness, strokes, heart attacks, there were no rules. They came; they took. End of story. "I guess we just have to wait to hear from the doctor."

Wynona sat down beside her, threaded their hands together. "And pray."

CHAPTER 11

Minutes crept by as they waited. Charlee paced the floor until her legs ached. She knew Ian was keeping an eye on her even though he stood back, gave her room, gave her space, but he was right there to catch her if she crumbled again. Finally, she curled up in a stiff-backed hospital waiting room chair, settling into Ian's arms. King Edward was visiting with a nurse in the corner—someone he'd seen earlier and said he'd recognized from the art store. She was a budding artist and Edward was giving her tips.

"Flirting," Ian whispered in Charlee's ear and nodded toward the two.

Charlee chuckled. "She is. King Edward is oblivious to it."

When the doctor stepped in, they all rose. He walked toward Wynona and the rest of the group gathered. "Are you here for Arnold Gruber?"

Charlee felt Ian's arm lace around her waist. "Yes."

"We're taking him into surgery. He has blockages in his heart. Suffered a massive heart attack, but no stroke. He's diabetic so the surgery can take longer than normal." The doctor paused just long enough for the group to digest the words. *Massive heart attack. Surgery.* He hooked his hands in the pockets of his white coat. "We're optimistic, but the surgery is risky."

"Has he regained consciousness?" Wilma's face was a mask of concern, but she mustered her strength to ask.

The doctor's dark eyes dropped for an instant. "I'm afraid not."

"He will, though," Wynona supplied; it was both a question and an answer. "I didn't know he was diabetic."

"Not sure he knows either. Like I said, we're optimistic." And that was neither a question nor an answer.

Frustration threaded through Charlee's system. "What does that mean?"

The doctor pulled a breath. "There's a thirty-percent chance he won't survive the surgery. And there's always the possibility he won't regain consciousness. Now, I have some paperwork. Who is immediate family?"

Charlee sucked a breath. Mr. Gruber's daughter. She hadn't even thought to let her know. "None of us. Mr. Gruber lives at my artists' retreat."

The doctor rocked back on his heels. "Oh, the one just out of town? Used to be the old kids' camp?" He'd shifted right into casual conversation, eyes friendly and focused on Charlee. She wanted to be angry at him for so quickly leaving the intense conversation about Mr. Gruber. But, she supposed in his line of work, dealing with life and death, one had to grow rhino skin. Still, she didn't bother to answer.

"I know his daughter lives in Kansas City. I need to get a hold of her. This won't hold up the surgery, right?" Charlee couldn't believe she'd been so selfish, so lost in her own fear that she hadn't bothered to let Mr. Gruber's daughter know.

"Not at all," the doctor assured. "Just have her swing by admitting at some point."

Charlee turned to find Ian's waiting arms. She clung to him as the doctor walked back through the white doors that for so many people offered either hope or despair—sometimes both.

Ian rested his head on top of hers. She listened to him breathe. "I can't believe I didn't call her."

A wide hand swept up and down her back. "It's better that you waited. You have something to tell her now."

That was true. At least they knew. Knowledge was power. And power could get you through the toughest of times.

"Here, I have Arnold's cell phone." Wynona dug it out of her bag.

Charlee took it and hit a button. Outgoing calls. All to Ian's numbers, first to the phone in his cabin, then his cell. Cold shot into her chest. Her eyes went to Wynona. "Did you all try to call us after you found him?"

"Not from Arnold's phone."

Ian snatched the phone from her hands and stared at it. "Oh no."

She grabbed the cell when it nearly fell from Ian's hand. He'd gone pale. "He tried to call you?"

His mouth hung open, eyes filling with tears. "I didn't know." His hand came up and covered the lower portion of his face and Charlee focused her gaze on him as the soldier who'd watched his friends die on the battlefield, watched her father die on the battlefield, crumbled. His giant shoulders quaked and when she thought he'd implode, he stormed away from them to the sanctuary of the nearby window where he could look out on a world that continued to spin even though theirs was falling apart.

Too many emotions raced through Charlee. If Ian had answered the call, would it have made a difference? Mr. Gruber had reached out, called when . . . when what? The scenarios ran through Charlee's mind, leaving a wake of shattered possibilities too painful to neglect. She imagined Mr. Gruber lying on his floor, gasping for air and reaching out for a cell phone only to be put off. She imagined his eyes closing, slowly realizing no one was there for him when he needed them most. Charlee thought she might throw up. She forced the images from her mind. She had a job to do. She needed to contact Mr. Gruber's daughter. But after scanning the phone, she realized there was no number listed. Gruber's phone had all of ten contacts. The art store, Charlee, Ian, Wilma and Wynona who shared a cell phone because they didn't like to use them claiming they could give you brain cancer, King Edward's cell, Pizza Hut, and the four cabin landlines. That was it.

"How can his daughter's number not be in here?"

Wynona stared at it as if the look would elicit the number's appearance. "Well, he hasn't had the cell that long. I'm sure her number is at his house. Let's go. King Edward can drive us."

Charlee considered leaving versus staying. On the one hand, she wanted to be there for Mr. Gruber. On the other, he would be in surgery for hours and Charlee needed to contact his daughter. Reluctantly, she nodded. Her eyes drifted to Ian, still at the window. She crossed the room to him and placed a hand on his arm.

He jolted, surprising her because Ian wasn't typically jumpy—except, of course, when he was waking from a nightmare. When he turned to look at her, the bewilderment shook Charlee to the core. His eyes were haunted and hollow. She had to swallow before trusting her voice to speak. "Wynona and I are going home to find Mr. Gruber's daughter's phone number. Do you want to come with us?"

As soon as she said it, she wished she hadn't. The last thing in the world she wanted was Ian on his bike in his present state. He looked like a stiff wind could do him in. It was a while before he answered, his gaze going from her to the door and back as if his mind was trying to catch up and couldn't quite get there. "He called me, Charlee. And I didn't answer."

She closed her hands over his strong upper arms. "It's not your fault, Ian. You couldn't have known anything was wrong."

"He needed me."

"Ian, you can't blame yourself." She squeezed, hoping beyond hope the pressure of hands to arms would send assurance through his system. "We couldn't have known."

He didn't exactly nod, but more jerked a slight movement that let her know he understood . . . maybe didn't believe it, but at least understood. "I'm going to stay here. In case."

Charlee nodded. "We'll be right back. I don't want to be gone long."

Charlee stood on her toes and pulled Ian's head toward hers. He came easily, but for the first time since they'd met, when she pressed her lips to his, there was no reaction. His mouth was a hard line that didn't alter as she touched hers to him. As Charlee walked away, casting one quick glance back at him, she had to wonder how much this event might change him. Ian was no longer the soldier come home, ready to start over. Ian was the man on the battlefield who'd survived when others hadn't. And that created a strange detachment she wasn't sure she had the power to reconnect.

———

"Not here, either." Wynona dropped her hands to her hips. They'd scrounged through Mr. Gruber's things until they found an old phone bill. But there were only a handful of long-distance calls on the bill. "It's got to be one of these, right?"

Wynona nodded, pulling her long hair over her shoulder and out of her way. "Yes. He told me just the other night he talks to her every week. Do you know the Kansas City area codes?"

Charlee shrugged. "Here, we can pull it up on his computer. Find the area codes and narrow these numbers down."

Wynona went to the desktop and moved the mouse. "Just a minute, he's on Facebook. Oh, this is Ashley's page."

Charlee crossed the room to gaze over Wynona's shoulder. There on the screen, a beautiful woman with Mr. Gruber's eyes held a chubby baby girl in her arms. Charlee was about to destroy her world and hated that fact. "Is there a phone number listed in her contact information?"

Wynona clicked around like a pro. "No. She works at Bradley and Baker on the plaza. Maybe we could call there?"

"It's Saturday. Worth a try, though. I mean, at this point we don't have anything else." Before calling, they checked the numbers from Gruber's phone bill, but none of them was a Kansas City area code.

Charlee called Bradley and Baker and got the answering service. She explained it was an emergency and please to let Ashley know it was concerning her father. She left her number.

Wynona had disappeared from the living room and came out of the bedroom looking as if she'd seen a ghost. Mr. Gruber's favorite robe hung from her hand and she nearly tripped over it as she stumbled out of his room.

Charlee rushed to her. "Wynona, what is it?"

She didn't speak, but pointed to the bedroom.

Fear shot into Charlee, but she had no choice but to go. There, posed beside the bed on an easel was a picture of Wynona. Charlee's heart jumped into her throat. A ray of dazzling light held the woman in silence. Her head was back, long white hair a silken shroud splayed over her shoulders, long flowing gown clinging to her legs in a night breeze you could practically feel. It was beautiful. Breathtaking and almost unearthly. With her head tilted, a beam of illumination caught the soft shade of one eye, making her look as if the light wasn't surrounding her, but was born from her. It was a masterpiece like no other.

"Oh, Wynona, it's incredible."

The woman who'd been frozen only a moment ago seemed to disintegrate. Hands came up to her face to collect the tears that flowed freely from her eyes. And it hit Charlee. "He must really care about you." Because this kind of painting wasn't just paint and canvas, brush strokes and planning. This kind of painting could only be created from the purest and deepest of love.

Hollow eyes found Charlee. "I don't . . . I don't want to lose him." And then the crying became sobs while Charlee wrapped her arms around Wynona and let her melt.

CHAPTER 12

Jeremiah McKinley stopped at the ice cream shop as he entered town. While deployed, he'd craved chocolate sodas, and when he got stateside, had scoured every ice cream shop to find one. None of them compared. The Dairy Flip was in a class all its own and he'd learned to appreciate the little things in life. Like the perfect balance of chocolate syrup, ice cream, and soda water. He stepped out of his brand-new Ford Ranger and slid the window open to peer inside the Dairy Flip. Just the same as he remembered. Some things never changed and for that he was grateful. Some things you could count on. "Rodman!"

Rodney turned, eyes wide, and Jeremiah realized his old friend hadn't gained back the weight as quickly as he'd hoped. "Miah!"

He'd been called Miah by half the town for half his life. When he first went into the army, guys made fun of him for his girly nickname. But Jeremiah McKinley wasn't above teaching respect when it was needed and soon no one joked about the name.

Rodney wiped his hands on a towel as he strode right past the window and out the side door. He grabbed Jeremiah in a bear hug. Miah grunted. "I gotta say, for being skinny, you're still strong as ever. I think you cracked my ribs."

Rodney laughed. "Wouldn't that be a kick? Spend years in the military and come home to get injured at an ice cream shop. I hear you're coming back for good."

Jeremiah nodded. "Eventually, yeah. I think."

"You here now because of the commotion?"

Jeremiah frowned. "What commotion?"

"At the artists' retreat this morning?"

Jeremiah's heart dropped into his stomach. He hated that his sister was alone out there with a bunch of crazy artists. He shook off the instant frustration. "What happened, Rod?"

He raised his shoulders and dropped them. "Don't know exactly. One of the artists took sick and they had to call an ambulance."

Jeremiah pulled his cell from his pocket.

Rod pointed down the road. "I'm sure they're at the hospital."

Jeremiah nodded and ran the few feet back to his truck. "Be back."

"Tell Charlee hi for me." Rodney continued to wave as Jeremiah pulled out.

Tall, wide shoulders, towering over six feet, he filled the entryway. Charlee sat up straight when Jeremiah entered through the far door. Her mind must be playing tricks on her. He couldn't be here. He was in North Carolina. She shook her head to clear it.

As his piercing golden gaze scanned the room and landed on her, she knew it wasn't her mind. Long legs made short work of getting to her. And she knew, oh she knew the look of concern on his face. So many times as a kid she'd witnessed it. When she tumbled into a raging river and he'd stripped instantly from his shoes and shirt to rescue her, when the captain of the high school football team took her to Murder Rock—where all the kids went for drinking and make-out sessions and Jeremiah plucked the jock from his car like one grabs a suitcase from a conveyor belt. The captain of the team had dangled there, full of fear and all the testosterone of the game draining from him. Charlee remembered it vividly. She had climbed out of the car and silently gotten into Miah's truck. Mortified, but also a little relieved. Rumor had it Brice, Mr. Football, had even wet his pants when dragged from his car by the infamous Jeremiah McKinley. Her brother, her larger-than-life big brother had wrestled a bear, for heaven's sake.

"What happened?" he ordered as he grabbed her up in his arms. Trapped there, against his stone-hard chest with her feet three inches off the ground, she couldn't speak if she wanted to.

Suddenly, Charlee became aware of another presence beside her. Ian. Oh. Oh dear. She gave her brother a quick hug and truly, it was great to see him, feel him. Alive, whole. Of course, he'd been in North Carolina for six months, but knowing and seeing were two different things.

When he finally released her, flicking a dismissive look at Ian, his golden gaze scanned her face.

"It's Mr. Gruber. I wrote you about him months ago. He's become like a grandfather to me and . . ." And Charlee's eyes misted because she had a grandfather she barely knew, a man who was flesh and blood and lived no more than thirty miles away. But in the time Mr. Gruber had been with her, he'd been more like family than the man who'd raised her mother.

When her mouth opened to explain more but nothing came out, she felt Ian's strong hand slide into hers. His other hand thrust out in front of him. "Ian Carlisle."

Jeremiah blinked, frowned, eyes seeming unable to decide where to light, on Ian or Charlee. Finally, he pointed to him. "Is this the one who lied about knowing me?"

Charlee's words came out in a rush as she tried to take a step in front of Ian. He sidestepped, of course. Stupid soldiers, always ready to go to war. "It was a misunderstanding, Miah."

"Miah?" Ian whispered and Charlee cut him with an instant sharp glare.

Charlee's grip tightened on Ian's hand, but found his muscles slack. He was relaxed and not the least bit intimidated by her brother. Well, he got props for that. *Everyone* was intimidated by Jeremiah McKinley. "Ian knew Dad. They were pretty close. He was with him . . . right to the end."

And now Jeremiah looked at him in a whole new light. Something flickered there, in his golden gaze, and Charlee knew he was considering how this young man might have spent their father's last days with him. That tended to melt all the ice chips of anger. Jeremiah's lip curled for an instant, as if his face were rejecting the thoughts that persisted. "You knew Dad?"

Ian nodded. "He was a really great man. The best. The best I've ever known."

Charlee's eyes went from Ian to Jeremiah, two men, two soldiers, both rejecting the emotions that threatened, and yet both understanding the other's need to do so. Ian's hand still hung in the air between them. Finally, Miah shook it. "Good to meet you."

Charlee explained what had happened to Mr. Gruber and the prognosis, the risks; she repeated each word specifically, as if doing so would tip the scales and give Mr. Gruber the best fighting chance.

They sat for a while as Jeremiah told her how he'd come to know where they were and how he still hadn't had a decent chocolate soda. Then he took hold of Ian's shoulder and said, "Sounds like it's going to be a while; why don't you and I go for ice cream?"

There was a glint in Miah's eyes Charlee didn't like. And a smile on his face, too wide, too toothy. Good heavens, did she need to worry about her brother trying to scare the life out of Ian? She released a long exhale and pressed a hand to her newly aching head. "Gird your loins," she mumbled.

Ian stood from beside her. "Huh?"

She cast a glare to her brother. "Nothing, Ian. You two be careful." That was all the warning she'd give.

Ian would agree to go, of that she was certain because she knew how guys were. She'd raised four of them, three older than her. And guys didn't back down from a dare. And this was most certainly that.

Ian pulled her up from the seat and planted a lingering kiss on her mouth—a territorial kiss—for her brother's benefit. The air around Jeremiah filled with electricity born of annoyance . . . or frustration . . . or some unnamable sensation that men felt when protecting their own. Whatever. She really didn't have the energy to dissect the male ego. She'd save that for Dr. Phil.

King Edward came scurrying over. "I'll have a milk shake. Chocolate, extra whipped cream. No cherry. God help them if they put a cherry on my milk shake."

Charlee watched Jeremiah's gaze level on Edward, then drift down, down, down to the edge of his kilt, over his knobby knees, to the hairy shins and finally stopping at his ankles. Her brother's face was unreadable, except for the tiniest spark of curiosity in his eyes and a smirk at the edges of his mouth. Jeremiah and Edward had never met. Edward was traveling in Europe when her father passed and hadn't made it back for the memorial service. Which, in retrospect, could have caused a ruckus with all the army brass wondering why Charlee was being consoled by three crazy artists and a man in a dress. Edward had even offered to return from his trip to be there, but Charlee had told him no. She was surrounded by the other artists and her brothers. All was well.

Jeremiah's tongue came out and moistened his lips. "Milk shake," he repeated. Eyes, two glass golden balls, revealing nothing.

Ian cleared his throat. "Edward, you want to come along?"

Beside her, she felt her brother stiffen.

"No." Edward waved a hand through the air, dismissing them. "I'll stay here with Char Char Baby."

Miah's nostrils flared for a quick second. Ian bit back a smile. He was *enjoying* this. Evil, evil young man.

King Edward reached to the hem of his kilt and fanned it. "Besides, it's scorching out there. And I'm chaffing a bit."

Ian took orders from the rest and she watched him walk out, leading her brother who—in Ian's own words—was now shell-shocked, thanks to King Edward. Miah's presence helped fortify her. Though she wished she'd known he was coming. He'd probably been planning to surprise her. That's how Miah was. Arrive, consume. But today he'd been derailed by a leg-flashing artist and the man she . . . the man she'd hired to fix her property and who was fixing her heart in the process.

Still no word from Ashley Gruber. Charlee almost hoped she wouldn't call until he was out of surgery. Things were up in the air right now and she hated having to give Ashley so much noninformation.

Charlee froze when her phone rang. "Hello?"

"This is Ashley Gruber."

Charlee swallowed; the woman sounded calm. Too calm to have received an emergency message about her aging father. Of course, she was an attorney and that had to create a stiff front.

"Ashley, I'm so sorry to tell you your dad has had a massive heart attack. He's in surgery now."

Silence.

Charlee counted to three. She needed to give the woman a bit of time to absorb, then she could offer her details, a place to stay while she's here. Even could help make travel plans. Would Ashley fly or drive? Oh yes, Charlee was good in a crisis. It was *after* when she fell apart. But the silence became deafening and Charlee realized the woman should be asking questions by now. Had she lost the connection? "Are you there, Ashley?"

"Yes." No emotion. No fear. No . . . anything.

"Uh, the nearest airport is about forty miles, but I'd be happy to come meet you there if you want to fly. It looks like you're about a five-hour drive, so I can get directions for you if that works better. Just let me know your travel plans—"

"I'm not coming."

Charlee must have heard wrong. "What?"

A long exhale. "I haven't spoken to my father for eight years and now I'm supposed to just drop everything and come?"

Charlee pressed the phone to her ear. This was all wrong. Could it be the wrong daughter? "But—"

"I'm sorry, Miss McKinley. He's a man I don't know. And I buried him a long time ago."

The phone went dead. Snippets of memories passed through Charlee's mind. Mr. Gruber only had one daughter. One daughter and one granddaughter, Ashley and Vivi. Charlee would know them anywhere; they were in practically every painting Mr. Gruber created. A sickening feeling rushed through her system, one that knocked the world right out from under her, causing her to ease her body down onto the seat. Still, she couldn't assimilate.

His daughter sent chocolates and candy and gifts from her Caribbean vacations. He frequently told them stories about Vivi, his granddaughter, after visiting with Ashley on the phone. How Vivi'd taken her first steps, their trip to the zoo where she repeated, "Muntee," for weeks after watching the chimps in the monkey hut.

Wynona sat down beside Charlee. "Was that—?"

"She's not coming."

"What?"

Charlee looked over to find Wynona's kind eyes wide with shock. "She says she hasn't spoken to him in eight years."

Wynona's hand came up, fist resting against her cheek. "Oh dear. Oh no." They were pitiful words because as the reality was settling in for Charlee, it also was for Wynona, a woman who knew Mr. Gruber perhaps better than any of them.

The older woman's head shook slowly, sadly, as if she both understood and had known all along.

Charlee grabbed her hand. "Did you *know* he hadn't spoken to his daughter?"

"What?" Wynona blinked as if trying to bring Charlee into focus, but Charlee could see her mind, her thoughts; her very heart was far away. "No, of course not. But Arnold is a proud man. And I don't really know what to say except when you reach our age and you look back . . ."

"There's a lot you would change?" Charlee supplied and wanted Wynona to stop talking, just stop because it hurt to see her in so much pain. Old. They were old. All of the artists except King Edward, who was in his fifties. And old meant years of ghosts and regrets. And Wynona—the woman who floated on clouds and slept in angel's wings was allowing herself to look back and see the should-have-beens.

Wynona squared her shoulders. "I don't regret my life. By the grace of God, I made it through some tough times, some hard times, losing a husband. I don't know why God smiled on me, but I feel certain he did. Arnold . . ."

"He lost a spouse too."

Wynona nodded. "I don't know where Arnold took a wrong turn, how he ended up an alcoholic, I just know that in his eyes there are many, many regrets. Oh, he tries to hide them. But your past will find you."

Like it had today. Charlee should say something, but there just weren't words. She thought of Mr. Gruber and all the times he walked to the mailbox and carried back boxes from his daughter. "But why the dishonesty?"

Wynona's mouth was a straight line. "Maybe not so much dishonesty as living the fantasy he wished could be."

"And knowing it never would unless he created it." Her heart broke. For all the injustice of it. Even for Ashley, a woman whose father was alive and desperate for a relationship—and she'd have none of it. And herself, a woman whose father was dead and the best part of their relationship was unfolding through a journal of her dad's letters to her. It was no wonder Charlee and Mr. Gruber had found each other; they offered to one another that thing they both desperately sought. Her chin tilted defiantly. "We're his family now."

Wynona patted her hand.

"*We* won't let him down."

"No, we won't," Wynona echoed. "We're truly all he's got."

———

Ian sat at the ice cream shop table, staring down Jeremiah McKinley. He was tall, like his father, commanding and powerful, something he thought the McKinleys must come by naturally. Their strong defiance was more than just bred. It was made.

Jeremiah's attention was on his drink. Or shake. Or sundae. Whatever that thing was with the mound of ice cream balanced on the edge of the cup and the disgusting-looking sludge, brown bubbles surrounding it. He took a drink and sighed. "I couldn't find a decent one of these in North Carolina. You certainly can't get them in the sandbox. It's been forever since I had a good one."

Ian knew what he meant. You also had a hard time finding a decent hamburger or French fries. "Sorry, dude. That looks terrible."

"You have no idea what you're missing."

"I'll stick with a hot fudge sundae." Ian took a bite and over his shoulder could see Rod making the drinks they'd take back to the hospital with them.

When the chocolate drink was half gone, Jeremiah got to the real reason he'd asked Ian along. Ian had been waiting for it. "So, my sister."

Ian nodded.

"You care about her?"

"Very much."

"Can you get her off that ridiculous hunk of land?"

Ian blinked. Figured Miah was going to insinuate himself into their lives by way of bullying. He hadn't expected a conspiracy. "The artists' retreat?"

Jeremiah's eyes widened. "You mean the freak show?"

Ian stiffened. "They're good people. Harmless."

Jeremiah let out a humorless laugh. "These are. But how long until some freak comes along who means her harm?"

Ian never thought of that. She opened those doors for anyone and everyone. He hadn't considered it because he always imagined himself right there. But summer was ending and his time as Charlee's handyman was coming to a close. And she hadn't made any more of a commitment to him than she had when they first met. Cold sliced his spine at the thought of her out there . . . all alone . . .

And Miah waited. Letting all those horrible scenarios run through Ian's head.

Ian shook them off. No. That was just fear and fear was as powerful as you let it be. He wouldn't give it that kind of hold over him. He leaned forward and narrowed his gaze on Jeremiah. "Your sister has been there for years now. She's a grown woman and no one, man or brother, is going to tell her what to do."

Jeremiah tapped his hand on the table.

"I know you worry about her. She worried about you too when you were deployed but that wouldn't have given her the right to tell you not to go."

Jeremiah worked the muscles in his jaw.

Ian thought a moment. "Besides, aren't you planning on doing something with the adjacent property? That'd put you right there, right? To watch out for her."

"I was thinking about it, then a man contacted me about buying the whole two hundred acres."

Ian's eyes narrowed to slits. "So this isn't about her safety?"

A flat hand landed on the table. "It's always been about her safety. Man. Why can't she just have a normal life and a normal job?"

Ian shrugged. "Like you?"

The irony was not lost on Jeremiah. "Curse of McKinley blood, I guess."

"Would you be saying the same things if she'd joined the army?"

He watched Jeremiah ponder this thought, chew it around and see how it tasted. "No. She'd be trained."

Ian leaned his weight on his forearms. "She *is* trained, Jeremiah. Believe me, she can hold her own. You did good. You and your brothers and your dad. In fact, I've never met a woman who was more aggressive."

This last comment turned Jeremiah's eyes to fury. His teeth gritted. "What?"

Ian held his hands up. "No, that's not what I meant. Aggressive, in life, in an argument." He shook his head. "Not the other. I don't know about that. Not . . ."

Jeremiah's wide eyes stayed so tightly fitted to him, Ian almost couldn't breathe.

"We aren't. I mean we *are*, but we haven't . . ." He threw out a breath. "Your sister's honor is safe."

Reluctant at first, Jeremiah finally let the tension drain off him, which Ian easily saw and appreciated.

Ian tapped his licked-clean sundae spoon on the table. "I love her."

Jeremiah remained quiet.

"I love her and she's not looking for that. Some guy named Richard did a real number on her and she isn't ready. But that didn't keep me from falling." There were grooves in the table, it was weatherworn and sun beaten, a little like Ian's heart. Jeremiah had mannerisms that mimicked Major McKinley, making him both easy to confide in and difficult to be around. Ian missed the major. And here, at the Dairy Flip, a part of Major McKinley was alive and right in front of Ian. Yes, Jeremiah was a lot like his father. The quirk of his cheek, the tilt of his head, that deep, intense stare.

Jeremiah rested an elbow on the table. "Would you at least talk to her about selling? Please. She'd have enough money to do whatever she wanted. If the offer comes through, it's a doozy."

"It won't do any good. But I'll talk to her. You know how stubborn she is. Even put up a fence to separate your property from hers." As soon as he said it, he wished he hadn't. Real hurt entered Jeremiah's eyes, but he flicked it away like a champ . . . or like a guy who'd spent too many years fighting his sister's battles when she'd rather war with her own two hands. "It isn't personal, Jeremiah."

He huffed. "Not personal? It's completely personal and I totally get it." His gaze landed far off. "She was all we had, you know? After Mom died. She was it. The great equalizer for all us boys."

"You just wanted to protect her."

"Still do. Come on, let's get their drinks back to them. I'd hate for that Edward guy's skirt to fly up in a rage."

Ian chuckled. "You have no idea."

CHAPTER 13

Charlee was going to take first watch. Mr. Gruber had survived surgery and would be in recovery for the next six hours then moved to ICU. She'd sent the group home to get some rest. Ian had wanted to stay with her, but they'd all already been there for more than five hours and since Ian and Jeremiah were getting chummy, she sent Ian to help Miah settle in. Keep them both out of her hair.

"Charlee? Charlee McKinley?" The voice was deep, vaguely familiar, or maybe the ease of words was what was familiar about it. Through bleary eyes she saw the white-coated man in dark loafers walking toward her. His steps quickened as he came closer. "It's me. Wesley Giles."

The past flooded her, high school, Mr. Harner's science class. "Wes?"

He stopped at her feet, boyish smile and eyes filled with joy at seeing her. His hair was darker than she remembered, but the eyes remained the same. "Wes, I haven't seen you for . . ."

He chuckled. "Eight years, probably."

When he opened his arms, she hugged him. He'd been her height during high school even though he was a senior when she was a sophomore. Now he was a good six feet. She stepped back. "What happened to you?"

"Grew." He laughed. "It's great to see you. Are you here with someone?"

He hung his hands on the stethoscope around his neck.

"Yes, Arnold Gruber."

He nodded, brows tilting into a frown. "Yes, the acute MI. He's recovering well. Looks like he'll pull through."

Relief flooded Charlee. Every time they said, "he'll pull through," it was as if tension was being peeled from her back. "Are you a—?"

"Oh." He rolled his eyes as if he'd been rude not to explain. "I fast-tracked through med school. I just transferred here after my residency. It's great to be home."

"You're a doctor?"

"Mm hmm. That's what they tell me," he said, as if it wasn't any big deal. "ER, but a small town ER doctor covers a multitude of duties. Yesterday I had to fix a leaky faucet." And then he laughed again while Charlee tried to rapid-age her short, squirmy lab partner and turn him into a physician. She couldn't quite get there. Until a nurse stepped through the glass door and toward them.

"Dr. Giles, I'm sorry to interrupt, but Mrs. Avers is being discharged and you said you wanted to speak with her before—"

"Oh, yes." He turned to Charlee. "Sometimes, I feel like I'm a preschool teacher."

This made the nurse smile as if they were sharing a joke Charlee could only guess about.

"Shellfish. If you're allergic to shellfish, you don't eat shrimp. Even if the shell has been removed." He rubbed a hand over his face. "Now I have to go explain that little bit of science to someone who's been in here twice in the last two months."

She said good-bye to her old friend, remembering the smile he'd had for her every morning in the accelerated science class they'd dropped her into when the other classes were full. She'd passed, thanks in no small part to Wes. He paused at the door. "I'll personally keep you posted on Mr. Gruber's progress." There it was, that sharp fervency of a physician;

his look had gone from friendly to deadly serious in a flash. He softened the somber words with a light smile.

"Thank you, Wesley." He was good at this, Charlee realized as he disappeared though the glass door. And he loved it. Like she used to love the artists' retreat before the work became too much. Like she was starting to love it again with Ian there to lift the pressure from her shoulders and do anything and everything she needed. But Ian was leaving soon and she already dreaded both the work and the loneliness that would accompany her after his departure.

She had no choice but to let him go. She'd thought this through. Saying good-bye was for Ian's sake as much as her own. Because in her heart she knew she had nothing more to give him, and maybe she never would. And Ian deserved better than that. He deserved the best. She just wasn't it.

She'd kept expecting to wake up one day and all the hurt would be gone and she could move forward, really move forward with her life. Maybe even with Ian. But "one day" hadn't come. Every morning, she still felt the sting of Richard's betrayal. And what right did she have to ask Ian to stay on a hope and a prayer that one day she'd be able to forget what Richard had done to her? His had been the worst kind of betrayal, because he'd never cared about her. Just what he could get from her.

And in a way wouldn't she be doing the same thing to Ian? Charlee's head ached. She tried to get comfortable in the hard-backed chair; soon, her burning eyes drifted shut. The room was cool and quiet, the sun warming a spot on her side. If she just kept her eyes closed for a few short seconds—

She woke with a start and could see a whitish blob hovering over her. "Miss McKinley?" The female voice soothed.

Charlee tried to move but a mass of white cotton material obstructed her hands.

"Miss McKinley, Dr. Giles asked me to wake you. You can go in and visit Mr. Gruber in a few minutes."

This announcement snapped Charlee awake. "How is he?"

"He's doing well. Made it through the night." The nurse glanced down at her watch. "Five a.m. Dr. Giles will meet with you soon to give you an update. Someone named Wynona has called to check in every hour. I told her he was stable and doing well. She said she'd be here in another hour or so."

Charlee shook off the sleep and the chlorine-scented blanket.

"I can take that." The nurse slipped the cover from her. She grinned. "Dr. Giles has a fantastic bedside manner, but I have to say, he's taken awfully good care of you even though you're not one of his patients."

Charlee ran her hand over her bed-rough hair. Her teeth felt furry. "We know each other from high school."

The nurse smiled down at her. "He knows almost everyone here. Trust me. You're getting top-shelf care."

"It's very sweet of him."

The nurse nodded. "It is. He's good to all of us." She rolled her eyes. "You should have seen the doctor he replaced. We nicknamed him the Troll. Horrible. No one liked coming to work. It's better now."

Yes, Charlee could see that this nurse was not only happy now but thrilled, overjoyed to be working with Wesley. Skinny little Wesley from science class. "And Mr. Gruber is doing okay?"

The nurse nodded over her shoulder. "Come see for yourself."

———

It's not that Charlee was particularly scared of hospital rooms, but they made her uncomfortable. All that artificial life being administered. The smell of medicine and death. As she stepped through the door, she thought of her mom. Seeing her so thin and frail on the white bed with cancer devouring her body. She always mustered a smile for Charlee. Was always upbeat and full of love. The nurse gave Charlee time to enter slowly. Much appreciated because the room spun for a quick instant as memories from all those years ago flooded her.

Her skin heated. Air from the ceiling vent hit her and the flesh that was hot, chilled. Charlee drew what strength she had and stepped inside. A drape covered the bed, extending from floor to ceiling. But the sounds and scents were all the same as if she'd been deposited into the past and the nurse would pull the curtain and there her mother would be. Beeps echoed off the still walls, the lights had been turned down, giving the room an odd green glow, the buzzing and humming of mechanical equipment gave the room its own rhythm. A rhythm she didn't like. A rhythm whose beat meant death, not life.

The nurse took hold of the curtain both low and high and slowly, as if unveiling a priceless work of art, began to drag the drape along its rail. Charlee swallowed as bit by bit, Mr. Gruber—not her mother—came into view.

A small balding head lay against a blue pillow that looked too full to be comfortable. In his nostrils tiny tubes offered oxygen, his arms were flat at his sides, both with tubes running under white bandages and into his veins; there was bruising along his arms. Charlee stepped closer and gave a questioning glance to the nurse. "Bruises?" she whispered.

The nurse stepped beside her and pointed to one. "He came in with a few, must have tried to catch himself as he fell to the ground."

Charlee pressed her lips together, staving off tears.

The nurse gave her a sympathetic smile. "These." She took Mr. Gruber's hand in her own and ran a finger a few inches above his flesh, pointing out certain spots. "These are from missed veins while trying to put in the IV."

A flash of fury ran down Charlee's spine. "Was it someone who didn't know what they were doing?" She hadn't meant to sound so aggravated, but really?

"No, no," the nurse assured. "Elderly people sometimes have veins that become roll-y, meaning they will roll beneath the needle. They can actually harden with age. We see that a lot."

Charlee gripped the silver bar at the bed's edge.

"Here," the nurse pointed to a deeply bruised spot on his inner arm, "we hit the vein; it was good for a while then the vein blew out." Her soft brown eyes met Charlee's questioning ones. "It happens sometimes, I'm afraid. They can pop from the pressure or even the toxicity of what's being injected. Once we found a good vein, we wanted to keep it open as long as possible, but you always run this risk."

Charlee nodded, appreciated the nurse's time and gentleness and frank explanations. Before leaving she asked if Charlee needed anything. "No, thank you. It's good to see him."

Mr. Gruber hadn't moved, but it didn't matter. He was alive, through surgery, and the prognosis looked good. Things were going to be okay. She quietly settled into a chair. She'd stay with him as long as they'd let her. As soon as she got comfortable, her eyes were heavy.

Movement woke her. Charlee stiffened, felt a killer catch in her neck, groaned and tried to move to work it out while her blurry eyes fought for focus.

A medication-influenced voice made her blink and work to find the source. "Doesn't look like that chair's too comfortable."

There, against the white bed, she found Mr. Gruber. She stood and came to his bedside. Relief flooded her. "I'll manage." Seeing him with his eyes open and focusing on her made her feel a little lighter and the world around a little brighter.

He raised his fingertips and then dropped them in a shrug. "Guess I caused quite a stir."

Charlee was grinning like a fool. For so many hours she'd thought she'd never again hear his gravelly voice, see those bushy brows shoot up on his face. "I guess you did. If you wanted attention all you had to do was—"

"Trade in my trousers for a kilt?" He chuckled, but must have instantly regretted it. His hand came up to his stomach and a wince twisted his face.

Charlee wished she'd gotten some instructions for when he woke.

Should he move, not move? She started to turn toward the door but a cold, bony hand clasped hers.

"Glad you're here, girl."

Girl. Her heart warmed. It was a term of endearment, one sometimes reserved for daughters or granddaughters. And now, now looking at him there on the bed, she knew she was all he had. No real daughter. Not for years. Just her. Just Charlee. "Me too," she croaked.

His eyes were clearing and for a short time, the two of them stayed right there. Then, his eyes closed and he exhaled a long breath. "Tired," he mumbled. "What all happened to me?"

Charlee shot a look to the door. She wouldn't withhold information because she'd had that done to her and there was nothing worse. At the same time, she didn't want to scare him. She opened her mouth but words didn't come out. She cast a glance to the door again, willing the nurse in.

Mr. Gruber sighed. "Heart attack, right?"

She nodded.

"I knew it. Knew it was comin'. Felt the pressure on my chest then the pain."

Charlee swallowed the lump in her throat, reliving the moments with him.

He gave her a weak grin. "Why don't you head on home? I'll be resting. Those dark circles under your eyes say you could use some rest too."

She had to smile. "Thanks. But I think I'll stay awhile."

The door flew open. Dr. Giles swept through the room, pausing at the hand sanitizing station. "How's our patient?" He winked at Charlee.

"Must not be too good if you think I can't answer for myself," Mr. Gruber said and Charlee laughed, surprised at the tear that trickled down her cheek. A happy tear. Wow. How long had it been since she'd had one of those? Happy, relieved, a cyclone of emotions swirled, leaving her dizzy, but content.

Wes stopped at the bed and planted his fists on his hips. "I see you didn't lose your sense of humor."

Gruber peered at him with one eye. "I see you didn't lose your sense of sarcasm."

Wes threw his head back and laughed out loud, the sound seeming odd in the stillness of the room. The echo bounced off the walls and cracked the heavy atmosphere. "Any pain?" He set to work checking numbers and looking now and again at a chart he'd snagged from the wall.

"'Bout as much as I can take, I reckon."

Wes's pen hovered over the chart, eyes sharp on Mr. Gruber. "You a war veteran?"

"Yes sir. Navy. Chief petty officer of the Coral Sea."

Wesley tipped an imaginary hat to him. "In that case, I'm going to increase your pain meds a bit. You military men are tough. And I don't want you taxing your heart just because you can manage the pain."

Mr. Gruber closed his eyes. "I guess I don't mind that." Neither Charlee nor Dr. Giles was surprised when a light snore came from Mr. Gruber.

"He's doing great, Charlee. Vitals are all strong, really came through like a champ."

Charlee pulled a deep breath and expelled all the fear she'd collected after the last several hours. "Thanks so much, Wes. Or should I call you Dr. Giles?"

"Just call me," he said with a quick grin. "Oh, I forgot." He turned back to Mr. Gruber and shook him gently to wake him.

Groggy eyes opened.

"Your daughter called to get an update on your progress."

Blood turned to ice in Charlee's veins. Wes gave her a last glance and left the room.

Charlee watched him go but could feel Gruber's eyes—daggers—penetrating her shell.

"What'd he mean, my daughter called?"

Charlee raised a hand to wipe the back of her neck and to block those spears for eyes. "Maybe he confused you with someone else."

"Charlee, what'd you do? You call my daughter?" There was anger in his tone, but something else. Fear. When she finally looked at him, she wished she hadn't. His eyes were wide with mistrust, like a man who'd built a beautiful fantasy world only to watch it fall to pieces around him.

"I'm sorry. Yes. I called."

His age-weathered hand fisted into the sheet. "And?"

Oh no. She wouldn't tell him. And maybe there was some hope because after their conversation, Ashley had called the hospital to get an update.

"You answer me, girl. You called. Stuck your nose in my business. Now that it's getting messy, you want out?"

Nausea roiled through her stomach. "I told her you were in surgery. She said she wouldn't come." After saying it, Charlee looked at him. Because he deserved her eye contact.

He remained stoic for a moment, but then the marble shell cracked, eyes crimping, mouth quivering. "Wouldn't expect more than that."

"I'm so sorry."

When she reached to take his hand, he pulled away. "I didn't give up on her, mind you. She gave up on me. And I don't blame her that." The ghosts and regrets of the past hovered in his gaze. "At least you're the only one that knows. Please, don't tell them. I couldn't live with it."

Charlee's gaze dropped to the floor. "Okay," she squeaked out.

And those eyes were piercing her again, like two little needles penetrating her flesh. "They don't . . . they don't know, do they?" It was as if he could barely get the words out.

The remaining portion of Charlee's heart broke into tiny pieces. "I'm sorry. Wynona was with me when I called."

His gaze jerked around the room, lighting here and there for short moments then moving on as if everywhere he looked, something was accusing him of the lie he'd been living. When his breathing spiked and a new machine started beeping, Charlee moved closer to him. "It's all okay, Mr. Gruber. No one cares about that."

His hands clenched and unclenched into the bedsheets. "Get out," he ordered, and the strength of his voice pushed Charlee back a step.

This only fueled his resolve. He pointed to the door. "Get out. Don't . . . don't come back. I . . ."

The nurse came rushing in, took one glance at the scene and headed toward the bed. "We need to get your blood pressure down." Her voice was soothing, but fervent. "Calm down."

He stretched to look around her, ignoring her plea. "I don't want to see any of them here. No one."

Charlee—being the source of his pain—left the room. Giant tears accompanied her hurried steps as she raced down the hall. She finally found a women's restroom and tucked inside. Mr. Gruber had been living a lie. Making a big deal out of all the things his daughter sent when he was sending them to himself. All the conversations about how he thought his daughter should save her money, not blow it on candy and chocolates for him. It all rushed into Charlee's mind and settled there. How lonely he must have been to do that. How embarrassed he must have been that his own daughter wouldn't have a relationship with him. And the embarrassment he'd suffer now. Now that the truth was out and he'd have to face everyone.

Charlee pressed a cold, wet paper towel to her cheeks. She couldn't have known. How could she have known? It didn't matter. The damage was done. She'd tried so hard to protect the artists from the world outside of the retreat gates. But the destruction came from within. Charlee stared at her face in the mirror, swollen eyes, mouth bent into a frown. *Is there nowhere that's truly safe?*

Of course there was. Staring at the reflection, she considered her options. Pain could be managed. It could be dulled, and she knew just how to do it. Her mind trailed to the wedding, the tent, Brenna's fiancé sliding that seductive glass under her nose. Charlee's tongue darted out and licked her lips as if she could still taste the liquid. Fresh and fire. Just for her.

No. She slammed her fist on the bathroom counter. She'd made a promise. She wouldn't go there. Not after last time. She thought of how badly it had hurt everyone—the artists who'd searched for her. Rodney, who'd finally found her. Charlee drew from the well of strength and support around her. This time, she wouldn't let them down. After several minutes the invasive voice quieted, no longer driving her, no longer in control. She'd stilled the beast. Even though she wanted to leave, just run to her Jeep, Charlee had to make sure Mr. Gruber was okay. She left the sanctuary of the ladies' room and walked back down the hall wishing she felt more victorious about calming the monster she knew dwelt within her.

There was no commotion at Mr. Gruber's door. She hoped that to be a good sign. A woman dressed in a colorful scrub top of tiny top hats and walking sticks looked up from the nurses' station.

The woman gave her a smile and said, "Can I help you?"

She didn't answer, but cast a glance to Mr. Gruber's door.

Understanding entered the woman's gaze. "I'll go get his nurse. You can talk with her."

Charlee's fingers threaded together on the cool countertop. She felt so tired, so spent, but who cared? She'd messed up everything by trying to help. The nurse arrived and pointed to a door down the hall. It was a consultation room and Charlee's heart kicked up as they neared. Once inside, the nurse rubbed her fingertips over her eyes. "I've got to stop agreeing to these double shifts."

Charlee swallowed the ball of cotton in her throat and waited.

"Arnold is resting. His heart rate went dangerously high, as you witnessed. Blood pressure is under control now." She tilted her head and regarded Charlee like she was trying to figure out a puzzle. "What happened?"

Charlee laughed without humor. She wouldn't tell anyone else about Mr. Gruber's secret. "I said the wrong thing."

"Must have been epic to get that reaction."

Charlee nodded. It was.

A sympathetic smile crossed the nurse's face. "We have to do what's best for our patients." The words were careful, deliberate, words that could elicit a bad reaction if not delivered delicately. Charlee's heart froze. What was this woman saying? Were they not going to allow her to visit Mr. Gruber ever again?

The nurse placed a hand on Charlee's shoulder. "He's refusing to see any visitors. Anyone." With that, the woman's chin tilted downward as if it solidified the request.

"But—"

Of course, she'd planned to leave him alone for a time, but she was all he had. She and Ian and the other artists. "I'm sorry. He is refusing. We can't force him. And we wouldn't. He is in his right mind and has every right to make decisions for himself."

Charlee couldn't breathe. Couldn't move. A choked, "I see," came from somewhere inside her. She shook off the shock. "For how long?"

The nurse turned to leave and cast a glance over her shoulder. "As long as he's here." It was so final, so conclusive Charlee couldn't gather the strength to follow her through the door, so she remained there, mouth hanging open and drying inside. Several minutes had passed when she realized she needed to leave the little room where news was given.

She'd had a bit of time now to consider her new world. A world where Mr. Gruber hated her and would never forgive her for letting him down. What if she never saw him again? What if once he was well, he sent a service to pick up his things at the retreat? Fear drove her back up the hallway to a spot along the wall where she could peek around the corner and see him through the window. Certain he was asleep, Charlee stepped out and stood there staring at him. *Trace my face with your eyes*, her mother had told her a few nights before she died. *Trace my face, then close your eyes and imagine me there. Can you see me? That's where I'll always be. Right there, locked away tight. In the eyes of your heart.*

Charlee closed her eyes and locked Mr. Gruber in that place too. A presence beside her drew her attention and Charlee opened her eyes to find a tall, slender brunette standing at her side. "Are you Charlee?"

Giant brown eyes blinked, hopeful. And Charlee's mind rushed to catch up. She knew her, would recognize her anywhere. "Are you Ashley?"

The woman's sad eyes trailed to the hospital room. "I had to come." She shook her head and the scent of magnolias flew off the long, mink-colored strands. "No matter what he's done to me, he's still my father."

Charlee tried to form words, but exhaustion and confusion refused to let her.

"I owe you an apology. The way I acted on the phone. I've mentally prepared myself for this. Expected it one day, even rehearsed my speech." She gave a toss of her head and readjusted the deep red designer handbag over her other shoulder.

"But you came." Charlee felt the first inkling of hope since the scene in Mr. Gruber's room.

"As soon as I hung up the phone, I made arrangements for Vivi, caught a few hours' sleep and here I am."

It took a lot of spunk for her to get here, Charlee could tell. "Thank you for coming. I think he needs you now more than ever." *Especially since he's refusing to see us. You're the only family he's got left.*

Ashley cleared her throat. "Please, understand. I'm not exactly here for him. I came because I needed to. For me."

Charlee's heart sank into her stomach. "But—"

Ashley held up a perfectly manicured hand. "Please don't make the mistake of thinking he and I will reconcile. I don't know what's going to happen. All I know is I had to come."

Confusion pushed against Charlee's mind, a mind that felt numb from everything that happened since yesterday morning when Ian showed up with a plate of oatmeal chocolate chip cookies. It seemed so long ago. Days, weeks ago.

Ashley tucked her hair behind an ear and leaned her weight on the wall at their back. Her feet were clad in mile-high stilettos—red, to match the purse. Big city girl, through and through. And tough. But there was also a softness that Charlee could only hope would surge to the surface so she and her father could start over.

From their vantage point, they watched as Dr. Giles stepped into the room. Charlee tucked back a bit when he woke Mr. Gruber. She glanced over to find Ashley mentally preparing herself for the doctor's report, for seeing her dad, for talking to him after all these years. Ashley, a woman who looked strong enough she could skewer you with her steak knife, then politely ask for seconds, fidgeted with the briefcase-style handle on her designer bag.

They watched Dr. Giles leave the room, just after pulling the drape around Mr. Gruber's bed.

His face was a mask of concern. Charlee's heart jumped. He stepped to the women after his nurse pointed in their direction. "He's stable for the moment."

"For the moment?" Ashley asked, leaning off the wall.

Dr. Giles studied her a few seconds without speaking.

She thrust out a hand. "I'm Ashley Gruber. I'm his daughter. I just got in; I'd like to see him if he's strong enough."

Wes's gaze darted to Charlee. "You didn't tell her?"

Ashley stiffened. "Tell me what?"

Charlee forced out a breath. "She's his *daughter*. Of course he will want to see her."

Wes raised his hands in a shrug. "I'm sorry. Truly. No one. He even said, no family."

A sound that was neither a laugh nor a cough came from Ashley. "I'm the only family he has." And the implication was not lost on Charlee or Wes. If he refused to see family, he'd specifically refused to see her.

Charlee turned to face her. "This is my fault, you see your dad . . ."

But the flat hand that rose to block Charlee stopped her words. "Don't. I should have known. Some things never change." Ashley turned her attention to Wes. "Will there be any expenses his health insurance doesn't cover?"

Wes pulled a breath. "I . . . I don't know. Medicare covers some, but not all."

Ashley popped her bag open and pulled out a pen and small notebook, all business now. Shoulder strap back in place along with every hair on her head. "I'll sign whatever you need me to, but the bills will be taken care of." There was such a tight professionalism to her tone, Charlee could only stand there stunned. Ashley was going to pay the bills for a man who refused to see her. She squared her shoulders. "If there's any change in his condition, please let me know. Here's my cell number. Or I can be reached tonight at the Carter Bed and Breakfast. I'll be leaving tomorrow." She turned a glare on Charlee. "I wish you'd never called me. I was okay. After trying to be in contact with him for a solid year and being rejected while he was too busy being drunk, I was okay without him. You didn't help anyone by calling me." Ashley spun and stormed off—attorney style—down the hospital corridor, leaving a speechless doctor to stare at Charlee.

Wes reached out to touch her, but she recoiled. "What was I supposed to do?" The words slid right from her mouth unguarded. "I didn't know. He never told me not to contact her."

"It's okay, Charlee."

Her eyes found him. "No. It's not okay by any stretch. *I'm* not okay." She needed to leave, go, get out of there. The walls were closing in, the oxygen was thin and dry and wouldn't satisfy her lungs. She had to go, now. Right now.

As Charlee ran from the hospital and out into the breaking sunlight, she thought of Ian. That was what she needed. She needed him. Charlee tried to call his cabin first, but it rang and rang. Then, she tried his cell and still no answer. Maybe he was still asleep. Her brother would be settled into the spare bedroom at her house, so maybe Ian was there with him, visiting about Charlee's dad. She didn't know, but she knew that in this moment, Ian was the only one who could help her.

When she got to the retreat, she found a note on Ian's front door.

Working at Mr. Gruber's. left phone to charge. come get me when you get back. Bring my phone.

Charlee pulled the tape from his door and wadded the note. She stepped inside to find the cell phone ringing, so she ran to grab it. By the time she made it around the table and to the small writing desk where it was charging, the ringing had stopped.

Her own cell phone was dead and she weighed calling Wynona to tell her the news about Mr. Gruber, but she didn't think she could take the disappointment without Ian there to hold her hand. Charlee hit the redial button, figuring whoever called was looking for news on Mr. Gruber. The call dropped. She grunted and started to slip the phone in her pocket when she realized a voice message had just come through. She hit the "play" button and listened.

"Ian, it's Miah, uh, Jeremiah. I know this isn't a great time to ask, but have you gotten a chance to talk to my sister yet about selling? The buyer is coming in on Saturday and if she's digging in her heels, I want to hold him off for another week. Gimme a call back. You know what, I'm just going to come find you. And uh, hope Gruber is doing okay."

The phone dropped from Charlee's hand as the world spun off its axis. Acid washed from her ears downward, scalding her system as it traveled. She closed her eyes, an attempt to block what she'd just heard. But there, in the darkness, the truth was a blinding light. Every emotion she'd suffered when Richard set her up to sell her property flushed into her mind, leaving her dizzy, off-kilter, equilibrium shot. Of course, Miah never knew the details about Richard. But how could he do this?

She shook her head, closing her eyes to the truth. Ian and her brother were conspiring to sell her property. The tiniest voice in the back of her head told her to give Ian the benefit of the doubt, but it was such a small little whisper, drowned out by the pain, she wouldn't give it a moment's thought.

Her world was trashed. Mr. Gruber. Now Ian. Jeremiah. Charlee backed away from the phone on the floor as if it were the beast of her torture. Her eyes raced around the room. Once again, she thought of the wedding reception. Seeing Ian dancing with Brenna and Brenna's fiancé with a drink for her. Under normal circumstances, she hardly ever thought about alcohol. But when everything spun out of control and the pain was unbearable, alcohol became her answer. It was life. At times like this, it was her god. Suddenly, calm ran from her head down. She had a plan. She needed to go. Get away. She'd known at the hospital that it was inevitable.

Charlee's breaths came in longer gusts of air as the plan formed and grew legs in her mind. She could escape all this. She knew how. She could go and no one would find her until she was ready to be found.

Charlee ran from Ian's cabin, leaving the door wide open. She'd make quick work of it. Stop off at the toolshed, swing by the grocery store in town, hardware store, gas up the Jeep, load her shotgun—just in case and go. She'd need to sneak past her brother, but he was looking for Ian, so that shouldn't be too hard.

Freedom was waiting for her. And it was only a short distance away.

CHAPTER 14

Ian found his front door wide open. "Hello?" he called as he stepped in. If King Edward or one of the sisters was inside, he didn't want to frighten them. He glanced around, found no one, and went to the sink to wash up. Movement outside drew his attention and he cut a glance through the kitchen window to find Jeremiah mounting the steps. "Come on in," he hollered, hands dripping with soapy water.

"You hear from Charlee?" There was concern in Jeremiah's tone and that caused concern in Ian.

"No. But my cell was almost dead, so I left it here while I worked at Gruber's."

"Well, no one's heard from her."

"Call her."

"I have. About ten times, goes straight to voicemail."

Something unsettling crawled over Ian's skin.

"Helloooo," Wynona called from the front door.

Ian motioned her and Wilma in and wiped his hands on a half-clean kitchen towel. "Charlee with you?"

She shook her long white head of hair. "No. We haven't heard from her, but King Edward thought he saw her pulling in an hour ago. We figured she would freshen up and then let us all know details about Arnold. We were about to head back to the hospital, but it's not like her to not check in."

Ian's heart squeezed. "No one has heard from her at all?"

Wilma stepped past her sister to sit at Ian's table. "No. And there's been a problem at the hospital, I'm afraid. Mr. Gruber isn't seeing anyone. His daughter showed up, but he won't even see *her*. And he won't see any of us. From what the nurse said, it was quite a debacle and Charlee took it very hard. Both Arnold and his daughter blamed her for the fiasco."

"Oh no." Ian sank into the kitchen chair. His mind raced, hoping to figure out where Charlee might be. She'd come back here—if Edward was correct—but where was she now?

Jeremiah tapped the table. "She better not run."

A hand came up to Wilma's mouth. "Oh good heavens, you don't think?"

Ian's gaze shot from one to the other, trying to decipher what exactly they meant.

Wynona pressed her hands flat to the table. "If she has, we have to find her. Quickly. Before . . . before any damage is done."

Ian stood from the table. "Stop. What are you all talking about?"

Knowing gazes shot from one another, leaving him the odd man out. He gritted his teeth. "Someone needs to tell me what's going on."

"It's Charlee, dear." Wynona pulled a breath before continuing, as if the motion would fill her mouth with all the right words. "When things get too difficult, she runs."

"Yes, I've been told that, but what does it mean?"

Jeremiah rubbed his hands over his face. "She disappeared for three days after our mom died."

Ian shook his head. "Disappeared?"

"Yeah. We found her in the next town over. Staying with a drug family that *graciously* took her in off the street and didn't bother to let the police know they were harboring a runaway."

Ian's heart sank. He knew she had a tendency to run, but for *days*? He'd thought maybe she just stayed away from everyone, locked herself in her cabin or something, but not physically run away, leave town.

"Alcohol is the problem, Ian." Wynona's eyes filled with pity.

Okay, this was a bad, *bad* dream. Worse than any from Afghanistan.

Wynona gave him a moment to digest, then continued. "She uses alcohol to self-medicate; it's her crutch."

Now, things were coming into focus. Her telling him at the Neon Moon that they don't drink in respect to Mr. Gruber. He must have mumbled the name.

"Yes, Mr. Gruber is the textbook recovering alcoholic. I believe his journey began when his wife passed. Heaven knows what that can do to you." He remembered that Wynona spoke from experience on the losing a spouse front. "They were strong for each other, Charlee and Arnold. Very strong. She hasn't touched a drop since Richard."

And now Ian was beginning to understand why Charlee was so reluctant to get involved with him. If things didn't work out between them, it could quite easily lead to her complete destruction. Another memory entered his mind. The wedding. "Brenna's loser of a fiancé shoved a drink under her nose, didn't he? That's when you all stepped in. Gruber . . . took it from her hand. And . . ."

"And we left. It was time to go. No matter what Charlee thinks, she's in love with you, Ian. And that means big trouble for her if she loses you." Hearing Wilma say that should have sent his heart soaring, but it didn't. It only made him ache because where love was concerned between Charlee and him, there was the risk of failure. He'd failed a lot of people in his life. Ian pushed the thought aside and turned to Jeremiah. "Where would she go?"

Realizing her brother probably had no clue, he turned to the group of artists. "Where would Charlee go? We gotta figure this out, then we have to split up and find her."

He went to the table to retrieve his phone and practically stepped on it; the toe of his work boot connected and the cell went spinning under the desk. He dug it out, stood, and turned to the group. "She was here. Must have come here first. Man, probably looking for me." Had he already let her down?

Jeremiah pulled the phone from his pocket and stared down at it, face going pale.

"What?" Ian demanded.

"Is there a message from me?"

Ian opened his phone. "No new messages. One saved." Which was weird because he had cleared all the messages from his phone a day or two ago and it wasn't like he had a full social circle that called. Ian hit the playback button and blanched. His knees almost buckled when he heard Jeremiah talking about a buyer and Charlee selling her property. He cut him a harsh glare, but no words were necessary. Jeremiah already looked like he'd backed over the neighbor's new kitten. Ian shook his head. "She ran."

"What are we going to do?" Hopelessness choked Wilma's words.

They really needed to stop discussing it and put a plan in action. They had a mission. Find Charlee before . . . before she could hurt herself. And to do that, they needed recon. "Okay, I need to know everything about where she's gone in the past. Any friends she might call on, any detail."

King Edward put a pot of coffee on as Jeremiah filled them in on the places Charlee had run away to as a kid.

"As far as friends, Charlee knows everyone in town, but we're her friends. She doesn't really associate with anyone else."

Ian scrubbed his cheeks; a five o'clock shadow was getting itchy from the sweat he'd accumulated at Mr. Gruber's place. He'd meant to take a shower as soon as he got home. "Anyone? What about neighboring towns?"

They all shook their heads. And Ian asked the thing he hadn't wanted to because he hadn't wanted to hear the words. "Where'd she go after Richard?"

Again, those knowing, annoying glances shot around the table, but wouldn't make contact with Ian or Jeremiah. Ian leaned forward. "We have to know."

King Edward dropped into one of the chairs. "Okay. We're sworn to secrecy, but really, that's a crock because everyone in town knows Charlee went off the deep end and spent two weeks hanging out in bars one county over."

The words hit Ian's heart with enough force to make him feel as though he might vomit.

Wilma raised her hands in defense. "She's mortified about what she did. Absolutely mortified. I don't think she'd ever do that again."

And Ian was sickened by the scenarios shooting through his mind. Charlee. Gorgeous blond, perfectly shaped Charlee getting trashed in dive bars. He drew a couple steadying breaths to keep the lunch in his stomach.

"No, she wouldn't do that again," Wynona agreed with her sister. "It was too costly. Too dangerous. Charlee wouldn't. She swore to us."

Ian wasn't a strategist, but he had to take the information given and assimilate it into the probable possibilities. "What about family?" He shot a look to Jeremiah.

He shook his head. "Caleb, Isaiah, and Gabe are all deployed. We have grandparents on my mother's side, but she'd never go there."

"You sure about that?" Ian leveled him.

"Positive. She's looking for a place where she can quietly medicate herself and get rid of her pain. Those people are only more pain. No. It's not an option."

"I can check hotels within a hundred-mile radius." Wilma rose. It wasn't much, but it was something.

King Edward rose too. "Jeremiah, why don't you and I go into town and ask around? If she stopped for gas or something . . . maybe she mentioned what direction she was headed."

Ian could tell Jeremiah wasn't thrilled with the prospect of running around town with a man in a dress, but for Charlee, he was willing to do it without complaint.

Jeremiah agreed and added, "I'll go back to the house and see if she was there at all. I ran into town and could have missed her. Maybe we can tell if anything is gone. Suitcase missing, whatever."

Ian stood and tucked his phone in his pocket. "I'm going to look around the property and see if anything seems strange, out of place. See if she left us any clues."

Wynona dropped her gaze. "I'll call the Neon Moon and see if Rayna's seen her . . . again, a long shot. She'd never stay right here in town. Too easy to find." She said on a long exhale, "Once they're open, I'll call the liquor store."

There was only one in town.

They split up to scour for any clue as to which way she might go. But after searching through the buildings, Ian had nothing. The only sign was a few paper bags strewn on the kitchen counter in the big building. He headed back to his cabin, but something made him stop. Ian turned and glanced behind him, and tiny hairs prickled on the back of his neck as if someone—some specter—was pressing cold fingers there. He focused on the toolshed. Shook the thought from his head and started toward the cabin. He didn't even make it a step when the sensation returned. He huffed and changed direction to the shed.

When he opened the door, allowing the light of the compound to illuminate the small room, he found his first real clue. The scent of grease and tools rose in his nose as he scrutinized the empty spot on the far shelf. It was about two feet wide. He searched his mind for what had been there. A tarp? No, but something similar, taller. When he stepped fully in, he noticed another empty space, this one on the floor. He knew the square plastic container that sat there, but didn't know what it had held. His eyes fell on the tool belt in the corner. What had been in that plastic container? *Need your help, Major Mack.* Ian had slid the deep green container out of the way a time or two. It was heavy. Why hadn't he ever opened it? His gaze fell on the tool belt again. *I bet if you were here, you could tell me.*

A thought struck him. He rushed out of the shed. "I'll have to get the next best thing."

Jeremiah and King Edward had returned from town with little info and that wore on Ian as the day dragged. Yes, Charlee stopped to get gas at the station in the late morning hours and the guy was fairly certain she'd gone into the hardware store next door, but couldn't guarantee it. The hardware store was across the street from the ice cream shop and Ian was headed there next to question Rodney because of something he'd said when they had their little man-to-man talk.

Ian collected Jeremiah and pulled the string on the light inside the shed. "Look around. Something's missing."

Jeremiah nodded. "Dad said he organized all this when he was here visiting."

Ian waited while Jeremiah took his time examining the spot. "Why don't you just ask the artists what sits here?"

Ian's brows shot up. "Dude, they didn't even know where Charlee kept the spare lightbulbs. They don't come in here. What would your dad put there?" He then turned and pointed to the spot on the floor. "And what would he put there?"

Jeremiah stepped to the spot.

"It was a deep green plastic container, you know like the ones you get at Walmart."

Jeremiah knelt down. "Look at the ring beside it."

Until it was pointed out, Ian hadn't noticed the perfectly round ring where the dust had settled. Jeremiah slid out a bucket beside the empty spot. He held up a package, a smile on his face. "Wicks for a lantern."

"A tent! That's what was there on the shelf; I was thinking a tarp, but no. It was a tent."

Jeremiah nodded. "My dad always kept our camping gear in a big plastic container. That's what was sitting there. That's what she took, and a tent and lantern."

King Edward interrupted them, pausing at the door. "And her shotgun."

Ian spun on him. "What?" Frozen spikes of fear shot through him.

Jeremiah put a hand on his shoulder. "Calm down. Dad told her to never go into the woods without her gun. Shotgun, rifle, handgun."

Ian crunched his face. "She has all those?"

"Guess you don't know everything about my sister."

"No. In fact, it's starting to look like I don't know anything about her."

Jeremiah lifted his hand then brought it down with a smack on Ian's back. "Good job. You figured this out. She's in the woods. Now what?"

"Since you and I are trained in all types of environments, I say we split up and start searching."

"What about us?" King Edward asked.

Jeremiah gave him a quick look. Edward—and his devotion to Charlee—must have melted Jeremiah's heart a little. He was actually warming up to the kilt-wearing guy, evidenced by the light smile of his face. "You all should stay here in case she comes back. There's a bad storm moving in. I wouldn't want you guys out there."

He raised his brows in Ian's direction. Yeah, Ian didn't want the artists out in the woods either; one of them might get distracted by a colorful butterfly and wander off a cliff. "He's right, Edward. You guys hang here. At least for now, then we can regroup."

Edward sighed, and for a man who worked so hard to get out of manual labor, he seemed bitterly disappointed he'd not be tromping through the woods.

Jeremiah patted him on the shoulder. "Besides, the worst sticker bushes are just about . . ." he raised a flat hand hip level near Edward, ". . . this high. It'd be murder on your . . . skirt."

Edward sucked a deep breath and pivoted his ankle out as if protecting his attributes. "We'll stay here," he said and they all left in their respective directions. Jeremiah was headed to Four Rivers, where their dad had taken them camping as kids, and Ian was headed to town. It was already five in the evening by the time he got to the ice cream shop. He drove the old work truck with only one thing on his mind. Find Charlee.

———

Rod was cleaning the awning when Ian got there. He lowered the bucket and scrub brush when he saw him.

"Hey, Ian." But as soon as he said it, Ian watched his demeanor change. Rod knew something was wrong.

"Charlee's missing."

Rod swallowed, Adam's apple bobbing as his eyes shot left and right as if she'd be right there in his periphery. "What happened?"

"Something about Gruber at the hospital blaming her for . . ." Ian threw his hands up. "I don't even know what. I just have to find her."

Rod nodded, worked the muscles in his jaw. "Okay. Sit down."

They sat at the picnic table, the sky dark and the wind soft. Rodney raised his hands. "What do you know?"

Ian had the details in exact order in his mind; a man used to giving information in high-stress situations, he spoke the words mechanically. "She gassed up. Stopped at the hardware store. Took camping gear, tent, lantern." He had to swallow before continuing. "And her shotgun."

"Well, thank God she's not out there without it."

Ian frowned. Was he the only one concerned with Charlee doing harm to herself? "Where would she go, Rod?"

He rested his hands over his face, blocking out the present, drawing the past. Ian could see him trying to remember. "You got something?"

Rod shook his head. "I don't know. Maybe. When I found her after Richard—"

Ian leaned toward him, fisting his hands because he wanted Rod to hurry up and it seemed if he shook him like a rag doll, that would help. "What do you mean, *found her*?"

"She'd been gone a couple of weeks. Longest ever. I took three days off and went searching. Have a friend in the sheriff's office in Laver and he found her Jeep. She'd been spending evenings in a hole-in-the-wall bar for a few days. Walking to the cheap motel next door. I got to the bar and went in after her. Thank God I had the sense to call my buddy. She was just getting ready to walk out with some redneck in camo pants and a Hooters T-shirt."

Ian closed his eyes, blocking the image of Charlee with someone like that.

Rod shook his head. "It didn't even look like her, you know? Gray and thin and just . . . just beat down."

Ian had to swallow.

"Charlee loves so deeply. She feels everything to the very core of her being. And is all-in when she loves someone. She lost her mom. Lost her dad. Richard was a poor replacement, but to her, he was everything."

The guilt swelled to a place where Ian could no longer contain it. "It's my fault she's gone."

Rod leaned back. "What? You said . . ."

He sniffed. "I know. That was just the beginning. She came looking for me and heard a message from her brother on my cell phone. He was asking if I'd talked to Charlee about selling."

For a thin guy, Rod flew out of the seat and landed on the balls of his feet, fists in the air.

Ian stood too, hands out in surrender. "Look, I wasn't planning to convince her—"

He stopped talking when the first fist flew at his face. Ian ducked right and Rod found his footing and threw another punch. He grunted. "Do you know what you did?" It was a scream and a growl and Ian didn't blame him for it.

"Rod! I wasn't trying to convince her to sell; that was never my intention. I don't want her to sell. It's her connection to her mother, and Major Mack remodeled the shed and built outbuildings. Jeremiah wants her to sell because he and her other brothers worry about her."

Rod's fists were still up, but Ian could see him tiring, even trying to digest the words. "Miah wants her to sell?"

"Yeah. I told him it'd never happen."

Rod's hands dropped. "Sit down."

Ian mustered a tiny smile. "You sure you're not going to go all Jason Bourne on me again?"

"You need to hear the details about Richard."

Hear about the man who'd broken the heart of the woman Ian loved? No thanks. But he knew he had no choice.

"Richard didn't love Charlee. He was after her property. That's it. End of story. Never cared about her, just the land. Wanted her to sell and open a joint account. Then they'd get married and blah blah blah."

"How'd she find out?"

"She heard he'd been spotted at the Neon Moon with a busty red-head. She didn't believe it, so she slipped on a camo jacket and a ball cap, tucked her hair underneath and slid into a booth where she could hear him talking. Jerk bragged about it. Right there. In the Neon Moon. Idiot didn't even have the sense to go somewhere out of town."

Ian frowned. "How do you know all this?"

"I was with her."

Jealousy shouldn't have been a sensation shooting down his spine, but there it was. Fresh and hot and disappearing as quickly as it came. "You're a good friend, Rod."

He lifted and dropped one shoulder. "She ditched me. Hit the road. Once I could get away from work for three days, I went looking for her."

"That's when you arrived at the hole-in-the-wall?"

"Yeah," Rod said, but his voice sounded far away. "After almost two weeks."

And though Ian needed to know what happened next, he also knew recall could take time and he shouldn't interrupt.

"We went back to her hotel."

Ian swallowed, fisted his hands at his sides.

"I put her in the shower." His eyes flashed to Ian's. "Dressed. She was in jean shorts and a tank."

Ian drew long, slow, steady breaths. This man may well have saved Charlee's life that night. Still, it was nothing he wanted to hear.

"She kept talking about . . ." His words trailed off. And Ian leaned forward.

"She kept talking about . . . Murder Rock."

Ian's world closed on the words. "Murder Rock?"

"Yeah." Rod blinked several times and Ian could see him trying to put it all together. "Murder Rock is at the base of The Mountain of Tears. It's maybe fifty miles from here. She kept talking about how the Indians must have felt when they'd been told they would have a safe place provided for them, only to find out they'd been drawn into a hol-ler where they were trapped by a renegade group of militia. It's one of the worst historical tragedies in our area."

"You think she'd go there?"

"I think she was going there when I found her. If she survived that barrel-chested hulk of a mountain man." Rod shook off the image. "Yeah. That's where she is. I'll go with you."

No. That wasn't what Ian wanted and wouldn't be what Charlee needed. She needed him. "I want to go alone, Rod." It was an impos-ing statement that left little room for discussion.

Rod stood, stared up at the early evening sky. "You love her?"

Ian came to rest at his feet. "I'd die for her."

Rod laughed without humor. "You will. Over and over and over again."

Ian frowned, something so cryptic in Rod's words. Then he remem-bered. This man had loved Charlee for a long time. Years, probably. And if Ian was reading the signs right, he'd already died for her once or twice.

Rod pointed an accusing finger at him. "You make this right, sol-dier. You make it right or I'll kill you myself."

And Ian knew it was true. Rod followed him to the work truck to mark the place on the atlas. He held the end of the pen in his mouth and positioned the map on the steering wheel. "Watch the roads going in. We've had a lot of rain and there can be slide-offs. Also, if you hear rocks falling or see pebbles dropping, get out of the way. Rock slides happen there all the time."

Wow. Was there any good news?

"Only one road in and out, so she can't get away."

There was that.

"Good luck." Rodney stuck out his hand for Ian to shake.

But Ian surprised Rodney by grabbing his shoulders and trapping him in a hug.

"Find her."

Ian smiled. "I won't let you down."

CHAPTER 15

Ian put in a call to Jeremiah as he drove the winding road to Murder Rock. "I think she's at The Mountain of Tears. I'm headed there now."

Though the reception was sketchy, with Jeremiah's voice growing fuzzy, then clear, then fuzzy, Ian made out the reply. "Okay. Not sure how long phone service will last. If you find her, try to let me know. I'm at Hercules Glades, but no sign of her or the Jeep."

"I'll keep you posted." Ian hung up the phone then decided to check in at the retreat.

Wynona answered on the first ring. "Any news?"

"I think I'm on the right track. Not sure I can call once I've gotten to her, though."

"Goodness, where are you, Ian?"

"Mountain of Tears. Any word on Mr. Gruber?"

"He's stable. Still won't see anyone. I'm headed there now. Darn stubborn man. He can't have me thrown out of the hospital."

"Why'd he tell them no visitors? I never got that part of the story."

"Arnold has been living a lie. He hasn't had any contact with his daughter for eight years. The gifts, the phone calls, none of it was real."

Ian rubbed a hand over his face. "He was sending presents to himself?"

"Yes, Ian. And now everyone knows. Poor man. He's humiliated. But he's met his match if he thinks a little request for no visitors is enough to keep me away."

"You really love him, don't you?"

There was a long pause. "I love everyone at the retreat. They're my family."

"But you're in love with Mr. Gruber, aren't you, Wynona?" He'd seen it. At the wedding when Gruber and Wynona floated around the dance floor and she practically glowed.

"I never thought I'd feel that way about another man. And certainly not a crusty, cranky old oil painter."

Ian chuckled.

"When Horace died, I thought I was dying right along with him. If not physically, emotionally."

Ian held the phone a little closer to his ear. "How'd you survive it, Wynona?"

Because he really needed to know this in case he made it to Murder Rock and his worst fears were realized. What if Charlee . . . what if . . . He squeezed his eyes shut and blocked the image.

"Prayer. I survived it with prayer."

Ian swallowed the cotton in his throat. "You think you could offer up a few of those powerful words now?"

He could almost see the sweet smile appearing on Wynona's face. "I already am, young man. Now go find her. And let her know she's loved beyond measure."

That he could do.

At the base of Murder Rock, a cattle gate blocked the road leading up into the mountain pass. He jumped from the truck and was relieved to find no lock. Ian shoved the gate to the side, mud caking along the bottom as he went. He pulled through then reclosed the gate to discourage anyone else from taking the road.

The truck was a four-wheel drive so he figured it'd navigate the mountain fairly easily. The engine droned louder as the grade increased. A full moon hung above as the setting sun trekked downward. He got stuck once and had to jam some tree limbs under the tires, making him wonder if the four-wheel drive no longer worked. The ruts in the road narrowed to one slender line snaking through the trees and brush that continually feathered the sides of the vehicle. Near the mountaintop, the landscape cleared a bit, allowing him to see more. But the sun had set, and only its haze from the horizon gave light. He stopped where the road seemed to end and spotted the Jeep through the brush. Ian's heart beat faster as he pulled alongside.

He cut the engine and jumped from the truck, eyes focusing on a golden glow deeper in the woods. He cupped his hands around his mouth. "Charlee?"

No answer. But he knew she had to be there. He jogged into the tree line where the campfire burned bright and shadowed a domed tent just to the right. He couldn't see anything but rocks and the tent. Then, one of the shadowy stones moved, coming to life, head and legs appearing first. It was Charlee; she'd been curled up into a ball.

"Are you okay?" He was out of breath from fear of what he'd find. Now, seeing her, alive, all the adrenaline raced out of him.

She mumbled an answer.

"Charlee, you scared me to death." He knew the last thing she needed right now was someone scolding her, but the words rushed out before he could stop them. He made quick work of getting to her, but she stumbled back as he neared, so he stopped, put his hands up and waited.

Her eyes flashed in the fire, throwing sparks around the darkened campsite. There was a partially empty bottle of something sitting near where she'd been and when the fire moved, it flashed upon it like a beacon. "How'd you find me?" Her words weren't slurred, but they weren't exactly clear either.

"Talked to Rod."

Surprising him, she threw her head back and laughed. "Oh yes. Your new friend. My, haven't you been making the friends since you've been here?"

The air thickened with accusation.

"First Rodney. Then my brother." Charlee bent and grabbed a large stick from beside her.

"Charlee, your brother wanted me to talk to you. I told him I'd do it."

"Of course you did. Because that's what the men in my life do. Run around behind my back making decisions for me." She moved dangerously close to the fire and used the stick to stoke it up. With each jab of the branch, the fire threw off sparks that rose then disappeared above the ridge.

"I told him I'd do it, but I also told him it wouldn't do any good. You weren't leaving. And nothing he'd say or do could convince you to."

Inquisitive eyes studied him over the flames. She worked her jaw. "Really?" There was no warmth, no measure of surrender in the word. There was also no sarcasm. Just a flat word revealing nothing.

"I don't want you to leave. The retreat is all you have of your mom. And now your dad. I mean, his handprint is all over the place there. I can't imagine leaving it."

"You mean *me* leaving it."

Ian had been staring at the fire when he said that. He looked over to find her head tilted and her hip cocked. "Yeah, that's what I said."

She dropped the stick, its blackened point landing in the fire and creating another gust of golden sparks. "You said *you* can't imagine leaving it."

No he hadn't. His mind retraced his words.

She lifted her hands and dropped them. "So what's your play here, Soldier Boy? You going to try to convince me to go home tonight? What's the mission? What's your objective?"

He raised his hands in the same fashion. "My mission was to find you." The wind picked up around her, tossing her hair over her shoulder.

"And then?" She gathered it at the base of her neck.

Ian shrugged. "That's all I got."

She snorted. "Some soldier."

Ian took a tiny step closer. "Charlee, all I could think about was getting to you. Making sure you're okay. After that, we could figure out how to lessen the pain."

Her eyes, usually blue-gray, were golden globes in the firelight, taking on the orangey hues of molten sun. She shook her head. "I already have a friend for that. Name's Jim Beam."

Ian's heart ached at the acid in her tone. "That's not the only way to deal with pain, you know."

She squared her shoulders. "It's the best way I've found."

Ian moved past her and picked up the bottle. Charlee stiffened. He gauged the amount she'd had. No use arguing with someone who'd been drinking. His eyes went from the bottle to Charlee. "You've been here a while. My guess is in your heart you know you don't want to do this. You're fighting yourself on it."

Her mouth quirked and Ian knew he'd hit a nerve. He plunged deeper. "Maybe there was a time when you felt like this was all you had. The only way to deal, but I think now you know it doesn't answer the questions. Just shoves them aside for a while."

When the breeze kicked up again, bounding off the mountains and shifting the smoke, Charlee folded her hands over her arms, hugging herself and holding herself together.

"What happened when you were twelve?" He dropped down at the edge of the fire and placed the bottle between him and Charlee. A motion he knew would confuse her, but if he tried to put it out of her reach, it would only make her want it more.

"When I ran away?"

"Mm hmm."

Slowly, she sat down beside him, letting a long exhale accompany her. "I just started walking down the road. We lived on a dirt road and it was dark. I remember being scared and even the road looked . . . I don't know . . . broken." She stopped talking for a few moments and Ian wanted to drag her over and hold her in his arms. He fisted his hands to keep them from reaching.

Charlee breathed beside him. He tuned in to the sound of each inhale and exhale. "I was scared that I'd let them all down. Mom was gone. And it was up to me."

Her hand flattened on the ground, fingers splayed, then tightened into a ball. "I knew I could never fill her shoes. I just had to get away."

"Someone picked you up?"

"No. I just kept walking. It was so dark and so scary, I was afraid to turn around. It felt like there was some monster or something behind me and if I turned, I'd be a goner. I just kept putting one foot in front of the other. I could hear coyotes in the distance. Twice, I could see the outline of animals along the roadside where the woods met the gravel. The more I walked, the stronger I felt. Less afraid. I walked right past those animals. Nothing attacked me."

They sat quietly for a while. "Then, a car picked me up at the edge of town. There were girls in back, a little older than me, teenagers, and a mom and dad in front. It was a beat-up old rusty car and it smelled like motor oil and sweat, but I remembered feeling safe. And envious that these girls had two parents. And I wondered if they knew how lucky they were."

"So you went with them?"

Charlee's words were soft, as if speaking too loudly would bring all the pain right back to her. "Yeah. That night, we were watching TV and it was really late. A school night. And the late movie was on. I never got to watch the late-night movie at home."

Fire flashed down Ian's spine. "Charlee, did they hurt you?"

"What?" Her eyes were haunted, so far away. "No. I felt warm and safe and in a little while, the pain didn't hurt as bad."

Ian bit the inside of his cheek to keep the anger down. What kind of people picked up a twelve-year-old and didn't report her to the police? Flying into a rage wouldn't help Charlee. He just needed to be still and let her talk. *Shut up and talk*, Mr. Gruber had once told him.

"The next morning they were all gone. Girls to school, parents to work. They left me a note to make myself at home and so I did until my dad finally found me."

"Then?"

"For a few years, I could just run away when things got bad. Sometimes, no one even knew. I'd tell my dad I was staying at a friend's house. When I hit high school, running wasn't enough. I needed more. When I'd drink, it dulled the hurt."

"And it still does," Ian said.

She nodded.

Ian's phone rang, causing them both to jump. He answered. "Yes. She's with me . . . We'll be home tomorrow morning." He glanced over at her. Her eyes had gone darker and he hoped the call hadn't undone the progress he was making. Of course, he should have called as soon as he spotted her. But his mind had blanked.

"My brother?" she asked.

Ian shook his head. "No. Wynona."

Charlee's mouth turned into a bow. Her gaze was troubled. "I've caused them all so much pain," she whispered.

"Yeah." He hadn't meant to say that. It just popped out of his mouth. "You scared us all to death, Charlee. My heart nearly gave out when I found out you'd left with a gun."

Her gaze turned to ice on him. "I'd never harm myself."

He snagged the bottle and held it up between them. "Really?" The liquid sloshed inside. "Because this would suggest differently."

She turned back to the fire and drew her knees to her chest. "I guess you wouldn't understand."

At that, Ian's hands fisted, his knuckles whitened, grip tightening on the bottle so much he thought it might break beneath his skin. He flew up from beside the fire, drew back and flung the bottle so hard it shattered against a nearby tree while a myriad of painful memories skated through his mind. "I've watched my friends die on a road when I knew I couldn't get to them in time. I held your dad in my arms while he drew his last breath. He was my hero, Charlee. He was the kind of man I didn't know existed."

Charlee stood too, arms slowly falling to her sides.

Ian took a few angry steps toward her, teeth gritted. "And he died saving me. So, please. Don't *ever* say I don't understand."

Silence filled the air around them. He stood at her feet, looking down into sobered eyes. Her mouth made a motion before the word could slip between her lips. "What?"

All the air left Ian's lungs. And all the pain of that day rose from that deep hole in his heart he'd locked it into. "He . . ." But he couldn't say it. Couldn't utter the words because if he did, the universe would know it was he who should be dead and Major Mack alive.

Charlee grabbed his arms, short fingernails digging in. She shook him. "What did you say?" Her voice rose with her insistence.

And Ian knew. He knew he'd have to tell her. Once again, he'd let the major down. He tried to form words, but couldn't. Scattered memories threatened to take shape but he'd worked so hard for so long to stop them, there was no energy left to complete the task. A voice, softer now, Charlee's. Her grip loosened on his arms.

"Ian, tell me what happened."

He squeezed his eyes shut. Blocking out the memory, blocking out the pain. But even in the darkest part of his mind, it was there. The sound of gunfire, he and the major both seeing the man dressed in dirty clothes and stepping into the doorway where they'd been pinned down. They didn't know where he'd come from; the other shooters were across the road and also inside a makeshift bunker. "He just appeared in the door."

Somewhere above them, an owl called. The woods were darker, moonlight crowded by clouds. Ian had to swallow before he could continue. "First the guy just stood there. It seemed like forever. No one moved. A dusty cloth wrapped around his neck and shoulders, his eyes were black and first frightened, then they changed as he raised the gun. Major Mack screamed and jumped in front of me. I raised my rifle and shot just as the bullet hit his throat."

He had to stop, to breathe, because the world was going black around him. Hands on his arms became a vise, not hard, but clinging. He felt her knees buckle beneath her and she fell toward him. But he had no strength to catch her, so together, they slid to a seated position as if the words he'd spoken had shocked the life from both their bodies. The fire crackled, a log perched above another dropping deeper into the brilliant glow where wood had become embers.

Though Ian expected Charlee to run away, she didn't. She stayed, closing her arm around his giant shoulder as he tried to talk, but words became tiny gasps for air until his shoulders quaked and tears streamed down his face. "It might not have even hit me. It might not have . . ."

Charlee rolled onto her knees and the weight of her staring at his profile was unbearable, more than he could take because he should have told her sooner. She had a right to know and he'd kept it from her. Her hands touched his face and he couldn't understand why she wasn't screaming at him. Telling him she hated him. It was his fault her father was dead.

Time stood still while she stared at him. Ian's heart was a black hole. Empty, dark. The only sounds were the crackling of a campfire and Charlee's breathing.

The words she whispered were so soft, he wasn't sure he'd heard them. "You killed the man who killed my father?"

One by one, each word registered and Ian slowly swung his gaze to her expecting to see all the hate he deserved. "Yes."

Charlee readjusted on her knees and took his face in her hands. There were tears in her eyes and when she blinked, they ran unbidden down her cheeks. "He'd be proud of you."

The words cut a jagged wound as they made their way to Ian's heart. He couldn't answer so he shook his head.

Her voice was stronger this time. "He'd be proud."

How could she say that? If it weren't for him, her dad would be alive.

Charlee released him and rolled over onto her bottom. She stared at the fire. "My dad died the way he always wanted to live."

Ian forced himself to look at her. The campfire danced across her features making her look unearthly, angelic.

When Charlee met his gaze, there was a certainty there. A look he knew, one he'd seen on her face every time she'd made a decision and dug her heels deep to defend it. He also knew that same look from her father. Charlee's chin tilted back. "He died taking care of his men."

Ian tried to swallow. Pain seared his heart, but there was something else there too. A tiny splash of hope, a droplet of optimism. Things he had no right feeling, but couldn't stop them as they bounced around inside, shaving off the jagged edge and offering . . . in a word . . . healing.

"What else happened at the end, Ian?" It was a demand that left no room for backtracking.

Ian tried to judge the merits of telling her versus keeping that secret inside.

"What else?" This time it was a plea, so full of need that he couldn't have stopped the words from tumbling from his mouth if he'd wanted to.

"He said to teach you how to stop running."

The air changed. First cold, then electric. And Ian was sure she'd jump up and run into the woods at any moment. But she stayed. Breathing beside him. Lungs filling with and releasing air.

"I didn't even understand what he meant. But it's what he wanted for you. I thought if I came here . . . I don't know." Ian turned to face her; now he was the one who would plead. "Charlee, you have to stop running."

She stiffened. "Do you think I like this? Do you think I enjoy it?" She shook her head. "I don't know how to cope. I'm fine until things get really, *really* bad, then I just . . ."

"You just start walking down that road in the dark and see where it takes you."

She laughed without humor and pushed away an angry tear. "Yeah. And it always leads me to the same place. Where my senses are numb and I can survive."

"There are other ways to deal with hurt. Charlee, it may be a broken road that leads to healing, but there's hope along the way."

"Hope gave up on me."

"No one's giving up on you except you. You're better than this."

"From the man who still has nightmares. It doesn't look like you're dealing so well." Now her gaze was fire upon him. "So talk to me about success after you experience it. Until then, I don't have a whole lot of other options." She stood and walked away from the fire, where the edge of the woods danced in the shadows of light off the nearby rocks. And there she looked small, helpless. A thin, scattered shadow of Charlee played on the nearby rock ledge.

"You choose whether to do this or not. It's your *choice*, Charlee. No one is forcing a drink into your hand."

She spun on him. "Sounds easy, doesn't it? But I've only had myself to rely on for a long time."

He walked to her, reached out to touch her arms, and on the wall of rock beside them, the two shadows became one. "But that's not true anymore. You've got me."

It flickered in her eyes, the realization that she wasn't in it alone.

"I'll help you. I'll be right with you. But—"

She sunk her teeth into her bottom lip. "But?"

He'd avoid the stipulations for now. If he pushed her too hard too fast, she might never come back. "We can do this together, Charlee. I'll stand right with you." And Ian's heart felt lighter for the first time in hours. Because the possibility reflected in her eyes was one of hope.

The first crack of thunder caused them both to jolt. They looked heavenward as the wind changed direction and cooled. A bolt of lightning shot across the sky.

Ian glanced at the tent, then to the truck. He didn't want Charlee driving and wasn't sure she wouldn't try to insist if he suggested going home tonight. "I think we better tuck in for the evening. Is that tent waterproof?"

She shrugged. "Guess we'll find out."

When the first drops of water fell, she hurried to gather up her things. Ian secured the lid on the plastic container and followed her into the tent with the lantern dangling from his hand.

Charlee zipped him inside and it was only then that he realized the error in his decision to stay. His eyes scanned the small domed room with the narrow bed taking most of the space. She'd been drinking and whether she'd had a little or a lot really didn't matter. He'd never take advantage. Especially since he knew things had the possibility of changing once she was completely sober and he told her what he had to.

"Lie down," he said and when her eyes flashed with either excitement or instant regret—too hard to tell with the lantern light casting eerie little shadows on her face—Ian moved to her and took the light source, turned the knob so it gave a gentle glow to the space. The shadows on her face softened, as did her eyes. He stood at her feet and placed the lantern on the floor. When he rose to look at her, the earlier apprehension was gone. Her hair smelled like strawberry shampoo, enhanced by the rain droplets on her. He touched her arms; the skin was smooth, slightly wet, and when he drew his hands down to her wrist her mouth opened to release a long sigh that feathered against his flesh. The lingering scent of alcohol on her breath made him take a mental step back. Her mouth was open, lips dotted with rain, lashes shading her beautiful eyes. She was everything in the world any man could ever want. And everything in him wanted to take. Her eyes drifted open as his fingertips spasmed against her wrists. She searched him, those gray-blue eyes flashing on different points of his face as if imagining . . . imagining . . .

Ian pulled a breath and started to step away, but her hand found his shirt and fisted there against his chest. Her gaze had gone from sweet to lingering, seducing. Oh Lord. No one should have to endure this.

He let out a long breath, hoping it would equalize the balance of the room. When thunder cracked above their heads followed by a brilliant flash, Ian found Charlee's body pressed tightly to his. Her breaths warmed a place on his neck. The tiniest chill ran over her skin and he closed his arms more tightly around her. She fit there, so perfectly, so right. And she was right. She was everything he would ever want and this . . . *this* was right. He closed the distance to her mouth until he felt her lips against his. Soft, sweet, hands and arms moving, caressing first his chest, then his neck, drawing him ever closer. It only took an instant for them both to be breathless. With great effort, Ian dragged his mouth from hers. But his body refused and in a second, they were one again, him drawing every exhale from her. The lack of fresh oxygen dizzied his mind, caused a haze to blanket every thought.

Lightning flashed against the tent as if snapping little pictures of his glorious torture. When the room brightened, his senses returned just enough to remember why he couldn't go through with this. At least not yet. Not until he heard the words from her he needed to hear.

Her fingers had found the way to the hem of his T-shirt, causing his stomach to spasm with anticipation. Ian closed his hands over hers. "Charlee, I—"

Her face was down, but when he spoke, her eyes shot up to meet his. "I love you, Ian."

And the world stopped spinning. Up was down and down was up and whatever he'd planned to say was gone because Charlee McKinley loved him. Loved him. Devoid of strength, he whispered, "What did you say?"

A brilliant smile kissed her face. "I love you. I have for . . . I don't know how long, but I do."

His mouth was dry. His forehead slick with sudden perspiration. Ian tried to tick off the words in his head, but they kept getting stuck. "Say it again."

Her look changed to complete desire and that didn't help anything at all because he needed to hear it, then he needed to process it, then he needed to . . . to take the woman he loved to bed. All the thoughts of propriety, honor, were gone. Only one thing mattered. Charlee and Ian were in love.

"I. Love. You." The smile again, the one that lit his world and had completely altered his path. And everything that could be right was right. Except . . .

He moved in closer, spreading his stance to allow an even tighter press of their bodies. "I love you too."

Charlee giggled and he was reminded she'd had . . . well, he didn't know how much she'd had to drink. Had the bottle he busted been the only one? Was it the first? Cold sliced his spine as Ian tried to forget she wasn't fully herself right now. And then he said the one thing he had to. The thing he'd been dreading because the outcome could alter everything for them. He took her face in his hands and held her a few inches away, disconnecting his body from hers, and it hurt, *physically hurt*, to push her away. "Charlee. I need you to promise me you won't ever run again."

At first she chuckled, but he watched the weight of his statement settle over her, a cloak, a blanket of cold. "I . . . I can't."

The troubled look that entered her eyes strengthened his resolve. "Charlee." The word was short, dominant, intrusive. "I've never been more scared in my life than when I realized you were gone. And believe me, that's saying something."

She recoiled, body stiffening.

"Listen to me. You're not alone anymore. You can't just wander off down a dirt road and assume everything will work out. It killed me, Charlee. Not knowing."

Her eyes darted, as if there were something to see other than green domed walls. On an exhale, she whispered, "I can't."

Ian readjusted his footing because he knew he was losing her, losing the woman he loved because she was mentally unable to break away from the one thing that could destroy them both. "Sweetheart, you have to."

He watched the walls come up. Watched the doors of her heart slam shut. She didn't speak, but her head shook from side to side, slowly, like one might do after seeing the aftermath of a horrible accident.

Ian hated that he'd given her such an ultimatum, but he couldn't live with the uncertainty. "I spent months and months not knowing if I'd survive the next day. If the guy beside me would survive. Every moment alive is precious, Charlee. Every one. I can't live knowing I might come home and you'll have disappeared. Good Lord, surely you wouldn't expect me to."

Her hands fisted at her sides, the only clue that she even heard him. Her face was flint, eyes glass. Posture, marble. She swallowed. "Please." And she blinked, first once, then several more times as if taking in information there was no room to store. "Can we just talk about this later? Tomorrow, maybe?"

Ian worked his jaw; on one hand, it was unfair for him to expect too much tonight. She'd been drinking, and alcohol affected everyone differently. On the other hand, Ian's heart was already breaking because he knew Charlee and knew she couldn't make that promise. Not tonight.

Not tomorrow. And maybe not ever. But he also knew he couldn't live without it. He loved her too much, and as long as there was an easy way out for her, it'd eat away at him until there was nothing left. He'd made a promise to Major Mack. Teach her how to stop running. This was in his power. He could teach her. He just figured it'd break his heart to do it. He forced a sad smile. "Sure. We can talk about it later."

When Charlee stretched out on the thin camping mattress, Ian unzipped the edge of the tent's window and peered outside. Rain came down in sheets, graying the world.

"Will you lie beside me?" she asked, slipping her hand into his.

He looked down to find her on her side, fingers twining with his. "Yes."

She scooted to the edge to make room for him and Ian stretched out behind her, his chest to her back. Their fingers unlocked and he wound his arm around her and pulled her up against him where her hair tickled across his face and neck. He reached up and drew a hand through the nearly dry strands, causing the scent of strawberries to fill the space around them. He buried his nose in her hair and pulled the scent deep, so deep into his lungs he'd be forever changed by it. A tiny swatch of her skin was visible on her neck and when he could take the scent no longer, he tilted up and dropped a kiss on the spot.

Charlee melted against him. His fingers spread and ran through the length of her hair again, causing a little moan to escape from her mouth. He swallowed the heated sensation that shot through his system. In a whispered voice he knew she could barely hear above the rainfall, he said, "Have you ever seen the Grand Canyon?"

"No," she whispered back.

He continued on, talking softly, the drone of his voice a vibration against her. "I never knew there were so many shades of brown and red. Like layers and layers of painted cardboard all piled on one another and cut with a jagged blade. It's beautiful."

She mumbled something in reply, but Ian didn't try to decipher. If he had any hope of surviving this night, he needed her to fall asleep.

"The water at the base of the canyon is so clear and smooth you'd swear it's glass."

Her breathing was slow now, deeper.

Ian pulled his hand through her hair again, this time tuning in to the sheer feel of soft, silken strands gliding over his fingers, against the delicate skin on his palm, sifting over the webs between each digit. And he wanted this. Forever. He wanted for her to fall asleep the same way every night, locked in his arms where she was truly at home. But Ian had promises to keep. First to Major Mack. Second to himself.

He went on talking. "When the sun rises, it's like you're watching the world being painted. Color bursts from where there'd been darkness. Light shines into the canyon, bouncing off the water beneath."

Charlee nuzzled deeper into Ian. When she spoke, her voice was groggy, filled with sleep already. "Will you take me there?"

He dropped his lips to the side of her head. "One day." And he closed his eyes because he knew it was a promise he might or might not be able to keep. And that all depended on what Charlee did in the next few days.

CHAPTER 16

Though Wynona wasn't supposed to be visiting Mr. Gruber, she'd slipped in a side door, bribed the nurse with a pair of bling-y sunglasses, and now she stood sentry outside the room of the man she loved. She supposed the hospital security guards could try to make her leave, but she'd seen one of them as she'd entered and figured if need be, she could take him. He weighed less than her and was stuffing his face with a chocolate-covered donut. Plus, she'd have the element of surprise. Wynona had never been afraid of going after what she wanted. Raised in a generation when girls were expected to be demure, she'd discovered quiet reserve had never won any contests and sedate behavior was highly overrated.

A nurse paused at her feet, and Wynona glanced up. She had two choices—give her the sweet-little-old-lady look. Or the don't-mess-with-a-woman-in-love look. She opted for the latter.

The nurse shook her head and disappeared. If she was calling donut-guard, Wynona was ready. But to her surprise, the nurse came back into the hall dragging a chair.

Wynona gave her a smile and mouthed, "Thank you."

The nurse shot a look down each direction of the hall then leaned toward her. "He's bound to come to his senses soon. He's got too many people here who love him."

Wynona nodded.

The woman disappeared and Wynona watched her round the corner. When she did, she saw another woman standing, almost hesitating, at the end of the corridor. Long dark hair lay over her shoulders and spilled along her collarbone. A deep-red briefcase-looking purse was clutched in front of her and instantly Wynona knew this was Arnold's daughter.

Her shoulders rose and fell in a deep motion and she started moving in Wynona's direction, feet clopping on the hospital floor. The sound bounced like a beacon, conveying intention, purpose. This woman wasn't planning to stay long. She had the distinct posture of a frightened cat ready to shoot off at any moment.

Wynona rose as the woman neared her. "You're Ashley, aren't you?"

She blinked with confusion, casting a look behind Wynona to her father's room. "Yes."

Wynona shoved a hand out toward her. "My name is Wynona. I stay at the retreat where your father's been living. I'm so glad to meet you."

Perfectly manicured hands and a perfectly fitting blouse and skirt all seemed out of place with the woman who was so uncomfortable. "I was leaving town when the doctor called."

Wynona's hand went directly to her heart, where fear rushed into her like hot acid.

Noticing her reaction, Ashley put out a steadying hand. "No, there's nothing wrong. He just . . . explained to me that when someone comes out of heart surgery, their temperament can be affected. He also told me my dad had called out my name in the middle of the night." The lovely woman with the giant dark eyes threw out a breath. "You're a friend of his?"

Wynona smiled. "Yes. A close friend."

Ashley reached a trembling hand to her head, dragged her fingers through the strands, messing up the perfect tresses. "What's he like?"

Wynona's heart broke for her. Right then and there. "He's a very good man, Ashley."

When the same nurse appeared with a second chair, Wynona motioned for Ashley to sit.

"He's giving, caring. He'd go any distance to help a friend. But he's no pushover. Intelligent. And . . ."

Ashley leaned forward. "And?"

Wynona looked away when she said it. "Lonely."

If the words were meant to melt Ashley's heart a little, Wynona figured they'd had the opposite effect. "Well, that was his choice, not mine."

"It must have been very hard to lose your mother."

Ashley settled her hands on her lap, bag tightly gripped like a life preserver. "I was seventeen. It nearly killed us both."

Wynona reached over and patted her hand. "I lost my husband. We'd been together since junior high school."

Ashley shot a sharp look to her. "My parents were together since they were twelve years old, neighbors, grew up together. They were older when they had me. In their late forties."

She needed to be careful how she worded this. "What did your father do to push you away?"

Ashley's gaze fell to the tiled floor. "Everything. He started drinking. At first, he still tried to be a father, but the more he drank, the worse it got. My mother's life insurance policy was supposed to be set aside for my education. I've always wanted to be an attorney. He spent it. Every dime."

Wynona reached over again, this time leaving her hand on Ashley's. "Oh dear."

"I was still hurting. I needed a parent. When my mom died, I lost both of them."

"Yes. I can see that you did."

Ashley turned to stare at her for a long time. And Wynona realized the young woman was wondering how she could be so sympathetic to

Ashley when her loyalty should be with Ashley's father. "What, dear?" Wynona shrugged. "I'm not going to make excuses for the man. What he did was wrong. Utterly wrong. There's no excuse for it."

Ashley opened her perfectly lined red lips to speak, but nothing came out.

Wynona raised and dropped her shoulders again. "People always try to tell you he was in pain, he was hurting, don't they?"

She jerked a nod, face unreadable except for the frown furrowing an otherwise smooth brow. "I've heard excuses from the whole world. But it doesn't help. I've read books on grieving, read books on alcoholism. I have a lot of knowledge, but no closure."

"Maybe the books and the words don't have what you need."

Ashley took her time staring into the room where her father lay, practically swallowed by the bed. Arms at his sides, needles protruding like he were some kind of science experiment. "It hurts to see him like this," she whispered. "How can it hurt when I hate him so much?"

Wynona's hand brushed back and forth over Ashley's. "Because you still love him. Not because he deserves it. Not because he was the model father, but just because you love him and nothing can change that."

A fat tear rolled down Ashley's cheek. She didn't bother to brush it away. "I don't want to love him."

Wynona nodded. "Understandably."

"I had to do everything on my own. At eighteen I moved out. I worked my way through law school; I'm raising my daughter alone. And I don't think I can forgive him."

Wynona sighed. "Unforgiveness. It's such a poison. Tell me, Ashley, if you could just go on with your life without ever seeing him again, could you do it?"

She thought before answering. "Yes. I really believe I could."

Wynona smiled. "Well, if you have that kind of power, you certainly have the power to forgive him."

Ashley's face paled as she digested the words. She pointed to the room. "He won't even see me."

Wynona waved a hand through the air. "Oh poo. Who cares what he wants. This isn't about him; it's about you. And your daughter."

The confusion on the younger woman's face made Wynona bite back a smile. "So, go off to your big city job and forget about him for a while."

Ashley gave her a frown and Wynona was pretty certain the woman was judging her mental stability.

Wynona stood. "Go off." She shooed her up out of the chair.

Ashley staggered to a standing position.

Wynona pressed her lips together. "Perhaps you could come back in six months or a year."

Ashley shook her head as if to clear it.

"I'll walk you to your car." She grabbed Ashley's hand and started dragging her along. At the end of the hallway she stopped. "He was a good father before your mother died?"

A sad smile touched her face. "A great father."

"Hmm." She walked on. At the front door, she stopped again. "I suppose you'd love to have that man back in your life?"

Ashley scrounged around in her bag for the keys. "Yes."

"He's been sober for eight years," Wynona said as she followed her to her car.

Ashley's eyes narrowed. "He hasn't tried to contact me in those eight years."

Wynona tapped a finger to her mouth. "No. I suppose he didn't trust himself to stay sober. I guess a good man wouldn't drag his family into his battle with alcoholism if he thought he could protect them by staying away."

Ashley pressed a button on her key fob, even though the door handle was right beside her. She opened her mouth to say something, but Wynona cut her off.

"You should be on your way. Have a safe trip."

Ashley stood looking at her like she couldn't decide if she was friend or foe. Was she helping her dad's case or hurting it? "It was nice to talk to you." It was more question than answer and Wynona was pleased with herself.

"Hope we meet again." She turned, started walking away, counted to three and spun back around. Yep. Ashley was standing right there, one foot propped in the car doorway, hand on the door. "By the way, before you leave town, there's something I think you should see."

Ashley's gaze narrowed.

"It won't take but a few minutes." Sweet-little-old-lady smile would do nicely here. But when she saw the fight-or-flight look enter Ashley's eyes, Wynona knew she couldn't mess this up. She moved quickly to the opposite side of Ashley's car and slid, uninvited, into the passenger's seat.

Rather than sit in the driver's seat, Ashley bent at the waist and stared down at her.

Wynona rubbed her hands over her thighs. "Oh. Well, I need to get back and since you're going that way."

Ashley got in quietly. "I think I'd rather not go. I'd be happy to get you a cab."

Wynona's chin tilted back slightly; if the hotshot attorney wanted a battle of wits, she better be armed. Wynona wasn't likely to go down without a fight. She heaved a breath. "A cab? That would be fine." She placed a hand on the door handle and Ashley seemed to sigh in relief. "But, I just wonder how much it's going to drive you crazy not knowing."

Again, the giant brown eyes narrowed to slits and Wynona figured big-city lawyers on the other side of the table from Ashley Gruber were desperately outmatched. But there were few powers on the planet stronger than life experience.

"Ashley," Wynona's tone changed to motherly. She never felt particularly good at that voice, but it forced Ashley's eyes and attention. "You *need* to come with me."

Keys slid into the ignition. A stiletto-heeled foot pressed the brake pedal. Gearshift slipped into reverse, and there they were, backing out then headed in the direction of the retreat.

———

Ian and Charlee broke camp at daybreak.

She had a headache, her stomach hurt, and she was embarrassed at the fool she'd made of herself. She watched Ian kick dirt onto the embers of a long-gone fire. "I think the rain did the trick." She had to wonder how much was nervous energy. He seemed filled with it this morning.

"I just don't want to take any chances." His gaze leveled on her as if there was more to his words than their surface meaning.

"Smokey Bear would be proud."

"We still need to talk, Charlee. I wasn't kidding last night."

She sidestepped the fire and stopped at his feet. "I've been doing some thinking about that. And I've decided I don't want to talk about it." Why should she? Make a promise knowing she couldn't . . . wouldn't keep it.

"What makes you so stubborn?" He moved forward until the tips of his boots bumped hers.

"The same thing that keeps me alive." She didn't back down, didn't flinch. If Ian thought some magical promise could keep her from diving off the deep end headfirst, he was dead wrong.

He turned away from her.

She tromped around him and faced him again. "Don't you think I've made those kinds of promises to myself? Over and over and over again? To the people who care about me? I just let them down, Ian. Every time."

"But it's different now."

She shook her head. "No, it's not. I love you. You love me and that is incredible. But if you really believe one spoken promise is going to magically make this monster disappear, you're more gullible than I would have thought."

It burned. She could see it in his eyes. But what could she do? "Let's go home," she said, and turned away to head to her Jeep before he could stop her.

————

Ian's heart felt like a giant empty hole in his chest. By noon, he was placing clothes in his bag and gathering his belongings. He knew the inevitable and though on every level he'd let the major down, this was the one place he wouldn't. He pulled the journal from the drawer and opened it to the last page. It was cryptic, in a sense, and made him think of stories of people who knew their own deaths were imminent. It was the only page Charlee hadn't read. It was the last hope of her coming to her senses. *Teach her how to stop running.* That had been Major Mack's plea. He hadn't asked Ian to be there with her. To protect her. He asked him to teach her. Like Major Mack had taught him so many things. Ian was in tears by the time he finished reading. He used the back of his hand to swipe away the streams of moisture on his face. He'd talk to Charlee, then go see Gruber—whether the old man liked it or not— then, if Charlee didn't relent, he'd ride to Oklahoma.

When the hair on the back of his neck prickled, he knew she was standing there, in his doorway. He turned to find her, hands on hips. Concern framed her features. "What are you doing?"

"I need to talk to you, Charlee."

The screen groaned as she shoved it open and stepped inside. It clanged shut behind her, but Charlee stood stoic, neither entering the room nor leaving it. Her gaze shot to his military backpack and stalled there.

"I'm packing."

Her brows shot up. "I can see that."

He lifted a hand in her direction. "Don't jump to any conclusions. This is just in case."

"In case what, Ian?"

He pulled a breath, let it out. "In case you won't agree to stop—"

She threw her head back and groaned. "Are you still going on about that? I told you last night and this morning, I can't."

Ian moved to the edge of the table, where he could anchor his body. Hands flat, he leaned on the solid wood. "If you won't promise, I have to leave."

She shook her head, long hair floating around her. "I don't know what happens to me, but there's this voice that won't stop telling me to go, to just get out. I don't have control over it."

He pushed off the table, stepped around the chairs, and landed at her feet. "I know that, sweetheart. But you have to find the way. You have to learn how to stop the voice. No one can do that but you. Not even me."

Her eyes filled. "I love you, Ian."

The words cut deep, but they were also a soothing balm. How four words could cause such pain and such joy all at once, he couldn't understand. "I'm counting on that." In fact, he was banking everything on it. In his mind, this was the only way, and he knew Major Mack would agree.

"But you're willing to just throw it away?"

"You can stop me by promising me that no matter what, you won't run."

"You know I can't. So, you're just quitting on me?" Her tone was acerbic.

He pleaded. "I'm trying to give us a chance."

Her hands fisted and he knew her well enough to know she'd like to throw a punch at him right now. "There's one last entry in your dad's journal. We're at the end of it, Charlee."

Her gaze darted around the room until landing on the book.

"Will you sit down? I'll read it to you."

———

The air in the cabin was thick, making it hard for Charlee to breathe. This would be the last entry. The final words of her father before . . . before . . .

She lowered her body into a chair at the table.

Ian slipped into the chair across from her and when her eyes met his, she knew he was drawing strength from her, strength to open the journal of the man they both loved. And Charlee really did love her father. She knew that now. And she missed him. He was so much more than the drill sergeant she'd known. He'd not been able to open himself up to her because he'd always felt it was his job to make her strong. And now she'd garner that strength to read the very last words her father had penned. Ian reached to take her hand, but when she felt his flesh against hers, she withdrew. If his love could be switched on and off with the refusal of a promise, she didn't need him.

But when he blinked and she saw the moisture filling his eyes and making them swim, all her anger melted. Ian was in pain. He drew a breath, flattened his hands on the table as if the motion would force courage into him. She watched him war with his body. She watched as he lost the battle before it even began. Ian opened the journal with a trembling hand.

He cleared his throat. "March 11. I met a man this morning whose eyes were filled with regret. I stared at him for a long time, and as the suffering became too great, I took a long look at my own life. Many a man is alive because of my commitment; that I know. But who pays the price? My own flesh and blood. Jeremiah, Isaiah, Gabriel, and Caleb. And more than the others, Charlee. Because her heart is so tender and she is so strong. Like her mother. Charlee, you don't know the depths of the power within you. You only have to reach and it's there. I met a man with regrets. I looked into his eyes and my own world was mirrored back at me. Charlee, don't end up like me."

Ian stopped reading, his voice having cracked on the last word. And Charlee knew why. Her father was almost perfect in Ian's sight. And here he was, a man so larger than life he became the standard for which all men could be measured. He'd died to protect Ian. He'd lived to make young men and women strong enough to survive in war.

Ian continued after several deep breaths. "What greater gift can a man give than to lay down his life for his friends?" Tears streamed down his face. "I am no special man. I am simple, Charlee. I loved your mother. And I still love her and will one day die loving her. She was the light of a shadowed world. She was a warrior, a fighter, a leader. She was the universe in a beautiful flesh package. I know the disservice I've done to you. For all the men I've trained to live and survive and thrive, I've not done that for you. I didn't know how. You're like your mother and she was so much stronger than I could ever be. Does the sky help the sun to shine? Does the bank help the river to flow? What could I have offered you? And yet, I know I've let you down. I love you, Charlee. Whatever obstacles may be in your path, you have the power to destroy them. I met a man this morning with regrets. But I closed my eyes and the image in the mirror disappeared. In the darkness, I saw your face. And you became my light. I am a man with regrets, but I'm also a man with hope. Charlee, find the way."

Slowly, Ian closed the journal.

"When did he write this—?" She couldn't finish because her heart was breaking.

"A few days before he died."

She breathed in, trying to create calm in a world senseless with sorrow. She'd known her father loved her. But she'd never seen their relationship through his eyes like she did now.

"Your dad used to tell me a story." Ian squared his shoulders. "About a man and a fishing hole."

A laugh surprised Charlee by slipping right out of her mouth. "Yes." She wiped the renegade tears off her cheeks. "I remember this story."

"The man lost his eyesight. But he still knew the way to the fishing hole. He didn't need any help. Didn't need anyone to lead him." Ian leaned forward, resting his arms on the table, giant shoulders dwarfing the space. "Charlee, you know the way to the fishing hole; you just have to get there."

She bit into her bottom lip. Did she? Ian might think so. Even her father might have thought so, but Charlee wasn't as strong as they believed. "I don't know the way."

Ian reached over and squeezed her hand. "Then it's time for you to find it. You're not blind, Charlee. You can find your way. Put one foot in front of the other."

She knew what this meant. He wasn't going to be there to help her. "And you're still leaving?"

He blinked several times, as if hearing her say it shot daggers into his heart. "You have to find it in yourself, Charlee. I can't do this for you."

"If you leave, how do you know I won't run?"

"I don't."

"And you'd be okay with that?"

Ian pressed his hands to his face. "I'm not okay with any of this. But I know it's what I have to do. What you do is up to you."

She thought about that. If Ian left . . . broke her heart, would she run? Probably. She couldn't imagine being without him. She was in love. Real love. Love that wasn't based on a lot of empty promises and plans for the future like Richard had given her. She'd been in love with him, but more with the ideas he'd put in her head. Traveling the globe, romantic getaways, she could paint and he would . . . would what? Be there with her. That's all he'd said he wanted. To be with her no matter where she went or what she wanted to do.

Her love for Ian was different. They'd never even talked about the future. Never even discussed the tomorrows. Their love was based in the now. It was built on work and sweat and mutual respect. It was real. "I don't know what I'll do, Ian. I don't know if I'll run. I guess we'll find out." Slowly, she stood from the table and walked—putting one foot in front of the other—until she was at his front door. "Do me a favor," she whispered, uncertain if he'd hear the words or not.

"Yes," he croaked.

"Miss me while you're gone."

But he was right behind her and placed his hands on her shoulders. He was breathing hard, and, she knew, fighting off the tears, but she felt strangely detached from the whole thing. Like she was watching it from above as it happened to someone else. Empathetic, yes, but not *her*. It wasn't happening to her.

He didn't seem able to let go. Charlee's eyes drifted closed. She didn't want to ask him where he was headed, but needed to know. For some inexplicable reason, she had to know. "Do you want to tell me where you're going?" It sounded so formal and unscathed, she paused to make sure it was her voice.

"I'm taking the job my dad offered." Words shouldn't have the ability to be so filled with pain and uncertainty. They were only words, for heaven's sake. They shouldn't be able to show such despair. But there they were, telling Ian's secret sorrow. "I'll miss you," he said when she only nodded in answer.

"Good-bye, Ian." She started to turn, but he stopped her by crushing her against him. His arms came around her, head buried in her hair.

"You know you could just promise not to run." His voice was filled with pain, hopelessness, and one last dying effort.

Promise? What good would it do? In the real world, the world she lived in, Charlee ran when things got too hard. When something cut too deep or hurt too much. It would be an empty promise. It would be a lie.

After a little while, his grip loosened. Charlee's eyes were closed and when he started to move away from her, she had to fight not to wrap her hands and arms around his. She felt him reach behind them. A moment later, he slid something into her hand. Charlee looked down at her father's journal. Silently, she left the cabin.

CHAPTER 17

"Oh my goodness," Ashley Gruber whispered; her heart nearly leapt into her throat as her eyes rested upon the painting of her and her daughter at the edge of the ocean, head thrown back, Vivi laughing, her baby belly round and shining in the sun's rays. It was as if the two of them were bathed in angelic light. Ashley's eyes sought and found Wynona, who stood on the opposite side of the painting. "I don't understand."

Wynona reached behind her. "Here's another."

In this picture, Vivi played at the edge of a stream in the park. She knew this picture and the other, but . . . "These are from photographs?" Her mind worked to understand.

Wynona nodded. "Yes. I found some of the photos on your Facebook page. Your father has been living your life along with you . . . just not bothering you in the process. He painted these from the Facebook posts."

Ashley's world spun around her. This wasn't the father she'd known after her mom died. This was . . . this was more like the man who had raised her. Older than the other dads. Wise. Full of experience and wisdom he loved to pass along to her. They'd always had grown-up conversations, she and her father. Even when she was very small. He never talked down to her. He'd been interested in her perspective on things, her opinions. "He's why I wanted to be an attorney."

Wynona led her to the kitchen table, where Ashley dropped into a chair. "He taught me that my voice could make a difference." Her eyes found Wynona. "Why didn't he reach out? Once he was sober, why didn't he try to have a relationship with me again?" And suddenly, Ashley was jealous for all the time she'd missed. "He obviously was able to have a relationship with you. With everyone here."

"I don't think he wanted to risk hurting you again." Wynona's mouth pressed into a straight line. "Before my Horace died, do you know what he told me?"

Ashley shook her head.

"He told me he wished we'd never met."

Ashley's mouth dropped open.

"He said he could deal with dying if he didn't have to watch me suffer. He said that if he could take the pain away of me having to watch him die, he'd do it. Even if it meant us never meeting in the first place. That's how strong love can be."

"You said you found *some* of the photographs on my page. Are there more paintings?"

"Yes, dear. Dozens."

"Will you show me?"

Wynona nodded and stood from the table. With the soft light of a summer sun shining through the window, she led Ashley to the loft where Arnold Gruber experienced his daughter's world vicariously through a lifetime of paintings.

———

Ian had barely settled into his temporary room when his dad knocked on the bedroom door. Ian turned to face him. "Can you put me to work right away?"

His dad, dressed in a flannel shirt with rolled-up sleeves, Dickies, and steel-toed work boots, let his weight fall against the doorjamb. "Good to see you too."

Ian dropped the T-shirt he held and looked at his dad. "Sorry. Just anxious to get started." He attempted a smile.

"I can see you are." But his dad didn't answer the question, so Ian went back to folding the wrinkled clothes from his pack.

"So?" his dad finally said.

Ian looked up again.

"The girl?"

"Charlee?" Even her name on his tongue caused splinters in his heart. Ian had to turn away to keep his dad from seeing the truth. "Summer's over. Job's done." And even to him, it sounded so final, so absolute.

His dad drew a breath and let it out, and Ian couldn't imagine what was going on inside the man. He was usually all business. Get the job done, not hover in doorways asking personal questions. That would suggest he cared what had happened, and Ian didn't really believe he did. "None of my business, but when she was here . . ."

Ian turned on him. "That was an act, Dad. Charlee wasn't my girlfriend; she pretended to be because Brenna was here and Charlee thought that was a lousy situation for me to be put in. It was, by the way."

His dad frowned. "Worked out, though."

Ian laughed without humor. "Yeah. Worked out just fine." He didn't try to stop the bitterness in his tone.

"Girl must care quite a bit about you to put on a show like that." His eyes darted around the room Charlee had shared with Ian. "Even stayed in here with you."

Ian closed his eyes, wishing the memory of Charlee there could be erased. "I slept on the floor." Of course, Charlee had slept there with him, but he didn't mention that.

His dad nodded and Ian continued unpacking. When the silence reigned, he thought his dad must have left, but when he turned, he found he'd walked in and sat down at the small corner table.

Ian cocked his hands on his hips. "What?"

"What happened between you two?"

Really? His dad wanted a heart-to-heart?

Thomas motioned with the crook of his thumb to the doorway. "Your mother said I should talk to you."

Ah. Now the inquisition made sense. Ian dropped into the chair ready to stick to his summer's-over-job's-done spiel, but when his gaze landed squarely on his father's, he saw it—the shreds of interest reflecting in his dad's eyes. "I'm in love with her."

"That's not news, son. Any man with eyes could see that."

"And she loves me too."

His dad nodded, didn't speak. No biting words of sarcasm. No criticism. Just silence.

"She has some things she needs to work through if we're going to be together."

His dad frowned. "And she's working through them, now?"

He shrugged. "Don't know. I hope."

That's when it happened. His dad reached across the table and took hold of Ian's forearm. "She'll come to her senses. And if she doesn't, she doesn't deserve you."

Ian's mouth hung open.

"I mean that. You're a good man. I hope . . . well, I just hope I can be a better part of your life than I have in the past."

Ian didn't know what to say. "We all make mistakes, Dad. Let's just move forward and not look back."

His dad smiled, eyes softening, crinkling around the edges. Before the moment could become too tender, he stood and walked to the door. "Of course, I'm not going to put together your benefits package until

I know for certain if you are or aren't going to stick around, so don't expect any paid time off."

Ian laughed. "Got it. Can I count on you to give me a good recommendation if I leave?"

His dad closed one eye and pointed at him. "You leave to marry that girl and promise your mother some grandbabies and I'll consider it."

Ian nodded. His dad disappeared down the hall whistling. Grandbabies. He'd love to make his mom a promise like that, but the thought of him and Charlee together grew farther and farther away. He wanted to believe she'd work through it; he just couldn't convince himself it would actually happen.

———

Wynona sat at the hospital in a chair where she'd spent many hours. She'd had to fight not to bling out the arms, but had opted to make sets of sunglasses instead. Now, almost every nurse on the floor owned a pair of Wynona originals. Her gaze drifted from the shades she was working on to Arnold's room. It had been three weeks since the surgery. When her gaze skittered from the doorway to his bed, she found him watching her.

Her heart did a little flop, but she blinked, offered a polite smile and went right on with her blinging. From the corner of her eye, she noticed him reach for, then press, the nurse's button. For days and days, she'd sat in the hallway. He'd mostly ignored her. Ashley was planning a trip back in a few more days. She planned to bring Arnold's granddaughter for the weekend. Because at the end of it all, Ashley still loved her dad and believed that a miracle could happen. He might come to his senses—which was what Wynona had told her repeatedly.

Moments later, the nurse arrived and over her reading glasses, Wynona watched Arnold speaking to the nurse, who turned and looked directly at Wynona. She swallowed hard and felt the onset of tears, but she gritted her teeth. This was a public hospital, for heaven's sake. He couldn't physically make her leave. Could he? Her stomach lurched at the thought.

The nurse came out and Wynona didn't know what to do with her hands. She'd dropped the glasses and rhinestones in her lap and now, palms sweating, she awaited the sentence. Carol, the nurse, gave her a bright smile. Too bright. Too happy.

It didn't matter. Wynona would stand her ground. She'd lived through the sixties. She'd done her fair share of fighting the establishment. If she had to leave, God and all his angels would know she was fighting it with every fiber of her being. And if they had to physically drag her out, so be it.

Carol smiled. "He'd like to see you."

Wynona swept the rhinestones into her plastic container. "This is a public place. He doesn't *own* the hallway."

Carol blinked, tilted her chin down and crossed her arms over her chest. "Wynona, I said he'd like to see you."

Wynona stood and met her toe-to-toe. "And I said . . ." She took hold of Carol's arm when the words caught up to her. The hallway swayed. "What?"

Carol nodded.

Wynona's world spun. Could she have heard right? Her hand spasmed on Carol's arm.

The woman patted her hand. "He'd like to see you. And you know how impatient he is, so get in there."

A sound slipped from Wynona's mouth, it was neither a laugh nor a sigh, but something in between that reflected all the hours of waiting and all the hope that he'd come around.

She pulled a deep breath and took tiny steps until she was just inside the room.

He was using a hand to comb his hair over. Her heart smiled at the thought of him trying to primp for her. "You look fine, Arnold."

He grunted, small frame squirming beneath the white bed cover. "And you look tired. Stubborn woman."

She stopped at his bedside and dropped her hands to the cool metal rail. "Obstinate man."

He tried to frown, but there was too much warmth in his eyes for it to really be convincing. "Why don't you go home?"

"Well, you know what they say. Home is where the heart is."

His lips were dry and cracked, his flesh held that grayed look of illness, but his attitude seemed almost back to normal.

Aged hands slid back and forth over the blanket. He dropped his gaze. "Guess I should appreciate you watching over me."

"You'd do the same for me."

He grunted. "You think too highly of me, Wynona."

When his legs moved, she reached down to the blanket and tucked the edge around his knee. "And maybe you don't think highly enough."

He nodded toward the hall. "What have you been doing out there all this time?"

She cast a glance behind her. "Oh, this and that. All the nurses have Hollywood sunglasses now."

"Should have known you'd sink to bribery to get your way."

Wynona tilted her head back a bit. "I'd sink to any depths or climb to any heights for someone I love."

Arnold blinked, sparse lashes flickering. When a thin, cold hand closed on hers, Wynona's heart began beating faster.

"I've done nothin' to earn your love." Faded blue eyes were rimmed with red and Wynona knew he was fighting his own tears.

She drew in a long breath through her nose, lips pressed together. "That's the great thing about love. You don't have to earn it." She squeezed his hand. "But you *do* have to accept it."

A frown deepened the lines around his eyes and across his forehead. "I've been horrible."

She sniffed. "An absolute beast."

"And you've been so good."

She cocked her head. "Why yes, I'm almost a saint."

He appreciated her trying to lighten the mood, she could tell, but the look turned to concern. "Ashley was here?" When he said that, he turned as if hearing it stripped away his carefully placed facade.

"She's coming back."

His hand released from hers and fell against his mouth, big blue eyes filling with hope. "She is?"

Wynona nodded. "With your granddaughter."

A puff of air escaped his mouth and now, tears fell unbidden, sliding down his cheeks into the grooves on his face. "After all I've done. She's coming back? To see me?" His eyes searched hers as if the notion was impossible.

"As I said . . . love."

He sat up in the bed. "She's bringing Vivi. I . . . I get to meet Vivi." His legs started moving beneath the covers, body tilting from side to side, and it seemed he might come apart at the seams if Wynona didn't do something.

She squeezed the lever on the side of the bed and dropped the railing. Without asking or waiting for an invitation, she sat down on the edge of his bed, facing him. One hand rested on her knee, the other propped against the railing on the opposite side.

Arnold took hold of her hand and placed it against his heart. "I'm so sorry. I just . . ."

"It's okay, Arnold. No explanations necessary."

But he was lost in the regret, eyes going far away. "I was just so ashamed."

"We all have skeletons in our closets, Arnold. I'm not proud of everything I did in my younger, wilder days. But that doesn't mean I'm any less of a person now. I have regrets. I have pain. But today, I choose what kind of life I'm going to live. Today, I can start fresh. The past has no power except what we give it. I refuse to let skeletons rule my life."

"Life's too precious to not give it the honor it deserves."

"That's right." She kept a soft touch against his heart. The bandages beneath her fingertips reminded her she'd almost lost him.

He frowned. "And you really think you could love an old bear like me?"

Her free hand cupped his cheek. "I already do."

He closed his hand over hers and pressed hard, as if imprinting her fingers on his flesh. "I sure don't deserve it. But I'm sure glad I got it."

Wynona tossed a look behind them. "Scoot over."

White, bushy brows shot up on his head, but he did as instructed.

Wynona stretched out beside him, tucking into the crook of his arm. Arnold settled around her, one arm closing over her shoulder where he could caress the long strands of her hair.

"Think we'll get in trouble for this?" he said, and rested his cheek against the top of her head.

"I hope so." She giggled.

"People are gonna talk."

She tilted back to look at him then shot a glance to the door where Dr. Giles was just entering. "Well," she said and leaned closer. "Let's give them something to talk about." And she dropped a kiss on Arnold's mouth while she felt his arms close more tightly around her.

CHAPTER 18

There was no possible way to remove Ian from the retreat. His footprint was everywhere, his memory in every direction she looked. Even her favorite spot was now tainted with him. It was horrible torture. Three weeks. Three weeks he'd been gone and she'd been so sure that life would make sense for her and one day she'd awaken and now that ever-important promise could be made. But the war on the outside was nothing compared to the war on the inside. Charlee was having to dig deeply into her being to make sense of the reasons she ran, the reasons she kept others at arm's length and the reasons it all had to stop. Deep inside her soul, there was a scared little girl. A child who wasn't brave enough to walk the road because of the monsters. And Charlee had allowed that part of her to control her actions. But also inside Charlee there was a warrior. A fighter who kept moving forward when the monsters closed in. She just had to learn how to give that part of her control, how to quiet the frightened child who had run unguarded for too long.

Her first opportunity came when she got a message from Wynona to please get to the hospital as quickly as possible. Charlee let the scenarios rummage through her head as she drove to town. Upon arrival, she threw the Jeep into park and practically ran inside.

Charlee found Wynona sitting in the hallway. She rushed over, terrified at what she might learn, but as she neared Wynona, the woman seemed casual, not tense, happy even. "Is everything okay?"

Wynona stood, eyes wide. "Yes, dear. Oh, heavens. I worried you with my message. I didn't mean to. It's just that . . ." Wynona motioned into Mr. Gruber's room. "He's been asking to see you."

Charlee reached out and took Wynona's arm to steady herself. "What?"

Wynona nodded and her scarf of silky white hair fell around her shoulders. "Yes. We had a nice, long chat. And well, he's choosing to leave the skeletons where they are and just move on."

Leave the skeletons. Maybe that's what she needed to do. Charlee gripped her with both hands now, her focus on Mr. Gruber. "He's okay? With us? With me?"

"Yes. Everything is okay." She leaned closer to Charlee and a bright red stain appeared along Wynona's cheeks. "The doctor caught us kissing."

Well. What do you say to that? "Oh my. I guess things really are better." Charlee felt the tinge in her own cheeks as well. "Can I go in?"

Wynona motioned toward the door. "He's sleeping now. Can you stay awhile? I had the nurse bring out an extra chair."

"Yes." They sat, and Charlee's thoughts turned to Ian. She hadn't run. Oh, there'd been a temptation, but she'd fought it. And succeeded. Still, she didn't fully trust herself. Even when she'd gotten the phone message Wynona left and she'd feared the worst, running had flashed into her mind. How could she ever trust herself? Maybe she'd never be free of this.

Charlee watched as the older woman's hands worked the rhinestones onto a key fob. "It's beautiful."

Wynona held it up and the stones caught the light, casting off rainbows. "Special order. The nurses all have bling-y sunglasses now. Guess my business is expanding."

"When did you start decorating things, Wynona?"

"When my Horace was sick."

"How did you deal with . . . I mean, how did you handle—?"

"His passing?"

"Yes."

Wynona dropped another dot of glue and a sparkling stone onto the key fob. "The same way I handled his illness."

Charlee knew he'd been sick a long time and Wynona had stayed at his bedside much the way she was staying at Mr. Gruber's now.

She stopped working and angled to face Charlee. "I couldn't handle it. Not on my own. I was shattered. And each and every day while I watched the man I loved deteriorate, it was like being broken again and again. Held together by sheer human will."

"How'd you survive?"

"Horace was in St. John's Catholic Hospital, room 702. Every day the chaplain came. He never spoke, just sat down beside me and held my hand." Wynona blinked. "Not one word. But, as he held my hand, the atmosphere changed. The room felt brighter, the world better. And when he'd leave, I noticed my heart was a little lighter inside my chest."

"You're saying you believe in God. That's what gave you strength."

Wynona tilted her head. "No. It's not a question of if I believe. I simply can't unbelieve." And then Wynona reached over and took Charlee's hand. Maybe Charlee had spent too long letting a scared little girl decide her actions. Maybe she'd spent too many days letting a frightened child run amok inside her psyche, dictating how to handle a crisis. Maybe it was time for that child to die. And as Wynona held her hand, Charlee closed her eyes and said good-bye to the skeletons of her past. When she opened her eyes, the hall was a little brighter.

———

Within an hour, Mr. Gruber was awake. Charlee entered his room slowly; the memory of his anger at her for calling his daughter flashed through her mind, trying to take root, wanting her to turn and run, but she didn't. She stopped at his bedside. He looked thin, gaunt against the harshness of the white sheets, but better than when she'd seen him last. His eyes were clear and rimmed with appreciation. "I got a whole bushel of folks that care about me."

Charlee smiled. "Yes. And I'll admit you gave us all quite a scare."

His demeanor became serious, one hand fumbling with the edge of his tray table. "A man doesn't know the number of his days."

Charlee's gaze moved to the spot where an aged hand lifted the corner of a leather-bound Bible. It was trimmed in gold and looked new. "Was that a gift?"

"Wynona. Said I ought to read it if I hadn't before."

"And?"

He rubbed a hand over his head. There was a cotton ball taped below his wrist where an IV had been. A brick-red stain darkened the area around the cotton, remnants of the bruising. "It's easier to read than I remember. She said it was written in today's language. Easier for a simpleton like me."

Charlee reached out and took his other hand, careful of the line that snaked from his forearm to a bag dangling overhead. "You're certainly not a simpleton, Mr. Gruber. You're one of the most intelligent men I know. You've traveled the world, studied in Paris."

This awarded her with a laugh. He sobered and gave her hand a light squeeze. "I'm sorry about all that stuff after surgery. Said some harsh things." And the burden of his words still weighed on him; that was plain to see.

"No need to apologize. We're family." She meant it.

His eyes lit. "I'm going to get to meet my grandbaby. She's three now. I talked to Ashley on the phone. She's forgiven me . . . all those horrible things."

"That's great."

"And I was wondering if it'd be okay for me to let them stay at the retreat for a weekend every now and again. I mean, if they want to. I'm hoping . . ." But then his words ran out. And Charlee could see the hope filling his eyes, a new hope, a light that had all but been extinguished.

He had to blink to keep the tears at bay. "Well, I'm just thinking that if I'm to be left on this earth for a few more years, I ought to make the best of it."

Charlee wanted to agree, but didn't trust her voice. She was overcome watching a miracle happen right before her eyes. What was the saying, "old dog, new tricks"? That certainly wasn't the case here. Mr. Gruber was ready to meet life head-on, with all its beauty and all its tragedy. He was letting go of the past and grabbing hold of the future. A future he could carve. "They're welcome at the retreat anytime they'd like to come. We've got plenty of room."

His lips pressed together hard enough the lines of his face deepened. He nodded. "Thank you. I feel like I'm getting a second chance."

Charlee sniffed. "Yes. I'm so happy for you. Now, please hurry up and get out of here so we can all go home." Of course, *all* was incomplete. Because all could only be all with Ian. And he was gone. Maybe for good.

"I could use a rest," Mr. Gruber yawned. He was still regaining his strength and deep discussions like this one probably took a lot out of him. They certainly took a lot out of Charlee.

She bent at the waist and kissed him on the forehead.

He grumbled at first, and she chuckled as she turned to walk away. When she cast a look back at him, there was a contented smile on his face.

The entire hospital looked a little brighter as she left. She'd make sure the cabin by Mr. Gruber's was clean and ready for Ashley and her daughter, Vivi. It was good to keep busy and Charlee felt the best she had since Ian left. She was just getting into the Jeep when she heard someone call her name. Sliding the blinged-out sunglasses off her face, she turned to look behind her. There, slamming the door on a slick black Mercedes, was Wes Giles. She smiled and waved.

He jogged the last couple rows of cars to get to her. There was no smile on his face. "Charlee, I need to talk to you."

Fear zapped her strength. This wasn't a friendly conversation or reminiscing. Something was wrong. He came around the opposite side of the Jeep and got into the passenger seat.

Tension flew off him in waves, causing Charlee's heart to beat all the faster. "Wes, what?"

He pulled a breath, let it out. Pulled another as if the words he needed were somewhere out there in the atmosphere. "I could have my license revoked for this."

She frowned. The words weren't specifically to her, more an internal argument he had no hope of winning. "Wes, what's going on?"

"It's Mr. Gruber. I was concerned with some of the test results so I did some digging to figure out what was going on. I . . . uncovered something."

Charlee gripped the steering wheel to maintain her equilibrium. "What?"

"He has a condition. His heart . . . well, essentially, it could give out at any time."

The world grayed then funneled down to one thin path. It was hard to breathe. "What do you mean?"

"In simplest terms, it's like a ticking time bomb."

Pain speared right through her chest. Her grip tightened. "How long does he have?"

Wes shook his head. "That's just it. There's no way of knowing. No warning."

She pulled her glasses off, tossed them on the dash, and pressed her palms to her eyes. It was hard to breathe, stuffy, no oxygen in the car. "Are you saying he could just drop dead at any moment?" And that seemed so unbelievable and wrong when he'd just decided to take life by the horns.

"Yes."

Everything in her sank into the floorboard. All the hope, all the joy.

"The surgery and heart attacks have put him at even greater risk. He's already overdone it. It's almost a miracle he's—"

She put a flat hand up between them. "Stop. Just stop." Why didn't doctors ever know when to shut up? Either continually giving you too much information or not enough. Another thought occurred to her. "Does he know?"

Wes shook his head. "Not yet."

And her heart sank a little more.

"No one knows but you."

Complete goo. They'd have to scrape her off the floor mats to get her out of the Jeep. Indignation rushed over her. "Why did you tell me?" She hadn't meant to sound so mad, but, well, mad she was.

Wes shook his head, eyes scanning her, obviously trying to gauge the reaction. "I just . . . You're so strong, Charlee. I figured you'd want to know so you can be there for him. He's going to need you."

She pointed at the hospital entrance. "Up until a few minutes ago, he wasn't even seeing me."

Wes nodded. "I spoke with him this morning after I caught Wynona stretched out on the bed with him. I knew he planned to reconcile with you today."

There weren't words. Deep in her heart, she knew her anger and frustration were not directed at Wes. But the things deep in her heart were . . . well . . . deep, and the news and the frustration about it were right on the surface. "Oh, so as a bonus for reconciliation, you decided to tell me he could drop dead at any second. Thanks, Wes."

He sat quietly, long, manicured fingers threading together on his lap. "Well," he said, "I've taken enough of your time." She heard the handle of the Jeep click. When the door didn't open, Wes threw his shoulder into it. "I'm sorry I told you. I really thought it was what you'd want."

He slammed the door shut. Charlee's fingers gripped the steering wheel so hard they ached. She loosened her grip, tightened it. Loosened it again. Tightened it again and dropped her head to the steering wheel. Her mind raced, snippets of scenarios running like silent movies in her head. Mr. Gruber, dying. Telling him that his second chance was going to be cut short. Her heart ached. Her head pounded. And then, she saw another scenario. Herself, sitting alone in a hotel with a bottle of Jack.

Charlee swallowed, mouth going dry and thirsty. She squeezed her eyes shut and tried to erase the image, but it wouldn't go. Couldn't go. It was her answer. It would ease the pain. Her breath came in short gasps and spurts as she started the Jeep, a plan forming in her head as if she were on autopilot. No one would know. No one had to know anything yet and besides, it was none of their business. She could slip away for a few hours. Not days. Just a few hours and no one would know because they didn't know about Mr. Gruber.

She pressed the clutch, ready to make her escape, ready to go, to run. But only for a little while this time, not for long. And wasn't that progress? She let the clutch out too quickly and the Jeep bucked and died. Feverish now, she reached to the ignition switch but stopped abruptly. Her hand, slick with sweat, was shaking. Her fingers trembling. And Charlee was reminded of Mr. Gruber a long time ago telling her that he'd get the shakes when he was drinking. His body would quake almost as if he were in withdrawal.

Charlee stared at her fingers, willing them to calm. Then, she tilted the rearview mirror and looked at herself. There was desperation in her eyes. Weakness, a frightened child trying to run. She wanted to look away, but wouldn't allow herself to do so. For a long time she stared at the person in the mirror, and the words of her father's last journal entry floated through her mind.

I met a man this morning whose eyes were filled with regret. I stared at him for a long time, and as the suffering became too great, I took a long look at my own life. Charlee, you don't know the depths of the power within you. You only have to reach and it's there. I met a man with regrets. I looked into his eyes and my own world was mirrored back at me. Charlee, don't end up like me. You're like your mother and she was so much stronger than I could ever be. I love you, Charlee. Whatever obstacles may be in your path, you have the power to destroy them. I met a man this morning with regrets. But I closed my eyes and the image in the mirror disappeared. In the darkness, I saw your face. And you became my light. I am a man with regrets, but I'm also a man with hope. Charlee, find the way.

She squeezed her eyes shut, looking for the image in the dark. Charlee let the silence inside the car surround her, absorb her. It was quiet. Like it had been earlier when Wynona held her hand. Unearthly quiet. Silence that promised peace. Rest. A long exhale escaped her lips, its hissing sound soothing, cutting through all the voices and all the noise. There, in the dark, an image took shape. Charlee's heart jumped. As darkness became one tiny pinprick of light, she could make out a face. Her light. Her hope.

Her answer.

Charlee's eyes snapped open. She knew what she needed to do. One quick stop at the retreat to grab the supplies she needed—she avoided everyone there—and now, she was on her way.

"Not running," she whispered to herself as she drove. "This isn't running."

With a mixed cassette of nineties country tunes, Charlee drove out of her past and into her future.

CHAPTER 19

After Charlee called Rosy to find out where Ian would be, she drove straight to the construction site. She first spotted him as she whipped the Jeep onto the narrow street. Ian was standing on the skeleton roof of a building at the end of the block. Her heart leapt when she saw him, then excitement turned to horror because he wasn't harnessed to anything. When she downshifted, he cast a look in her direction, the sun glinting off the yellow hardhat on his head. He raised a hand to shade his eyes—as if not really believing the image.

The road was paved, but littered with dust and bits of gravel from the construction site. Charlee couldn't stop the smile on her face. It appeared, big enough to cause her cheeks to ache, and when Ian hurried to the extension ladder and descended, the smile grew even bigger. Her lungs wouldn't fill. He looked amazing. Just amazing. More so than she even remembered. T-shirt, jeans, work boots. He was perfect.

Something to the right caught her attention. She dragged her gaze from Ian to find someone . . . some woman . . . walking toward him, a lunch box in her hands.

Charlee's lungs squeezed out all the air. Brenna. Brenna was hurrying to him, oblivious to Charlee and the Jeep and the fact that, *excuse me, this is the man I love.* Charlee's gaze went from the sashaying Brenna to Ian. Had he actually been coming down the ladder for her? Had he even seen Charlee driving up? *Oh God, I'm going to throw up. Please help me not throw up.*

When Brenna got to Ian first, he placed his hands on her arms. Charlee wanted to close her eyes, but train wrecks and all that. The coffee in her stomach roiled. Ian was talking, fast, a hundred miles an hour. Then he pointed toward the Jeep. Brenna's mouth dropped open. The lunch box dropped to the ground. And Charlee's heart dropped into her stomach.

Two steps and Ian was running toward her. She couldn't move. Stunned. Her feet wouldn't work. All her energy was going into figuring out what Brenna was doing there. It had only been three weeks.

Ian flung the door open and snatched her from inside. She drifted along, easily; there were no more bones in her body to hold her steadfast. He smelled like sweat and man and hard work and oh Lord, she'd missed that. Arms closed around her, but she was still a puddle of goo. Words came at her. She needed to key into them. What was wrong with her?

And then, someone else was there. Right in the middle of their moment.

Brenna. All the haze and all the confusion cleared in one quick shot of jealousy. Charlee's gaze narrowed on Ian. His eyes darted to Brenna, giving her a warning look. What the heck did that mean?

Brenna cocked her hip, opened her mouth to speak, but Charlee cut her off. "Don't." Charlee lifted a hand. "Unless you're wearing his engagement ring, don't say a word to me."

Brenna closed her mouth, but the warning was there, in her eyes, flying off her body.

Ian held both his hands tightly around Charlee's forearms. Maybe excited to see her, maybe just keeping her from running away.

But the attention made Charlee bold and whatever was going on between Ian and Brenna—or whatever had gone on between Ian and

Brenna—wasn't what mattered to him. This she knew because as he'd neared her, his eyes lit with the same fire, the same love hers had when she saw him. Charlee cut a look to Brenna. "Are you?"

She frowned.

"Wearing his ring?"

Brenna's nostrils flared, eyes flames on Charlee. "No."

"Then, this is my man—if he'll still have me—and if you ever come near him again, I'll skin you like a hog."

Brenna's quick intake of air was accompanied by a look to Ian— *Aren't you going to defend me?* it said. But he just smirked, slid an arm around Charlee, and shrugged. "You heard her. Believe me, I know this woman. She'll do it. She's got the tools."

Brenna stormed off and Charlee was ready and willing to watch every step of her retreat, but she couldn't. Ian. He was all in her face, eyes filled, those beautiful eyes so filled with so many emotions she couldn't begin to name them.

"You're here." He squeezed her arms as if not really believing his senses.

"Will you still have me? I love you, Ian. I love you so much."

Through his joy, his eyes narrowed. "I thought I could live without you. I was wrong."

"You could have come back, you know?" Her hands closed over his arms, both of them holding the other up.

His smile faded. "I couldn't. I made a promise to you and your father."

She moved to stand closer to him. "I know you did."

"And that's why you're here now?" There was so much hope in his voice, she could only laugh, nod. Laugh again.

His hands found their way to her face, then her hair, and she drank him in—the feel of his sun-heated flesh on her skin, the smell of pure man and pure love. "I'm sorry about Brenna. She's been hanging around the jobsite for the last week. I told her there was nothing between us and there couldn't be—"

Charlee shut him up by pressing a quick kiss to his lips. Big mistake. He trapped her there, mouth opening, body angling to meet her more fully, to pin her against his torso and legs. And . . . oh, she was lost. His muscles were full and tight from work, his lips and tongue danced over her mouth, and, for a few hot seconds, there was no one in the world but them. When the catcalls became loud, Charlee broke the kiss. Her lips were swollen and rough from his whiskers and it felt incredible and tingly and alive. Her body was alive when Ian Carlisle was around. Gloriously and unashamedly alive. And right now all she wanted to do was get him alone.

She shook her head to clear it and had to take an excruciating step away from him. There was business to tend to, after all. They couldn't be standing around sucking face while there were important items to discuss.

She reached into the back of the Jeep. "You forgot your paintings."

Ian's fingers reached for her as if not wanting her out of arms' reach. To keep from grabbing her again, he closed his hands into fists. "And you're returning them?"

She nodded. "Here's the one Mr. Gruber painted and here's the one I painted."

When she pulled the painting of the big red splotch titled *Blue* from the wrap, he frowned. "*You* painted this one?"

She nodded. "Yes. And you chose to keep it in your cabin, proving you have excellent taste."

"I chose you too." He came at her, crushing the painting between them.

She cast a glance skyward. "Proving we can all be misguided at times." With great effort, she pushed him away.

He took the painting of the red splotch from her and stared at it. "Will you do another one for me one day?"

She reached into the back of the Jeep again. "I already did." When she pulled out the painting, it was a black canvas.

"Let me guess. You call it *White*."

"No. I call it *Life Without Ian*." Charlee lowered the canvas and rested it against the Jeep's tire. "That's what my world is without you. It's just a big, dark, empty hole."

He took a step closer, setting *Blue* with the other canvas. "Yeah, know the feeling."

"Ian, I have to tell you something." And before she could stop herself, she dove into the story about Mr. Gruber and his new lease on life and his daughter. And the doctor. And his death sentence.

Ian crushed her against him. "I'm so sorry, Charlee. He should never have come to you with that first."

"He meant well," she mumbled into his chest.

He tilted her out to look at him. "What did you do?"

"I ran. To you."

On his exhale, he pulled her back into his arms.

"You were wrong, Ian. It isn't all in me. I needed a source to draw from and I found it."

Again, he looked into her eyes.

"My dad. And you. You gave me the strength to stop that frightened little girl inside. I'm not going to run. Not now. Not ever. Fear isn't going to rule my life anymore. I'm free. And I swear to you, I'll never run again."

There were kisses that touched her heart and there were kisses that made her feel loved, but this kiss was something else, something different. It was the world and the universe; it spun the stars away from her and anchored her feet to the crumbling earth. It both lifted and dragged her. High and deep. And in all the times Charlee had been kissed in her life, she'd never felt anything like it. It was the future. It was a white picket fence and a toddler hugging her leg. It was a Fourth of July display and a quiet, snow-covered Christmas morning. It was life and it was good.

And if she had her way, it would be the first of many. When Charlee opened her eyes to look at Ian, it was as if she'd already lived that life. Her heart was content, her mind at peace, and if she lived to be a hundred, she figured there would never be a moment more precious than this one.

Until he said the next few words.

"Charlee, will you marry me?"

And the whole amazing series of emotions began again.

———

Charlee sat at the edge of Mr. Gruber's bed. He'd be released later today, but she'd taken on the job of explaining about his heart and the condition that could kill him. Ian sat beside her, holding her hand, and Wes Giles stood in the far corner of the room to answer questions. Wynona was on the other side of Gruber's bed, hand on his shoulder. Charlee had already told Wynona.

The crusty, loveable old man stayed quiet for a long time after she explained. The muscles around his mouth ticked. Then his watery blue eyes drifted up to hers. "Is that all?"

What? Charlee leaned toward him. Maybe he hadn't understood. "Uh, yes. Mr. Gruber, isn't that enough?"

He reached back and squeezed Wynona's hand. "It's no surprise that an old man is going to die one day."

Charlee repositioned herself, gearing up to explain.

His upturned hand stopped her. "I'm old, Charlee."

Something hit her solidly in the chest.

"If I die tomorrow, I die tomorrow."

Charlee closed her eyes, shutting out the thought.

Gruber turned to face Dr. Giles. "But you don't know how long I'll live, right? 'Cause you're just practicing."

Jokes, Mr. Gruber was making jokes. Charlee tried to wrap her head around it.

Wes took a step toward the bed. "There's no way to determine. And yes, I'm just practicing."

Wynona cleared her throat. "Charlee, dear, I think what Arnold is saying is that life is a gift every day. No one knows the number of his days, but we have charge over the quality of the days we're given."

Gruber ran a hand over his face. "I'd like to stay on a little longer. Don't get me wrong. I've got more to live for now than I've had for years." He angled to look up at a smiling Wynona before turning back to Charlee. "My daughter is back in my life. Coming to visit in another week. I'll get to spend some time with my granddaughter. Even if this ticker only holds out for another month, I've gotten every blessing a man my age can hope for."

Charlee nodded. She was beginning to understand. It wasn't quantity of years. It was quality.

He closed one eye. "Now, on to more important things. You have a promise to keep to your father, little girl."

"Spreading his ashes."

Gruber sat up straighter. "That's right."

"Well, I'd like to do that when my brothers are here." She looked over at Ian, whose smile could light up the abyss. "I'm hoping they will all be able to come for the wedding. But maybe a small preliminary ceremony would be nice."

"Later today," Mr. Gruber said.

Charlee flashed a quick look to Ian then turned her attention back to Mr. Gruber. "Are you sure you'd be up to that?"

"Yep. Already got a present to mark the occasion."

"All right. This afternoon. At my favorite spot."

———

Charlee stayed in the hospital room while Ian slipped downstairs to the cafeteria. He poured a cup of coffee at the help-yourself station.

Jeremiah's voice caused him to turn. "I hadn't gotten a chance to tell you thanks for being here for my sister."

Ian smiled. "I'm the one who's grateful."

Miah ran a hand through his hair and Ian noticed two nurses stopping to watch him. "I'm really sorry about the property stuff."

"What? The message you left about her selling the property?"

"Dude, I didn't do that on purpose. I didn't know about what Richard did to her."

Ian slapped him on the shoulder. "I know you didn't. Forget about it. Besides, I told you it would never work."

They both chuckled.

Ian pivoted to face him. "A crisis was probably the only way for Charlee to realize alcohol isn't her answer. Everything happened the way it needed to, Jeremiah, so don't beat yourself up."

Miah's eyes grew troubled. "How is she?"

"She's got a handle on it. I know she had to dig deep, search her soul, understand that being independent and headstrong is great, but you can't let it control you. It's okay to need others."

"I guess I can understand that." Jeremiah slipped his hands into his pockets.

"Maybe it's easier for us because we're soldiers. You're only as strong as the men surrounding you." Ian took a sip of the coffee, made a face, and went back for more cream. "So, what happened with your investor?"

Miah shrugged. "Only interested in the whole plot."

"And your brothers agreed? You only needed Charlee?"

Miah nodded. "I'm glad things worked out like this, though. I've been checking out the big building on my stretch of land. It's in need of repairs, but it could be a pretty cool lodge."

"Really? Going to open your own artists' colony?"

Miah laughed; the sound drew the attention of three women walking by. "Hardly. I was thinking a hunting and fishing lodge."

They took the stairs instead of the elevator and started down the long corridor. Charlee stepped out of Gruber's room and Ian's heart melted. Just like it always did when he saw her. He was vaguely aware of Miah saying something about the nurses' station, but Ian barely heard. The woman of his dreams, the woman he loved, the woman who would soon become his wife was right down the hall waiting for him. As if she knew he was there, she turned and smiled.

And Ian smiled too and said a silent thanks to Major Mack, the man who brought them together. In the farthest reaches of his mind, Ian had to wonder if this had been Major Mack's plan all along. Ian had once asked him why he'd taken such an interest in him. The major answered that if he could reach Ian, he could reach anyone. Did Mack mean anyone, even Charlee? "Thanks, Mack," he said, then added, "You had my six."

EPILOGUE

Charlee McKinley, soon to be Charlee Carlisle, stared out over Table Rock Lake. The small gathering at her favorite spot reminded her of all the things she had to be thankful for. Beside her, Mr. Gruber was holding Wynona's hand; the two were an official couple now. King Edward—dressed in his finest kilt—was flanked by Jeremiah to his right and Wilma to his left. There'd be a more formal memorial later, but Charlee knew some things were ending and some were beginning and monumental moments needed to be marked with a ceremony. She'd made a silent promise to her father that she'd spread his ashes when she knew where to do it. Mr. Gruber knew that as well, and that's why he'd insisted they gather today.

Charlee reached down and found her strength by taking Ian's hand. This was hard for him too, she knew, and for Jeremiah, though both men stood soldier straight, hands clasped behind their backs until she interrupted Ian's at-ease pose. He gave her a sad smile. Her gaze fell across the path beside the pergola where Ian had placed the painting Mr. Gruber had done for her from a photograph he'd snapped of Charlee and her dad during his last visit.

In the painting, Charlee and her father sat side by side on the oak stump with her favorite spot in the background. Her dad looked so alive in the painting, it felt as though she could reach in and touch his face.

The sun warmed her cheeks and the peaceful quiet of woods and water surrounded her. This was a safe place. She gave Ian a nod and he opened the journal to the passage she'd chosen.

Ian cleared his throat and began to read. "What incredible gifts come from the love two people share. When I first met the woman who would become my wife, my heart stopped beating. She was the most beautiful thing I'd ever seen and though we were from different worlds, we fit. We fit as if we'd been created to be one. I never understood real love until I met her. I never understood loving unconditionally until tiny Jeremiah was placed in my arms. I never understood the power of a father's love for his daughter until I held Charlee, her soft baby skin against my battle-calloused hands. Love is a gift. It is to be cherished. It is to be nurtured. And most of all, it is to be enjoyed. If I could give my children one piece of advice, it would be this. Find it. Capture it. And never, ever let it go."

Charlee opened the lid of the small urn. They'd spread the remainder of his ashes when her brothers could be there, but this was her way of telling her dad that she'd gotten the message loud and clear, that she'd never again run, and that everything was going to be okay. She tilted the urn and the breeze grabbed the ashes and carried them to the lake. Charlee closed her eyes, offered up a prayer. She turned to face Ian. "I do miss him," she whispered. "I was wrong when I said I only missed what we never had. I miss him, Ian. So much."

"I know, Charlee." He dragged her into his arms as the others remained silent. "I miss him too."

She looked up at him. "And he knew I would. And that's why he sent you. You rescued me."

He cupped her cheek. "Everyone needs someone to rescue them."

She nodded. "He took care of me. Even after he was gone."

"Yeah," Ian said and pulled her closer. "Me too."

She turned to the lake and watched the ashes drift with the current. If life were a river, she'd found her shore. If life were an ocean, she'd found her moon. And if life could go on forever, she'd want to capture this moment and put it in a bottle. It was the moment when everything came together, everything made sense; it was the moment she'd actually realized that things may not be as they appeared, but if one was willing to continue along the broken road, they'd land at the most amazing of destinations.

NEXT IN THE ROADS TO RIVER ROCK SERIES BY HEATHER BURCH

Read on for a sneak peek of *Down the Hidden Path*,
the next Roads to River Rock novel by Heather Burch,
coming winter 2015.

DOWN THE
HIDDEN PATH

Dear Dad,

It's fall here and the leaves are changing. The colors are unusually vivid this season, the deepest red, the brightest yellow, and richest orange I've seen. Or maybe it's that I've been gone so long, staring at endless shades of olive drab, I'd forgotten the beauty of autumn. I drove out to the cemetery yesterday to visit the Havinger family plot where Mom's buried. I wondered if we should contact Grandfather Havinger and see about having your urn placed there by Mom's grave; it just seems wrong that the two of you aren't together.

But I know that's not what you asked for. Your words echo back to me. "We had your mother in life. We can let them have her in death." You were always so strong, so fair—even with those who didn't deserve it. Of everything you taught me about life, three things stand out. How to be a good man, how to be a good soldier, and how to be a good father.

The first, I daily strive for. The second, well, I suppose I've done. The third . . . the third I hope to one day do. And I guess that's what this letter is about.

I've put in my time for Uncle Sam and though the journey was both long and radically difficult, I find myself missing it and wondering what life would be today had I never signed up. I don't know how to be a civilian, Dad. I'm a little bit scared I'll fail at it. What advice would you give me if you were standing here at the water's edge, enjoying the grand display of colors and life? I really wish you were here. I really wish I could hear your voice one more time.

Your son,
Jeremiah

Jeremiah McKinley wadded the letter and dropped it on the last embers of the early-morning campfire. It had been the pre-dawn hour when he left his house and walked down to the lake's edge, where he'd started a fire with wood and kindling he'd gathered earlier in the week. There was still a chill in the air and it went straight to his bones, because for the thousandth time, he wondered what he was doing back in River Rock. Fog rolled off the lake, great billowing clouds that rose and disappeared as the sun trekked over the mountaintop.

Jeremiah turned to walk back up the winding path to his house, the place he'd throw his time and attention into until he figured out how to be normal again. When he thought of the road ahead, though apprehensive, he was also excited. He'd open a hunting and fishing lodge right here on Table Rock Lake. And instead of carrying a gun to kill insurgents, he'd carry one for hunting deer or wild pigs or turkey. Plus, he was near his sister, Charlee, and that made him happy.

Jeremiah shot a glance in the direction of Charlee's land and her ever-odd artists' colony. She'd found happiness, and that was something Miah wanted as well. Happiness. Contentment.

Peace.

An hour later, he headed into town with the weight of all his questions still heavy on his shoulders. When he spotted the breakfast taco truck, he whipped into the Dairy Flip's parking lot.

He counted four people in line and glanced down at his watch. 7:25. Miah chewed the inside corner of his cheek. Since he'd been in River Rock, he'd come to love the breakfast taco truck that showed up wherever and whenever it chose. He hated the fact that you could stand in line and at any given moment, the man inside would say, "Sorry, we're out," and close the little window. Just like that. It had happened to him twice. Miah tapped his foot and waited behind a guy with three kids in tow. In front of him, a woman with long, ink-black hair stood on the tiptoes of her tennis shoes, arms folded and propped on the counter while she chatted with the guy inside.

Miah had no patience for morning chitchat and was just considering the merits of telling her so when her laugh split the air.

Something shot straight into his gut. The sound from her lips was deep, rumbling, almost smoky, rich as warm butter and sweet as mountain honey. He knew that laugh.

A slender hand reached up and captured some of that silken hair. Jeremiah's mind rushed to catch up. This couldn't be her. But that voice. When the guy in front of him moved and blocked Miah's view, he sidestepped so he could see her fully, if only from behind. He was completely out of the line now and a heavyset woman rushed up to take his spot.

Who cared? His eyes trailed over the brunette, assessing the possibility. Right height. But wrong body shape. This woman had long, slender legs, a perfectly shaped rear end, a small waist. No, it wasn't her. Miah stepped back into line a little surprised at the disappointment rising in his chest.

And that's when she turned around.

———

"Gray?"

Mary Grace Smith almost dropped her tacos. She'd spun from the counter to hurry back to her car when a wide chest stepped out from the line and nearly body-slammed her. Her bottle of Coke teetered on the edge of her makeshift food tray. Choice words shot into her mind. What kind of idiot jumps in the face of someone carrying food? But then something registered as her gaze slid from the tray between them up over his chest, neckline, chin. He'd said her name. Finally, her eyes found his. And her heart stopped.

"Miah?" It was one word. Just his name. But having it on her lips and looking into that golden gaze caused a flurry of unwanted sensations. *Run. Run, run, run, run, run.*

This was a bad dream; that was all. A bad dream where she'd awaken drenched in sweat. Of course, she'd known the odds of seeing him. She'd heard he was returning to River Rock. And suddenly, with Jeremiah in front of her, blocking her exit, River Rock seemed smaller. Too small.

He was all wide smile and animated eyes as he said, "Wow, I . . . I didn't know you were living here. Are you just visiting?"

Those eyes she'd watched for hundreds if not thousands of hours. Eyes that had, at one time of her life, entranced her. Eyes she'd drowned in. Of course, everyone who met Jeremiah was hopelessly trapped in his golden gaze. Add to that the ridiculously chiseled features of a Greek god and that bubbling personality. He was the triple threat. Miah made you feel like you were the only woman on the planet. Even if you were the checker at the Piggly Wiggly and all you were doing was scanning his food. She'd actually seen women swoon. And that right there was why Gray took a full step back.

He didn't seem to notice as he waited—perfect smile in place—for her to answer. Gray mustered her composure. "I just moved back. A few months ago."

"It's great to see you." His brows were riding high, all excitement and anticipation.

Gray steeled herself. "You too." She nearly choked on the words getting them out, and as quickly as she'd run into him, she could run away. "Well, better get going."

When she stepped around his wide shoulders, he caught her arm. *Don't look up. Don't look up.* But her eyes had a mind of their own and trailed to his. The tiniest of frowns creased his forehead. He stood not more than a few inches from her, her shoulder pointing like an arrow at his heart.

"Gray," he whispered, and the sound shot down her body and right into her soul. "We need to catch up."

Gray bit her cheeks hard until she tasted blood on one side. She painted on a wide, cheery smile. "Oh, sure. Yes, you know, I'm so busy, these days, Jeremiah. But I'm sure we'll see each other in town now and then." And she blinked, once, and again. The gentlest tug liberated her from his hand. Her feet fell into motion and before she knew it, she was at her car door.

She fumbled with the keys and the tacos and the cold drink until she managed to get in. Gray slammed the car door shut, closing out everything she couldn't deal with. Closing out Miah McKinley and his smile that melted hearts. When she shifted to put the keys in the ignition, her hands were trembling. Gray squeezed her eyes shut. The fact that one brush with Miah could thoroughly wreck her, even after all this time, bit into her pride.

She glanced in the rearview mirror to find him standing in the same spot, one hand lifted to his forehead to block the sun, but from the safety of her car, it resembled a salute and that shot into Gray's heart and settled there. Miah'd lost his dad not much more than a year ago. And at that time, she hadn't been able to stop her mind from trailing to him. How he was handling the news. Was he okay?

"It doesn't matter," she grumbled as she started the car and backed out of the parking spot. She cast a fleeting glance to him and waved as she drove by. Gray breathed deeply, the scent of tacos a good replacement for the regret she tasted, even now.

She reminded herself Miah was just a snippet from her past. And as she put her foot on the gas, she let the past go because it was her future she was interested in. Four miles down the road, David was waiting for her.

ACKNOWLEDGMENTS

A huge thank-you to my family. John, Jake, and Isaac. I couldn't do any of this without you.

To the folks at Montlake. I've never known a more enthusiastic group of professionals. I'm so honored to work with all of you. You make me better at what I do and you constantly challenge me to dig deeper. JoVon, Hai-Yen, Charlotte, Kelli, Jessica, and Thom. I hope our partnership lasts a lifetime.

A special thanks to Jamille Twedt for medical information on heart attacks and for being one of my biggest fans.

ABOUT THE AUTHOR

Heather Burch writes full time and lives in Florida. Her debut novel was released to critical acclaim in 2012 and garnered praise from *USA Today*, *Booklist Magazine*, *Romantic Times*, and *Publishers Weekly*. Her epic love story, *One Lavender Ribbon*, was an international bestselling novel in 2014. Living in a house where she's the only female, Heather is intrigued by the relationships that form among men, especially soldiers. Her heartbeat is to tell unforgettable stories of love and war, commitment and loss . . . stories that make your heart sigh.